Moonshine

A Post-Apocalypse Romance

Kat Bostick

ISBN 978-1-7350097-0-4 (eBook Edition)

ISBN 978-1-7350097-1-1 (Paperback Edition)

For everyone who believes love can conquer the darkest days.

I'd given him one of the softer pieces of myself, the kind that breaks easily in someone else's grasp. I looked down at Joshua's hands. Thick, calloused fingers clutched his knees. They were capable hands but rough, so very rough. He could just as easily hold me safe with them as he could crush me.

Content Warning

Moonshine takes place during the end of the world. The lights have gone out and life teeters on the brink as Liv struggles to survive. Sensitive readers should be aware that the story includes the following potential triggers:
-depictions of violence
-discussion of sexual assault
-depictions of starvation
-mentions of physical and emotional abuse

Living on a Prayer

No one knows why the lights went out. Except maybe some secret branch of the government. They always know stuff like that, don't they? I suppose it doesn't really matter now. Six months after the blackout, they went dark too. Government officials disappeared and with them, government aid.

It was like someone took the seams of the entire nation and started tugging. At first there was only a little pilling; a handful of looters who thought they could get away with stealing—they usually could—and soccer moms fighting over the last package of toilet paper at big box stores. I thought the people stockpiling had to be out of their minds. The power was out. Why bother stocking up on groceries that won't keep?

One month in, I suddenly understood the appeal of buying sixteen cases of canned vegetables. Food was food in the end of the world and those of us without it found ourselves at a disadvantage that could serve to be deadly. On the other hand, those who had it also found themselves facing death by the hands of those without.

I still remember the sickening dread I felt over the first report of someone killed over supplies in the city. It seemed so barbaric, so inhuman. Unfortunately, it was only the beginning.

Despite having no lights, no fridge, and no running water, the blackout felt inconsequential during that first month. Moving from my duplex to one of the disaster relief camps was like going to summer camp. Most of my bunk mates were friendly enough and though the food wasn't amazing, it would keep me going. We even made a game of conspiracy theories, trying to figure out how we'd gotten in this mess.

People at camp said it couldn't be an EMT—or was it EMP?—because there wasn't a weapon big enough to knock the whole country off the grid. And plenty of technology still worked. My cellphone had power—though no signal or Wi-Fi—and most older cars ran just fine. It wasn't like airplanes suddenly fell from the sky. Not that I saw, anyway. We just didn't have electricity.

There were plenty of other theories: a massive solar storm, rapture, Russians, super intelligent sentient computers, aliens...the list went on. You name an apocalypse movie, and someone believed we were living in it. As for me, I didn't think the world was ending. I was naïve enough to believe that someone somewhere was taking care of it for me.

That was how I ended up in my current predicament. I didn't even bother to pack the right shoes when I left for camp. I believed my stay would be temporary. Those trendy low impact, brightly colored barefoot shoes were great right up until you stepped on a pointy rock. Make that six hundred pointy rocks on the gravelly shoulder of a back-country road in middle-of-nowhere, Washington State.

Or, as one of my former travel companions charmingly referred to it, Bumfuck, Washington. In my mother's household that phrase would have earned me a mouth full of soap. That was before though, and as much as I could use the laugh, I needed to keep my mind on track.

And I couldn't risk the noise. Making too much noise got you killed in the end of the world.

Boots. I needed boots and for the first time in thirty miles, I might have found somewhere to acquire them. Shimmering before me like a beautiful oasis in the desert was a sporting goods store.

Alright, fine, it wasn't shimmering. In fact, the weathered building looked like it had seen better days *before* the world ended. The yellow sign advertising live bait was practically crushed under the weight of creeping moss that made its way down the roof, threatening to cave the whole thing in.

The second I saw the place I wanted to sprint to the door with tears of joy in my eyes. Experience taught me better. After grocery stores and gas stations, outdoor gear stores were the next to become hotspots for looting. There was that handful of eager people who attacked shopping malls and jewelry outlets but somehow, I doubted they were sitting pretty on a throne of Twinkies. No one cared about diamonds and designer bags now.

Stuff was useless in the end of the world unless you could eat it, wear it, or defend yourself with it. A shame, really. I loved stuff. I missed throw pillows and fingernail polish and sparkly tops that had no practical purpose. But there was no use lamenting over the past. It could swallow you up like a black hole if you weren't careful.

It was three days ago that I last spotted human activity and even then, the trail was fairly cold—based on my very lacking knowledge of such things. Still, the store was surrounded by a concrete lot and left me wide open to anyone inside or scouting from the trees. I could wait until night, but my flashlight ran out of batteries, and it would take me forever to fumble around in the dark.

Was I going to risk it? I sat in stillness for another minute, listening for any sign that I wasn't the only one here.

That was the thing about the end of the world. It wasn't the earth ripping in two or cities consumed by tsunamis. It wasn't hordes of zombies wandering the streets. Most of the time it was...empty. Quiet. Sometimes just quiet enough to trick you into thinking it was a Sunday morning and everyone was sleeping in and any moment the smell of fresh baked goods would waft down the road from a café like nothing had changed.

That feeling was a lie. Everything had changed.

I'd learned the hard way that sometimes, quiet doesn't mean empty. Quiet doesn't mean you're alone. Quiet can be much more dangerous than gun fire and raised voices. Quiet means you're being watched. As much as I desperately hated being alone, I would rather not have company.

Even if there were others nearby, I wasn't in any shape to run from them in ripped up shoes. I glanced down at my sneakers with a sigh. There wasn't really another option.

Looks like it's now or never.

Up until the world ended, I wasn't one for prayer. Growing up in the Bible Belt, you'd think I would have been well versed in religion, but my parents weren't the type to believe in anything that didn't make them wealthy or make them look wealthy. One man back at camp claimed God had abandoned us and we were what was left after the rapture took the good ones. Maybe that was true. Maybe there was no God, but when it's just you and the eerie silence of an empty town, you start asking for guidance from anywhere you can get.

Please God, let there be size five and half boots in there. And please God, don't let there be raiders in this town. Don't let there be anyone but little old me.

Prayers sent and parking lot scouted, I took off at the fastest pace I could manage, my backpack slinging back and forth as I went. I wasn't sure if it kept getting heavier or I kept getting skinnier, but the darn thing nearly toppled me. By the time I reached the glass door my heart was pounding so fast that my head felt light. That was happening a lot more often lately and I couldn't always blame it on fear.

Please God, let there be a box of granola bars in this shop.

Based on the smashed glass, which I hadn't noticed from a distance, that was unlikely. This store was already hit by other travelers, maybe raiders if I was especially unlucky. They always trashed what they didn't take because, hey, why not? If you're going to stoop so low you attack fellow humans with blunt objects, knocking over mannequins and lighting useful stuff on fire is only to be expected.

Not ready to give up hope and terribly uncomfortable being so exposed, I ducked through the glass-less bottom half of the door. Shards crunched beneath my sneakers, and I winced. There were at least three holes in the soles of each shoe and there was no avoiding the glass. I would have to tip toe and hope nothing large embedded in my skin.

There were no windows in the shop, making the broken door the only source of light. I could easily make out a dusty counter with an open and empty register, two shelves of disturbed fishing rods, and a toppled clothing rack that used to hold hunting attire based on the label. The air inside was stuffy, and the place had a dull fish smell to it, likely from bait that was not-so-live anymore.

If someone was in here, the glass skittering under my feet would have immediately alerted them. I held still for three breaths, listening intently for any sign that someone was coming to shoot me and take my stuff. Maybe there was a God after all. No one came for me and as my eyes adjusted to the shadowy interior, I spotted a sign marked "shoes."

In my experience, the first thing people went for in this kind of store was the guns. This one was a tiny place in a tiny town and didn't sell firearms but there were several empty shelves that previously held knives. After guns, people usually took anything else they could carry. The boots in the back were picked over, obviously visited by more than one person or group in the past.

On the bright side, my shoe size was small enough that most people couldn't wear it. Unfortunately, that also meant that retailers in nowhere towns didn't typically carry it. I'd found that a six was doable if I doubled up on socks but currently, I was lacking in the sock department, and it didn't look like there were any left here.

Just behind the furthest shelf was a door marked "employees only." Feeling more desperate than brave, I twisted the handle and tested the lock. The door opened with a creak. Inside appeared to be storage shelves, most of which were as disturbed as the rest of the store. It was nearly pitch black in the stock room, but I propped the door open and crept inside anyway.

I'll be honest, I'm afraid of the dark. Of all the things I'd seen in the end of the world, darkness wasn't all that bad, but for some reason my brain just went haywire every time the lights were out. Five steps in, I started imagining clowns hiding behind the shelves. Not raiders or someone desperate enough to eat me like wild game, but *clowns*. If I could go back in time and warn my sixteen-year-old self how many nights I'd be spending alone in the dark, I would have skipped every single one of those horror movies.

I barely managed to stifle a scream when the plastic crate I was reaching for fell off the shelf and dumped shoe boxes on top of me. I got a cardboard cut on my forehead and several scrapes on my arms but, because God was real *and* feeling the love for me today, I found brand stinking new boots in size six. The only pair, too.

It took serious guts, but I pushed myself further into the room in search of socks. My bravery paid off. There was half a crate of wool socks hiding under a bunch of the duck toys used for training hunting dogs. It was tempting to take all of them but even if socks were lightweight, I knew I shouldn't add too much extra bulk to my pack. These days I was lucky if I found more than a picked over blackberry bush or two. The hungrier I got, the harder it was to carry anything besides my own body.

Once back in the relative safety of the shoe section—and once I'd closed the gaping clown hell door—I sat on the floor and hastily exchanged my ripped up tennis shoes for hiking boots. The fit wasn't perfect, and I was probably going to have blisters for days. Nothing to be done about it.

The longer I stayed inside the store, the antsier I got. With only one obvious entrance, I was trapped. Despite my nerves, I forced myself to check the back shelves for food or any other useful items. I found a collection of books but sadly none of them detailed wild food or how to identify it, which would have come in real handy. There were dozens of discarded beef jerky, protein bar, and snack mix boxes but not even crumbs were left to pick through.

I would have felt better if I'd never discovered those boxes. Seeing colorful pictures of food brands that I recognized made my stomach rumble painfully and my mouth water. I needed to get out of here and find somewhere to settle down before nightfall. Then I could worry about sustenance.

The new leather boots were rigid around my ankles and toes, but holy cow did it feel good to walk over that glass without worrying about any of it getting through the holes in my shoe. It was about time something went right.

I was less careful coming out of the store as I was coming in because if someone was watching, there was no way I would avoid their gaze. Once out the door, I powerwalked—running risked using up the rest of my energy for the day and I needed to do some serious hiking to get far enough away from this town—to the tree line and located the road I'd been following for the last three days.

Without a compass or frequent road signs it was hard to say exactly where I was. I was fairly certain that I was still going east or at least east-ish. Based on the way the towns were gradually shrinking and the elevation was rising, I was getting closer to the Cascades. Mountain wilderness would be great for avoiding other people but considering what a poor job I'd done of keeping myself fed on wild food, this didn't bode well for me.

Not to mention, the weather was getting colder. It was subtle right now, but the sunny, dry days were giving way to cooler and cooler nights. Without a tent or proper clothing there was no way I would even make it through autumn in the mountains.

That didn't leave too many options. Whether or not I headed back west, I would have to deal with winter. While I might be lucky enough to find more supplies, maybe even some canned food, I risked encountering raiders. Thus far I'd seen signs of others heading this way but most of it looked to be from a single person or small groups. Raiders travelled in numbers, and they were quickly overtaking urban areas.

From what I'd seen, many of their groups were pre-existing gangs or younger men with no qualms about committing horrible acts of violence. They swept through cities, towns, and camps like knife wielding locusts, taking whatever—and whoever—they wanted. By now Seattle was probably split up into territories, each maintained by one bloodthirsty raider group or another. Returning to the city was less desirable than freezing to death in the mountains.

East-ish it was then. Sooner or later, I would have to come upon a town that hadn't been abandoned or perhaps another FEMA camp that wasn't ravaged by raiders. I slipped as far into the trees as I dared, noting that the afternoon sun was already beginning to hint at that golden evening glow. I wasn't going to make it much farther today. That was the struggle of travelling on foot.

When I wasn't gathering meager amounts of food or sneaking through towns, I was walking. I couldn't really say what my goal was with all that walking. Maybe I was headed for the fabled camps in eastern Washington, the ones supposedly untouched by raiders and blessed with wind energy. Maybe I thought if I just walked far enough, I would find some normal place that wasn't affected by the end of the world and be welcomed by kind strangers. Or maybe I simply wanted to survive and so far, the only way I knew to do that was to keep moving.

I didn't encounter any berry bushes for the remainder of the day. The invasive Himalayan blackberry proved to be an ally on my journey through the wilderness—when I wasn't getting painfully tangled in it, anyway—but it seemed to grow scarcer as I neared higher elevations. I picked several dandelion plants throughout the afternoon, chewing the bitter leaves and grimacing. That was hardly enough food to fill my mouth, much less my stomach.

By twilight I was wandering aimlessly, barely aware of the road, feeling lightheaded and like my legs were made of pool noodles. That sprint to and from the store took its toll. Once upon a time I was a cardio-bunny, but my days of track and field were long over. Though I struggled to walk, I forced myself on until I found a patch of evergreen bushes tucked around the back of a Douglas fir. It wasn't the ideal place to sleep but it would conceal me.

Settling between the bushes with my backpack in my lap, I clenched my jaw in an attempt to ignore the painful emptiness in my gut. I didn't want to consider what my frail state meant. I didn't want to think about what would happen if I didn't wake up with enough energy to walk tomorrow. It hadn't been this bad before. I was hungry, sure, but I never stopped.

Darkness gradually closed in around me and my heart tripped with the familiar terror that accompanied the night. Even with my knees tucked to my chest and my location hidden, I never felt safe. It was going to be another restless sleep, waiting for any sign of a hunting predator or a bold group of raiders. Any of the hope I earned from my successful scavenging trip in the sporting goods store was quickly fading and I found myself praying once again.

Please God, don't let me die out here.

2

Yellow-Bellied

I fell into a deep sleep for short but blissful hours. While I slept, my brain created a glorious dream of a brightly lit restaurant where I sat eating tray after tray of sushi. I don't think I even like sushi but once it's gone, all that stupid stuff you didn't give a chance becomes appealing. What if I actually *do* like sushi and now, I'll never know?

The four other people I ended up sharing a tent with back at camp joined me in a daily whine-fest, listing all the foods they never tried, places they never travelled, and the expensive shoes they wished they'd bought. We had competitions to see who could come up with the best first world-problem. We were still living in the first world. We had infrastructure and a big, rich government. We just had to wait it out. The right person would put the right plan in place and boom, no more power outage.

Our naivety was laughable.

My back was stiff from sleeping in a fetal position and an all too familiar ache in my joints told me I overdid it yesterday. Fortunately, I was able to get up and move around without passing out—always a good sign when you're low on sustenance—but the telltale shake in my hands made it clear I needed to make food my biggest priority.

Maybe that was how I got lost. Or maybe in my exhausted haze yesterday I wandered further from the road than I thought. Either way, twenty minutes into my search for any kind of edible berry or dandelion—one of the few wild plants I knew I could eat—I realized that I couldn't see the road. I tried to backtrack to the tree I slept beneath but I must have been wrong about which direction I came from because another twenty minutes had me standing among totally unfamiliar surroundings.

"Don't panic, Liv," I ordered my very much panicking self.

The only reason I managed to make it this far without getting totally lost in the wilderness was following the road. I never found much in terms of supplies, but those few bags of potato chips and soggy fig bars were my saving grace. With no road, how was I supposed to know which way was east?

The sun rises in the east, dummy!

Duh! Oh. Wait. Or was it the west? Where was Google when you needed it?

I instinctively fingered the back pocket of my jeans where my cell phone used to sit. I was mostly certain the sun rose in the east. Scanning the forest, my eyes found a faint glimmer of light. The sun hadn't yet crested the tops of the trees, but it was clearly visible through the branches.

Okay, my new plan was to follow the sun. If I kept going east, I could find a good camping spot and make markers so that I could explore the area until I found the road again. That would also be an excellent way to look for food. Maybe I'd even come upon an empty house with a full pantry.

Yeah, and maybe I'll find a unicorn that lets me ride on its back all the way to Disneyland.

"Don't be sour," I chided myself. "This is a good plan. This is fine. I'm fine. Everything is going to be fine."

Three hours later—or something like that because how do you even measure hours without a clock?—I was totally not fine. My body ached, the spot where a shoebox hit me in the face throbbed, and I was weaker than I'd ever been. Imagine drinking six cups of coffee on an empty stomach then running up twelve flights of stairs. That was what I felt like just shambling through the understory. Earlier I'd found one lone dandelion plant growing in an open patch of sunlight and eaten every single visible part of it, right up to the flower.

All that did was make me feel like vomiting.

I was about to give in to my body's need to rest and lie down wherever I was standing when I spotted train tracks. Train tracks would intersect with the road and maybe even lead me to a town. This close to the mountains the towns might still be inhabited and well stocked. God, maybe I would even find someone to lend me a bed.

At this point sleeping on a rug would be more comfortable than sleeping against a tree trunk.

Taking a bet and hoping my instincts were correct, I took a right and started following the tracks. I walked as far as I possibly could before the lightheadedness came again. A clearing ringed by ferns and bushes appeared fifty feet from the tracks and I knew I'd found that perfect camp spot for the night. Using my very last scrap of strength, I collected a handful of branches to cover a cozy nook at the base of a maple tree.

And cleared the spider webs from the bark, of course. Even in the end of the world, a girl doesn't want to wake up with spiders in her hair.

It wasn't the most inconspicuous shelter I'd ever made but it was enough. From there I had the perfect vantage point to see the tracks and the opening in the trees where I'd come in.

Unlike the night before, I didn't dream. Huddled against my tree, I fell into a heavy, dark sleep and when I woke, I was more than a little afraid that was my first taste of death. Was my body on the brink and only the minuscule calories from yesterday's dandelion plant kept my weak heart beating? I didn't see any tunnels made of white light or hear the voices of angels but then again, maybe I really was just another bad one left behind by God.

Dying or not, I decided it would boost morale to change my clothes. I hadn't done that in almost four days and while all my clothes were dirty, the ones I picked were cleanest.

I'd successfully washed laundry in a creek before but the few trickles of water I encountered lately were barely enough to fill my bottle. It seemed more prudent to worry about hydration rather than hygiene. Who was around to smell me, anyway?

I was almost finished repacking my bag when I caught sight of movement near the train tracks. I froze, holding my breath and watching with dread as two vaguely man-shaped figures wandered along the tree line.

Once upon a time I was a people person. I loved talking to strangers and making new friends. The end of the world broke me of that. I learned the hard way what people were capable of when it was every man for himself.

Of all the things that would get me killed, I never imagined it was my favorite color being yellow. My bag was almost full, and I was frantically repacking when the men spotted me, no doubt because the shirt under my jacket was vibrant yellow and caught the rising sun in a gilded show.

They were a good distance away, but I could make out their expressions just fine. They were smiling. It was not a friendly, glad-to-see-some-one-else-out-here smile. Bestial excitement glittered from filthy faces. Even before the world ended, I knew that look. I'd simply been too innocent to recognize when I was prey.

The stakes were lower then. I wasn't happy about a hand shoved down my shirt or an unwanted pinch on the rump but that was nothing compared to what I saw in these men. We were living in lawless times now and there would be no repercussions for their actions. Remembering that was what got me moving. A quick glance over my shoulder showed they'd increased their pace and were jogging my way.

Unlike me, they didn't have big packs to weigh them down. They seemed to be dressed for hunting, rifles slung over their shoulders and camo jackets to disguise the upper half of their body. Why only jackets? I wasn't a hunting expert, but the effort seemed useless if any passing wildlife could see their denim clad legs.

What was wrong with me? These men were hunting *me*, and I was wasting precious brain power wondering about their jeans.

"Where are you going, sweetheart?" One called after me. "We want to talk to you!"

I didn't look where I was going, I just ran. I ran until cool air burned the lining of my lungs and my ears were pounding with blood. I ran until the world around me blurred not from my speed but from dizziness. I was too weak to run much further. What remained of my leg muscles were on fire. I stumbled, twisted an ankle, crashed through branches, scraped against tree trunks.

The men gave chase. They reminded me of starving dogs, ravenous at the sight of a rabbit. Even when I couldn't see them, I could almost feel their breath on my nape. I heard them too, crashing through the brush with much less effort than me. In the beginning I had a good lead, but they were rapidly gaining on me.

They were going to catch me. There was no way out of this.

I thought of the bus then, recalled the swarm of men just like these two. Flashes of blood painted my memory. The gore was far more horrifying than any movie I'd seen. The wailing pleas of a woman whose name I couldn't remember resounded in my skull as I replayed those haunting images. No one would remember her name now. No one would remember mine either. I couldn't go on any longer. Even if I pushed my body, my brain was failing.

Starved of nutrients and adequate rest, I struggled to maintain consciousness. The exertion from running took the last crumb of energy I had left, and my vision was tilting. My thoughts went from panicked overdrive to a sluggish confusion.

Why was I even running? I should let them catch me. Maybe they'd be merciful and kill me quickly. I wouldn't live anyway. If by some miracle I got away I was still doomed to starve to death. A slow death that I would see coming but could do nothing to prevent.

I'd heard that your life flashes before your eyes when you die but I always thought it would be more mystical, all my best memories floating by like a dreamy river. Instead, I was visited by all the things I shouldn't have done. Shouldn't have argued with my mom the last time we spoke, shouldn't have said no to the million social events I turned down, shouldn't have avoided fried food because I was scared to gain weight.

There were the "should haves" too. I should have gone to school in Texas so I could go home to my parents during the blackout. I should have packed better gear when I left my house in Seattle. Should have done something when raiders attacked my group instead of running like a coward—like I was now.

I should have become a gosh darn Girl Scout, so I knew how to navigate the woods and find my way east. Then I wouldn't even be in this mess.

I was deliberating my choices—that last ounce of will to live warring with the fatigued desire to give up—when something darted in front of me. My vision was too far gone for me to identify the dark shape. I skidded to a halt, tumbling forward without my momentum. I shoved my hands out but it was as if they moved in slow motion, unable to catch me before I landed face first in the dirt.

Thirty seconds passed before I managed to lift my head. My gaze met a mouthful of sharp teeth. Just above those curled lips and fangs was a shimmering wet nose and a snout carpeted in silky black fur. At first, I thought it was a bear. Then my eyes focused enough for me to realize it was a dog; the biggest dog I'd ever seen. Probably bigger than me.

Men behind me, a dog—maybe *dogs*—in front of me, and I wasn't sure which was worse. Dogs could be harmless and sad, looking like some starving, wet mess from an SPCA commercial after their people died or left them. They could also be vicious predators. Packs of dogs roamed the roads and claimed territory near previously inhabited areas. I'd seen them from a distance—even saw a rather gory dog fight once—but had thankfully been able to avoid them.

A dog, much like a person, was a wild card. Would they wag their tail only to bite you when you got too close? Would they surround you and attack you from all sides? Would they eat you? Okay, I was pretty sure people hadn't devolved into cannibalism—yet—but the same couldn't be said for dogs.

The canine rumbled a low growl. A gruff sound followed, this one unmistakably human. I raised my gaze past the dog and saw a man looming over me. He was the biggest *man* I'd ever seen. From my position on the ground, he appeared implausibly tall, a dense tree trunk carved into the shape of a person.

He could have been a walking tree. Unlike my pursuers, this man was dressed head to toe in camouflage. Even the lower half of his face was covered with leaf patterned cloth. Inky hair was tied back at the nape of his neck. That was the only human part of him I could make out beside dusky eyes, barely visible under furrowed black brows.

Taking a gamble, I lifted pleading eyes to the monstrous stranger. "Please, help me." My voice was a raspy croak. It sounded like death.

There were thundering footsteps behind me and two rapid cracks ringing in my ears, a storm coming to climax right above me. Then I was sinking, my head falling to the cool earth, my body becoming oddly weightless. The sensation was confusing, like floating on air and slowly dropping to the bottom of a lake all at once.

Distantly, I wondered if this was what dying felt like.

3

Axe Man

There were birds singing. In the forest there were almost always birds singing. At one point I thought the sound was beautiful. Eventually, I began to feel as if the birds were mocking me. What was so thrilling that they had to tweet about it all day? The world was ending, a crushing weight that grew heavier and heavier until my body threatened to buckle.

I became conscious of the feel of my body and realized that the weight was gone. I was cozy, all the aches and pains easing as I rested on the softest surface I'd felt in...God, how long had it been since I'd been in a bed?

There was warmth too, gentle and subtle on my face. Now that I was rousing, I could hear the quiet crackling of a fire. That delicious mingling of aromatic smoke with damp summer air invoked nostalgia for a childhood I didn't have, one spent roasting marshmallows over a campfire and sleeping under the stars. My parents wouldn't be caught dead in a tent, and they hated going anywhere with bugs.

There were other smells, layers of scent that painted a million possible surroundings in my mind. The zesty hint of fresh cut wood danced with cinnamon and a mix of herbs that reminded me of a new age herb shop—the ones that sell incense, crystals, and artsy glass bongs. Beneath that was the delicate aroma of flowers, not sweet and floral like a perfume but earthy like a botanical garden.

I hesitantly pried my eyes open. Dim light danced over dark blurs with fuzzy outlines. I blinked lethargic lids until finally—yes, thank God—my sight sharpened. I was staring at a wall. It held no paintings or windows, only aging grey-brown boards. I shifted my gaze to a cherry wood nightstand. The piece was weathered, like an antique that someone found at a garage sale but hadn't restored.

I moved my gaze the other direction—at least as far as I could from my resting position. I was too afraid to raise my head yet. It felt heavy enough to snap my neck. And I didn't know where I was or who I was with. I wasn't ready to alert them that I was awake.

There was a door on the far side of the wall. It was at the very edge of my peripherals, so I only caught a glimpse of it. If not for the worn brass handle I could have mistaken in for another wall panel. Was that the way out? I should probably make note.

I rolled from my side to my back with way more exertion than it should have taken. The ceiling above me, as old and weary as the walls, tapered down from a peak. Firelight flickered across the beams, causing my eyes to lose focus again. I lowered my chin to my chest so I could look at myself instead.

A patchwork quilt covered my legs. The squares were varying shades of fading blue, some decorated with embroidered flowers. Very homey and not what I expected to wake up to after running through the woods to escape raiders. Past my feet was the end of a wooden bedframe. It was crafted out of small logs, one of those furniture accents usually featured in kitschy vacation cabins with deer heads on the wall.

There was nothing kitschy about this space. The rustic appearance felt too real to be intentional. The place seemed like it fell together that way organically. A country home assembled one piece of old wood at a time.

Just beyond the foot of the bed, I noticed him. The low light almost hid the small dining table. It couldn't hide the man seated in the chair furthest from me. His hulking shape filled the room, drawing my attention not only because of his imposing presence but because he made the table look comically small. The shadows in the room seemed to gravitate toward him, making his unruly head of black hair and matching beard into a shade of midnight. The darkness clung to his already reticent features, painting his face in mystery.

How long was I unconscious with him staring at me like that? The strained, clumsy ticking in my brain built up into a whirring of anxiety. Anything could have happened while I was blacked out. A hand slipped over my legs and stomach found my clothing intact. That didn't necessarily mean it hadn't come off at some point but surely there would be some sign of that.

I dragged that same hand up to touch my hair. It was dry. There was a steady drizzle when I ran from the clearing and my hair had been damp for hours before that.

Okay, so I'd been here for more than an hour. I swallowed. My throat was scratchy and dry. Up until the clearing I'd done a good job of staying hydrated. Water kept my energy up and filled my complaining stomach. I was thirsty now but not painfully so. That gave me a window of time that fit within four or five hours. Unless he gave me something to drink, and I forgot. Or he gave me something that would make me forget.

Somehow, I doubted a man that big would need to use anything if he wanted to...yeah, not going to complete that thought.

My eyes finally lowered to the contents of my backpack, neatly laid out on the table before him. Even my collection of tampons were sorted into an organized pile with the other bathroom items. Pretty methodical for a guy who looked like he might behead a hiker with an axe.

I gulped down my apprehension and did my best to sit up. Even that was enough to make my head spin. The man tensed as if I was about to leap out of bed and attack him. An odd clicking resounded off the wooden floor and then a huge dog rounded the corner of the bed, growling viciously.

"Kuna!" The man growled a warning back at the dog. The rough grate of his voice almost made me jump out of my skin. That dark gaze never left me. "You're awake."

"Yes." Fear clawed at my throat, making it feel raw. I was going to lose it if I didn't chill out.

"Water?"

I gaped at him helplessly before squeaking out another "Yes. Please."

Now that I wasn't face first in the dirt, both man and dog weren't quite as big as I initially thought. He rose from his chair to retrieve a cup from a cabinet, proving that not *as* big was still darn big. Like taller than any man I'd ever met by half a foot with at least fifty pounds more bulk than the bulkiest. And with all that black hair, I was surprised I hadn't mistaken *him* for a black bear.

There was a rushing sound when his back was to me, one I hadn't heard indoors in a year or more. Running water. He had running water! Where was I and who the heck was this guy? I instinctively flinched away when he stalked from the kitchen to place the full glass on the nightstand. His brows pinched in a harsh frown, and I flinched again.

"Thanks," I murmured. He grunted and returned to the kitchen, his hips resting casually against the counter. I took the glass with shaking hands and swallowed as big a sip as I dared.

"When was the last time you ate?" It was more accusation than question, as if I'd been starving myself for the fun of it.

"Oh, I don't know. Yesterday, maybe." I tried to keep my voice steady, but it trembled as much as my hands. I took another sip of water to gain some composure.

"You're malnourished."

"I figured."

"Olivia Sophia Bryant." I sat up a little more to see he was holding my driver's license.

It was probably silly to keep it. My wallet and cell phone too. The phone had been dead for over a year and the sixty bucks in cash was worthless. They were little tokens of faith, my hope that someday they might mean something again. I didn't really care if the money had value or if any of those stupid apps on my phone still worked. It was the security of a future that was like the past I knew.

It wasn't a perfect life. I didn't have great friends and there was no boyfriend that might be thinking of me from somewhere far away. My parents probably presumed me dead and had come to terms with it, if they weren't dead themselves. Still, I liked that life. I was going to make something of it.

That life was gone now. Olivia Bryant was dead. She withered away out in those woods and someone new took her place. I didn't know this girl yet, had no idea what to expect from her. It's a wild thing, becoming a new person. I had to be different if I was going to survive the end of the world. And I was going to start by growing a backbone.

"Only my father calls me Olivia and only when I'm in trouble. It's Liv." I sat up as straight as I could, shoulders back, fragile chest puffed out.

"Can you get up?" He ignored my response.

"Yes," I said knowing full well that I probably couldn't.

He crossed his arms, his raised brows daring me to prove it. His face wasn't as harsh without that frown. That wasn't to say he was *friendly* looking. With a face that square and rigid, it was nearly impossible for him to appear any way other than dour. The thick beard that covered the lower half of his face and stretched down to the top of his Adam's apple made his jawline seem even broader. Those murky eyes were lighter without the shadow of a scowl, more of a cocoa brown than dark umber.

I heaved myself out of bed with a stifled groan. For a second, I wobbled there dizzily before steadying myself. My walk to the table was more of a shamble and I had to brace myself on the wall twice. Just about every part of me hurt. My knees ached, my legs were sore, and my ribs smarted with each subtle shift of my torso. The skin from my collarbone to my sternum was burning but I was too scared to look down and see the damage from my run and the resulting tumble to the ground.

My axe murderer friend studied me as I made my journey into the kitchen, his face showing nothing but unimpressed displeasure. After a treacherous and snail-paced journey to the table, I had to catch my breath before pulling out a shockingly heavy wooden chair. I tried to hide my exhausted panting when I lowered myself into the seat across from him.

Up close, his eyes reminded me of a perfect mug of hot chocolate. How could a man with hot chocolate eyes be frightening? With that lethal scowl, that was how. No amount of melted chocolatey goodness could make up for the hard edge that practically cut the air between us.

It didn't help that he had so much hair. It made him look wild, almost feral. He reminded me of those rugged men who wander out of the city to spend the rest of their days alone in a cave in the mountains. By the looks of it, he kind of was. Only difference was he lived in a shack instead of cave.

"Your friends are dead."

I gaped at him, completely clueless as to how to respond to that. *Backbone, Liv. Grow that backbone.*

"What an awful thing to say to a person. Did you kidnap me just to make me feel bad? What's next? Are you going to tell me my parents didn't love me?"

Now he was the one slack jawed. "I didn't kidnap you."

"I didn't think so either but now I'm second guessing myself because you're glaring at me like a scary murderer and reminding me that most of my friends are dead."

"A scary murderer? How fucking old are you?" He shook his head. "*You* asked for *my* help."

"I did but I was half sure you were a walking tree, and I was hallucinating. I hadn't realized you would be so rude."

"I'm not—" he bared his teeth. Feral man. "Stop changing the subject. You can't distract me that easily." Rough fingers scratched a familiar line through his beard. "Were you willing bait? Did they offer you something in return? Food? Shelter? Protection?"

It felt like we were having two different conversations. "Look, Mister...what did you say your name was?"

"I didn't."

"Fine. Here's the thing, beard boy. I have no clue what you're talking about. Bait? Bait for what? Who are 'they?' I'm grateful that you helped me, but I'm starting to wonder if maybe you've confused me with someone else. Are you sure it wasn't another starving blonde lady lost in the woods that you're thinking of? I mean, we can't be that rare."

What was I saying? Why was I arguing with a potential axe murderer? Part of me felt I should be demurely thanking him and hunching down in the chair, but it seemed pointless. I was trapped in his house, God only knew where. My chances of survival were as good here as they were out there.

"You're telling me that you didn't know those men? They just happened to chase you into *my* woods? And you just happened to run into me while running away from them?"

"Sounds about right," I nodded. "And for the record, they're not *your* woods."

"My property, my woods."

"Who's going to enforce private property laws now?"

He propped a meaty hand on the butt of a gun holstered on his belt. "Me." That was about as close to a threat as I wanted to get.

"I realize that it might seem suspicious that our paths crossed in the middle of nowhere while I was trying to escape raiders but I promise you, it's purely coincidental. If anything, I should be the one suspicious of you. I've gone weeks without seeing a single person and suddenly I encounter three men in one instance? How do I know you weren't working with them to herd me into a trap so you could go all Donner Party on me?"

"I don't even know what the hell to say to that." He rested his elbows on the counter behind him, relaxed body language warring with his brusque tone. "First of all, fuck those assholes. Second, is that what you think raiders do? Eat people?" He pursed his lips, considering. "You haven't actually seen raiders eating people, have you?"

With a shrug I replied, "It just seems like something people might do in the end of the world. At my hungriest, I can't say with absolute certainty I wouldn't have eaten a fellow traveler." I wrinkled my nose. "On second thought, I couldn't do it. Gross."

"Are you crazy? Did I bring a crazy person into my house?" He seemed like he was asking himself more than me.

I answered anyway. "I think I'm doing pretty swell in the mental health department, all things considered. On a scale of chill to psycho, I fall right about at the hungry squirrel mark."

Silence thickened the air around him like fog, not just uncomfortable but a bit suffocating too. Dark eyes were shadowed by even darker brows, making his brown irises into black wells. They were terrifying and mesmerizing. It was only when the expression turned from scrutinizing to menacing that I realized I was staring at him. Staring at him staring at me.

"Okay, Squirrel." I jumped when he spoke. "What story do you expect me to believe?"

My nerves returned with trembling hands. What happened if he didn't believe me? "What part of the story do you want? It's a long one."

"What are you doing out here?"

"You brought me here."

"What were you doing in *my woods*?" He was quickly losing his patience, I could tell. For some reason that only made me want to prod more.

"Maybe you should consider putting up a sign, since you're so sensitive about the whole woods thing." When he growled like his dog, I decided to not to push my luck and answered. "I was following the railroad tracks. Figured they might take me near a town where I could get some food."

"Nothing left around here. If there is, you'll have to fight off raiders to get to it. Don't seem like you're in any shape for fighting." His next stretch of silence was contemplative, but it didn't make me any less uncomfortable.

I did my best to smile. "So, I'm Liv. What's your name?"

He ignored me again. "Were you with anyone?"

"No, I'm single. I played the field, but I guess I just never found the one."

"Other people. A group. Were you traveling with anyone?" His volume rose. I had to flex my weak muscles to keep from ducking away from the roughness of his words.

"No. I was alone," I admitted. "You going to tell me your name yet?"

"Why do you care?" The creases on his forehead sunk deeper, almost completely obscuring his eyes.

"I'd like to know the name of the man that saved my life." I swear he recoiled at the sentence.

He considered, jaw flexing and shoulders tense. I'd never met anyone that felt threatened by pleasantries before. "Joshua." It was more grunt than word.

"Nice to meet you, Joshua." If saying that he saved my life made him uncomfortable, hearing his name on my tongue was downright painful.

"This all you got? You got a camp somewhere?" And we were back to the interrogation.

I waved my hands with a flourish, putting on my best game show host voice. "This is all of my worldly possessions."

My enthusiasm fell flat when I actually looked at the contents of my pack strewn before me. I was more prepared for a weekend getaway than surviving in the wilderness. There was a stainless steel water bottle, a beach towel, colorful leggings, flowy yoga pants with some tribal pattern, a collection of t-shirts, many of which were pink and yellow, a purple and white striped bikini, piles of underwear, a new package of hair bands, a handful of tampons, two tubes of sunscreen, and four pairs of sunglasses.

Both of us stopped on the sunglasses at the same time. I shrugged and explained, "Sunglasses break easily, and they were the least picked over item in gas stations."

None of the items were useless but few of them had proven to be particularly useful either. The tampons were quickly becoming a precious resource, but I hadn't gotten my period in...shoot, I couldn't even remember. Otherwise, I hadn't used much else recently. Bathing took too much energy and walking in the trees, I didn't usually need sunscreen or glasses. The leggings and shirts only served as layers, and they were poor layers at that.

I was doing this survival thing all wrong.

"This your only weapon?" He raised one hand above the table and waggled my folding knife. I hadn't even noticed it was missing from my pocket.

"Other than my samurai sword? Yup." I tapped my pointer finger on the table. "I'd hardly call that a weapon, though."

"It could be if you had the skills to use it."

"I didn't exactly have time to teach myself knife fighting. I was kind of busy trying to survive."

"You weren't doing a very good job."

"Did you rescue me just to insult me?"

"You need to eat." He ignored me—*again*—and gave me his back. It was only when he yanked open the door to a tiny fridge that I realized what it was. Running water and a fridge? A working fridge?

I gasped. "How do you have electricity?"

"Same way I've always had electricity."

I waited but he didn't give me anything more than that sarcastic quip. Since he was preoccupied and apparently not concerned with what I was doing, I took the time to repack my bag.

Joshua watched me in his peripherals as he added something to a hefty cast iron skillet and clanged it onto a stove by the sink. The stove was black and metallic and took up a quarter of the kitchen. Just like the nightstand by the bed, it looked like some antique thing that desperately needed a polishing. How did it even work?

I understood when he opened a groaning hatch beneath the burners and added a handful of wood strips. It was a wood burning stove. I didn't know anyone still used those.

Was I rescued by a pioneer? He lived in a wooden shack—probably built by hand—and cooked his food over a fire. I didn't realize people like him were real. Except for maybe Amish people. Joshua didn't look Amish. He was wearing Levi's and a grey flannel, and he had a hunting knife strapped to his belt.

And a gun.

Somehow, I doubted Amish people carried guns. Oh, and duh, they didn't use electricity. Then again, no one used electricity these days. No one but Joshua. He was growing more mysterious by the minute.

He didn't say a single word when he was finished questioning me, which left me to stare at him as he cooked. He didn't come across as a kindhearted stranger but so far, he hadn't leered at me either. On the creepy scale he was more "murder you because you're disturbing his peace and quiet" than "follow you home at night and climb through your window."

Not exactly the most reassuring assessment.

"You're too skinny." I couldn't say what kind of man Joshua was just yet, but he was a pro at breaking quiet spells with rude comments.

"Didn't anyone ever tell you not to comment on a woman's figure?"

A familiar smell wafted from the stove to hang in the air. Though I hadn't eaten a significant meal in days, maybe longer, the scent of whatever food he prepared made my stomach turn. I wrinkled my nose in recognition when he scraped greasy brown lumps out of the pan. "Um, no thanks. I'm a vegetarian."

Joshua snorted derisively and set the plate of meat on the table in front of me with a clatter. "That's why you're so scrawny."

I pouted. "You're kind of mean."

"And you're whiny," he snapped back.

"I am not!" I whined.

A minute ticked by, and I made no move to touch the plate. I glanced up in a cautious survey of his features. He was scowling. When I crossed my arms and leaned back, he mirrored the movement. I was playing with fire, I knew that, but what better way to get a gauge on the type of person Joshua was? By his expression he was definitely an impatient type. Would that impatience lead to rage? Violence? Not the best idea to provoke him but if I knew what I was up against, I could decide if I needed to try for an escape sooner rather than later.

Another minute passed. My stomach growled painfully but it was drowned out by Joshua's angry noises as he crouched to dig through the cabinet closest to him. There was a series of scuffling sounds and a curse word I wasn't sure I'd even heard before, then the cabinet door slammed. I heard the click and scrape of a can opener, then Joshua thumped a dented can of black beans in front of me. Liquid sloshed over the side and onto the table.

"It's cold." I complained, though mostly to judge how upset he actually was.

"And all the meals you've eaten until this point were hot and fresh, I'm sure." He threw his hands up. "If you quit bitchin' and eat that damn rabbit it might still be hot."

"That was a rabbit?"

He fixed me with a look of pure contempt. I pushed the plate of meat in his direction. He caught it, glared at me some more, then pinched a piece of meat between his fingers and plopped it into his mouth.

His mustache wiggled back and forth when he chewed. It was so odd and fascinating to watch, like a living carpet on his face that moved in its own rhythm. Suddenly I was giggling, my own laughter a foreign sound to my ears. I guess I was finally losing it after all that time alone.

"You are crazy."

"Probably." I covered my mouth with two fingers, but more quiet sounds of amusement tickled their way out of my throat anyway. Joshua frowned—big shocker—and took another piece of meat. As soon as he bit down, I was chortling again. Now he looked more confused than anything else.

"Eat." He nodded at the can.

I heaved a dramatic sigh and brought a small spoonful to my mouth. The beans were cold and bland, but I *was* hungry. So unbearably hungry. I'd gotten past the point where my stomach hurt. There was just a pit in my gut where hunger used to be. Before I knew it, the can was empty, and I was instinctively scanning the table for extra food.

"More?" Joshua asked quietly. I was so fixated on the beans that I hadn't noticed him watching me. My ravenous frenzy was embarrassing.

Not embarrassing enough that I didn't eagerly nod. "Please."

He turned back to the counter. A minute later he was serving bread with a tray of butter and a jar of jam. My mouth started to water.

"Why didn't you start with the bread and jam?"

"Protein."

"Did you bake this yourself?" I picked up a piece of bread and inhaled. Crumbs dotted my upper lip and nose. Joshua wasn't quite frowning anymore but there was still not a smile on his face. That lack of hostility was good enough for me. I grinned at him, much more genuine than before.

"Yup."

"And the jam?"

"Homemade too."

"Where did you get butter?" I eyed the creamy stuff warily. It was wetter than I remembered butter being.

"Butter comes from the goats." He explained, returning to his seat.

"Goats? You have goats? Are you a farmer?" I left out the word "Amish" because I wasn't sure if it was rude to ask.

"Something like that."

"Can I meet them? The goats I mean. I've only ever seen goats in a petting zoo. Well, through the fence of a petting zoo. I wasn't allowed to actually pet them because goats are dirty, and my mother hated dirty." I was oversharing. Side effect of spending too much time alone.

"Maybe. Eat."

"You don't talk much, do you?" I started smearing butter on a slice of bread. Now that I knew where it came from, I swore I could smell the goat.

"Don't have anything to say."

"Somehow, I doubt that. Are you out here all alone?"

"Why are you asking?" The suspicion returned in full force.

"I'm making conversation."

"Or you're gathering information."

"Yes, usually when you get to know someone you are gathering information on them. It sounds unfriendly when you say it like that." I started buttering another piece of bread. The goat butter was different, but I was dumping on so much jam I could hardly taste it.

"Why are you asking?" He repeated.

"Sorry, I was only curious. I didn't see anyone else here and there's only one bed, so I assumed you live by yourself. Seems lonely, not having anyone to talk to. I haven't had anyone to talk to for months." I explained, trying to sound innocent.

"How did you end up in my forest?"

I set the half-eaten slice of bread back on the plate and looked down. I really didn't want to revisit those memories just then. Or ever. "I was running from those men."

"Before that?"

"I got separated from my group when we were following the interstate. I was trying to go east. That's where my group was headed."

"Thought you said you didn't have a group."

"I don't. Not anymore." I snapped, though I felt like a housecat hissing at a lion. I was surprised that I'd even been brave enough to add the edge to my voice.

"How did you get separated?"

Separated was a terribly tame word for what happened. "We stopped to camp. Raiders attacked. They had knives, big ones, like the ones that people use to cut open coconuts." I picked at the crust of the bread and tried to think about the way a knife like that looked cutting a fresh coconut on the beach instead of the arm of a man attempting to ward off an attack.

"Machetes?"

"I think so."

"How many men?"

"I don't know."

"Estimate." He demanded.

"Fifteen?"

"How far from here?" He was doing a good job of hiding it, but he seemed alarmed.

"I-I don't know." I stammered. I saw him preparing to snap the question again, so I quickly gave another answer. "We were still close to Seattle. Maybe forty miles out of the city? Far from here. I've been through countless towns since then."

"When did this happen?" Joshua crossed his arms and leaned back, relaxing slightly.

"It's hard to say. I lost track of time. Four months. Or maybe six? I couldn't keep up with the days." I rubbed my hands over my face to ease the dread that prickled in my stomach when I recalled losing my group and the months that followed.

"And your group? How many?"

I recounted every face and name I could until I had a number. "There were twenty-four of us. We all fit on one bus."

"How did you get away?"

"I was using the bathroom in the bushes when I saw the men coming and I ran." It wasn't like I could have helped. That didn't stop me from feeling guilty. "I left them." Seemed like ever since the blackout, all I'd been doing was running away.

"That was the smart thing to do."

"I guess." I took another bite of bread to distract my mouth and keep my lip from giving away how close I was to tears. I wouldn't cry in front of Joshua. He already thought I was weak. I had to prove him wrong.

"Why were you going east?"

"We heard there were more camps further east. Bigger ones with power and food. I think we were headed for Yakima or the Tri-Cities."

"You think?"

"I was just following everyone else. I didn't know what to do."

He huffed like he didn't expect any better of me. "Why were you looking for other camps?"

"Ours was destroyed. It started as a riot. People were shot. All the supplies were stolen or ruined. One of the National Guard guys helped my group escape with a few crates of packaged food and—what do they call those?—oh, right, MREs, some water, and fuel. We took a school bus from a nearby high school."

I closed my eyes and recalled that day. I heard the pop of gunshots, remembered wondering why fireworks were going off. I thought it was a celebration. I thought maybe the power was coming back on.

"You got any family?"

"My parents are in Texas."

"You didn't head south to meet them."

"No, it appears I didn't."

"You don't like them?" That hardly seemed like useful information.

"Is that any of your business?"

"Is it your business to ask if I'm alone out here?" He countered.

"Touché, big man." I puffed sigh and finished my slice of bread. "I like my parents just fine. Not enough to walk twenty-five hundred miles only to find they've left home. There's no point in looking for people when we can't communicate. I might walk south, and they might travel north, and we'd pass each other on the same mission." And I knew that they would never come looking for me. They might not even be relieved to see me if I made the perilous journey and showed up on their doorstep.

Joshua seemed satisfied with that answer. He didn't ask any other questions, only finished the meat on his plate, watched me finish my bread, and said "You need a bath."

"I'm too skinny and now I stink? Gee, you're delightful."

The look I got was the type of exasperation that led to murder, I was sure of it. "I'll get the water ready. No more food. Need to let your body get used to eating again."

There was a long silence that gave me ample opportunity to argue. I don't know why I had the urge to because he was right, I *really* needed a bath. Part of me wanted to disagree with him because I felt powerful when I did. Being defiant annoyed him but it didn't earn me any of the awful retaliation I anticipated from a man like Joshua.

Well, I couldn't really say that, could I? I didn't know much about him yet, but I was pretty sure there weren't any other men like Joshua.

4

Stranger in the Mirror

Without so much as a backwards glance, Joshua stomped out of the house. Was that a sign of trust? Or was I such a lack of threat that he wasn't worried I'd grab a knife from the block on the counter and ambush him at the door?

If I had any intention of exploring his shack and satisfying my curiosity while he was gone, I quickly changed my mind when I noticed the dog was still inside with me. She sat on a rug on the other side of the room, boxed in by two worn leather recliners, ears alert and eyes focused on me like laser beams. I swear she growled when I even thought about moving.

I decided to restrict my exploring to eyes only. My room in the three bedroom duplex I shared with two roommates in the city was only a little smaller than this place. There was the bed where I woke up—queen size, taking up a good quarter of the room—and a nightstand on either side of it. In the corner beside the bed was a guitar and a short chest of drawers that was as in need of some TLC as much as the rest of the furniture.

The kitchen and dining room combo where I sat was mostly occupied by the wood burning stove. There was barely space for the countertops and the sink. The sink was deep but narrow and by the look—and smell—it hadn't been thoroughly cleaned in a while. In the corner between the cabinet and that mysterious door was the fridge, quietly humming a noise that was now at the top of my favorites list.

How was it possible that he had power? In the middle of nowhere? Add it to the growing list of questions.

The dining room table and chairs were solid wood, and the set might have been pretty once. The table was petite and round, perfect for a breakfast nook. It was this nice chestnut color too, but it was riddled with scratches, dents, and water marks. Joshua wasn't a coaster guy.

I was beginning to get a better picture of him. He was a bachelor escaped from the city. Maybe a hipster barista that threw down his apron and disappeared into the mountains. It would explain the flannel and the beard.

Nope, that man had never touched a latte in his life. The word "Frappuccino" probably wasn't in his vocabulary.

He was a redneck type, then. Maybe this was his family farm. It would explain the outdated appearance. He inherited a goat farm and didn't have the money to fix it up. Or he might not have had the time to before the power went out. Either way, there was no chance this guy was new to living out here. He looked the part too much. He even had the ugly, mean dog.

I looked back over at the black beast in the corner of the room. She was standing now, jowls vibrating but no growl escaping her throat. She was a beautiful animal, actually. A hundred pounds or more with long legs and a thick, muscular chest. Her eyes were that same dark brown as Joshua's and her fur a similar sleek black as his hair.

The dog perked her short, floppy ears up and whipped her head around to look at the door. A few seconds later footsteps pounded outside, practically shaking the whole shack. The front door swung open, and Joshua returned with—what in the world was it? He had some kind of metal tub in his hand that—Oh. No way. Not happening.

He was holding a steel water trough. There was absolutely no chance that he was going to get me to bathe in it.

"I'm not scrubbing down in a goat's water bowl," I said as soon as he closed the front door. He looked at me like he was surprised to see me there, or maybe just surprised I was still bothering to speak to him.

"Yes, you are."

"Gross! No! What's the point of bathing if it's in a dirty goat thingy?"

"It's not dirty. Stop whining." Once again, he moved on, changing the topic before I had a chance to continue my complaint.

"You got any bad injuries besides that one on your chest?"

"On my chest?" My hands reached for the painful spot I'd all but forgotten about. I winced when my fingers pressed the fabric of my shirt into a thin cut. "How did you know that was there? It's under my shirt."

"It bled through."

"I'm bleeding?" I tucked my chin to my chest and sure enough, there was a rust-colored line across my shirt. The mustard yellow top had gone from fashionable—if not filthy—to making me look like a hot dog.

My concerns were ignored as Joshua carried the trough between the two recliners to rest in front of the fireplace. I hadn't given much notice to it before because the dog was in the way. She sat beside it, enjoying the heat from the sparkling logs. Of everything in the shack, it was the most charming.

Like the rest of the tiny structure, it appeared to be made by hand. Uneven and multi-colored stones were stacked together to form a small arch and a half circle hearth. It looked like the perfect place to sit and enjoy a cup of coffee on a snowy Christmas morning.

"You're not bleeding anymore. Might need stitches though. And I need to check for any other wounds that could get infected." He rearranged the chairs to make a path to the kitchen. Joshua must've spent a lot of time talking to himself because he barely raised his voice loud enough for me to discern what he was saying.

I cleared my throat. "I can check. Do you have a mirror?"

He eyed me for a minute. "We'll see."

"Hey, wait," I put a hand up when he marched back into the kitchen to retrieve one of the pots off the stove. Steam was rising from it now. "Don't you have anywhere else you can put that? I'd like some privacy."

"Don't have any."

"You don't have any privacy?" I fisted my hands on my hips.

"No."

"What about in there? Is it a closet? Or a room? Maybe you could just put the tub in there and close the door while I get clean." I waved at the door next to the kitchen.

"No."

"Why? Is that where you keep the bodies of all the other women you rescued?" It was supposed to be a joke, but it sounded a little too accusatory.

"No."

"Is 'yes' even in your vocabulary? It's the opposite of no? Spelled Y-E-S?" Big surprise, he ignored me.

I didn't get up from the table until Joshua stepped through the secret door—it definitely led to a room and not a closet because he disappeared inside for more than five minutes—then returned with a full-length mirror. It was oval shaped and looked to be another garage sale antique that was left to collect dust. He placed it against the wall beside the fireplace and waved me over impatiently. I scooted across the wood floors on socked feet, not trusting my wobbly legs to carry me that far.

I couldn't bring myself to stand in front of the mirror when I was close enough. I was more afraid of what I would see than I was curious about how I'd changed.

I knew my eyebrows would be a little out of sorts since they hadn't been waxed in ages. My hair was probably tangled because I lost my brush. I'd seen a shadowed reflection of my face in puddles and still water from time to time, but I had no idea what I would be confronted with in that mirror. I wanted to look in and see my old self looking back at me, that friendly girl with healthy blonde hair and lively green eyes. Not beautiful but cute. Nice enough to look at.

I doubted I would even recognize myself now.

Joshua made an impatient grunting noise and I startled. He was so quiet and still that his presence had faded out of my awareness. I don't know how that was possible since he was looming over me, his frame twice as wide as mine and his arms probably thicker than my thighs. I'd never considered myself short yet I felt microscopic next to him.

"You're seriously going to stand there?" His only response was to huff, cross his arms, and turn his back to me.

Maybe he didn't trust me to be alone in his living room. Though, his living room was also his bedroom and kitchen so it wasn't like I would be alone if he was in either of those "rooms" anyway.

"Joshua?" He kept ignoring me. "Joshua!"

"What? Would you get it over with? This isn't a damn hotel. I have better things to do than babysit you while you primp in the mirror!"

I was so taken aback that I took a step away. At least that answered the question I hadn't yet asked. "I am not *primping*. Who raised you? Just because it's the end of the world doesn't mean you no longer have to utilize your manners." Of course, I had to be rescued by the only person in the world who managed to make my blood boil with a single sentence. "Why are you helping me? What do you get out of this?" Why was he *babysitting* me if it was such an inconvenience to him? I hadn't found people to be particularly charitable after the blackout.

His mouth was half open like he was ready to make another brusque remark when the question I wasn't asking, the one glaring between the lines, became clear to him. Joshua softened more in that brief moment of recognition than I'd seen since I woke up. A series of emotions played across his face. Understanding shifted to something that was almost sympathy. Then just as quickly it became horror.

I'd never been happier to see a horrified expression on someone's face. Joshua was rude and ill-tempered, but he wasn't expecting any...*compensation*.

I couldn't believe I even had to clarify that. What a time to be alive.

The softness vanished and Joshua was flicking impatient fingers at me. I flicked my hand back at him. I waited until he'd turned again to grab the bottom of my shirt and tug it over my head. I fumbled with the button on my jeans next. It took me three tries to get it undone because of the shudders that still wracked my body. This time I wasn't sure if they were from exhaustion or nerves. Did I really take Joshua's word when he couldn't give me an explanation for why I was here?

I'd promised myself I wasn't going to cry in front of him. It was proving to be a difficult promise to keep.

I was standing in my underwear in some strange man's home while he was only three feet away. I had no clue where I was or who he was. Did it even matter anymore? I wasn't sure. I was so tired of running, of being afraid.

No more fear. I inhaled a huge breath for bravery and stepped up to the mirror.

Despite the fire, the air was cold, making goosebumps rise on my skin. My *pale* skin. That was the first thing I noticed when I saw my reflection. I was ghostly white, which made all the bruises on my legs, arms, and chest look even more apparent.

There were a lot of them. I was dotted with purple and green spots. There were also fresh scratches all over my forearms and neck. None of them were as bad as the angry red line slicing from beneath my collar bone to my left breast.

My hair, once straight and sleek and shiny, was a tangled mass. I'd done my best to comb through it with my fingers but there were still several clumps that were going to take forever to work out with a brush—assuming Joshua owned one. It was greasy too, making my dark blonde into a mousy color.

My eyebrows weren't as bushy as I remembered them getting when they were grown out. At least there was that. They were brown, a shade darker than my hair, and when they were full like this, they made my face too serious.

Beneath those bushy brows, I met my own eyes. The color was the same light green—seafoam green if I was feeling fancy—but they were unfamiliar. Something was missing, some spark that made me look alive. The rings around them were so dark it appeared I had bruises there too. My normally round face seemed misshapen now that my cheeks had lost their plumpness.

Considering how long I'd gone without a full meal, much less three in a day, my body wasn't as bad as I thought it would be. I probably lost twenty pounds.

It might have looked worse if I hadn't gained that freshman fifteen last year and never worked it off. Still, I *was* scrawny. Bony. My breasts, which used to be, in my humble opinion, the most attractive part of my body were pointy little triangles. There was empty space in the fabric cups of my bra.

In another time, before the world came crashing down, some women might be envious of my body. My hip bones stuck out and my stomach was flat. I almost looked like one of those fashion models, the ones bordering on skeletal but making up for it with huge breasts and defined abs. Subtract the breasts and abs and that was me. Well, take away the glossy, airbrushed skin too. My knees were scabby. I was battered and sickly.

Disgusting. I looked disgusting.

Those tears I was desperately trying to hold in arrived with a horrible croaking noise. The croak was followed up with a whimpering gasp that startled Joshua and made him twist in my direction. He had resting bitch face dialed up to a thousand percent. I ignored him, even if he was looking at me in my vulnerable state. All I could do was stand there, sobbing at my own reflection, wrapping my arms tight around myself.

I didn't think I could feel any worse until Joshua asked, "what's wrong with you?"

"What's wrong with me?" I wailed. "The world is ending and everyone I know is probably dead and I look like a walking corpse! And to top it all off, you're asking me what's *wrong* with me? What's wrong with *you*?"

He didn't have a response to that. Joshua made a slow circle around me, inspecting every inch of my skin in the most perfunctory way possible. He was the first man to see me naked and he was looking at me like a used car.

Joshua stopped when he got to my chest. I felt the heat of his hand hovering over my skin but never touching. At least he was respectful. I could be dead in the forest after those two raiders were finished with me. That thought made me cry harder. Behind me, Joshua's every exhale was a cloud of annoyance. I glanced over my shoulder when I heard a floorboard creak and saw him already across the room.

He returned from the kitchen with a boiling pot of water for the trough. Once the tub was full, he stepped through the secret door again. He came back out with a handful of glass bottles, a hairbrush, and a bar of soap that looked homemade. It smelled like lilacs.

By the time the bath was ready, I was less concerned with the lack of privacy than I thought I would be. Joshua had already seen me—most of me, anyway—and he was making a conscious effort not to look. I ignored the nerves as I stripped the last of my clothes off. He took a seat in one of the worn leather recliners, his gaze fixed on the fire like I wasn't even there. My gaze was fixed squarely on him, just in case.

He never snuck a peek, not even in his peripherals. The trough was a bit of an awkward shape for reclining but the water felt amazing. It was the perfect temperature and he'd splashed some fragrant oil in that soothed my aching muscles. I didn't think I would ever get the chance to take a hot bath again and there I was, soaking in luxury.

I spent a few minutes hunched low in the water, trying to get as much of my body submerged as I could. When that got uncomfortable, I sat up and reached for the soap. I smiled the faintest smile, took a rag he'd left for me, and got to work scrubbing.

Next, I had to tackle my hair. It was much longer than I realized. By the time I brushed out all the knots, the water was cool. The bottle of what was presumably homemade shampoo smelled like citronella. It wasn't very sudsy, but it spread through my hair easily enough.

I wanted to cry again when my hair was finally clean. It would have been a good cry this time. I hadn't realized just how dirty I was and just how bad that made me feel. Being clean was an instant boost to morale. And soaking in hot water? I was like a whole different person.

"Thank you, Joshua." It came out on a relaxed sigh. He jerked his chin up in a sharp acknowledgement of my words.

I wasn't even concerned with whether he saw me when I stood to dry myself off. It wasn't like there was anything exciting to see unless he was into toothpicks. I wiped as much water from my skin as I could before stepping onto the rug. I tucked the towel under my armpits and wrapped it around my body, stooping to pick up a pile of clothes beside the tub.

"These aren't mine." I said when I realized I was looking at a pair of men's long johns and an enormous thermal shirt. The long underwear looked fairly new, but the shirt had a fraying hole on the left side and what I hoped was only dirt stains. I gave it a wary sniff.

"Your clothes need to be washed."

"So, you expect me to just go commando until I find a laundromat?" Joshua didn't answer. That was the answer.

Fine. Commando it was. I had to tie the strings on the waistband of the pants in a tight bow to get them to stay up. They were so long that only my toes poked out of the ankle holes. It looked ridiculous. The shirt could be a dress on me. Oh well, at least I didn't smell bad.

"Let me see your chest."

He stood from his chair, his imposing shadow spilling across the living room, and pulled a tin out of his pocket. I turned to face him, eyes downcast as I lifted my shirt. When his hand made contact with my skin I almost jumped. The feel of his fingers was jarring. It was the first time another person had touched me in months, maybe longer.

I sighed louder than I intended when he pressed gauze onto my skin. If he noticed, he didn't care. He only pointed to the bed. I didn't immediately react because I didn't understand. He waved his hand more impatiently. I quirked an eyebrow at him and slowly trailed to the bedside. He gave a nod when I sat on the mattress, then busied himself with something in the kitchen.

"Do you want me to—"

"No." Jeez, he didn't even know what I was going to ask.

The fire was dying down and the room growing darker, but I continued to watch him, my curiosity only increasing as he pulled a collection of jars from a cabinet and started scooping spoonfuls of their contents into a mug. He had to break up small pieces of wood to grow the fire inside the stove before adding another pot of water onto the surface. It seemed an awful lot of effort just for a little hot water.

Steam billowed from the pot within a few minutes. Joshua carefully gripped the handle and poured it over the contents in the mug. When he was finished, he plopped down into a dining chair across from the bed and eyed me suspiciously.

I could only meet his eyes for a heartbeat before averting my gaze. He didn't avert his. I wiggled further up onto the bed and tucked my knees to my chest. Joshua stared at me for an uncomfortably long time. I couldn't figure him out. First, he avoided looking at me and now he wouldn't look away. Eventually he turned his attention back to the mug and I exhaled shakily.

Satisfied with his hot concoction, he strode to the bed, handed me the mug, and hurried back to his spot at the table. I sniffed the liquid warily. Whatever he brewed was pungent and sweet. The smell was so strong it made my lips droop in an involuntary grimace.

"What is this?" I asked quietly.

"Tea," he responded.

"Not hibiscus, I'm guessing."

"Just drink."

I did as he commanded. The first sip was the worst. That pungent scent tasted just like it smelled. There was a bitter aftertaste too. My throat tightened and I had to hold the tea in my mouth for half a minute, mentally arguing with my gag reflex until it finally agreed to give in and let me swallow. I did my best not to make a disgusted face as I drank but the flavor never improved. If this was an acquired taste, I hoped that I didn't drink it often enough to acquire it.

"Thanks," I coughed when the mug was empty. All I got was another sharp nod.

I set it on the nightstand and resumed my upright fetal position. It was mostly to keep myself warm now rather than an attempt to hide from Joshua's one-sided staring contest. Fifteen or twenty minutes passed in silence before I broke it with a loud yawn.

I didn't get much sleep these days and when I did it was interrupted every hour as I jolted awake in fear. For the first time in weeks, maybe months, I was safe from any outside threats—unless Joshua was one, but I was fairly convinced that he wasn't—and it was like my body knew it.

My eyelids were heavy, head foggy, muscles relaxing. Relaxing a little too much, actually. It felt the same as the subtle drowsy haze that I got when my mother poured me half a glass of wine during our last Thanksgiving together.

Did Joshua put something in my tea? I was watching him the whole time. If it was drugged, the effects were mild enough for me to fight against them. I blinked back sleepiness and straightened.

"What kind of tea was that?"

"Herbal," he grunted.

"Did you put something in it?" Not that I believed he'd just come out and admit it if he secretly drugged me.

Joshua relaxed further into his chair, that same soft expression from earlier flitting across his face. "Only herbs to help you sleep and to ease pain. You fell hard. Surprised you didn't crack your ribs."

"Oh." I really needed to think of something else to say. "That's nice of you."

"Sleep," he rumbled.

I scanned the room until my eyes fell on the extra space in the bed beside me. "Where do you sleep?"

"I don't."

I waved a dismissive hand at him. "Of course, you do. You can die without sleep."

"I'm not dead yet."

That was the end of our conversation. He got up from the table and settled back in the oversized recliner by the fireplace. He must have sat in that one often. Compared to the twin chair on the other side of the rug, it was worn.

The leather arms were faded and fraying. When he lowered himself onto the cushion the whole chair creaked like it struggled to bear the weight.

What are you doing out here all by yourself, Joshua?

Joshua watched the fire, and I watched him for as long as I could stay awake. He was still, almost unnaturally so. There were several times where I couldn't even tell if he was breathing.

This isn't a damn hotel. I flipped his words around in my head, trying to make sense of them compared to his actions.

He was being awfully hospitable to a stranger in the end of the world. I hugged the pillow beneath me. It was a pretty good one, not too floppy, not too firm. The bed was warm, the mattress soft. My belly was full, and I was clean. All of it thanks to him.

If this wasn't a hotel and he wasn't being charitable, then there *was* a price, even if Joshua hadn't named it yet. I drifted off wondering how I would end up paying for my stay in his little cabin.

5

Snake in the Grass

A sense of urgency roused me, but I was just so comfortable. I was finally in my own bed, in my own room. That shouldn't be possible. The day I left for college my mother converted my bedroom into a guest room. I wasn't about to question it. I was cozy and everything smelled like cinnamon.

A loud clang startled me from my dozing state and suddenly my brain was screeching. *Get up! Someone found me! I need to get up!*

That panic didn't translate into motion right away. It took me five solid seconds to open my eyes. I saw greying wood above me. I heard unfamiliar clattering noises. I smelled that spicy scent, food too. Then I was bolting upright and screaming.

I don't know why I screamed. Maybe if there was an animal poking around me, I would spook it?

There was an animal, as it turned out, but I didn't spook her. A big black dog sat a few feet from me. When I shot up, she stood, fur bristling, and growled.

"What the fuck?" There was another clang as the man in the kitchen beyond the foot of the bed set a heavy pan on the stove a little too hard. Once Joshua recognized me as the source of the shrill sound, he scowled. "What the hell is wrong with you?"

I gaped at him. Despite the rush of adrenaline, I wasn't fully awake. Collecting one thought in my head was like walking through molasses. My brain finally clicked on as I recalled last night. Joshua frowning at me, feeding me, bathing me. Oh. Yeah, he totally saw me naked.

"What's wrong with you?" He repeated.

I brushed hair from my face and straightened. "That's kind of a rude thing to ask, don't you think?"

"You always wake up screaming?" He turned his back to me and readjusted the pan he'd almost dropped. Something was steaming on the stove in front of him. I could hear the faint crackle of the wood burning inside the ugly steel thing.

"Only when I wake up in a stranger's house with his monster dog sizing me up for breakfast." I shot the dog the meanest look I had. She was unimpressed.

"Kuna, leave it." Joshua muttered without turning around. The dog, Kuna, shook her head until her ears flapped but eventually obeyed the command and trotted over to the fireplace. She plunked down on the rug with a loud sigh and an angry glare in my direction.

The room was brighter in the morning, but barely. There was a window over the sink, to Joshua's right with yellowing curtains. They looked like they could have been a nice shade of white at one point. Years of dust didn't do the color any favors. The faintest blue glow through the window told me the sun hadn't even crested the horizon. Dang, he got up early.

I surveyed the space a second time, hoping to see more now that I wasn't squinting in firelight. I spotted two additional windows. One by the front door and one to the right of the fireplace. They were as tiny as the kitchen window and covered by matching curtains.

Other than a small bookshelf that I hadn't noticed last night, there wasn't much else to see. All the added light did was reveal that the place was dirtier than it looked in the dark.

It really was just a shack. One tiny building with all the rooms of a house—minus the bathroom, which I really needed to use—combined into one. I did another cursory scan to make sure there wasn't a bucket or bottles of pee in the corner.

"Do you have a bathroom?" I twisted to put my feet on the floor. Sitting up still made me feel woozy.

"Outside."

"Do you just use the yard like the dog?" I didn't think it was an unreasonable question. He had no bathroom, and he cooked his food over a wood burning stove. Pretty primitive. I assumed his restroom habits might be too.

That was an incorrect assumption. Joshua frowned over his shoulder. This one was less frustrated and more of an, "is this girl stupid?" look. He abandoned his cooking, walked to the front door, and crossed his arms. When I didn't trot over there like his obedient dog, he cleared his throat and frowned harder.

You'd think someone so impatient would use words to get their message across more efficiently. I eventually grasped what he wanted and teetered over to his side. He yanked an insulated raincoat from a rack and handed it to me. Then he kicked boots in my direction. They were mine. I slipped them on without socks, wiggled into the oversized jacket, and followed him out the door.

The shack had a porch. It was the cutest part of the little structure. A wooden bench and two Adirondack chairs were tucked to one side. It gave the building a rustic, country-living look. All it needed was one of those bling crosses above the door and some chipping white paint.

Past the porch was a huge field full of plants. They didn't appear to be ordered in any specific way but there was a path snaking through them and beds made from river stones. If I hadn't noticed the tomato plants scattered throughout, I might not have known it was a garden. Beyond the garden there was a wall of massive evergreen trees, shadowing the surrounding area and making it impossible to see what else was back there, if anything.

I inhaled deeply. The air was fresh, cool, and clean. There was the faintest whiff of mulch and a scent that reminded me of a petting zoo—perhaps those goats he mentioned—but otherwise it smelled earthy, like the forest. Distantly I heard the clucking of chickens and what could have been a bleating goat. The rain was only a light drizzle today, but it muffled much of the noise coming from beyond the house.

We circled around the side of the cabin—I was training myself not to call it a shack, that seemed impolite—and passed a woodshed. The scent of sawdust and the sharp tang of pine permeated the air around it. I took another inhale and realized that same smell lingered on Joshua. Not that I was smelling him.

We arrived at our destination a few hundred feet past the woodshed. An outhouse. Joshua had a *real* outhouse. It was literally four tall planks of wood with a door cut into it, topped with a triangular roof.

Said roof looked less than satisfactory in the safety department. The wood was very, very weathered and it had a layer of moss pressing down on it. Hopefully I wouldn't be crushed while I was taking a pee.

Joshua walked me to the door, gestured with his hand, and waited. Yup, he was going to stand out there and wait for me. Not a particularly trusting fellow, I noted as he subtly rested his hand on the gun strapped to his right hip.

The interior of the outhouse was exactly what I imagined: a wooden porta-potty. There was a bench with a toilet seat in the middle. When I lifted it and looked inside, I only saw blackness. It was just a giant hole in the ground. I had no right to be disgusted since I'd been squatting in the woods and kicking dirt over my waste, but it still grossed me out.

That and I was slightly afraid I was so skinny I would fall down it.

I had to pee like crazy and yet, once I stepped into that outhouse, my urge dissipated. Joshua could probably hear me pee through the door.

He saw me naked last night. It doesn't get any worse than that.

I had to think about *every* waterfall I'd ever seen to overcome my performance anxiety.

When I was done, I retied my pants, looked around, and realized there was no way for me to clean my hands. Not even sanitizer. I wrinkled my nose at them and tucked them into my pockets. Joshua took off back to the house without even glancing at me when I shouldered the door open.

Inside, Joshua watched me wash my hands in the kitchen sink then pointed towards the bed again. Did he seriously want me to go back to bed? The sun was rising. I followed his finger to the nightstand and saw another mug waiting for me.

I nodded my understanding and plopped down on the bedside. Beside the mug was a toothbrush, a jar of grey powder, and two little green leaves. I was beginning to feel like I was staying at a bizarre bed and breakfast.

This isn't a damn hotel. Okay, big guy. Whatever you say.

I sniffed the mug first. That was the source of the spicy aroma. Two whole cloves and a slice of apple floated beneath the amber liquid. I sipped cautiously, unable to hold back a soft moan when I tasted the sweet cinnamon concoction.

Joshua peeked over his shoulder until I finished everything in the mug. "Brush with the powder, rinse with water, then chew the leaves. You can swallow or spit them out."

I did as he instructed. I had no idea what kind of powder this was, but I had heard of people brushing their teeth with charcoal and this looked similar. Other than a slight saltiness, there was no taste. It felt weird and made me drool a lot, but it also made my teeth beautifully clean. I couldn't remember the last time I brushed my teeth. I'd taken to scraping them with my fingernails—I know, ew—or abrasive plants.

I nibbled the edge of one leaf. Spearmint. Not seeing any obvious place to spit the leaves, I half choked in my attempt to swallow them. Trying to appear nonchalant while my eyes watered and my throat burned, I sauntered—no, it was still kind of a wobble—to the kitchen table and took a seat.

There were two pans on the stove top and a steaming pot. Joshua was making a feast by the looks of it. He stepped away from the stove to retrieve a small glass French press. On the bottom was an inch of dark grounds. Was that—no way!

"Are you making *coffee*?" I gasped as he poured boiling water over the grounds and covered the press.

"Chicory and dandelion root. No more coffee until next summer." He went back to the stove and stirred the other two pans with a wooden spoon.

"What's chicory? Wait, until next summer? Where are you going to get coffee?"

"Chicory is a plant." Oh, wow, couldn't have gathered that on my own. "Coffee grows in one of the greenhouses."

"You *grow* coffee?" I asked incredulously.

"Yes."

"Like they do in Hawaii? And you have a greenhouse? Where? How big is your farm?"

Joshua gave me that narrow eyed, suspicious scowl. "Why do you want to know?"

"Um, hello! It's cool! I didn't know you could grow your own coffee. How *do* you grow your own coffee? Does it grow in a pod? Can I see it?"

"Maybe." For every twenty words I spoke, Joshua had one.

He served me a plate of scrambled eggs, sautéed greens cooked with fresh garlic, a pile of greasy brown vegetables, and more mystery. I was so not touching that. Next, he put jam, butter, and a cute roll the size of my fist by my plate.

The final touch was a mug full of the chicory and dandelion root drink with a pitcher of milk on the side. It had to be goat milk. It seemed darker and creamier than what I remembered milk looking like but it was probably processed differently—if at all—than the skim milk I bought at the local convenience store for two dollars.

"Wow, this looks great. I don't know how to thank you." *Hopefully this meal doesn't add too much to my debt.* I smiled at him.

He sat across from me and dug into his food without acknowledging me at all. His mustache moved up and down across his lips. I quickly averted my gaze, so I didn't bust into another fit of giggling.

I went to bed feeling quite full after my first real meal in weeks, but the hunger had returned in full force this morning. Still, it was kind of odd that I went from running helplessly through the woods to sitting at some man's breakfast table with a plate of eggs in front of me. Could I be lying unconscious on the forest floor somewhere and making this all up?

I took a hesitant bite of scrambled eggs. A little too salty but that should be proof this wasn't a fantasy, right? If it was, I would have dreamed up French toast with powdered sugar and a latte loaded with whipped cream instead.

Another bite. Suddenly I was halfway through the plate. The greasy brown stuff turned out to be mushrooms. I devoured them. The garlic greens too. I practically scraped every crumb of food off the plate. Except for the meat.

Joshua looked up from his meal and raised his eyebrows when he saw how much I'd eaten. His plate was still half full, though he did have a much bigger serving than me. His eyebrows quickly sunk when he saw the meat on the edge of my plate.

I smiled politely and tapped my fingers on the table. He made a loud noise that he might have intended as a sigh and leaned over, stabbed the meat rather aggressively, and eating my portion.

After my plate was clear I fixed my mug of...tea? I added a splash of milk. Joshua noticed and slid a jar of honey in my direction, which I gladly added to the mug. If this was meant to replace coffee, it failed. It was better than I expected—rich, slightly bitter, full bodied—but left me craving a cup of coffee even more than when I started drinking.

It should have been awkward to sit at a stranger's breakfast table. It wasn't. The silence wasn't heavy or tense. When I felt the need to fill it, I did so with more eating. I reached for a roll, broke it in half, and was about to scoop some jam onto it when Joshua shoved the butter at me.

"No offense, I'm sure you put a lot of hard work into your butter, but I don't really like it. Goat milk is kind of weird."

Apparently, he wasn't offering. "No bread without butter."

"Is that a house rule?"

"You won't eat meat and you need fat. Butter." He explained through a mouthful of food.

"The food was greasy. I'm sure I got plenty of fat."

He snatched the bread from my hand, smeared a ridiculous amount of butter on it, and handed it back to me. I took it from him with a pout. I considered leaving the bread on my plate and refusing to eat it out of spite but considering that just yesterday I was fainting due to lack of food, I decided I shouldn't be ungrateful. Who knew how many more meals I might get after this?

Joshua finished eating, sipped thoughtfully from his mug, and resumed his staring.

"What?" I asked with a little more snap to my tone than I intended.

He took another long sip before responding. "You've got no one looking for you?"

"Not that I know of."

"And nowhere you were going?"

"I told you, east. And even that wasn't working out so well since I had no compass and map," I admitted.

"Alright."

"If you put just a few more words into your sentences it would be much easier to communicate with you." He didn't like my recommendation.

"You can wash your clothes outside after breakfast. It's raining so no point in putting a line up. There's a stand on the porch. Set it up by the fire."

"Okay." I pinched my lips together and nodded.

"I've got work to do. Come back in when you're done washing up," he ordered, rising from the table and taking both plates with him.

"And do what?"

"Rest."

"I'm not tired."

"Doesn't matter. You're weak."

That was that. Joshua cleared the table, rinsed the dishes, and left me sitting there to contemplate why he wasn't telling me to pack my bag and be on my way. As soon as he was done in the kitchen he tugged on his boots and opened the front door. The dog, Kuna, jumped up from her spot on the rug and bolted through the doorway after him.

I should have demanded to know why he was helping me. I should have asked what he wanted in exchange for this…I wasn't sure I could call it kindness. Joshua didn't have the demeanor of a person that did nice things for the sake of being nice. Saving my life was way more than nice. Following it up by clothing, cleaning, and feeding me?

Seemed like the kind of thing a person did to put you in their favor.

When did I become so cynical? I wanted to believe people were good, inherently so. Maybe they could be, even if their axe murderer demeanor didn't reflect it.

I gave up thinking too hard about my presence in Joshua's home and did as he suggested. Now that I was clean, I could see—and *smell*—how awful my clothes were. I

carried my armful outside and found a big metal bucket and a washboard on the porch. A real life washboard. Maybe Joshua was Amish, and he just made an exception for the fridge? Otherwise, why did he have all this pioneer stuff? He didn't seem like he was dirt poor. Solar panels and handguns weren't usually signs of poverty.

I pondered it more as I brought the rest of the hot water from the stove outside and poured it over my clothes. There was a tub of powder that I assumed was soap. I sprinkled a very generous amount over my clothes and mixed it around with my hands. I had to pause for a breather afterward.

Yes, pushing my clothes around in a bucket of water made my heart pound and my head spin. At least it kept me from getting too cold.

My jeans were caked with dirt, my shirts had sweat and berry stains, and my underwear—yeah, I won't even go there. It was pretty gnarly.

Once they were done soaking, I grabbed the washboard and stared helplessly at it for almost a minute. I'd seen people use them in movies. It seemed simple in theory. I gave up on trying to figure out the best way and just rubbed the crotch of my underwear along the metal. It was an awkward motion for me, and I kept dropping clothes but eventually, I found a rhythm.

I repeated the process with everything, pausing between each garment to rest. Even the slightest exertion had my heart racing. The scrubbing was hard on the arms too.

When I was finished, I lugged the laundry stand inside along with my clothes. I set the clothes up on the stand, placed two logs on the hot ashes from the last fire, and searched the surrounding area for matches. When I didn't find any by the fireplace, I took my search into the kitchen. Joshua came through the door right as I was opening a drawer by the stove.

"What are you doing?" He snarled.

"Oh, sorry, I was just looking for matches."

"Matches?"

"For the fire." I pointed uselessly at the fireplace, feeling like I'd been caught doing something much worse than looking for fire starting supplies.

He stomped over to the hearth, not bothering to remove his boots and tracking mud all over the floor. He knelt beside the fire and lifted a rectangular black stone. "You didn't see this?"

"How am I supposed to start a fire with a rock? I thought that only worked in movies."

"You're helpless." Joshua stuffed bark shavings under the logs, held the stone over the fireplace, and rubbed a piece of metal along it. A spray of sparks flew from the stone.

I rolled my eyes. "Well excuse me! Not everyone lives like Laura Ingalls Wilder."

He stopped his hurried fire-making to stare up at me, almost seeming surprised. Then he realized we were making eye contact—apparently that was not something he was fond of—and Joshua quickly finished his task.

He waved at the fireplace, somehow managing to make the simple gesture appear belittling and irritated all at once. Thankfully he left before I was tempted to make another sarcastic remark.

Well, at least he's only a jerk and not a serial killer. I thought, but not before giving the secret door a wary look. *Or at least I'm not his type if he is a serial killer.*

I didn't have anything else to do now that my clothes were clean. I gave the bookshelf a cursory scan, hoping the books that Joshua read might give me a hint about what kind of person he was. Most books had the word botany, permaculture, or agriculture in the title. A handful were about wildlife, and one had a complicated science-y title that translated to "how to tell the weather without a weather app."

If I decided I wanted to take a nap and couldn't fall asleep, I would pick one of those up for a read and would instantly be cured of my waking state.

A nosier person would have snooped in Joshua's absence. There were a lot of unanswered questions about him, and his lifestyle and I suspected he wouldn't be terribly forthcoming. Even the idea felt wrong. He'd done a lot for me, and I wasn't planning on repaying him by digging through his drawers. He trusted me alone in here, after all. He even left kitchen knives out in plain view on the counter. I took that as a show of faith.

We were both taking a risk with our miniscule amount of trust. Every part of my story could have been a lie. Any of the few details he gave me about himself could also be untrue. Once upon a time I probably wouldn't have even considered that. I had no reason not to trust people before.

Now, people were snakes. Their motivations were rarely clear and when they were, they were rarely good. At any moment they might rise from the grass and strike at you.

If I really thought about it, people had always been snakes and I had always been far too trusting for my own good. I wanted to think the best of people, to see the good in them. I couldn't afford to do that anymore.

I wasn't doing that with Joshua, was I? Did I already trust him without grasping what I was getting myself into by accepting his help?

I sat on the edge of the bed and looked to the door where he thundered through fifteen minutes earlier. Only twenty-four hours had passed since he brought me back here. Was it possible he was only waiting for me to regain a bit of strength before making a move?

I snorted. *What kind of move? He's more likely to break me up and use me as tinder than he is to touch me.*

I stretched out on the bed and stared up at the ceiling, which was about as entertaining as reading about growing seasons in the Pacific Northwest. I didn't think I was tired until I woke to the sound of heavy boots on the porch. Joshua stood in the doorway, scanned the room until he found me on the mattress, then left again.

This repeated every hour for much of the day. He must have been timing himself because I was counting too and each time sixty minutes passed, he would return. That schedule was interrupted twice when he escorted me to the bathroom—which didn't make me feel like a prisoner *at all*—and once when he came in to eat lunch. He insisted I eat as well.

Joshua and Kuna returned for the last time as the sun was setting, pretty late since I was fairly certain it was still summer. He carried in a chunky basket that he set on the table *before* kicking his muddy boots off.

No wonder it was dirty in here. He didn't bother shaking the rain off his coat either. I waited until he was finished removing his gear—and until the dog had wandered over to the fireplace and sprawled out on the rug—before rising from the bed and tiptoeing to the table to peek inside the basket.

I was a *little* nosy.

"Cold?" Joshua noticed goosebumps on my forearms when I rolled up extra long sleeves. I nodded. "More rain coming tomorrow. It's not getting any warmer. You got anything better than your jacket?" He asked as he moved the laundry stand so he could get the fire going again. That was the most I'd heard from him since breakfast.

My olive green jacket hung limply on the corner of the stand. It was an early birthday gift to myself the first fall I moved to Washington. Everyone warned me about the rain, but I thought they were exaggerating. It was polyester and fairly thin, so it didn't provide much in the way of warmth. I

t was also supposed to be water resistant, but I'd found that after an hour in continuous rain, it resisted zero moisture. It looked good with a pair of black skinny jeans and pumps though.

"No. That's all." I collected my clothes from the stand and dumped them on the bed to fold. They were crunchy and stiff but at least they were clean.

Joshua passed me on his way to the chest of drawers by the bed. His shadow pooled over me, blocking out the light from the fire. He was such a big person and not just because he was unusually tall. There was a weight to his presence, a potent self-assurance that came effortlessly to him.

I spent my life around my father and men like him; confident, well-spoken, and assertive. Men who considered themselves alpha males. They were the type of people who took what they wanted. None of them carried themselves like Joshua did. They were hot air balloons, powered by overinflated egos. It didn't take much to make them fall from the sky.

I got the feeling it would take a lot to make Joshua fall. He was solidly on the ground.

The middle drawer of his dresser squeaked when he yanked it open and pulled out a faded blue flannel. He tossed it onto the bed next to my folded laundry. "That'll do for now."

The fleece lined shirt was way too big for me, but it was cozy, and it smelled of smoky pine and cloves. I wanted to change into my own clothes but once again I was faced with the privacy issue. The whole house was condensed into one room. I had nowhere to go where Joshua wouldn't see me. Modest wasn't an option.

"I'm getting dressed." I kept as casual and confident a tone as I could muster. He was already at the hearth. I had to assume that his back being turned was acknowledgement of my warning.

My hands shook as I yanked Joshua's tent of a shirt off my shoulders and quickly fastened my bra. I tugged on leggings so fast I almost fell over. Relief only came once I was in my own clothes.

Being underweight already made me feel like I had the body of a child. Wearing huge men's clothing that hid the few womanly features I had didn't help. I was much more comfortable in the freshly laundered leggings and magenta tank top. The pink didn't go with my borrowed blue flannel at all but warm was better than matching.

The basket Joshua brought in was full of vegetables. There were hard yellow squashes with green stripes, heads of broccoli, cucumbers, tomatoes, carrots, beets, kale and a cabbage. I was thoroughly impressed, which I made sure to voice. His answer—which I was beginning to believe was the only response he was capable of—was to grunt.

He roasted most of the veggies with butter and some herb he picked from a pot on the windowsill above the sink. I hadn't noticed the six pots perched behind the curtain. There was basil—that one I recognized for sure—and maybe cilantro. Or parsley, I could never tell the difference without tasting them.

The breakfast Joshua cooked was good. The dinner was delicious. I wouldn't admit it to him, but his cooking was a lot better than I expected.

"How long have you lived out here?" I waited until he was distracted by food to begin prying again.

"Long time."

"When did you decide to become a farmer?"

"I didn't."

"Are you from Washington?"

He answered with a fork in his mouth so the "yes" came out muffled by food.

"Do you have any brothers or sisters?"

"Why are you asking so many questions?" He grumbled.

"I'm trying to make our conversation less one-sided. If I don't ask a question, you don't talk." I hid the tremor that the gruff snap of his voice startled out of me with a shrug.

"Sounds like you're gathering information."

"Yeah, you said that already. What do you think I'm going to do, steal your identity? I could hardly pass as you."

His dark eyes burned into me. I met his challenging gaze, still shaking. "Or figure out what I've got going on here and let your raider buddies know."

"Seriously?" The accusation was so absurd that I let out a deep belly laugh. It was his turn to be startled. Good.

"What's wrong with you?" Joshua masked surprise with his trademark frown.

"You should really stop asking that. It's not very nice."

"I'm not nice."

"Thanks for dinner." I said as a subtle disagreement. He was nice enough to cook for me. The laughter lingered on my face, and I gave him a very wide, genuine smile. It made him so uncomfortable that he returned his attention to his plate with a sharp jerk of his head.

The silence stretched on, and my good humor began to wane. I paused my eating, twirling a piece of squash in a pool of butter. "What did you mean when you asked about me being bait?"

He stopped mid chew, studying me. "You really just ran into those fuckers yesterday?"

"Yes."

"It's a tactic raiders use," he swallowed. "Sending helpless women, sometimes kids, to lure folks in. A woman begging for help is a good diversion."

"And when you asked if I was," I choked on the word, "willing?"

"I don't reckon most women in raider groups want to be there. Men who go around robbing and maiming don't make good company."

I set my fork down on my plate. "That's awful, really awful."

"That's the world now." He kept eating, unfazed.

A thought struck me. "How do you know so much about raiders? There can't be that many all the way out here." My voice rose an octave with cautious hope. Maybe the men that chased me yesterday weren't raiders at all, just two travelers with bad intentions.

"I hear things."

I narrowed my eyes. "Hear things where?"

He mirrored my expression. "You ask too many questions."

"And you don't answer enough of them!" I immediately snapped my mouth shut, fearing my raised voice would finally draw a reaction from him. I tried to justify myself. "You're the first person I've talked to in...I don't know how long. I don't know anything. I don't know the state of the world anymore."

"It's as bad as it gets out there." Joshua's voice was steady. He kept scraping food from his plate without so much as twitching at my outburst.

I breathed out an imperceptible sigh. "And in here?"

"Same as it ever was." I wasn't sure if that was a good thing based on the way he said it.

When Joshua didn't say anything else, I decided to try lightening the mood with more friendly conversation. "Well, I'm from Texas. Dallas, to be specific. That always surprises people since I don't say y'all or anything like that. My parents are East Coasters who moved to Houston for work before I came into their lives. They don't really have accents either. I moved here two years ago for school. It was scary, at first. I love cities but coming to a new one all alone was overwhelming. I was barely adjusted to life on the west coast when the blackout happened."

He glanced up at me but still said nothing. I paused to take a few bites of food before adding, "I've never been on a farm. I saw plenty of them as a kid, but it was mostly cornfields and feed lots. Those always made me sad. That's why I became a vegetarian. Do you take good care of your animals?"

"Hmm." I assumed that was meant to be a "yes."

"So, you were farming all day? That's why you were gone?" Asking if he was "farming" was a stupid question and based on the look he gave me, he agreed. "Yes."

"How much food do you grow?"

"Plenty."

"Is this like a *farm*-farm or just a hobby farm?"

Another "are you stupid?" look but he answered anyway. "I don't grow commercially, if that's what you're asking."

"I suppose even if you did, that wouldn't matter now. It's not like there's a farmer's market down the road."

Joshua cocked his head and his face twisted into an odd look. Perhaps that was meant to be a joke. I never found out. After my last comment he stood, tidied up the kitchen—not as thoroughly as I would have—and started boiling water for tea.

I wrinkled my nose when he brewed another cup of the pungent stuff from the night before and expected irritation. Instead, his face relaxed just a hint and there was a flash of something—dare I say—friendly in his eyes. I tried wrinkling my nose again, but he only gave a slight shake of his head and finished the tea off with a spoonful of honey. I wasn't sure if that added sweetness made it better or worse.

He handed me the mug, pointed to the bed, and retreated to his chair by the fire. Feeling brave, I ignored his command and carried the hot drink to the neighboring chair, carefully balancing it as I sat. Joshua and the dog both turned to give me matching glowers.

I cleared my throat. "I'm very grateful for everything you've done for me." I gulped too much tea, the liquid burning all the way from my tongue to my stomach. When I'd composed myself as much as I was going to, I continued with, "If you'll point me toward the nearest road or town, I can be out of your hair by sunup. I'd like to keep going east."

"East through the cascades?"

"Mhmm."

Joshua was incredulous. "On the cusp of autumn?"

"Yup." Not that I'd known just how close autumn was.

"You've got a month before you hit snow. Maybe less."

"I'll walk fast."

"And eat what?"

I was getting to the point where I felt he was poking holes in my plan because he thought he knew better, not because he was genuinely concerned for my safety. "Look, Joshua, I appreciate your help, but I'm not stupid." I tucked my feet under my legs and faced him. "Nothing comes for free anymore and I don't know if I can pay whatever debt it is I'm accruing by staying here."

The silence that followed was a lead weight on my chest. Somehow, Joshua's dark gaze managed to feel even heavier. It broke through my ribs and seared my lungs, making them struggle to suck in air. I'd never met someone so intense. Every expression, every twitch of his jaw muscle, every shift in his heavy brows, felt like it was done with this terrifying ferocity.

Watching him—and being watched by him—was akin to watching a predatory animal. There was no movement that didn't display the lethality he was capable of. For all that it was frightening, it was also mesmerizing.

"What do you think I want from you?"

I squirmed, not wanting to give an answer that he would agree with. "I-I don't know."

"Maybe you're not the one with debts to pay."

A sip of tea slipped down my throat, then another. Finally, I blurted, "what is that supposed to mean?"

"Penance."

That cleared exactly nothing up for me. Did that mean he was helping me to ease his own conscience? To get back in God's good graces? What spiritual debts did he have to pay that warranted giving up his living space and resources to a stranger? That was a heck of an imbalance on the karmic scales.

"I don't understand."

"Go to bed." He jerked his chin to the corner of the room. "You're safe here."

I hadn't realized that I obeyed him until I was sitting on the edge of the mattress, hands cupped around my rapidly cooling mug.

You're safe here. It had to be a lie. I wasn't safe anywhere, hadn't been since the blackout. Safety was an illusion and Joshua was as much a snake as anyone, coiled in my path, camouflaged as something innocuous.

But God, did I want to believe him. He was so sure of everything he did, so competent and capable and...safe. Whatever and whoever Joshua might be, he made me feel safe.

And that was the most dangerous part of all.

6

Handmade Isolation

It was mid-August when Joshua found me. That meant, much to my surprise and his, I survived on my own for almost five months. I felt like I'd lost time. Those five months were blended together in a haze of panic and hunger. I was a nomadic animal, scavenging as I went.

Joshua requested—or demanded depending on how you chose to interpret his tone—that I tell him the whole story of my survival, from the day of the blackout until the moment I fell at his feet.

None of the movies I watched about the end of days prepared me for the reality of what I saw before I left Seattle. No one wanted to think about what a hospital looked like when they finally ran out of fuel for their generators. No one wanted to describe the smell of death that hung heavy in the air when they carted body after body to the cemetery, dumping them in a mass grave with none of the respect our dead used to receive.

I hadn't realized how truly selfish I was in the beginning. I'd thought the worst a blackout did was make it impossible for us to charge our cell phones and cause all the chocolate ice cream to melt. If I'd really given it some thought, I might have considered that one or two comatose people plugged in at a hospital would pass away without electricity. Tragic but probably inevitable.

There were so many technologies I never had to bother with, so many intricate systems that kept people healthy and fed and safe. Without power, people began dying from simple ailments. Some of them passed from exposure to elements. It didn't matter that most of them were elderly. They were people and less ignorance and carelessness might have saved their lives. \

Joshua started that discussion three weeks ago. I knew for certain this time because I was careful to keep track of the days. I didn't go as far as ticking them off in notches on the wall. That would only make me feel more like a prisoner.

Joshua wasn't holding me captive, necessarily. He never said I couldn't pack up and leave. He was just being secretive, hovering around me when I went anywhere besides the kitchen.

He had goats and greenhouses and plenty more but all I saw was whatever was visible between the porch and the outhouse. I took in as much as I could during those bathroom visits, but the property was quite large. Joshua was also not too keen on answering questions.

Both the woodshed and the house had thick solar panels covering the roofs. I'd heard rumors about state governments rushing to install solar technology on essential buildings like hospitals, but they'd never been confirmed.

Apparently solar power worked just fine. Joshua's only comment on the matter was the anyone who blamed the blackout on an EMP was a moron, though the word he used was much less polite. The blackout wasn't exactly a blackout after all. Did that mean the rumors about abundant wind energy in the east were true too? I wouldn't know until I saw for myself if I ever made it that far.

A week into my stay I noticed a fence through the trees beyond the garden space. There were metal posts that caught the late summer sunlight in a dull glitter. It was a very tall fence made of very thick wood. More like a wall, really.

The garden visible from the porch was much more intricate than I'd initially noticed. Huge stones carved winding paths that twisted through clusters of green. The river rock raised beds each had a different shape and housed different varieties of plants. I couldn't discern any type of order to where each plant was placed but there had to be one. Joshua wasn't the most organized and tidy person in his home but in his garden, he was meticulous.

I didn't recognize much of what was growing beyond the apple trees that were loaded with pink and yellow fruit. Even then I only identified them because the apples were a dead giveaway. Maybe if I asked nice enough, he would let me pick a few. After three weeks of doing nothing but eating, napping, and flipping through plant books, I was slowly going mad with cabin fever.

Joshua sensed it before I ever voiced my frustration. For someone who lived alone in the wilderness, he was very intuitive about people. I told him that once and got a snort that I think was a laugh.

It wasn't an inaccurate assessment though. On day twenty-one he wordlessly carried our breakfast plates to a little white table on the porch.

The sun was never up when Joshua was—which he made sure was also when I got up by creating a concert of clattering sounds in the kitchen—but it made breakfast on the porch that much more spectacular. We couldn't see the sunrise because of the tree line. That didn't mean the view wasn't breathtaking. The sky turned a pale shade of pink and washed the green and brown world in that same delicate color.

"Beautiful view you have out here," I murmured as I sipped my tea, knees tucked to my full belly, a wool blanket wrapped around my shoulders.

Joshua gave me one of those long, quiet looks that I was slowly growing accustomed to. "Yup."

That day I sat on the porch without so much as a wary glance from him. I watched as he carefully walked the stone paths between plants, touching and plucking leaves, clearing soil with his hands, raking wood chips, and shoveling compost from a wheelbarrow. I had no idea what he was doing and why, but I was fascinated regardless.

Eventually he retrieved a basket and got to work picking eggplant, butternut squash, carrots, celery, broccoli, cabbage—there was so much that I was beginning to feel like a rabbit—and beets. I hadn't gotten over how impressed I was by the amount of food he grew or the ease with which he seemed to do it. It was definitely a full-time job, but it looked like one he enjoyed.

Joshua disappeared around the side of the cabin when he was finished with his garden chores. I was extremely tempted to follow him but this porch sitting was my probation and I wanted to prove I was trustworthy. He seemed to finally be confident that I wasn't going to kill him in his sleep or make off in the night to tell a pack of raiders where his farm was. That was all the trust I got, and I was eager for more.

I retrieved a book on wild edibles from inside and occupied my mind for an hour or so, studying some of the pages Joshua bookmarked for me. My curiosity finally got the best of me when I heard a rhythmic cracking.

I skulked around the side of the house where I knew the woodshed was. Joshua was beside it, giant axe in his hands and his flannel discarded so that he wore only a filthy white t-shirt. There was a round stump in front of him with a smaller log in the center of it. He lifted the axe over his head and swung it down so hard I swore the ground shook beneath my feet. I was cemented to the spot, frozen in a state of awe.

Chopping wood had to be the manliest thing I'd ever seen.

There was another reason I caught myself appreciating it that I was much less comfortable with. My gaze followed the round of Joshua's biceps as he brought the axe down again and suddenly my throat was bone dry. Somehow, I hadn't noticed how strong he was.

I mean, duh, he was strong, but I hadn't been paying attention to his physique. It was impossible not to feel his size. He took up all of the surrounding space when he was near me. Beyond that I was only peripherally aware of his body. I spent most of my time studying his face, judging his expressions, differentiating his frowns from his scowls, trying to catch humor in his chocolate eyes.

I wasn't looking at his face now.

He replaced the log and swung to split it three more times before pausing to wipe sweat from his brow. I didn't have time to react when he spotted me standing there and lowered his axe. My brain jumped between thinking of an excuse for staring at him and justifying myself for leaving the porch, preparing my defense for the inevitable anger.

It never came. He nodded in greeting and waved me over.

I hooked my pointer fingers together behind my back and approached like a misbehaving child expecting a scolding. That did make Joshua's brow fall, puzzled by my slumped shoulders and downcast eyes. I guess it didn't occur to him that spending almost a month with someone who behaved like an ornery cat created certain expectations. Sometimes he was nice—in a very subtle, unspoken way—but most times he acted as if I was a nuisance.

Maybe because he was helping me out of some misplaced guilt. I still hadn't gotten a reasonable explanation out of him.

"Better?" He asked when I was within earshot.

"Huh?"

"Fresh air."

I was convinced that he was unclear on purpose to make it harder for me to talk to him. Joshua wasn't much of a conversationalist. "Oh, you mean do I feel better now that I'm not cooped up inside? Heck yes!"

My enthusiasm pleased him, I think. "You know where it goes?" Ah, onto the next unclear question.

"Where what goes?"

He stooped to pick up four of the smallest logs and a handful of thin slivers for kindling. When he held them out it took me a few seconds to grasp that he wanted me to carry them. Despite my delayed reaction, there was still no impatience. I stretched both arms out and let him stack the logs on my forearms. They were heavier than I anticipated, and my arms dipped down before I steadied myself.

Joshua gave a satisfied nod when I didn't drop the wood, then jerked his head in the direction of the shack with a, "let's go, Squirrel," to prod me forward.

He followed me with the rest of the logs. His load was bigger and heavier than mine but by the time we reached the porch he passed me, breezing through the door with an annoying lack of effort. My breathing picked up a little and yet, as I handed the logs to him to stack by the fireplace, I noticed that my heart wasn't racing in that fluttering, too much caffeine kind of way it had a few weeks ago. I couldn't hold back a smile.

Joshua looked up at me from his crouched position for a breath, maybe two. That was a first. Usually he ducked his head, as if the sight of happiness made him lose his appetite.

Not an ornery cat, I thought. *Just a skittish one.*

"Hungry?" I sat up like a zombie rising from the grave when Joshua's rough voice rumbled through a dream and woke me. It had to be hours after I settled into bed for a "quick" nap because the light coming through the windows was dim and Joshua already had the stove lit for dinner.

I rubbed sleep from my eyes. "Sorry."

"Not an answer."

"You never answer my questions, so I guess we're even." I climbed out of bed and slipped into my borrowed flannel.

"You're eating."

My tease came out on a yawn. "Yes, sir." His lack of response was my cue. "Can I help?"

"Sit."

"That's a 'no' then?" I shuffled to the table and pulled out the chair furthest from the stove.

Kuna noticed me moving across the room and got to her feet but didn't come any closer. She didn't like me any more than when I got here but she had finally learned that it wasn't cool to stalk me. She still growled occasionally but it didn't scare me as much as it used to. I stayed out of her way and she—with a little nudge from Joshua—stayed out of mine.

Joshua didn't say anything else. That didn't stop me from talking. This was part of our routine. During meals—and any other time we were together, really—I would do my best to strike up a conversation. Usually, he would ignore me.

I kept it light, sharing basic personal information and asking the same of him. He was rarely forthcoming, but I got a word or two out of him. Those one sided discussions about myself got boring so I tried bringing up movies and TV shows. I'd never seen him look more irritated than when I mentioned the first season of Game of Thrones.

Eventually, I started doing whatever I could think of that might amuse him which included self-deprecating humor, quoting what little Shakespeare I knew, making up wild stories about my months on the road, and laughing hysterically at his mustache when he ate. I figured if he wasn't evil then he had to have a sense of humor.

So far, I hadn't gotten more than a snort. I was successfully amusing myself though and that alone was enough to motivate me.

Joking was a great way to cope with the feelings that left me almost catatonic the first week I was here. Under the safety of Joshua's care, with food and shelter in abundance, I finally relaxed. Relaxing meant my brain eased out of the constant adrenaline push for survival.

Suddenly I had time to think and there were plenty of things I'd rather not have thought about. The full weight of not just the last few months but the last year hit me like a tidal wave.

Violence. Death. Fear. I felt all of it fresh and raw. I recalled the bus and the raiders that murdered everyone I left behind. I'd replayed that memory before but in a strange, distant way.

It was a mental warning to myself: *That could have been me*. It was how I kept moving when I was too hungry, too tired, and too sick of being alone. I used all those people—good people, kind people—as a lesson to teach myself consequences and I felt sick about it.

Those thoughts provoked thoughts of my parents. What fate did they meet? Were they ravaged by violent people who wanted what they had? There were friends and acquaintances that crossed my mind too. My friends back home, people from my classes, my roommates. I even thought of the old man with the Yorkie who lived across the street from my rental house.

So many faces that I might never see again. Voices that would never say my name again.

It was almost more than I could take. Almost. I saw, bore witness to all of those that didn't make it, prayed for them, and then I pushed them away. They were dead. I couldn't change that. I was alive. I wanted to be alive. I wanted to be happy to be alive and that wasn't possible if I let my heart be ruled by ghosts.

I was dozing upright when Joshua dropped utensils on the table. His steadying hand on my chair was the only reason I didn't topple backwards when the noise startled me.

"Thank you," I murmured both for saving me from humiliation and for the plate of food he put in front of me. Gratitude made Joshua uncomfortable, but I offered it to him regardless. I *was* grateful to him. He was the reason I was sitting here.

The first few minutes of dinner were spent in silence. The nap I'd taken earlier had done nothing to boost my energy. Joshua occasionally stopped eating to watch me—I don't know why he did that—but I didn't give him any of my usual pouts or even wrinkle my nose. That required more effort than I could muster.

"I am," he suddenly said.

I lowered a forkful of squash and cocked my head at him. "You are?"

"Alone."

"Unless I'm a ghost and you see dead people *Sixth Sense* style, you're wrong." I guess I did have the energy for a little sarcasm.

"Out here."

"More words please."

"You asked if it was just me out here. It is. It was me and my Pops. Now it's just me." He didn't look up from his plate or stop eating as he explained, but that gravelly tone of his voice thickened even more, betraying some unidentifiable emotion.

I was tempted to point out that one, I inquired about that almost a month ago and he was very late to respond and two, I already knew that. It was obvious that he didn't have anyone else out here—unless he kept his cannibalistic monster of a brother in that secret room—but he never told me if it had always been that way. It wasn't as if he kept family photos on the wall. I kind of assumed he bought or built this place with the intention of being alone.

"I'm sorry. About your dad."

Joshua gave a half shrug in acknowledgment but didn't say anything else. I opened my mouth to add more, worried that my reaction to his confession was clumsy, when he spoke again. "Pops inherited the farm, but it was just a hunting shack in the woods then. He built the house by the creek and expanded from there."

"Your dad built this?" I waved my fork around the kitchen. "And you have a creek?"

"Yeah. The woodshed too. I helped him build the rest." Still no eye contact. "The creek runs along the north side of the property. On sunny days you can see it from the outhouse. I'll show you tomorrow."

"Where did he learn to do all of that? Did you grow up out here?" I kept my tone innocent. He was finally answering my questions and I didn't want him to shut down because I was too inquisitive.

"Taught himself, mostly. And yeah, I did."

"You live a very unique life."

"It's nothin' special."

"I grew up with the twinkling lights of buildings instead of stars. My morning started with the hum of car engines during rush hour traffic. And I'm pretty sure if I put my hands in the dirt like you did today, my mother would have made me take a bath. To me, your life is like an alternate universe."

Joshua finally gave me his gaze. It was a cautious look, head tilted down, brown eyes raised in...surprise? Or bewilderment? None of the expressions I'd seen him make before were quite like this.

"You're not."

"Not what?"

"Alone out here." I smiled around a bite of eggplant. "You have me."

I got another of those long, contemplative stares. With his mouth full, he said, "you talk too much."

"And you don't talk enough. Between the two of us, we can almost make a normal conversation."

The only other words uttered at the table that evening were under Joshua's breath. They sounded vaguely like "damn woman and her damn talking." I decided not to take it personally.

While grumpy-pants washed the dishes, I tip toed into the living room to soak up a little extra heat by the fire. Kuna was already in her favorite spot on the rug. When she saw me coming, she rolled to her feet and growled.

I widened my stance and squared my shoulders. She never lunged at me with the intention of biting, but I wouldn't put it past her to try, especially with Joshua's attention fixed elsewhere. I wasn't going to let her bad attitude rule me anymore than I would let his. With a deep inhale for bravery, I sauntered past the dog and to the chair that sat adjacent to Joshua's. The guttural vibration grew in volume and ferocity, but she never moved from her spot.

I glanced over my shoulder to see if Joshua was watching before sticking my tongue out at her.

Kuna stood, fur bristling and eyes blazing for about five minutes before giving up and settling back on the rug. I snuggled deeper into the chair, enjoying the heat on my face. I got so caught up in the light that I didn't notice Joshua come up beside my chair until his shadow stretched across the room. I bolted up, almost knocking the cup of tea out of his outstretched hand.

The noise he made this time was only a quiet huff, but it betrayed his near-constant annoyance. He put the mug in my hand with a brisk motion and grunted, "chamomile."

"Thanks," I whispered.

This was one of those subtle nice gestures. Several evenings ago, I mentioned that I was beginning to enjoy the taste of chamomile and every evening since he brewed that instead of the pungent concoction that helped me sleep. I watched him drop into his chair, his own mug dwarfed by his meaty hands. Steam billowed up around his fire-lit face, adding even sharper edges to his already hard features.

Joshua had the potential to be scary. Scratch that, Joshua *was* scary. At least, until you spent an evening in his living room, listening to him correct your Shakespeare misquotes—how did he know Shakespeare?—while sipping chamomile. Such an enigmatic man.

The absurdity of it—of my whole situation, really—was so ridiculous that an unbidden snort of laughter escaped before I could swallow it. Maybe I was dead, and this was all some bizarre afterlife. Joshua would make an excellent grim reaper.

He absorbed my laughter with feline focus. I was an unknown to him and he was just as busy trying to figure me out as I was trying to solve the mystery of him. His face softened when our gazes met, his eyes warming to rich chocolate.

The laughter died down, but my grin stayed. There were a few short seconds of eye contact, just like earlier when we were stacking wood. My lips held their curve between sips of tea until the mug was empty and my eyelids were heavy.

I see you, Joshua.

7

Thunder

There was a time where I took two showers a day. My roommates would get furious with me for hogging the bathroom in the morning, but it was the best part of my routine. Even after working a closing shift, I would wake up early enough to squeeze in that shower before all the hot water was gone. Some people like a cup of coffee first thing in the morning. I liked a steamy shower.

Emphasis on the *liked*. Showers, like most good things, were in the past.

Bright side? Hot water was not. Boiling bath water wasn't an easy task on a wood burning stove, but it was worth it for the luxury. That was Joshua's word for it, of course. He and I had very different definitions of luxury.

It took me three days to convince him to let me take a hot bath. Filling the trough required a lot of water and even more energy to heat it. Every time I brought it up, he suggested hot water and a cloth.

Or his method, which to ordinary people was a form of torture.

Apparently, his method was good for you and Scandinavian people seemed to love it but just because I looked Swedish didn't mean I was down for an ice bath. I might have been exaggerating a wee little bit when I called it that, seeing as it was only just autumn and the water wasn't *that* cold, but my opinion still stood. I'd had enough stripping down in frozen creeks for one lifetime.

Joshua didn't share my sentiment. He never divulged much information about himself but every once and a while he would drop a tidbit like the fact that he'd *never* taken a hot shower and didn't feel he was missing out on anything.

"Never? Not even one of those outdoor showers they have at campsites and public pools?"

"Nope."

"What about a bath?"

"I bathed in one of these a few times when I was a kid." He gestured to the trough as he positioned it by the fire.

"Wow, you seriously missed out." I was genuinely disappointed for him.

He shrugged. "Waste of energy. I like the creek just fine."

"You *like* freezing your tush off?" I sighed at even the mention of a hot shower. "You're only saying that because you don't realize what you're missing. There's nothing like taking all your clothes off after a long day of work and letting all that hot water wash the grit away. And the steam..." Joshua was making a weird face, probably because I'd started miming taking a shower. I blushed and refocused my attention on picking out clothes.

The trough wasn't the same as soaking in a real tub, but it was far better than crouching in a cold stream and splashing water up into my armpits with no soap. It didn't work for my hair—it was far too long and thick—which meant I had to wash that in the kitchen sink.

Washing your scalp in ice cold well water was pure agony. I quickly decided I would be going no-poo for the foreseeable future. Thank God for messy buns.

By the fire the water stayed warm for almost twenty minutes. I could scrub myself down and still have time to luxuriate in the heat. That meant sacrificing my privacy, but I wasn't all that worried about it.

Sharing a single room with another person didn't leave space for much privacy. Besides, Joshua didn't seem to have any interest in taking advantage of my nudity. If anything, he went out of his way not to look at me. Clearly, I wasn't his type.

I didn't know how old Joshua was but he was old enough to have seen more than one woman naked and they were probably all much more appealing than me. He didn't strike me as that type, but experience taught me that every man was that type when presented with the opportunity to have sex. He might not be dashingly handsome but Joshua was muscled and had a touch of that bad boy attitude that some women couldn't resist. I was sure he got plenty of offers back in the day.

Though, where would he meet a woman living out in the boonies? And if he brought a woman home, would he bring her back here? It wasn't as if his house was horrible but it wasn't exactly a classy bachelor pad. Then again, he did live with his father at one point and there was only one bed.

God, why was I even thinking about this?

Now I was picturing Joshua having sex on the bed where I slept—which made me uncomfortable for reasons I wouldn't admit to anyone lest they think I was jealous, because I definitely wasn't—while his father sat in the chair by the fire and pretended not to notice like Joshua pretended not to notice me.

Unless the secret door was hiding his *Fifty Shades of Grey* style bedroom. Even goat farmers had kinks, right?

Bathing. That's what I should be thinking about. Not sex. Never sex. Not when I'm about to get naked in front of a man. Unless I'm getting naked to have sex with him, of course. Not like that was ever going to happen now.

I couldn't hold in a groan when I *finally* slipped into the tub. Hot water was heaven. Joshua's cheek twitched but he didn't turn his attention from the flickering heat that licked at the logs in front of him. I took a deep breath, lying back and enjoying the water before I got to work scrubbing and rinsing suds away.

Once I was thoroughly clean, I kicked my feet up on the edge of the tub, making another loud groaning noise half because it felt good and half because it got a reaction out of Joshua.

"You know what I miss?" I breathed a dramatic sigh and stretched one leg out further, so the fire warmed the bottom of my foot. "Smoothies. I so did not appreciate my blender enough. God, milkshakes too. I would have drunk so many more milkshakes if I'd known I couldn't have them in the future." Joshua didn't respond so I continued. "And Frappuccinos? Coffee, whipped cream, caramel. What a luxury that was."

"It was a luxury before the power went out," he mumbled.

"Yeah, I guess you're right. Five dollars for coffee on demand ain't cheap. I took it for granted though. It was all so easy. Everything was at my fingertips."

"You didn't have to work for anything." I think that was intended as an insult to my character.

"Not gathering my resources like a caveman doesn't mean I wasn't working. I carried heavy trays of food for up to twelve hours a day. That was *hard* work." I pointed my toes indignantly.

"Tough."

"You know what else I miss?" I raised a hand from the tub and flicked a few droplets of water at him. His expression darkened but he kept his gaze forward. "Chocolate. If I'd known the world was going to end, I would have used my college fund to buy a chocolate farm in Florida and live on nothing but milk chocolate."

"A chocolate farm? Do the bars grow on trees?"

"Oh boy, I don't know how chocolate is grown. Just like I don't know how coffee is grown. Silly, clueless Liv." I deepened my voice sardonically.

"If you'd done that you would be dead. Eaten by a python or a crocodile or killed by a virus transmitted by mosquitoes. And if that didn't get you, a hurricane would." He was unfazed by my mocking retort.

I rolled my eyes but mostly for my own benefit since he wasn't looking at me. "Wow Joshua, you're so optimistic."

"I'm realistic."

"Not me. I believe in magic and happy endings. My glass is full."

"Half full," he corrected with a tilt of his head in my direction. He wasn't stealing a look—God forbid he act human enough to glance at my breasts, which were bouncy and soft now that I was gaining weight—but he was giving me his attention. I wondered if he actually enjoyed these conversations or if he was just getting better at hiding his annoyance.

"No, I meant full. I've got everything I need." I splashed him again. He whipped his head my way for a two second scowl before turning back to the fire.

"You're inexperienced. You don't even know what you need." Inexperienced? At what? Life? He couldn't just let something be a good thing. Did he want everyone to be as miserable as he was? Not happening.

I punished his sour mood by upping my cheerfulness to a level that could almost annoy me. I smiled and giggled and chattered on about my favorite brunch special at this café down the street from campus that I went to every Tuesday after my morning classes. He responded with a few grunts and one word answers and a frown that settled on his face and stayed there.

There was a line—invisible and almost impossible to find without running into it by mistake—and when I crossed it, he would be real mad, not this exaggerated, huffy annoyed that he made a show of. When I ran out of good topics to blather on about, I decided I'd gotten close enough to that line without crossing it and it was time to stop.

"Do you know what I miss most of all?" I murmured more to myself than to him.

"Hmm?" He was clearly still listening.

"Thunder."

"Thunder?"

"Mhmm."

"Last I checked the grid going down doesn't mean there are no more thunderstorms." He shifted his gaze again, not looking directly at me but focusing on my outstretched feet.

"It doesn't thunder here."

"Of course, it does."

"What like once every decade? I've lived here for two years and never heard thunder. Southern thunderstorms are so much different than the rainstorms here. They're chaotic. Downpours and flooding and blinding cracks of lightning. One of the most frightening and exhilarating experiences is waking up to thunder as it rattles your windows. The ferocity of it makes you feel so small."

My sigh this time was wistful, almost sad. "Not insignificant, just...like you're only a piece of something bigger than you can even fathom." Some days, it was hard to come to terms with how the world had changed. There were things I just wouldn't get to experience anymore. Things I would never see again.

Joshua finally looked at me then, *really* looked at me. I had adjusted to his staring, but I realized that until now, he'd only ever done it when I wasn't looking back. He really was like a cat, refusing to meet my eyes except in challenge, darting his gaze away if it was anything but that. This time our eyes met, and it made me feel oddly vulnerable; naked.

Of course, I was literally naked which might have contributed to that sentiment, but he paid no mind to my exposed breasts and bare legs. He was fixated on my face as if he'd never seen it before. The potency of his full attention made me shiver and wrap my arms around myself.

He must have thought I was uncomfortable with my nakedness because he turned away sharply when I moved. I supposed that was for the better because I continued to shiver once I noticed how cool the water had gotten.

The strange exchange passed. I waited until Joshua seemed hooked on the fire again and rose from the water. Towel tightly wrapped around my body, I made a hasty dash onto the hearth. That way the water would drip onto the stone and dry in the heat of the fire rather than dampening the rug. The warmth on my skin wasn't a bad feeling either. As soon as I was beside the fireplace Joshua was up and heaving the trough outside.

Once I heard him shut the door, I whipped open my towel and shimmied so any stray water would drop off my skin. I stood half naked and exposed to the fire until the first thump of a boot on the porch. I gathered up my clothes and scurried to the corner by the bed to get dressed. Joshua had his head down, probably worried he would walk in on me dressing.

"And they say chivalry is dead."

"Who says that?" His chair groaned beneath him when he resettled into it.

I gave a muffled answer through the fabric of my shirt as I tugged it over my head. "You know, *they*. The collective of mysterious people who say stuff."

"Ah," Joshua snorted.

"Are you tired?" I floated back into the living room on a total high.

"I'm never tired."

"Right, I forgot, you're a robot." I stiffened my arms and moved them up and down robotically, laughing softly at Joshua's bewildered look. How was it possible that he'd missed out on so much pop culture? "Well, I'm hungry."

"You just had dinner an hour ago."

"And now I'm hungry again. Can I have some bread?" He narrowed his eyes at me and opened his mouth to say something, but I cut him off. "I know, I know. No bread without butter."

He shook his head and waved me into the kitchen, muttering "locust" when he thought I couldn't hear him.

I stuck my tongue out at the back of his chair, picked some mold off half a loaf of bread on the counter, and smothered it in jam. If I forgot the butter, it was absolutely not on purpose. I would never do that.

8

Suspicious Minds

I woke to the unfamiliar sound of a door creaking. By now I was used to the rare groan of Joshua's chair as he rose from it in the middle of the night, but this new noise startled me. I bolted upright, eyes wide but vision blurry from sleep and the thick darkness that blanketed the surrounding room. I blinked until I could make out the dining table in front of me. To the left of it was the front door.

The open front door.

Was someone in here, someone other than Joshua? Was that even possible? My heart raced so fast it hurt. There was a loud, irregular rush of air coming from somewhere. I focused on it and realized it was my own ragged breath.

"Joshua?" He didn't answer.

I couldn't see him. The fire was out, and the room was pitch black but for a sliver of dull moonlight that peeked through the curtains in the kitchen. I tried to listen for any other noises but the more anxious I got the louder blood pumped in my ears. How did someone get in? There was a fence, wasn't there? It wasn't indestructible but it had to be pretty good because Joshua never seemed worried about it.

The front door creaked again as it slowly pushed further open. I froze, completely still—no, completely paralyzed with fear. I waited but no one came through. Maybe the wind blew it open. Shouldn't it be locked? It had a deadbolt, and I knew Joshua kept it latched at night.

"Joshua?" I whimpered his name again.

This time there was a response. Not a verbal one but a soft shuffling of feet on the porch. Then there was a figure in the door, so big and dark it filled up the whole entryway. My panting grew more frantic. The figure hurried from the doorway to the dining room table but stopped short of the bed.

"What?" Joshua's gruff voice snapped.

"Oh, God." I exhaled so hard I lurched forward. I'd never been happier to hear him snap in my life.

"What's going on?" His tone was impatient but there seemed to be a hint of genuine concern there, too.

"You didn't answer when I called you and the front door was open. I was worried. Is something wrong?"

"Just a feeling."

His honesty surprised me. "A feeling? Like a bad vibe?"

"Somethin' like that. Go back to sleep." He swept back to the door.

"Are you leaving?" I asked, sliding out of bed, and moving to follow.

"Stay put," he hissed.

I stood by the side of the bed and watched him slip outside. His steps, usually brisk thumps, were soundless. It unsettled me as much as him saying he had "a feeling." The only noise was the scrape of Kuna's nails as she trailed at his side. And just like that, I was alone.

Not really, I reassured myself. This was no different than when he and Kuna went out to work. He was out there on the property, probably within shouting distance.

Fire starting remained a mystery to me, but it gave my trembling hands something to do. I abandoned the flint after bloodying my thumb on the first attempt. Instead, I used the fire poker to dig around in the ashes until I found the tiniest glimmer of a spark. It took lots of blowing and maneuvering to coax a wispy piece of bark to light.

Getting that ember to ignite into an actual fire was a challenge. I carefully added more kindling, graduating to larger and larger hunks of wood until finally placing a log in the center. I almost thought I ruined my chances when the log appeared to smother the flames. It caught with a startling whoosh if air and a satisfying crackle.

I let pride and the warmth of the fire ease my anxiety enough to stop pacing and settle into the chair across from Joshua's. Knees to my chest, I practiced breathing deeply and consciously. By the time I heard footsteps on the porch, quieter than usual but much closer to the familiar hammering I was used to, I'd calmed enough to settle my heartbeat.

"Everything okay?" I whispered when he filled the space between the chairs.

"Fine. Go to bed."

"What exactly happened?"

"I told you."

"Tell me again." I looked up at his shadowy face then added a quiet, "please."

"Just had a feeling I ought to check on something." He shrugged and flopped into his chair with a heavy sigh. For the first time I noticed the lines on his face, the deep indentations under his eyes. Joshua looked tired. Not the kind of tired that happens when you miss a night of sleep. It was a weary tired and it triggered an urge for me to fix it. He took care of me. I should be taking care of him too.

"Check on what?"

A sudden and unexpected hostility flickered to life on his face like the flames devouring the wood. "You set this up?"

"What?" I twisted in my seat so I could look at him more directly. "Set what up?"

"You got someone waiting out there? Are you the distraction?"

"Am I—oh for God's sake! Are we still on this? I've been here a month, Joshua. Four weeks! Don't you think I would have done something by now if I planned to rob you?"

"Unless you were waiting until I trusted you."

"You don't trust me!" I stood from the chair too quickly, causing Kuna to snarl at me.

Joshua stood too. For the first time since he brought me here, I was almost afraid he would hurt me. "How can I?"

"Gee, I don't know. How can you trust me when I've done nothing but tell you how grateful I am and offer to help you manage your chores?" I threw my hands up, my anger warring with my uncertainty. "I'm about as bad as they come."

I skirted around Joshua, stomped to the door, and yanked my boots on. "If you're so convinced, I'm untrustworthy then why not just kick me out? Your penance is done. Whatever it is you needed forgiveness for, you've earned it." I hesitated with my hand on the front door, twisting to look over my shoulder. "If I'm such a dangerous *distraction*, why don't you march me out into the woods and do whatever you did to make those two raiders go away? It would save you a lot of grief."

I was almost out the door when Joshua's icy tone stilled me. "What do you think I did to make those men leave?"

"I don't know, scowled so hard they got scared and ran away? You're a big guy with a gun. I'm sure they took one look at you and decided it was safer for them to find something else to do. Why does it matter? Is that a threat?"

"If I was threatening you, you'd know it." Would I?

"So, what are you trying to say? What do you want from me?" I snapped back.

He didn't answer. I didn't give him much chance to. Despite the storm of emotions threatening a tornado inside me, I closed the door softly and paused my escape on the porch. What was I doing? Where was I going? It was the middle of the night, and it was dark. Terrifyingly dark.

I hovered on the first step, watching shadows of tree branches weave across the garden and through the woods until I'd imagined every frightening scenario possible. Eventually I gave up trying to psyche myself into going out there and instead settled in one of the Adirondacks. The night air was humid and biting. Goosebumps dotted my bare arms and I deeply regretted not grabbing a jacket.

I was in quite the pickle, wasn't I? For months I had no one to rely on but myself. I knew *I* would take care of myself. I could trust myself. Somehow, I let that self-assurance slip away like sand through my fingers as soon as Joshua offered me a place to stay. He took care of me, gave me everything I could need.

But that nagging "why" behind his actions was a chasm that would always separate us. If he didn't want anything from me, had no use for me, then I was discardable. There wasn't a real reason for him to keep me around. I let myself get far too comfortable here and now I would pay the price for that.

I would have to leave on my own or he would make me. Either way, I was back in the wilderness with no supplies and no shelter with winter fast approaching.

I was doomed if I left, doomed if I stayed. Was this how it ended for me?

My spiraling panic was interrupted when the door flew open, spilling firelight onto the porch. "Come inside," Joshua growled.

"Why?"

"You're going to freeze out here."

I stuck my chin out stubbornly. "If I'm some evil raider spy that wants to ruin your life, why bother helping me? Leave me out here to freeze."

"If you don't get your skinny ass in here—" he pointed an angry finger at me.

"You'll what?"

His mouth opened and closed, a threat dangling on his tongue. It must have been one he knew he wouldn't make good on because he faltered, opting to go back inside and close the door. Great. Now it was just me and the darkness. The horrible, freezing darkness that was probably full of murdering clowns.

Just when I'd resigned myself to freezing to death, Joshua came back out with the quilt from the bed. He tossed it over my lap in a heap and plunked himself down on the porch step. The damp wind didn't seem to bother him. He leaned his elbows on his knees, feet bare and chest covered in only a worn thermal.

"You don't have to do this, Joshua." I broke the uncomfortable silence.

"I don't have to do anything."

"God, would you quit behaving like a stubborn teenager for five seconds?" I rolled my eyes, shuffling from the Adirondack to sit next to him on the step. Our shoulders almost touched. I was tempted to lean into him just to steal some of his body heat. "I'm trying to give you a guilt free out."

"I don't feel guilty."

"Uh-huh." That was why he came out here with a blanket and sat sullenly in the cold. Because he was decidedly not guilty. "Well that should make it easy for you then. I'll pack tonight and leave in the morning. If you want, you can blindfold me and lead me away from the farm, so I never find it again."

"Jesus, woman! I'm not kicking you out."

"Then what? I don't understand what you want from me!"

He mussed his hair with agitated fingers. "Why did you get up?"

"You were gone."

A glimmer of suspicion returned to his eyes. "So?"

"You're really going to make me say this?"

"Yes."

"I was scared! There. Are you happy now?" I swallowed back the crack in my voice. "You were gone, and I was scared. I'm afraid of the dark." Humiliation bloomed a hot red across my cheeks. "And lots of other things but it all stems from the dark."

"Is that all?" He glanced my way then back to the woods. "I reckon you know what's out there, in the dark. Probably smart to be afraid." Was that reassurance? From *Joshua*?

I watched him, chewing my lip, trying to figure out how he went from suspicion and back so rapidly. "So that's it? If I'd just admitted that I was being a chicken, you would have been fine?"

"No."

I tugged the blanket tighter around me and scowled at him. "Nothing about you makes sense."

"The feeling is mutual." He scooted as far from me as the step allowed. "What else?"

"This is one of those times where a few more words would get your point across a lot better."

"What else scares you?"

"Um, let's see..." I tapped my chin with my pointer finger. "Spiders, snakes, clowns, serial killers—"

"Real stuff."

Ridiculous, confusing man.

"Spiders are real!"

"What had you sitting up like you knew death was coming for you?"

I sucked in a harsh, frozen breath. Had I really looked that bad? And did I really have to answer this question? It felt like we'd gone from deciding if I was out to get him to midnight confessions at a sleepover. The change in pace was jarring and I found the vulnerability from earlier cracking me back open into a nervous, exposed mess.

"Being alone," I whispered it so quietly that the wind stole the words away.

"Huh?"

"Being alone." My voice sounded small. "I don't want to be alone anymore. I spent a lot of nights sleeping in ditches, under trees, behind old buildings, squeezing my eyes shut so I had less fuel to imagine my nightmares walking in the shadows around me. Worse than those nights though? Standing alone along a beautiful expanse of creek and having no one to share it with, realizing that I might *never* have anyone to share it with again. Even just to hear someone else describe the way the sunlight on the water made them feel, to see them pick up a pretty rock, would fill some void in me that's been growing since I lost my group."

That was a little too honest and we both knew it.

I talked about myself, shared stories about my childhood and my parents, but it seemed there was some invisible line neither of us crossed. Joshua was secretive about his life, and I mirrored that, to a degree. It was safer, kept us from getting too close. That way when he inevitably sent me packing, there would be less hard feelings. Less guilt or resentment, less loneliness. Hard to miss someone that doesn't trust you. Or even like you.

Now I'd given him one of the softer pieces of myself, the kind that breaks easily in someone else's grasp. I looked down at Joshua's hands. Thick, calloused fingers clutched his knees. They were capable hands but rough, so very rough. He could just as easily hold me safe with them as he could crush me.

"You're not." My words echoed from his mouth. He wouldn't look at me, but I could feel the tension leaving him. "Now get your squirrelly ass inside before your toes fall off. I'm not carrying you around if you get frostbite."

It wasn't an apology, not by a long shot, but from Joshua that seemed to be as good as I was going to get. For all that he could be hotheaded, he was also quick to cool. I didn't know how to get him to trust me but perhaps crossing that personal line was a start.

We were surviving the end of the world together. What harm could there be in sharing my most vulnerable pieces? I might not get reciprocation but at least I would get the relief of letting them out.

When Joshua stood and hovered in the doorway, holding it open for me, I followed him.

"It's definitely not cold enough for frostbite."

"Damn woman and your damn arguing."

9
Baby Steps

Joshua was pacing the kitchen when I woke. That in itself was unusual. Where was the clang and clatter of breakfast? The man was nothing if not routine and breakfast had to be done first.

"Joshua?" I sat up, tugging the quilt over me like a protective shield.

He made a beeline for the bedside, looming over me with an antsy vibe that wasn't like him. "You hungry?" He asked hurriedly.

"Ugh, I'm not starved."

"Put your shoes on."

"Where are we going? I'm not even dressed." I pulled the covers back to reveal his oversized shirt and a pair of leggings.

"I'll show you." Joshua almost sounded *cheerful*. And maybe a little strained. "C'mon, Squirrel. You're dressed fine."

He thrust my boots at me before I even made it to the entryway. I hopped on one foot, trying to cram the other into my boot without untying it. "At least squirrels are cute."

"I eat squirrels." He reached around me to pull the front door closed and shooed me down the porch steps.

"Oh...kay." I stumbled down the last step in my rush to keep up with him. Joshua already had a speed advantage over me with such long legs. Why did he have to powerwalk? "I'm just going to pretend you've got a bizarre sense of humor and not read into that."

The last sound Joshua made for the rest of our trip to wherever-the-heck-we-were-going was a snort that definitely counted as laughter.

The sun wasn't yet visible through the trees when we reached our destination, which was probably why I didn't understand what we were looking at right away. Joshua stopped a few feet away from a small hill where someone had leaned a bunch of glass windows on the grass. Or so I thought until I took a closer look and realized I could see open space through the glass. Joshua came around the side of the hill and pulled open a wooden hatch that I never would have seen. He motioned for me to follow just before disappearing.

I quickly came around after him and found a narrow staircase leading down to...another garden? Then it hit me. These were his greenhouses, and they were almost completely underground. Pretty clever if you were trying to stay off the radar. The air at the bottom of the stairs was surprisingly muggy and warm. The scent was fresh and earthy with a sweetness that hinted at some flowering plant I couldn't see.

"This is where the coffee grows." The words left him in an exhale that, again, sounded oddly nervous. It was so unlike the Joshua I'd come to know that it almost made me nervous too. "And plenty of other stuff that doesn't tolerate cooler nights. We built the original greenhouse structure to grow essentials in the winter, but I expanded it for the tropical plants."

"Tropical plants? In the Pacific Northwest?"

"I started with the coffee. Just wanted to see if I could do it." He scratched through his beard. "After that success I experimented with others, seeing what could handle the minimal sunlight. Thought I might turn it into an income someday. Folks love fancy shit."

He stepped further inside, and I followed him. The surrounding space had to be double the size of the cabin and there was another door at the other end of the room. A collection of potted trees and shrubs occupied the area by the second door. A path through the greenhouse was lined with river rocks that made raised beds just like in the garden. The plants growing within were tiny, only just planted a few weeks ago by the looks of it.

A rustic garden table took up the spot between two beds, covered in pots and plants of all sizes. The aesthetic matched something from a home and garden magazine more than it matched Joshua's rough lifestyle.

"Can I see?" I clasped my hands together under my chin. "The coffee?"

"It doesn't look like what you recognize as coffee right now."

"I don't care. I want to see it! Please?"

He shrugged and headed for the other door. "In here."

The next room over was even muggier. Every available inch of space was filled with potted plants or bright green trees. It felt like stepping into a tropical jungle. Somewhere I heard running water. Joshua led me closer to the sound until I noticed a teeny tiny pond with a waterfall that trickled over more river rocks. It was all so unexpectedly beautiful.

I trailed my gaze over every plant, then back to Joshua. His eyes met mine for the briefest moment and I saw something I'd never seen before. It wasn't quite happiness, but it was pretty close. He clearly took pride in the plants out here and had put a lot of effort into curating this space. It wasn't just a growing room; it was a sanctuary.

This was Joshua's peace offering and it was not one I would take lightly. He was letting me in on one of his secrets too. Maybe it wasn't the type of resource that people would fight him for, but he saw enough value in it to keep it hidden for more than a month. Now he was sharing it with me.

"This is beautiful, Joshua," I said breathlessly.

On instinct, I reached a hand out to touch his arm. It was innocent, only reinforcing my words with physical contact. Joshua jerked away, shock on his features before they hardened into their usual scowl. He side stepped away from me—not subtly—and cleared his throat loudly.

"This is Kona coffee." He pointed to the closest plant. It looked like any other house plant to me, but what did I know about plants?

I let him glaze over our awkward moment and searched my brain for a question to ask. "How much coffee do you actually get from them?"

"Couple pounds. It wasn't really worth the effort when you could buy coffee just about anywhere." He tucked his hands in his pockets, making such direct eye contact with the plant you'd think he was talking to it rather than me.

"Will you tell me what the other trees are?" I shuffled closer to him. Joshua's recoiling wasn't personal but that didn't make it sting any less. No girl wanted to go half a year without touching someone and then have the first person she meets act revolted by her affection.

Skittish kitty cat, I reminded myself. *He's not the type that wants to be pet.*

"Another time. Need to feed the chickens and pack up breakfast."

I watched him pretend not to notice me watching before realizing that the look I was giving him held a little too much longing.

It's only because he's taken care of me. It's only because the world is ending, and I just don't want to feel alone. Joshua doesn't even like me. I shouldn't have to remind myself any of this, but I did, over and over again, until I remembered that Joshua had said something and I hadn't responded.

I acknowledged him with a nod, recognizing how vulnerable it made him feel to show me this place. Unraveling the mystery of Joshua and maybe, just maybe, earning his trust was going to take the babiest of baby steps. This was a good one and I wasn't going to push.

"Pack up breakfast? Are we taking it to go?" My cheerful tone was only a little forced.

"Yup. Now get moving. We've got somewhere to be."

10

Snack

I was never going to understand Joshua's logic. Any normal person would have felt awkward after our blow up fight the night before. Instead, he was relaxed. Ever since our spat he'd been weirdly calm. All the tension that used to sit in his shoulders when he was studying me at the dinner table was gone. Suddenly I was trustworthy.

I wasn't foolish enough to believe he *trusted*-trusted me, but he didn't seem to think I was waiting to pull a machete out of my pocket and stab him either. I officially had rights to walk about the property and when I offered, I was given chores. Joshua even showed me the chickens, goats, and the lone pig he kept for reasons I didn't want to think about.

Goats, as it turned out, were gross and creepy. What was with those eyes? Pigs weren't much better. The plump creature Joshua was raising was scarcely reminiscent of the pot belly pigs that occupied petting zoos. I got the distinct impression that under the right circumstances, the thing wouldn't hesitate to eat me. The chickens were cute, at least.

None of that compared to what we were doing now. When he mentioned we were leaving the farm, I had to hold my breath to keep from jumping around with excitement. The place was pretty but jeez was I sick of sitting around.

I had no idea what snares were or why we were checking them, but I didn't really care. As much as I appreciated the safety and shelter of Joshua's home, I wanted to be out in the world. The longer we were isolated in that tiny cabin, the more acutely aware of it I became.

When I saw the fence around the property from the other side for the first time, I was shocked. If I didn't know it was there, I wouldn't have seen it at all. Joshua explained that when his father built it decades earlier, he was attentive to which part of the property was most easily concealed. He made a point to select local evergreen plants that he knew would thrive and planted them meticulously around the wooden wall. If someone was astute enough to see the wall beyond the bramble and somehow climbed the six-foot planks, they would be greeted by a hidden row of barbed wire on the other side.

Smart but also disturbing. Almost like Joshua's father was anticipating the exact situation we were in now.

We were only about a hundred feet into the woods when I noticed a shift in Joshua's demeanor. He kept his hand close to the gun on his hip, eyes up and scanning the trees from time to time, but none of it was wary. The behavior seemed innate. Otherwise, he was more at ease out here than he was in his own home.

"What is it?" I asked as he plucked a cream colored mushroom and tossed it into my basket.

"Chanterelle. It's a little early for them this far north but this patch is always reliable." He picked another and held it out for me to examine. "Plenty of mushrooms are edible around here but you should never eat anything you can't identify."

He went on to explain how he identified it and what to avoid if I was ever starving in the woods—again—and stumbled upon fungus. We didn't walk much further before stopping, this time for Joshua to point out blackberries. I nearly squealed with joy when I saw the massive thorny bush loaded with fruit. We spent about ten minutes filling a second, smaller basket that Joshua kept hooked on his backpack. I ate about as many berries as I picked. Some of them tasted like a glass of wine, fizzy and overly sweet, but I ate those too.

Joshua snorted when I lifted my juice stained palms with a grin.

Our journey into the woods continued like that for over an hour. We kept a pleasant pace, Joshua pausing often to point out plants, mushrooms, and even a few songbirds. There was no way I could remember everything he said but I listened regardless, fascinated by his vast knowledge and how easily it came to him.

Whenever I asked a question, Joshua answered. Out here, he was a different person. His eyes sparkled with excitement, and he spoke more than I'd ever heard at one time. I liked this side of Joshua. Part of me never wanted to go back to the farm. I was having fun with him and, maybe it was wishful thinking but, I was pretty sure he was having fun with me too.

"I can eat it? You're not just trying to get rid of me?" I asked, plucking a beautiful blue berry from a cluster of what he called Oregon grape.

"There are easier ways to get rid of you." He raised his eyebrows expectantly. Too expectantly.

I narrowed my eyes at him. "You seem awfully excited about me eating this."

He hardened his features, which didn't disguise the amusement in his eyes. "I don't get excited."

I popped the berry into my mouth. Two seconds later my lips puckered involuntarily, and I was pretty sure my eye was twitching. "It's sour!"

Joshua watched me struggle to swallow the tart red juice and for a sliver of a moment, he nearly smiled. "Sour's good for you."

"You think you're pretty funny, do you?" I yanked the water bottle from the side of his backpack and swished a mouthful.

He shrugged and kept walking, forcing me to jog to catch up to him. I almost tripped over Kuna when both he and the dog stopped abruptly. Joshua stooped to pinch a big, white, umbrella shaped mushroom and held it out for me.

I cautiously extended my hand, feeling wary after his last trick. "What is it?"

"Destroying angel."

I quickly recoiled. "That sounds poisonous. And terrible."

"Very."

"Put it down, Joshua!" I batted at his hand, too afraid to actually touch the mushroom.

"Won't kill you unless you eat it." His lips twitched.

"What if you lick your fingers?" The longer he held that thing the shriller I became.

My anxiety only heightened his amusement. "Guess I might be dead when you wake up tomorrow."

I glared at him, then at the mushroom, then back at him. "Not funny."

Joshua shrugged again.

"I have to pee," I grumbled before he could powerwalk away from me.

He crossed his arms and looked at me as if to say, "go ahead then."

"Not here."

"Why?" He groaned.

"You can see me."

"I won't watch you," he said, somewhat indignantly. "I'll turn my back. Go."

"I can't."

"Why?" He groaned again.

"I have a shy bladder," I whispered. He frowned like I'd spoken nonsense. "I can't go if you can hear me."

"If I can *hear* you? I'll know what you're doing whether or not I hear you."

"I know but if you can't hear me, I can pretend you don't. I'll be quick. I just need to find a good tree to pee behind."

Joshua sighed so loudly it was almost a growl. He finally gave in with a curt, "hurry up. Stay in sight."

"That defeats the purpose," I called over my shoulder.

I tip toed through the undergrowth for about ten feet. When I looked back Joshua was staring at me. I waved a frantic hand at him. He shook his head but turned around, so his back was to me. Even from here I could feel the impatience rolling off his body in waves. One interruption and we were back to regular ol' grumpypants.

I found a shrub that seemed suitable and squatted to test how well it hid me. I could still see Joshua and Kuna, which meant they could definitely see me. Not that it mattered if the dog watched me, I guess.

I hurried further back into the woods as quickly and quietly as I could, pausing to test out stumps and bushes. Eventually the ferns and shrubs thinned a bit, and I found a thick tree. I yanked down my jeans and exhaled in relief. I was pulling my pants back up when I caught movement in my peripherals. I whipped around, praying that it wasn't Joshua coming after me because I went too far.

It wasn't Joshua.

In front of me was a huge brown animal, as big as Kuna but lower to the ground and longer. I stared for a second, so shocked that I was sure my vision was failing me. I was face to face with a massive, tawny cat. He had a thick, diamond shaped head raised high in the air to investigate my scent. His ears were up, light green eyes locked on me.

I tried to think of what to do to scare off the animal, but my voice was shaking, and I could barely raise it above a whisper. "No, no. Stay back."

The big cat lifted a paw and held it there motionless for a second. Then he set it down, taking one step closer to me. I took a frightened step back. He took another forward. I panicked, stumbling backwards as fast as I could. The cougar advanced on me, shoulder blades straining against muscle and skin as it hurried silently across the forest floor.

"Josh-u-a!" I shrieked. A root jutted out in my path, catching my heel, and sending me back onto my butt.

I couldn't be more than five feet from the cougar now. He was crouching, head bobbing with excitement. I was going to be cougar lunch. A loud crash in the underbrush startled both of us. Joshua barreled through the trees, hands raised, voice booming an angry "hey!" at the animal. Kuna followed at his heel, teeth bared, a vicious growl rumbling from her throat.

The big cat put his ears back and let out a terrifying snarl. Joshua clapped his hands and shouted again. The cat backpedaled, turning tail, and sprinting off into the woods. Kuna tried to follow but Joshua gave her a firm command and she stayed. Every muscle in her body was tensed, her instincts warring with her obedience.

"What the hell are you doing? You don't run from a cougar!" He gripped my upper arms hard and yanked me to my feet. I winced both from the way he held me and the pain in my tailbone.

"S-sorry," I stammered. "I didn't know."

His brow was deeply furrowed, eyes alight with adrenaline, anger, or both. When he let go of my arms I teetered there, lower lip trembling—whole body trembling. Joshua opened his mouth to chastise more but he stopped, and his expression lightened to confusion when he saw my tears. Apparently, he couldn't understand why almost getting eaten by a cougar only to have him *blame me* for it would make me upset.

"You don't run from a cougar," he repeated, voice still rough but edged with less annoyance.

"Sorry." *Why am I apologizing? It's not my fault that a predator tried to eat me.*

We both stood frozen in place, me quietly sobbing and him floundering because he had no idea how to get me to stop. Kuna huffed loudly. I was still frightened, and the sound spooked me so bad I yelped. Without thinking I jumped forward and reached out for Joshua. My arms wrapped tight around his ribs, my forehead buried in his chest. He was so solid and safe that once I was there, I didn't want to move. I huddled against him, shaking for what felt like half an hour.

He seemed even more helpless in this situation. His body was so rigid it must have hurt, and he couldn't figure out what to do with his arms without giving me the impression that he was returning my embrace—or whatever you might call this terrified clinging—so he held them awkwardly at his side. Finally, he lifted a big palm and clumsily patted the top of my head like he was petting a puppy.

I pushed away from him and sniffled, "Sorry."

"Never run from a cougar."

I nodded, my gaze fixed on his boots. "Right."

Thankfully, Joshua decided now wasn't the time to give me a more thorough lecture, probably because he was as afraid that I would start crying again as I was of the cougar.

We continued in silence. I was humiliated and I wanted nothing more than to go back to the cabin and hide in bed. To say as much out loud would have been equally embarrassing so I had no choice but to follow Joshua and Kuna.

I was looking down, hyper-focused on where I was putting my feet, when Joshua slowed. I bumped into his shoulder and almost fell backwards. I didn't need catching but he caught me anyway. Fingers dug into my upper arm and anchored me upright. By now he was accustomed to my wincing at his unexpected movements and didn't seem to realize it was because he was hurting me.

"Joshua," I whimpered his name. He released me so fast that I did stumble back and had to catch myself on a tree. Then he shushed me. Because I was making noise for the fun of it.

I leaned against the tree, quietly waiting as he crouched to examine something. Only when I lifted my gaze did I realize that something was a flailing rabbit. I gasped, horrified, and quickly covered my face, not at all interested in seeing what he was about to do to the poor animal. When he gripped my elbow and tugged me forward so we could keep moving I made sure my face gaze was shoulder-level, so I didn't have to look at the dead rabbit hanging off his pack.

We stopped at five more snares, only two of which had helpless rabbits hooked in them. Steady rivulets of silent tears had begun to wet my face by the time we finished our task and turned back toward the farm. I couldn't believe that he'd brought me out here to hunt animals. How could he think I would want to witness *that*?

Though we moved briskly, the walk home seemed endless. My feet were lead as I heaved them up the porch steps. Joshua sent me into the house, disappearing with his creepy collection of rabbits. I wasn't about to argue with his silent order.

To my surprise, Kuna chose to follow me for a change. She kept her distance, eyeing me as I undid my boots, slipped from my jeans, and snuggled into my flannel. When I flopped into one of the recliners with a heavy sigh, she mimicked the action, tossing her body onto the rug.

"I'm never leaving this house again." I whispered pathetically to the dog.

She grunted at me.

"Cave-dog."

11

Territorial Predator

Joshua shooed me away from the kitchen when I tried to clean up the remnants of dinner. I wandered to the fireplace instead, sliding down onto the floor to rest my back against the cushion of the chair opposite his. I ignored the big black dog still stretched out on the rug near me, wrapping my arms around my knees and drawing them to my chest.

Normally she would growl if I dared to sit on the part of the floor that belonged to her. This time Kuna only raised her head to peer at me with something almost sympathetic in her dark eyes. She wasn't pleased to have me around, but she was beginning to tolerate my presence.

I let the flames lure me into their dance until I was transfixed on the red and gold light. My focus was so intent that I didn't notice Joshua cross the room to search the bookshelf. Even when he walked in front of me, his thumb pressed into the center of a book to save his place, his chair groaning a complaint as he sat, I didn't look up.

"They're territorial." When he spoke, it startled me so much I jumped, which startled Kuna and had her rising onto her front legs and making a noise between a grunt and a growl.

"Go ahead, eat me," I snarled defiantly at the dog. She blinked at me and lowered her head onto her feet. "Who?" Despite my sharp tone with Kuna, my question was murmured. I couldn't bring myself to meet his gaze.

I was as helpless and easily frightened as he thought I was. What was the point of my false bravado? He didn't believe it and no matter what I did, his opinion of me didn't change. That upset me more than I wanted it to. Why should I care what Joshua thought of me? He wasn't required to like me.

It wouldn't have bothered me as much if I hadn't convinced myself that he *did*. For a heartbeat he was talking to me, even being playful. I thought he was enjoying himself. I let that hopeful thought get carried away enough to imagine he was enjoying himself *with* me.

It was a mistake. I forgot that Joshua didn't like anyone, and he didn't enjoy anything. He was only trying to teach me skills that would make me more useful.

"Cougars," Joshua answered softly, handing me the book. It was a guide to mammals of North America. The page he'd saved was a chapter on the North American Cougar.

"Oh." I took the book, stealing a glance at him.

"I've crossed paths with that male a few times over the years. Probably more times than I've actually realized. Our territories overlap, it seems." I couldn't help but smile a little when he referred to his property as his "territory," as if he was no different than the cougar. "We stay out of each other's way. Plenty of deer to go around."

I skimmed the first page, muttering, "not enough skinny blonde ladies to go around, apparently."

"Most likely he was only checking you out before you tried to get away. You acted like prey, and it got him excited. When you ran, he couldn't resist the urge to chase. You never run from a cougar," he repeated for the hundredth time.

"So, you said." The sneer felt especially rude since, for once, he was genuinely trying to be nice.

"I wasn't angry. It surprised me is all."

"I'd hate to see you when you're actually angry."

"I *was* angry," he clarified. "I meant I wasn't angry at you. I shouldn't have let you get so far out of my sight. You don't know what you're doing out there."

That was another apology. It helped get the point across a better if you used the word "sorry" when you apologized. That was the thing about Joshua; he was never obvious with any sentiment that wasn't frustration or annoyance. I couldn't say if that was intentional or if it was simply because those were the emotions that were easiest for him.

He had to enjoy something. Maybe not me, but he had to like someone.

I pressed my lips together, finally finding the courage to look at him. He was staring at me. There was no sign of his usual frown, only that calm, neutral face he got when he was studying me. I could never figure out what he was thinking when he did that.

"I'm sorry for walking away." There I went again, apologizing when I did nothing wrong. It wasn't as if I was carelessly wandering off. I only wanted privacy. My incessant need to say I was sorry irritated me. It was a lifelong habit of mine—growing up with controlling parents will do that to you—and with Joshua it seemed to be elevated.

"Actually," I straightened my shoulders and gave him a hint of that defiant look I shot the dog earlier. "I'm not sorry. I won't go that far next time but I didn't do anything wrong."

His lips twitched and I might have called the glint in his eyes pride. "Good."

"Good," I echoed.

I returned my attention to the book, stopping to read a section, and noticed him in my peripherals. His expression had softened, eyes warmed over to a delicious cocoa color. I slowly closed the book, sliding my eyes across the floor, over the dog, then up his body until I was staring back at him. He blinked once before turning sharply toward the fire.

It was okay for him to stare but not to be stared at. That was a shame. When it wasn't shadowed with a scowl, Joshua had a nice face.

"I thought..." He cleared his throat. "I thought taking you on a hunt would help. Thought maybe if you knew how it was done, saw that we don't take too much and try to make it quick, you might feel better. That did it for me."

"Did it for you?"

"Pops started me hunting as soon as I was big enough to hold a rifle. Around that same time, I was learning to read. Peter Rabbit was a favorite of mine and when I realized it was rabbits we were and eating, I refused." He turned enough to catch me in a sidelong glance. I offered an empathetic smile.

"Pops took me out anyway. He wasn't a man who would be refused." There was a bitter twist to those words that tempted me to probe.

"That's sad, Joshua."

"It was necessary." The harshness was back. "He taught me that if I'm to survive, I have to be the predator."

Like the cougar.

"Pops showed me the hunt from nature's perspective. We kill for food, nothing more. That's the way it's meant to be. We don't live in a world where every creature lives happily ever after." That was a dig at me. To Joshua, I was like a Disney princess who spent the day braiding her hair and singing to sparrows.

"There's nothing wrong with wanting to live in a world like that."

"It's never going to happen and dreaming about it only makes you naïve."

"I'd rather be naïve than bitter," I snapped back, setting the book down so I could wrap my arms around my knees and bring them closer to my chest.

"Bitter is why I'm alive. It's why you're alive too."

"Lucky me." I was doing it again, that awful sneer. "I should go to bed." I stood abruptly, making Kuna stir again.

Joshua sighed so loudly it sounded more like an exasperated groan. "Good idea."

I stomped to the bed and threw myself down, flinging the quilt up so I could crawl under it. I lay there with my back to the fireplace—and more importantly, to Joshua—for what could have been hours. After a long, emotional day I was exhausted but my brain wouldn't shut up and let me sleep. There was this nagging, unresolved feeling that had me replaying my interactions with him over and over in my head.

I couldn't understand him! I tried so hard to be nice and make up for his lack of patience with an excess of my own and it did nothing. This morning I thought he was having fun with me, but it didn't last. Then he apologized for his outburst only to get annoyed again with even less reason than before. Was that just the type of person he was? Unfriendly and irritable and impossible to talk to?

My frustration was replaced with disappointment. It shouldn't disappoint me. Why did I care what kind of person he was?

For the same reason I cared if he liked me. He was all I had. The only one I could talk to, the only one I was safe with. Combine that with the fact that he saved my life, and I was finding myself more than a little attached to him. There had to be some psychology behind it, like Stockholm Syndrome.

I had no right to expect anything of Joshua. He didn't invite me into his life. I fell face first into it. The responsibility of me was thrust onto him and I should be grateful that he even accepted it. If he liked me, I would be thrilled. If he didn't, I was glad to be tolerated by someone who was willing to give so much, even grudgingly.

But what if I liked him? What if I liked him despite his worse qualities? What if the more I got candid glimpses of him, the more I was beginning to like him in a way that would lead to devastation? The feeling was unbidden, an escaped little glimmer of foolish romanticism that needed to be carefully contained.

After the blackout I had to compartmentalize. Certain emotions were locked away, never to see the light of day again. Then suddenly Joshua made me safe and in doing so, made it safe to feel.

Now I couldn't swallow down the tiniest flutter when I remembered the twitch of his lips—that almost smile that lit up his face. There was this thrill that bounced happily in my stomach after seeing him in his element, relaxed and as carefree as a man like him was capable of.

He was so unlike anyone I'd ever been with, so unashamedly and uniquely him. No ego or vanity ruled him. No self-indulgent desires drove his decisions. In all that he did, Joshua was true to his way of life, strange as it may be.

I squeezed my eyelids tighter, smothering the spark inside me before it became hope. Joshua was good to me, selflessly so, and that was enough. It had to be. If I dreamed I would ever get more from him than that, I was bound for heartbreak.

12

Burden

"I have to go to market today." Joshua announced to the eggs he was scrambling on the stove.

"Really? I was thinking of heading to the mall. Maybe we can carpool."

"Huh?"

"Oh, I just thought we were joking since neither of those things exist anymore."

"Pretty sure a building doesn't disappear just because the electricity doesn't work in it," Joshua shot back, finally catching on to my sarcasm. "And plenty of markets exist. They're just not what you're used to."

"Wait, you're serious? I thought you said everything was picked over by raiders. Does that mean there are other people in the area?" I shivered at the thought, recalling the men I'd encountered before Joshua found me. As lonely as it could be out here with just the two of us, I wasn't sure if I liked the idea of other people nearby.

I also wasn't sure if I liked the idea of him lying about it.

He didn't answer for so long that I began to feel nervous. "Yeah, there are a few folks in the area." I started to ask about them, but he kept going. "This particular market isn't that close."

I finished the last button on another borrowed flannel before twisting the spare fabric at the bottom and tying it into a knot. The shirt would have been too big on me anyway but with how thin I still was, it was like a tent around my body. I considered for a moment, deciding to be brave. "Sounds like fun. When do we leave?"

"You're not coming." He turned to set the cast iron pan on the table.

"Why can't I come? I can walk. Look at me. I'm full of energy!" I skipped over to the table to demonstrate.

He scowled at me and set a heaping plate of eggs, arugula, and mushrooms in front of my chair. When he broke a small loaf of bread in half, he dropped the larger piece next to my plate.

Of the two of us, Joshua had a significantly larger appetite. He probably needed six thousand calories just to maintain his regular body mass. That didn't stop him from indulging my love of bread, even if he pretended like he wasn't doing it on purpose.

"I've noticed." He scooped the meat from one of the rabbits onto his plate, ignoring me when I wrinkled my nose. I was disappointed to see my power move was losing effect.

"Don't be sour. That's what you wanted, isn't it? Now you can make me pay back my debt to you by working on your farm for seven years." I slipped into the chair across from him and reached for the jam jar.

"Who said anything about debt?" He asked through a mouthful of food. Whoever raised Joshua was not big on table manners.

"You act like I'm a burden."

"You *are* eating all my food." He shook a finger at me when I started to put jam on my bread and handed me the butter. I wrinkled my nose again and his eyebrows twitched upward.

"You're making me!" I pointed out as I grudgingly scraped butter across the jagged surface of the loaf.

"More."

"You might as well make me spoon the butter straight into my mouth." That earned me a look that said if I kept whining, he actually might.

"Can I trust you to stay here?"

I'd almost forgotten that was the reason I was arguing with him. We argued so often that it was easy to lose track of the cause. Now that I was becoming accustomed to his mannerisms and brooding, I enjoyed some of our heated discussions. Joshua was easy to tease.

"You never told me why I can't come."

"It's not for women."

My jaw dropped. "Are you kidding me? The power goes out for a year and we're reverting to some antiquated, sexist behavior? You can't have a men's only market. As a feminist, I disagree with that on so many levels."

He snorted. "I'm sure the folks at the trading post will change their tune if you explain your feminist agenda."

"Good. I'll bring notes."

"You're not good at sarcasm."

"No, *you're* not good at sarcasm. Otherwise, I would have known you were being sarcastic."

"You're not coming but if I can't trust you here then I'm not going." He poked at a piece of mushroom on his plate.

"Joshua," I gave him my best puppy dog eyes. "I want to come with you. Please?"

"No. It's not a place for women."

"So, you're a male chauvinist now?"

"No, I'm realistic. Trading is dangerous. And most markets have certain…expectations of women. Not all of them are there voluntarily. I've got to watch my back and I can't do that if I'm keeping an eye on you the whole time."

"Expectations?" I sputtered. "Voluntarily?" My brain couldn't seem to process anything beyond those two words.

"That's what I said."

"You mean like," I lowered my voice. "Prostitution? Or slavery?"

"A little of both. Apparently, there's a shortage of women." His words were so matter of fact.

"And you're okay with this?" I suddenly had a sick lump in my stomach. Was that the kind of man Joshua was, and I hadn't seen it?

"I never said that."

"But you're going to the prostitute slave market!"

He scooped a bite of eggs into his mouth and frowned at me. "It's not a slave market. There are very few people trafficking, if you can even call it that. Mostly folks trade scarce items like weapons and medicine. That's what I'm after."

"You're strong, though. You should do something to help those people! It's your moral obligation."

"I'm not obligated to do anything and I'm not here to be anyone's hero."

"You saved me. That makes you a hero."

"Don't be childish."

"Don't be cruel! You're just going to sit by and let people openly participate in slavery?" I slid my plate away and crossed my arms.

"If that's what it takes to survive. I'm not wasting my time and resources to save a bunch of strangers. It's already cost me enough caring for you." His words shot across the table, leaving me to feel like I'd been smacked.

I stood so fast my chair fell over and banged on the floor. Kuna leapt from her place by the fireplace and hurried into the kitchen, hackles raised. "Well, I'm sorry I'm such a problem for you. Next time you can leave me on the forest floor if it's so costly to help." I stalked over to the bed and flopped onto it. "You're the one that told me to stay."

It occurred to me that I was being slightly irrational. Even if Joshua's attitude was callous, he had a point. It wasn't his obligation to help anyone, and he was probably putting himself at risk if he did. I was hardly about to say that out loud and validate him, though. He was just too casual about the whole thing.

Shouldn't it bother him, at least a little? I wanted it to bother him. I wanted him to be a good enough person to care about things like that. I wanted to know that I wasn't wrong about him.

I jumped when there was a clatter by the bed. I lifted my head from the pillow it was buried in and saw Joshua marching back to the table. My plate was on the nightstand. "Eat. All of it."

"No."

"Fine. Starve. Your choice. I'm leaving after breakfast. I'll probably be gone all day. You have to stay in the house so if you need to do anything outside you better hurry up and get it done."

"What if I follow you?"

"Follow me and get lost in the woods again. Or get snatched by raiders."

"Couldn't that happen if you leave me here alone?" I sat up on the bed and crossed my arms again.

"Kuna will stay with you."

"No way! She's more likely to eat me than a cougar is."

"She's never eaten anyone who's alive." I wanted to think that he was joking but I didn't know if Joshua was capable.

I knew he could feel me glaring but he didn't look up from his breakfast plate. "You're serious."

"About?"

"All of it. You're going to some end of the world black market where all women are slave prostitutes? *And* you're going to leave me with your man-eating dog?" Okay, maybe I was being a little dramatic.

"Yup."

Quieter, I added, "and you kept this a secret until now because you don't really trust me." Selfish as it was, that part bothered me as much as the rest. He said there was no one else around and I believed him. What else was he keeping from me?

After breakfast Joshua left with a backpack that probably weighed more than me and a promise to be back "sometime before tomorrow." Kuna whimpered at the door, eventually settling down in front of it to wait. Every time I stepped off the bed she snarled until I sat back down. It was going to be a long, boring day.

An hour dragged on with nothing to distract me from the lingering sting of Joshua's words. A burden. That was how he saw me. A burden that for some ridiculous reason—a reason that he still hadn't divulged after two months—he accepted as his own.

You are not a burden, Liv.

I wasn't. Or at least, I didn't have to be.

My disappointment shifted into determination. I was not a burden, and I would prove it. An idea hit me almost immediately, one that would benefit both of us. Even if *he* didn't appreciate it, I would.

Besides, I was going to lose my mind if I had to spend the whole day in bed. The only problem was that I didn't know where he kept his cleaning supplies. Well, the only other problem. The first problem was the dog.

Kuna stood and growled when I slipped off the bed. I waited a few minutes until she sat back down in front of the door. Then I took a few steps toward the kitchen. She growled again but didn't stand. We repeated this dance for almost twenty minutes before she finally lowered herself onto her belly with a sigh. Dark eyes followed my movement through the house but apparently, I wasn't threatening enough for her to continue the effort.

I shouldn't have. I know I shouldn't have but as soon as the dog was off my back, I tried the handle on the door I was forbidden to open. It was locked. I stood on my tiptoes to reach the top of the door frame to look for a key. There wasn't one. I ducked down to the floor to look under instead. Faint light cast the shadows of furniture onto the floor. A threadbare red rug with faded gold filigree covered most of the floor. That was all I could make out.

It was obvious that Joshua kept supplies in there. He couldn't exactly hide that he went in empty handed and came out with bandages, balms, and food. That was why it remained a secret after all this time. If Joshua didn't trust me enough to tell me there were other people in the area, he definitely wouldn't trust me with his supplies.

When I couldn't pry the door, I dropped my curiosity and opened the cupboard under the sink. There was a hand broom, a dustpan, and a duster, as well as several cleaning cloths. There were no cleaning supplies besides a spray bottle of some unknown liquid that smelled like vinegar, but I could make do.

My first course of action was to clean the kitchen. It was by far the dirtiest part of the house, which was gross considering how often we used it. I wiped down the dishes and set them in the rack to dry. The countertops were next. They were coated with breadcrumbs, sticky jam stains, and grease spots. They practically glittered when I was done with them. The stove and the table weren't left out of my scrubbing frenzy.

After the kitchen, I went crazy with the feather duster. There was hardly a surface in the entire house that didn't sport a fine layer of dust. By the time I was finished with the furniture, I was having fun. This felt so normal. When was the last time I did something normal?

For someone so strange, Joshua had given me quite a few tastes of normal life.

Kuna became wary of me again when I started sweeping. The hand broom required me to crouch on the floor and it offended her that I was on her level. She never got up from her spot by the door though, only watched me with quivering jowls.

Joshua really was gone the whole day. The sun was barely up when he left. By afternoon I was still alone. That worked out fine. Despite the space being small, it took the bulk of the day to clean the cabin. I was going to have bruises on my knees in addition to a sore back after mopping.

I finished my cleaning spree with the fireplace. The hills of ash that accumulated there were so large they were beginning to spill out onto the hearth. It was a painstaking effort, but I managed to scoop most of the burnt debris into a filthy cloth I found under the wood pile. It was a great idea until I got to the part where I wanted to dump it out.

No way was Kuna going to let me open the front door. I had to devise an escape plan. I managed to jerk the window above the fireplace open but only after practically getting into a fist fight with it. I probably wasn't going to be able to get the screen back on and hide the fact that I climbed out. Joshua should have known I would need to go pee more than once in a whole day. It was his fault I had to climb through the window in the first place.

Jumping out a window, even on the first floor, was not as easy as it looked in movies. I went out feet first with my front facing in. I had a good grip on the windowsill, but it was higher up than I thought, and I was left with my legs dangling. I took one hand off to toss the ash cloth and fell on my butt. Bruise number forty-five.

Once outside, I made my way to the outhouse. First, I emptied the cloth into the pit. Then I took a really long pee. When I was done, I paused to inhale the fresh air and enjoy the cool hint of autumn. I hadn't been outside without Joshua, even if I was allowed to roam most of the time, and it felt kind of liberating to be on my own.

It also felt kind of scary. No one could get me out here, of course. At least, I didn't think they could. The fence wasn't impenetrable, but it was pretty dang close.

A big fir groaned as a strong breeze rocked the trees and I jumped. Time to stop thinking about bad guys and get back inside before I gave myself a heart attack. I was headed for the cabin when I caught a glimpse of yellow. In a grassy area on the outskirts of the trees was a patch of wildflowers. I quickly picked a few of the bushiest ones, the final touch to turn a clean house into a clean home.

Climbing back through the window proved even harder than climbing out. Eventually I gave up jumping for the windowsill and hunted down something to give me a step up. I found a thick cut piece of a log in the woodpile and rolled it up against the wall.

I finally made it through the window by clambering onto the unstable log only to find myself face to face with Kuna. I righted myself quickly and squared my shoulders.

"What are you going to do? Eat me?" I gave her my most ferocious look. I guess that was all it took to prove myself to the massive dog. She backed off and returned to her silent vigil by the door.

The sun was barely above the tree line when Joshua got home. I knew he was coming before I heard him because Kuna leapt up and pressed her nose in the crack of the door, whimpering and wagging her tail madly. What I didn't expect was for him to fling the door open, eyes wild with alarm. The moment he saw me reclining on the bed with a book in hand he straightened and quickly fixed the standard frown onto his features.

I saw that, I thought teasingly before realizing that alarm on Joshua's face might be something that should worry me.

"Is everything alright?" I marked my page and set the book on the nightstand.

"You left." He said it so coldly I almost shivered. I think I preferred it when he raised his voice.

"Not exactly."

"The window screen is on the ground. I thought you—" He shook his head sharply and closed the door behind him with a slam. "I told you to stay here."

"I had to pee." This wasn't the reaction I was hoping for when he got home.

"Hold it next time."

"I didn't realize I was your prisoner." I lowered my gaze to hide my disappointment.

"Good girl, Kuna." Joshua turned his attention to the dog and tossed her a strip of jerky. She scarfed it down, tail still wagging. He opened the door again to let her outside. She took off in a sprint. "At least one of you knows how to wait."

"I'm not some obedient dog." I rose from the bed and stomped over to him. "Why are you being such a jerk? It must be a day that ends in 'Y.'"

"You're too sensitive." He heaved his pack off his shoulders and onto one of the dining room chairs.

"Have you ever considered that maybe you're a little too *insensitive?*"

"Don't take it personally." He shrugged, much less irritated than he tried to appear now that he realized I hadn't made a break for it. Why did he care so much? I couldn't even read a compass. How was I going to remember where the farm was and tell someone else about it, assuming I could even find someone else to tell?

Joshua was unbuckling a pocket on the top of his pack when he noticed the flowers. "What's this?"

"Um, flowers." Picking them for him felt stupid now. Joshua didn't care about décor.

"That's goldenrod. It's in the book you were just reading."

"Is it useful? I thought it might liven things up in here."

"Everything *can* be useful."

"Even me?" The words tumbled out before I could stop them.

Joshua gave me a weird look. "'The hell kind of question is that?"

One born of the insecurities you've nurtured with your bad attitude. I shrugged and moved the flowers from the table so he could unpack his bag.

He focused on fixing up a fire before unloading. The temperature was dropping and soon the cabin would be chilly. He knelt beside the hearth, stared at it for a second, then frowned over his shoulder. "It's clean."

"I tidied up. I needed something to do." I swallowed. "And maybe you could think of it as a thank you."

He stiffened and I was afraid that he was angry. I'm sure he could find a reason to be. I snooped through his house or touched something that didn't belong to me or wasted precious calories. "You don't have to."

"I want to." I hooked one pointer finger on the other and looked down at them. "Thank you, Joshua. I know I'm taking up a lot of your time and energy."

"I, um," he cleared his throat and returned to his task. "I didn't mean it like that. What I said this morning."

"It's okay. I understand. I'm not exactly helpful." Truth be told, it wasn't okay, but how was I to express that to him? I didn't think it would go over well if I tried to explain that he hurt my feelings.

"You are."

I laughed softly. "I'm sorry I called you a jerk. You don't have to flatter me to make up for being short."

"I mean it."

I lifted my head hopefully. "Maybe when I'm strong enough I can be helpful as your market companion."

"Not a chance in hell."

"I'm going to get cabin fever." I blinked pleading eyes at him.

He fanned a spark, placing more kindling around it when it bloomed "Most trading posts will never be safe for women. I'll take you somewhere else. When you can carry your weight in supplies, that is."

"Really?" I squealed. Joshua scowled when he joined me at the table. Right, he didn't like enthusiasm. I pressed my lips together and calmly said, "I would like that."

Now if only he would tell me where *somewhere else* was. Two days ago, I had no clue there were trading posts. I thought maybe we were the only two people still alive in the foothills, besides the men that chased me into Joshua's woods.

He didn't expound on his vague promise as he began unpacking. Apparently good meat, especially smoked and properly dried, was becoming scarce. Not just because of the shifting seasons but also because not a lot of people knew how to properly process it. Illness from food was becoming much more commonplace simply because people tried to save meat or other food products and didn't do it safely. That meant Joshua was becoming a valuable trader.

To all these people that were apparently around. I was only a *teensy* bit bitter that he'd kept it from me.

He explained that meat used to fetch him small items like bandages, toiletries, and fabric. Now he was offered seeds, packaged food items, medicine, and in one case, ammunition. That was mostly what he brought home, bullets for his rifle, radish, beet, and turnip seeds, toilet paper, a roll of bandages, a small container of prescription antibiotics, and scraps of black fabric. He handed the fabric to me with a grunt.

I examined the familiar shape. "What is this?"

"To replace your tampons."

"These are period pads?" I withdrew and set them back down on the table.

"They're not used." If Joshua was the type of person to roll his eyes he would have.

"I prefer tampons."

"Good luck finding some."

"These are fabric. You have to," I paused for dramatic effect and lowered my voice, "wash them."

My discomfort clearly irritated him. "You have to wash your clothes too."

"Where did you even get these?"

"Trading post." Now he was looking at me like I was brainless.

"Yeah, duh! I mean where did you get them there? Who makes these?" I did roll my eyes.

"Frank's wife sews them. She makes underwear too, not that you need any."

"Glad to know you're keeping track of my underwear," I muttered, then straightened when I realized what he'd said. "Wait, so Frank's wife gets to go to the trading post? Why can't I?"

Joshua stared at me with that flat expression. He kept staring for what felt like ten minutes, studying me like he genuinely couldn't figure out how to justify himself.

"Joshua? Where'd you go?"

"Frank's wife doesn't come." He came around the table and strode past me. "And Frank's wife carries a gun."

Oh, right. Guns evened the playing field for just about everyone in the end of the world. They weren't really my cup of tea. I wouldn't be able to shoot someone when I needed to. I would probably just end up shooting myself by mistake.

"While we're on the topic, who's Frank? How did we go from there being no one around and everything being looted to you trading with people you're familiar with on a first name basis?"

Another blank expression. Too blank. That was a look I'd come to know as a dead giveaway for Joshua lying. Okay, maybe not lying. Omitting. He was keeping things from me, many more things than I initially suspected. Just when I thought I'd earned a modicum of trust. He'd only given enough to appease me. Apparently, I was easily appeased.

Why though? Keeping secrets about himself, protecting his own privacy, that I understood. Why hide that there were other people around? I couldn't understand his logic.

"I have something else for you. And something to show you." He successfully changed the subject when he headed for the forbidden door and unlocked it, beckoning for me to join him.

I wasn't so stupid that I couldn't see he was avoiding the conversation. For now, I would let him. He was never forthcoming with these sorts of topics. I would have to wear him down and this evening wasn't the right time to push.

Joshua swung the door open and stepped inside, disappearing into darkness. I tried to peer in from the doorway. There was one window on the far wall but with the sun below the horizon, I couldn't make out more than grey hues through dirty glass. A faint light flickered to life, Joshua lighting candles on a wall sconce. I crept toward the glow.

My expectations for this room were all over the place. I joked that it held everything from the bodies of his serial murder victims to the enchanted rose that made him such an angry beast. Whatever it was, it was private and suddenly Joshua was letting me see it. The line between trust and mistrust was confusingly blurry with him.

I was standing in a personal library. That had to be what it was because every inch of wall was covered in shelves and every one of those shelves was covered with books. *Overfilled* with books. Once a shelf was full, more books were squeezed in above the others. Even more books were stacked neatly on the very top of some of the shelves.

No two shelves looked alike. It seemed as if each time a bookshelf was full, a new one was brought in with no concern for how it looked or if it matched the other. When I made a half circle around the room, I realized one of the "shelves" wasn't even a shelf; it was a wooden bed frame for a single bed standing upright with shelves and sturdy feet screwed into the base.

I tried to scan the titles to see what kinds of books he read but all it told me was that there didn't appear to be a type of book Joshua didn't read. Some were fiction I recognized like *The Lord of the Flies*, but others were non-fiction, like one titled *Bushcrafting for Beginners*. Despite the untidy appearance, the books were carefully organized by author.

Based on the wear and discoloration, this was a collection built over a lifetime. I closed my eyes and tried to imagine Joshua as a little boy, lying on the floor in this room and reading by candlelight. Or perhaps, on the rug next to the fire with baby Kuna curled up beside him. It was a sweet image. Until now, I never could have imagined Joshua as innocent and hopeful. Maybe even happy.

Dang. He was *smart.* Not just street smart—or, um, survival smart—but book smart. If he'd read even half the material on those shelves, he was way ahead of me and my half-finished college education. The man was full of surprises.

"This was my room," he explained as he lifted the tattered red rug and messed with something on the floor.

"This is where you grew up?"

"Yes. I was born in this room."

"You were *born* in this room? Like your mom gave birth to you in here?"

He looked up sharply, bemused by my shock. "Yes."

"That is so *Little House on the Prairie*," I joked, though I'd never read any of those books. Joshua probably had. "You were born in this house, and you still live here. Do you like it?"

"Sure."

There was a loud squeak and then a groan as he pulled one of the floorboards and—I kid you not—a trap door opened. "Okay, so your old room has a secret passage. Does this take you to Narnia?"

"Takes you to the cellar. C'mon." He waved me over.

I took two reluctant steps forward and eyed the dark hole in the floor. "You promise this isn't your murder basement?"

"It's a cellar, not a basement." Not the part I was hoping he would clarify. God forbid I call his murder cellar a *basement* by mistake.

"Ah, how reassuring. Is there a light?"

Joshua plucked a small flashlight from his pocket and handed it to me. I clicked it on and shone it down the hole. I couldn't see much other than a metal ladder and a dirt floor.

Considering I was standing in a building that was little more than a shack, I shouldn't have been so surprised to see a dirt floor *inside*. It seemed like something from a peasant's house in ancient times. Or maybe I just didn't know as much about country living as I thought I did.

The feeling might not be mutual, but I trusted Joshua. Really, I did. That didn't mean I wasn't more than a little nervous about climbing down a rickety ladder into his secret cellar while he stood at the top and watched me. He trusted me enough to show it to me though, so I decided I should trust him not to lock me in there with his freak twin brother who ate human flesh.

I did spend a few seconds psyching myself up by going over all the times he had an opportunity to lock me in this cellar and didn't, including this morning when I threatened to follow him. If he'd really wanted me to stay, he would have thrown me in the murder dungeon, right?

The metal rungs on the ladder were icy under my bare feet. So was the air around me and the ground when I reached it. I wrapped my arms around myself and shivered. Now that I was down here and Joshua was holding the light, I couldn't see anything. It was scarier than I thought it would be.

I started recalling every horror movie I'd ever seen with a basement or a creepy trap door and all the monsters that lived in them. When Joshua skipped the last few rungs on the ladder and leapt down with a thump, I let out a startled scream.

He reached out clumsily in the dark until his hand landed on my shoulder. I'm not positive he was intending to touch me reassuringly or just making sure I hadn't toppled over. As soon as he made contact, he withdrew and asked, "what happened?"

"You scared me." I giggled nervously.

He shifted away from me to light more candles. I gasped again, this time in total shock at how big the space was. It seemed to be about the size of the entire cabin. To my right there were metal shelves loaded with jars of canned goods—probably homegrown and homemade—as well as several big ceramic crocks. Next to that were wooden stands with wide, tray-like shelves. One was filled with apples. The other had a variety of potatoes.

So, this was where he stored the food he grew.

Behind the ladder was two metal filing cabinets labeled "seeds." That was quite the collection of seeds and Joshua came home with even more today. I supposed seeds were pretty darn important for a farmer.

To my left there was more shelving. These ones, however, had massive plastic containers on them, labeled with a variety of grains, beans, and other pantry items. They had to be at least twenty gallons each and there were probably twenty five of them. It was a lot of supplies for just one man.

"So, is this like your medieval root cellar?" I turned to look back at him. He was staring at me. Why was he always staring?

"Why is it medieval?"

"Because the floor is made of dirt. Plus, look at all the candles. Totally medieval."

"I have a few history books for you to look at when you're done with the plant ones." Whoa, was that a joke? He was practically being a person.

I grinned. "Make me a reading list, bookworm."

There was a small wall separating the rest of the cellar from the food storage area. Joshua was still standing at the base of the ladder—and yes, staring at me—so I assumed he was letting me do the exploring. I stepped through the doorway and froze. The light from the candles was blocked by the wall that separated the two rooms.

"Joshua?" I couldn't hear or see him but the moment I said his name I felt him behind me. Even when he didn't have a shadow, I could sense him looming over me.

He lit more candles without a word. When the room was illuminated, he quietly said, "okay."

I wasn't sure exactly what he meant was okay, but he almost seemed nervous. Once my eyes adjusted to the candlelight and I saw what was in front of me, I understood why he might be. I also understood why he had to trust me before he let me see this.

"Whoa. Not so medieval after all." I couldn't believe what I was seeing. I knew he was prepared but not *this* prepared.

We weren't standing in a root cellar anymore. We were in a bunker. The walls were concrete and instead of a door, there was a thick metal hatch with a little round window that I hadn't noticed when I stepped through the opening. There were two vents on the ceiling that I assumed brought in fresh air from outside. Lining three of the walls were more heavy-duty storage shelves.

They had everything you might expect to see in a doomsday bunker. Sleeping bags and cots, dried food, potable water tanks, emergency medical kits, flashlights, hunting equipment, winter gear, toilet paper, and so on. You needed it to survive, Joshua had it.

The fourth wall was completely filled with guns, big military looking ones. There were gas masks hanging above them and boxes of ammunition. Lots and lots of boxes.

I followed the distinct hum of electricity to the far right corner and noticed a freezer chest. Joshua had solar panels on the roof and the woodshed but with how cloudy some of the days were, I hadn't imagined he got enough power for a fridge, a well pump, *and* a freezer chest. It would explain why there were no lights in the house. The electricity had more important places to be.

Well, if I had to pick a guy to rescue me during the end of the world, I picked the right one.

"Are you one of those survivalists?" Whatever reaction he was expecting from me, it wasn't the calm question I posed.

Joshua blew out a breath. "Grandad was. My Pops too. He raised me to be prepared for anything."

"Did you think the rapture was coming?"

His lips hitched upward. "No rapture. Dad was expecting something—tyrannical government, disease, famine, war, any of it."

"It's a shame he didn't get to see the world end. I bet he'd feel awfully proud of himself for being right."

"He did get to see it."

"Oh, I'm sorry. I guess I just assumed..." I stumbled through my words. It was rare for Joshua to talk about his father and when he did it was more to explain the source of his information. I realized now that it might be because he was still grieving. "How long has it been?"

"Eight months."

"How did he...?"

No! Remove foot from mouth, don't shove it in further. I finally got him to relax and trust me and now he's going to shut down again.

His reply was terse. "He left for supplies and never came back."

"I'm sorry, Joshua." He was quiet for a long time, leaving me to stare awkwardly at the gun rack with him at my back. I wanted to turn around so I could see his face but if he was upset, he wouldn't want me to look at him.

"He was proud," Joshua finally spoke, then added, "he thought everyone else was a fool for bumblin' around with no clue what to do without electricity. He was proud to be the man that would survive the end of the world—ironically."

I resisted the urge to laugh, half because I was relieved and half because I couldn't believe he said his father's death was ironic. "I bet he would be proud of you now."

I felt Joshua stiffen before expertly changing the subject again. "I have something for you upstairs. Help me bring the supplies down and I'll give it to you after."

That was all I needed to put the spring back in my step. "You have something for me? Something *useful?*"

13

Good Tears

I never would have imagined that Joshua liked surprises. Being the one to surprise, that is, not being surprised himself. After my tour of the cellar, I helped him unload supplies. Then he started on dinner without even mentioning whatever the something was that he brought for me. I tried to play it cool by asking him more questions about all that survival gear—without mentioning his father again—and chattered on about my uneventful day.

Despite the lull in his mood after talking about his dad, Joshua appeared to be in good spirits. It was hard to tell with him. A lack of a frown wasn't necessarily an indicator of happiness for most people, but I was beginning to believe that with him, it was a very good sign. Not only did he talk to me while he was cooking dinner, but he also let me help for the first time.

Okay, he let me cut a carrot and wash some chard. I wasn't exactly the sous chef.

It was another token of trust. I would take it.

"So," I swallowed a bite of venison. It took eight weeks, but I'd finally lost the battle over my vegetarianism. Joshua would stand his ground through a lightning storm.

Stubborn man.

"After dinner."

"You don't even know what I was going to say!"

"You were going to pretend like you haven't been wondering what I brought you this whole time and 'casually' ask about it." Joshua didn't smile when he made air quotes but there was a glitter of amusement in his eyes.

"I was not," I mumbled into my last forkful of food.

"Mhmm."

"You've read every book published in the last hundred years, you know how to survive in the wild, you're a successful farmer, and now you're a mind reader too? Impressive."

Joshua denied my praise with, "you're not impressed."

"Of course, I am." I took both our plates and rinsed them, saying over my shoulder, "and just because I'm easily impressed doesn't mean it's not a compliment."

"Sit," he commanded.

I practically leapt from the sink back to my chair. The legs screeched across the floor in my haste to be seated. More amusement played across his face. I grinned and folded my hands in front of me like a polite child. He didn't get up from the table. I tried to make my grin look more eager. He still didn't get up.

"Well?" I asked impatiently.

Joshua stood, making a painfully slow trip to his pack. He unzipped a pocket on the very top. A plastic bag crinkled in his hands, tucked behind his back and out of view. By the time he was back in his chair I was wiggling with excitement. I didn't even care what it was. I was just thrilled that he brought me something.

"A man came from further west today with a bunch of packaged food." He tossed the plastic bag onto the table and scratched his fingers through his beard. "It's not chocolate, not really, but it's about as close as we get these days."

I looked from Joshua to the bag of Tootsie Rolls and realized there were tears welling in my eyes. It wasn't *really* about the candy. It was Joshua. I had no idea he was paying enough attention to our one sided conversations in the evening to remember my chocolate lamentations.

Being isolated for an extended amount of time can warp your view on human interaction. The tiniest experience with another person can seem dramatically good. He *did* save my life which was pretty dramatic and definitely good, but his motivations could have been unsavory.

It was easy for me to romanticize his actions simply because he rescued me. Kindness and friendship didn't come as naturally to him as it did some people, but he was trying. How was I supposed to thank him without making him uncomfortable?

Was he happy that I cleaned the house? I could do that again. Or maybe cook dinner. Somehow, I didn't think breaking down into tears and gasping thanks was the right way to do it.

I rubbed my pointer fingers under my eyes to catch any stray tears—which wasn't exactly subtle but by now he'd noticed that I was crying—and smiled softly at him. "That's very sweet of you, Joshua."

Disappointment flashed across his face, but he hid it well, his words coming out neutral. "You don't like these?"

"No, no, I do!" Just as I opened my mouth to speak a single tear slipped from the corner of my eye. Joshua watched it slide down my cheek and form a droplet on my chin.

"You're upset?"

"Sometimes people cry when they're happy."

"I've never seen anyone cry when they're happy."

I couldn't help but laugh. "And it's only real if you've seen it with your own two eyes, right?"

"No."

"Thank you, Joshua, for the gift. It was really thoughtful. And for everything. Oh gosh, I'm sorry I know I already said that, and you don't like it when I...sorry." I wiped under my eyes again, my smile watery.

"C'mon." He grabbed the bag and headed over to his chair by the fire. I took a few deep breaths to calm myself before following him to the hearth.

Joshua handed me the bag when I settled cross-legged by the fire. "Thanks," I said again, quietly so it didn't sound like I was making a big deal of it.

I pinched the plastic and yanked it open. It smelled like childhood memories of piñatas and birthday parties and hiding under my bed to eat Halloween candy my parents didn't know I had. I plucked two candies out of the bag, one for me and one for Joshua. He took the offered candy very, very hesitantly.

"Do *you* dislike them?" I asked, untwisting the wrapper.

He turned the candy in his hand to examine it, eyeing it like it might bite him. "I've never had one."

"You've never had a Tootsie Roll?"

"No."

"Okay, what's your favorite candy then?" My mouth was watering but I was waiting until Joshua opened his.

"I don't have one."

I dropped my jaw in dramatic astonishment. "You don't like candy?"

"Never had any."

"You've never—yeah right. You're messing with me." I waved a dismissive hand at him.

"Nope. I've never eaten candy. Actually, I had dark chocolate at a movie theater once. It was bitter."

"That doesn't count! Only old people and chefs eat dark chocolate," I teased. "Wait, so you've been to a movie theater, but you've never had candy?"

"My parents thought processed food was poison."

"They're not wrong. Now open that up and poison yourself with me." I jerked my chin, rather impatient at this point.

Joshua carefully peeled away the wrapper, glowering at it suspiciously. He pinched the roll between his pointer finger and thumb and said, "you realize what this looks like, right?"

"Oh, come on! It looks like chocolate."

"It looks like dog shit."

"Just eat it already!" I popped the taffy into my mouth and winced when I tried to bite down. It was pretty hard—rock solid, actually. I picked up the bag and took a second look. There was a jack-o-lantern on the front and the date was from two Halloweens ago.

Joshua grimaced as he attempted to chew. He struggled with the candy for about thirty seconds before spitting it out into the wrapper. "You like this?"

"They're supposed to be soft. But yes, I do."

"It's sickly sweet." That was the first time I'd heard someone sound offended by a piece of candy.

I grinned and sang, "more for me."

Joshua watched in fascination—or maybe horror—as I unwrapped four more. When I'd consumed as many as I dared, I flopped backward onto the rug, tilting my head up to whisper more gratitude to him.

His lips twitched, curling up into the slightest self-satisfied curve. That was a Joshua smile, a really nice one. It made me notice something I'd seen on our walk in the woods. It was something I was noticing with growing frequency.

Joshua wasn't pretty like the clean-shaven, well dressed, country club boys I was accustomed to and that, I decided, was part of his appeal. He was what people called ruggedly handsome. It was a bit cliché, but I finally understood what the phrase meant. His beard was a little overgrown, his brow broad in way that made him look stern, his aquiline nose sported a bump from a previous break, but there was a hidden charm to those features.

The longer we were together, the more I got glimpses at Joshua's softer side. He wouldn't meet my gaze, but I could still see the way his brown eyes relaxed to that warm, melted chocolate color.

I'd take that over candy any day.

14

Honey-Do

Joshua

Damn woman was going to give him an aneurism. If Joshua had known there was such a nettling, stubborn personality hiding behind that skinny frame, he might have thought twice about bringing her home. He thought her silent, frightened demeanor meant she would be easy to handle.

Nothing about that damn woman was easy.

In between bouts of incessant talking, she went through these quiet spells. They lasted just long enough to lull him into a false sense of security. His noiseless peace wasn't at risk with a woman who lay unmoving in bed, blank gaze fixed on the wall.

Maybe he ruined it by checking up on her, unintentionally giving her permission to speak to him. It wasn't like he'd been cossetting and hovering. Joshua only wanted to make sure she wasn't sick. Then she'd get him sick and put even more stress on his routine.

Somehow, he gave her the impression that they were friends.

Helping someone when they were in a dire situation didn't make you their friend, it only meant you weren't a complete piece of shit. No one taught her that, unfortunately. She went on and on, asking personal questions. She could be entertaining—sometimes—but admitting that would only invite more talking.

Not that she needed an invitation. Maybe she would have given up a long time ago if she wasn't so damn good at reading him. Joshua didn't smile nor did he laugh and somehow, she still knew when she amused him. That seemed to nullify any of his excessively unsociable behavior because it convinced her he was faking it.

Which he wasn't, obviously. Joshua didn't have to pretend to be anything for anyone.

Being unfriendly wasn't an act. That was who he was, and she needed to get over.

Instead of accepting it, she accused him of being petulant. Petulant! Like he was a misbehaved child and not a grown man who outweighed her by a hundred and fifty pounds. He almost liked it better when she was scared of him.

On second thought, he didn't. That made him feel bad—guilty, even—and far too much like his father. Another way she irritated him without even *doing* anything. What business did she have coming into his home and making him feel guilty for being—what? Tall? Gruff? It wasn't like he'd done anything to her. In fact, he avoided touching her whenever possible.

The guilt must have made him too soft. As soon as she saw an opening, she was suddenly invading his life with far too much expertise for someone as innocent as her. Damn woman had assaulted him from every angle, and she was quickly winning battles.

One minute she'd been pale and exhausted, sleeping most of the day and night, too weak to even lift firewood. The next she was scrubbing his floors, washing his curtains, and threatening—or maybe offering—to do *his* laundry. She was even *climbing his countertops* to dust away cobwebs.

Joshua couldn't say why that pissed him off, but it was the final straw. He didn't think he could take it anymore. This was his cabin, *his space*, and she couldn't just show up and start changing things. For all she knew, he wanted those cobwebs in the corner above the cabinet. Maybe he liked mud on the floor and ashes spilling out of the fireplace.

Nope, he definitely wasn't petulant.

Probably the most annoying part about her was that she managed to wheedle him out of his shitty attitude, and in the strangest ways. When Joshua came in from the garden and caught her standing precariously on the counter, he was livid.

What if she fell and broke a bone or gave herself a concussion? That would be one more burden on his back. So, he dropped what he was doing, grabbed her by the hips, and tried to haul her off the counter.

Normally he wouldn't put hands on her, but she needed a reminder of who was in charge here. He wasn't against manhandling to make a point. If he said no climbing, there would be no climbing. Period.

Only, she didn't budge. She just *kicked him*.

It didn't hurt anything but his ego. Yeah, Joshua could admit that. He didn't like someone that small thinking they had so much power over him.

Maybe she wouldn't have felt so bold if he'd kept his fuse lit but the image of her standing with one foot on his chest, wiggling the duster like he wasn't there, was too damn funny. It was an effort not to bust out laughing.

Now she was at it again and based on the cursing—if he could call it that—coming through the kitchen window, she finally did hurt herself. After she harvested from the garden, fed the chickens, and picked what apples and pears she could carry, Joshua sent her in to rest.

She was intent on helping—his fault, really, because he made her think she wasn't pulling her weight—but that didn't mean she was physically equipped to. The damn woman was busy cleaning almost every evening.

That was one of two things that sent him storming up the steps. Joshua already intended to give her a verbal thrashing before he heard all her whimpering. If she hurt herself doing something as pointless as reorganizing the top shelf in the dish cabinet, he was going to be pissed. He stopped by the door and stomped mud off his boots before entering, per the demand of the woman who had appointed herself keeper of the floors.

He'd given up arguing with her over certain issues. The little masochist enjoyed it too much.

Through the open window Joshua heard her grumble "darn it," "stupid thingy," and, "this is so rotten." That was about as close as she came to swearing.

"Olivia!" Joshua flung the door open. "Where are my damn clothes?"

"Uh oh, I'm Olivia today." She lifted her green eyes, not to him but to the black dog standing in the doorway behind him, and smirked. "That means I'm *really* in trouble."

"What did you do with my laundry?" He ground out, kicking his boots off in a messy pile because he knew it annoyed her.

"I don't know if you noticed but it's raining." She gave his wet hair and raincoat a pointed look. "Correct me if I was wrong but I assumed you didn't want your clothes getting a second wash after you put all that effort into drying them. I put everything over there." She paused to point to the bed, where his clothes were neatly folded and stacked. "PS, I fixed your favorite shirt."

Joshua didn't have a favorite shirt. There was a flannel that he preferred over others because it had extra give in the sleeves and didn't lock his arms up. Last week he'd snagged it on something in the woodshed and popped half the buttons off. It was on his mental list to fix it, but he'd been especially busy trying to make sure he got transplants done in the greenhouse and hadn't gotten around to it.

Choosing to ignore what she said, Joshua slammed the door behind him and began dumping the contents of his pockets onto the counter nearest the entryway.

"If I learn how to weave a basket, will you put all of your stuff in it, so the counter doesn't get cluttered?" She asked, returning her gaze to the hand she had spread palm up over the table.

He grunted a "no" and kicked his boots out of the way a little harder than necessary.

A sound that could have been a laugh came from her as he made his way over to the bed, peeled his damp layers of shirt off, and pulled on a fresh t-shirt. When he picked up the newly mended flannel, he paused to examine her handiwork. Some of the buttons were slightly mismatched in color but they were all a translucent shade of brown. Excluding the one just below the collar, he realized.

Where the hell did she find a button with a heart on it? Did she seriously draw a fucking heart on a button just to piss him off?

"'The hell is goin' on in here?" Joshua circled the table where she was still messing with her hand.

She perked up and smiled at him. "How was your day?"

"You gonna answer my question?"

She smiled wider. "Are you going to answer mine?"

No, he wasn't going to, just as he hadn't every single day that she'd asked him that ridiculous question. What kind of question was that anyway? What did it matter how his day was? He got up and put himself to work. Same shit, different day. Why did she want to know? It wasn't like she cared.

Did she?

Joshua frowned at her. "What are you swearing about in here?"

"Splinters," she sighed sheepishly and held up a pair of tweezers before fixing her attention on her hand again.

"Where'd you get splinters?"

"Underneath the table." The tweezer clinked onto the wood surface as her clumsy left hand dropped them. "Aw poop!"

A snort escaped before he could stop it. He cleared his throat to disguise the sound. Based on the way her pink lips turned upward, she noticed anyway. Joshua refrained from doing anything she would consider sulky to hide his amusement and took the seat next to her.

"Let's see." He held out an expectant hand.

She narrowed those unusual green eyes at him, understandably apprehensive at his sudden gentleness. She might be much better than most people at seeing through his bullshit but Joshua still managed to throw her off balance from time to time.

It surprised her enough to let out a tiny gasp when he leaned across the table to cup her hand in his. He wasn't what she called a "touchy-feely" person. She'd noticed that early on, thankfully not making a deal of it.

The period in Joshua's life where he received any kind of affection was short lived. There were plenty of times when his father put hands on Joshua, but no matter what John claimed, it was never out of love. And even if no one had given him contact of any kind as a boy, he still believed he wouldn't enjoy the touch of another person.

It felt unnatural and invasive. Why would he want to give up his personal space like that? What could he gain from intimacy?

Of course, Joshua understood what people gained from certain forms of intimacy. The motivation behind sex was obvious. There was a craving to be satisfied.

As for the rest? How clingy did someone have to be to feel the need to hold their partners hand whenever they went anywhere together? They were walking around with a leash made out of human flesh. That was the purpose of hand holding between parent and child. What made a romantic relationship any different?

Overall, he viewed affection between adults as a type of possessive behavior for the insecure. In his experience, a man was typically affectionate towards a woman in his company when he felt threatened. Joshua saw it as more evidence to prove they were all just animals with big brains. He could acknowledge his own instincts and biology enough to recognize any longing for touch and closeness was merely a programmed behavior.

Perhaps he should be grateful to John. The bitter man intended to rid Joshua of all weakness and he succeeded. Joshua survived easily on his own out here because he had no need for contact with others.

Nope, there was absolutely never a time where Joshua pondered what his own voice might sound like responding to someone else's words. Not once had he found himself sitting awake in the dead of night and willing his mind to quit dwelling on the vacant space in his chest that came with such prolonged solitude.

Normally Joshua made a point to be honest with himself. Under the current circumstances, he was allowed a little denial. He absolutely could not and would not form a connection with this damn woman. Even if sometimes—fine, most of the time—he was becoming comfortable with her presence.

Even if he was relieved not to be—no, he wouldn't go there. No use considering this arrangement in too much detail because it could end at any time.

Then he would be alone again, and he would regret having let himself get tied in knots over it.

Anyway, just because he didn't want to be touched didn't mean that Joshua *couldn't* touch. He had no problem holding her hand. It wasn't intimate, it was a task. There were splinters to be removed and he would do it swiftly and efficiently. And her petite hand was pleasantly warm, soothing to his icy skin. Maybe that was why she gasped.

It had begun to rain during the last hour of chores and combined with a cool wind, it left him clammy and chilled. She must have anticipated that drop in temperature because she had fire burning hot in the fireplace and the stove.

"Give me those." Joshua snapped the tweezers from her and began plucking at one of about fifteen thin slivers of wood embedded in her skin. She yelped and jerked her hand when he pulled the first one out. "Hold still."

"Be gentler," she countered.

Joshua grunted and got back to work, gentler this time. At first, he was focused enough that he didn't feel it. Then the familiar tingling sensation made him uncomfortably aware that she was looking at him.

It was only fair. God knew he stared at her. Every chance he got he was staring at her. Joshua hadn't spent a lot of time with other people, especially women, and he'd been trying to figure this one out since she arrived.

Her gaze was much more direct than his. While Joshua might flit his eyes across her features, studying the pout of her lips, the freckles under her eyes, and the way she wrinkled her nose, she would boldly watch him with barely a blink. He risked a quick glance at her and saw astonishment.

So, he was touching her. What was the big deal? It was hardly more inappropriate a touch than when she flung herself at him after their run in with a cougar.

If he was a pettier person, he could point that out, but he was not eager to ever discuss the situation again. He would sooner forget the whole thing than revisit the sickening fear that clenched his gut at the sound of her shrieking his name, the anger he'd felt when he realized how careless he'd been, or the guilt—damn her—she *made him* feel when he didn't know how to give her something as simple as a reassuring touch while she wailed like a child. That entire day was a mess and, worse, a failure.

Joshua didn't fail at anything. Not until *her*.

The worst part was that prior to the cougar encounter, they were having a good time. Joshua didn't care what Liv thought of his lifestyle, his cabin, or his damn outhouse. Yet, he discovered that he did care, just a little, that she liked what he liked.

Growing up, Joshua didn't have friends. There were other children he occasionally played with in town when John was running errands but none that he could share interests with. His interests weren't those of a child, even when he was one.

The experience of introducing another person to his private world, the one filled with all the things that made him tick, was completely foreign to him. It wasn't his intention to share any of that with her, but she had a way of coaxing unexpected behavior out of him.

That day was supposed to be about hardening her off, showing her what she had to face if she wanted to live in his world. He realized too late how stupid that was. She'd spent nearly half a year surviving on her own.

Whatever dark and horrible world was out there, she'd seen it. She'd *lived* it. And somehow, she still greeted each moment brightly and eagerly. Joshua expected Liv to be a lot of ways—none of which were flattering—and so far, she hadn't met many of those expectations. Every new plant, mushroom, or bird that he introduced her to absolutely thrilled her.

Wasn't that a damn shock? It didn't matter what random fact or survival tip Joshua was droning on about, she was captivated. That pleased him more than he wanted to admit.

Then the damn cougar happened and the whole thing went to shit. There was no fixing it after that. Liv's happy mood vanished, and Joshua was helpless to bring it back.

Hoping to lessen some of the uneasiness that pressed at the nape of his neck, Joshua spoke. "You have small hands." And that was why he didn't talk to her. His conversation skills were nonexistent.

"Joshua, your hand is as big as my face." There she went again, saying his name like it belonged in her mouth. Did such familiarity come so easily to others or was it just her?

"What's your point?" He tightened his fingers around the sides of her palm as she jerked it a second time. They were only splinters. She could be so dramatic sometimes.

"I don't have small hands. You have monster hands."

"But I don't have monster sized mugs and you can barely fit those grabbers around one."

"Grabbers?" She snickered and wiggled the fingers on her trapped hand, making it impossible for him to see the last splinters. "You have a very unique vocabulary."

"Says Miss *Phooey*," he countered. "You gonna tell me how you got so much wood in your skin?"

"I was trying to scoot the table and my palm slipped. You should really sand that rough wood under there." She knocked underneath the table with her knuckles.

"Waste of time when you could just not move the table."

"But the floor is sticky, and I don't want to crawl under it to mop." She pushed her lips out in that signature pouty way. If he was petulant, she was whiny.

"So don't."

"Wouldn't it be nice to sit down for dinner and not have your socks glued to the floor by whatever old food or God only knows what else is spilled down there?"

He worked his jaw, avoiding an immediate answer because the honest one would be "yes." It would be nice, just like it was nice that the curtains were no longer yellow from age and dust and his nose wasn't constantly stuffy from the ashy debris floating into the living room from the fireplace.

As exasperating as it was to suddenly have someone occupying his space, there were a lot of perks. Joshua was never the tidiest person, but he did prefer a certain standard of clean. It had been months since he'd had time to do more than rinse off his dishes and wash his clothes.

Conceding that would guarantee that she kept doing it, thus putting him in the awkward position of having to feel grateful towards her. Maybe he needn't thank her for doing something she chose to do.

When Joshua didn't say anything more, avoiding the conversation altogether rather than giving her an answer, the scheming blonde decided that his silence meant "yes." That was how it usually went with her. Ignore her prodding and she would push on as if they were having a two sided conversation.

"Good, I'll get it extra clean as soon as you move the table for me." Joshua quickly turned his focus back to the last splinter.

"No more rearranging my furniture." He returned the tweezers to the first aid kit on the table and circled two fingers across her palm. Because he was checking for any stray splinters that he missed, of course.

Not because her skin was buttery soft or because the motion seemed to hypnotize her, drawing her further across the table toward him. Which was why he stopped the second he was certain he'd done his job. Or a few seconds after, anyway.

"Thank you, Joshua." Her tone was breathy. He got up from the table without responding. That soft smile was too much for him to face just then.

Joshua groaned when he pulled open the drawer beside the stove to return the first aid kit and found all the contents had been rearranged. The scissors were neatly stacked to one side, the clothespins were tucked in a little plastic basket that he hadn't realized he owned, the needles were returned to the pincushion, and the thread for repairing torn clothing was ordered by color, based on the rainbow if he wasn't mistaken.

What was next? Did she plan to go through his underwear drawer and sort the garments by fabric type? He considered griping at her for messing with stuff that didn't belong to her, but he had to admit, the drawer irritated him in its previous state of disarray.

"Do you want dinner? I already made the salad." Damn woman and her damn salad.

Somehow, she'd convinced herself that Joshua was going to have a heart attack if he didn't start eating more leaves. The little vegetarian hadn't been too impressed when he explained that he didn't have a need to eat rabbit food when he could just eat the rabbit. Not that Joshua had a problem with vegetables.

If he was being honest, it was mostly out of stubbornness that he grumbled about it. And if he continued to be honest, he would admit that his exaggerated disdain for her salads was no different than when she complained about all the butter, he forced her to put on her bread.

On second thought, there was a difference; it was his cabin and his kitchen and his food, therefore he was the one responsible for the decisions. Joshua was supposed to be in charge, and it wouldn't do for him to submit to some scrawny woman just because she smiled at him like an innocent doe. He was not a man to be influenced by feminine wiles.

Once again, Joshua didn't answer. This time he hadn't intended to ignore her, he was just too distracted by her sudden presence beside him in the tight confinement of the kitchen.

He seemed to have a heightened awareness of her whenever she was near. There was a prickling along his skin, almost like he could feel her aura of heat from more than a foot away. The sensation was disconcerting enough to draw his attention from whatever she was saying.

"...didn't have anything particular in mind I could pull out one of those cookbooks from your room and try a new recipe."

"No." His answer was automatic.

"Okay...I'll just get out of your way then." If he hadn't spent the last nine weeks with her, he might not have picked up the note of dejection.

Ah shit, that was what he got for speaking without thinking. The cold voice in his head hardened at the sight of her disappointment. It wasn't his job to entertain or satisfy her. What did he care if she was unhappy?

John was a cold bastard too, he reminded himself.

Not influenced by feminine wiles? Yeah, right. She might not be the evil vixen his father warned him of, but she certainly had her ways of beguiling. If her displeasure wasn't so genuine it might not have the stirring effect that it did. But the damn woman was so naturally effervescent and sweet that when Joshua's attitude shattered her good mood, he felt guilty.

Guilty! How the hell did she manage to make him feel so Goddamn guilty without a single nagging word?

He frowned down at her sad face and muttered, "fine. Go pick a book."

"Really?" The smile she gave him was so bright it was almost blinding. "This is going to be so fun!"

While she was perusing the shelf in the other room, Joshua unloaded vegetables from his basket and cleared the table. He scooped up several colored pencils and a notebook full of scratch paper, noticing a note written in red, blue, green, and purple. Since it was sitting on the table, he assumed it wasn't private and that it was acceptable for him to read it.

Even if it was private, he would have read it anyway.

As it turned out, it wasn't a note. It was a to-do list. Instead of a number or a box to check beside each task, there were doodled hearts and smiley faces. At the very bottom of the list in sloppy, barely legible writing she'd written "sand underside of table." Based on the tasks she'd written, Joshua suspected this list was meant for him and not her.

"What's this?" He waved the paper at her when she returned to the kitchen with a thick book sporting a rainbow of vegetables on the front. It would be just his luck that she found the only vegetarian cookbook in his house.

"It's a honey-do list!" She answered in a sing-song voice.

"What's a melon got to do with it?"

That earned him a rush of laughter. "No silly, honey-*do*. As in honey do this for me, please." Honey? Now she was calling him honey? If that wasn't the most patronizing shit— "It's not all urgent but I've noticed a few things that could use some love. I thought if I made a list, we could work through it and get some of that done before winter."

We could work through it? Well, that was better, but it didn't mean he wasn't pissed that she thought she could order him around. "You think I don't have enough to do around here?"

"I know you're busy, which is why I was going to offer to take over more outdoor chores so that you would have time for these. I could cook dinner more often too, since you're going to send me in early anyway. I can probably get some of the smaller tasks done but I have no idea how to fix a leaking faucet. I know you do." She winked and flopped the book open on the table.

Huh, that wasn't such a bad suggestion. Wait, was she mocking him? It sounded like a compliment but what reason could she possibly have to compliment him? There didn't seem to be a manipulative bone in her body.

Fine, she was right. Some of these were important. The faucet *did* need fixing because even a few drops a day was a waste of a precious resource. And that damn kitchen window had been stuck open since early summer, letting far too much cold air in, and making Liv shiver at the breakfast table. It made her look even more pitiful than she already did with her thin body wrapped in his oversized clothes.

But there was no way in hell he was going to sand beneath the table just so the little squirrel could drag his furniture around.

"Do you have any sweet potatoes in the murder dungeon?"

What the hell did I get myself into?

An hour later, after being sent down to the cellar *twice*, Joshua was sitting at the table, sipping a glass of moonshine, and watching blondie dish out some vegetable casserole thing with a ridiculous grin on her face.

Was it fair to be annoyed that just about everything made her happy? It shouldn't be that easy to please someone.

At least her happiness meant that she wouldn't be whining. And if she was going to stick around, he should be glad that she enjoyed cooking. It took weeks to teach her to use the stove without burning the shit out of everything, but she seemed to know her way around it now. It was hard to complain about enjoying a drink while someone else served a hot meal at the end of a long day.

In fact, this was a first for him. From the time Joshua was big enough to walk and carry dishes, he was made to help with meals. He'd never really had the pleasure of relaxing while someone else took care of him. It was...comfortable.

He'd been worried when he saw the vegetarian cookbook in her hands, but Joshua had to give her credit. In addition to the salad and the casserole, Liv cooked up a serving of elk without him even asking. On top of that, she cooked it *well.* It was tender and moist with just the right amount of seasoning. And she only did that silly nose wrinkle twice.

Not that he was paying attention to her nose. Or her lips and the way she puckered them when she was concentrating. He definitely wasn't admiring how she carried herself now that she was putting on some weight.

When she set a steaming plate in front of him with a helping that only a man his size could eat and still go for seconds, Joshua grunted a noise that was close enough to a "thanks" that he didn't feel rude. She just smiled. She did that a lot.

"Jesus, woman."

Liv froze with her fork halfway to her mouth. "Did I do it wrong? I thought you liked it rare."

"Where the fuck does a vegetarian learn to cook meat like that?" He cut off another bite. "Maybe I will make you cook dinner."

Was she blushing? "My dad." She looked back at her plate, her lips pressed together to suppress a smile. "I cooked dinner for my parents every Sunday. Dad had expensive taste in meat cuts. I learned quickly not to overcook them." Chewing thoughtfully, she added, "It would probably taste a little better with real butter."

"I wouldn't change a thing." The rosy tint darkened on her cheeks, snagging his attention away from his plate until she noticed him staring and he quickly averted his gaze. That was new. Liv wasn't shy and not much seemed to embarrass her. Who knew being nice turned a woman pink? Joshua couldn't seem to shake his fascination with her.

As soon as they finished cleaning up dinner, Liv collapsed onto the rug in the living room, her feet pointed at the fireplace, mouth full of Tootsie Rolls, and another of those ridiculous grins stretching her lips. Joshua couldn't suppress the lingering satisfaction and surprising smugness that he felt for finding something she liked.

He hadn't intended to bring her anything that she didn't absolutely need. Packaged food was nutritionally lacking and a waste of space. The farm provided all the food he could need and then some. But it didn't provide chocolate and for some bizarre reason, he couldn't seem to forget the longing in her voice when she talked about it.

Liv would like this, he'd thought before he could catch himself. Liv? Since when was she Liv? She wasn't. She was that woman—that *damn* woman. That scrawny woman with big pleading eyes in a mint color he'd never seen eyes take before. She was another responsibility that he'd accepted. So, what did he care if she liked anything? Why should he trade for something with no value simply to please her?

He shouldn't.

Joshua must have lost his damn mind because he did. And he spent the whole hike home excited about it.

Joshua also spent that hike trying to justify himself. It was an apology for yelling at her about the cougar or accusing her of being a thief. It was an apology for all the times he yelled at her unnecessarily. That explanation didn't really fit. Joshua didn't apologize.

The reason folks left him alone, the reason he was a scary motherfucker, was because he was unapologetic in all that he did. Well, being half a foot taller than the average man and weighing in pound for pound with a black bear added to the scary appearance too. Dangerous men didn't get excited about giving Tootsie Rolls to the interlopers that invaded their kitchen. So, when did he knock his head without noticing?

"Where are you going?" Liv asked, yanking him from his thoughts as he hovered in the doorway.

"Checking the gate." He quickly swung the door closed behind him.

There was no need to check the gate. It was locked. It was always locked. There was this sensation in his gut that drove him to do it again. And hopefully if he was out for a few minutes, she would finish her candy and go to bed. Not that he was avoiding her.

He was only...avoiding her. Sometimes she overwhelmed him. He hadn't fully adapted to having another person around all the damn time.

And no matter what he did, that uneasiness that came from touching her wouldn't pass. Spending fifteen minutes walking the eastern portion of the fence would cool him down. Otherwise, he was afraid Liv would start one of her blabber sessions and instead of having a normal conversation he would snap, hurting her feelings in the process.

Joshua hadn't realized he was headed home until he quietly closed the door and nearly tripped over the sleeping figure sprawled out on the rug. Great, she was out but not out of his way.

Though, if he was the type of person to smile, he might do it now. It was funny to see her and Kuna tangled up together in front of the fire. That mean old dog hated Liv for weeks and suddenly they were the best of friends. She had a way of getting under the skin like that.

Who the hell was he kidding? That damn woman was not just some woman. They weren't friends, per se, but Joshua really ought to be honest with himself. She'd grown on him. There was no way to let her stay in his home without making any kind of connection.

They slept in the same room—well, she slept, and he kept vigil—and ate every meal together. It wouldn't be possible to remain completely walled off while spending that much time with someone.

With expert stealth, Joshua made his way into the living room and knelt beside her. Kuna almost ruined his sneaking with the loud thump of her tail. He cocked his head and listened for Liv's even breathing before using two fingers to brush a curtain of amber blonde out of her face. Just to make sure she was asleep, of course.

And his motivation for running those same two fingers from her temple to her chin? Curiosity, of course. He only wanted to know if the skin on her face was as silky smooth as the skin on her hands.

It was even softer.

Joshua believed in God. He'd been raised to, and no amount of ill treatment ever made him lose that one belief. The only difference was he ceased thinking God was good. God *could be* good when he felt like it, but he could also be fickle. Only a capricious God would drop someone as fragile and gentle natured as Liv in his lap. It was a tease, maybe mockery.

See how sweet she is? How opposite she is to you? You're the perfect person to break her. That was all Sutton men could do to other people—break them. That was the only way broken men knew how to behave.

Someday soon she would see how destructive he was. She would be strong soon, too. Strong enough to pack up and find somewhere else to be. That was the way of a relationship like this. Joshua had seen it with his own two eyes. No use getting attached to someone who wouldn't be there much longer.

Kuna wagged her tail again, raising her head hopefully. He gave the dog a pat and whispered, "she's trying to tame you too, huh?"

When Liv didn't stir at the sound of her name being called, Joshua decided he could leave her there for a while. Sleeping on the floor was hardly comfortable and sooner or later she would get stiff and wake.

He slumped into his chair, letting the old leather and worn cushions soften the ache of his overworked muscles. The joints in his knees were particularly unhappy with him today and reclining with his legs outstretched was all he could do to ease the discomfort.

There was a breathy sigh from the floor and then tiny, warm fingers were resting on top of his foot. Joshua stilled, every muscle in his body taut as he waited for the hand to recede and for Liv to sit up. After two whole minutes of barely moving, he finally relaxed. It was such a trivial touch, so lacking in intimacy. Strangely, he had no desire to shy away from it as he usually did when an unwanted hand was on him.

Instead, he felt warmth. That wasn't necessarily an emotion, but it was the only way he could describe the sensation in his gut. Warm and bordering on that same smugness he experienced when he succeeded in making her happy.

The faintest tremor of Liv's pulse vibrated from her wrist across the top of his foot. She was one person, a one hundred pound addition to the tiny cabin, yet somehow the place felt so full now.

The heavy silence of night wasn't quite as heavy or silent anymore. In between the crackle of the fire, the buzz of light rain, and the rush of autumn winds was the gentle hum of Liv's sleeping breaths, lightening the air around her as she always did.

Eventually he gave up waiting for her to wake, carefully slipping from his chair. It took a moment to psych himself up enough to actually touch her. Joshua was terrified she would open her eyes to find his hands on her and wonder what the hell he was doing.

Liv trusted him—probably too much—but that didn't necessarily mean she would be okay with him doing what he was about to do.

Maybe she wouldn't care. He hoped not because after a frustrated groan, Joshua scooped her up in his arms and gently moved toward the bed. She wasn't as light as the first time he carried her like this, unconscious and pale and teetering on the edge of death. She could be heavier though. It bothered him to feel the bones in her hips so easily and to see her collarbones emphasized on her narrow chest.

Was he doing enough to keep her fed? Was he letting her work too hard on the farm? She hardly covered any of his chores, but he didn't know shit about recovering from starvation. Exertion might be the opposite of what was good for you. Getting her to sit still was a hell of a task, though.

Joshua thought he was safe once he laid Liv out on the mattress and covered her with a quilt. He started his retreat only to freeze at the sound of the blanket rustling and a soft groan from her.

"Joshua?" She said it so quietly, yet so earnestly he couldn't help but turn back to her. Liv was sitting up in bed, clutching the quilt and looking at him with wide, unfocused eyes.

"Yeah?"

"Will you be here in the morning?"

What the hell kind of question was that? "'Course I will."

"They left. Please don't leave me." Joshua stared at her, trying to decide if she was awake. The tone of her voice made her seem so small and the panic sounded so real that he felt the need to reassure her but wasn't really sure how. "Joshua?" She repeated.

"Nothing to worry about, Squirrel. I'm not going anywhere."

Liv nodded and slid back down onto the pillow. Joshua stood by the bed, quietly waiting until her breathing calmed and she was undoubtedly asleep. Even after he knew she was, he stood there, watching her brow crinkle in response to whatever she was dreaming.

What he was doing, Joshua couldn't say, but he knew that he was going to keep doing it. Probably a lot longer than he should. He had this feeling deep beneath his sternum that he didn't know how to describe. It had him wondering if he would make it out of this in one piece.

I'm not going anywhere, but she will, he reminded himself before settling back in his chair to watch the night pass.

15

Easy Lies

"**Y**ou don't trust anyone. Not unless I say you can," Joshua ordered as we stepped past the gate. He woke me before dawn this morning to inform me that we were taking a trip to Rockham Falls. The populated and well organized town that he conveniently forgot to mention for two months.

Rockham Falls was another trading post, safer than the one Joshua visited last month. People came to trade every day. Attendants and items available varied but most of the time, the place was hopping. Or so I'd been told an hour earlier. Before that, Joshua made it out like this area was desolate, save for the raiders hiding in the shadows.

He hadn't even been that clear. He simply said that everything in the area was picked over. I guess that was technically true, if you excluded the town that had thus far managed to keep itself safe by forming a militia to patrol and guard the tiny sanctuary. Why he felt the need to keep any of that a secret from me, I had no idea. Sometimes Joshua's motivation was clear cut and sometimes he was a mystery.

I peppered him with questions as soon as he told me what we were up to, but I got the usual grunted half-answers. Obviously, I'd misjudged the mutual trust I thought we shared. I should've known better than to be hurt by anything Joshua did, but it stung to find out there were even more secrets between us. I'd been kidding myself to think we were somehow in this together, becoming partners of a sort.

Nope. It was Joshua and the nuisance that he occasionally offered a speck of information so she would stop pestering him.

"How do I know you're a good judge of character?" I panted.

I practically had to jog to keep up with his long stride and with a pack full of supplies, that was a challenge. I might have overestimated by ability to carry as much as I took on. I had my regular pack—not a massive one like the backpacking one that Joshua carried—but it was probably a good twenty pounds.

It held a small collection of dried meats, late season apples and pears, a variety of nuts, wild mushrooms, and a handful of other farmed and foraged goods. More than enough to make my back ache and we'd only been walking for two minutes.

Joshua fixed me with one of his "that's a stupid question" frowns but he answered anyway. "I'm still alive."

"Fine. Trust no one. I can't believe you've never watched the X-files."

He ignored my comment and took a sharp turn around the side of the fence, stopping abruptly when he came upon a rusted piece of metal under a filthy tarp and a bunch of debris.

"Uncover that side." He pointed to the corner of the tarp.

I cautiously approached, looking for snakes or spiders or any other creepy creature that might want to live under an old tarp. When my slow pace earned me a scowl, I quickly yanked the crinkled brown thing to reveal a Dodge truck that looked older than the pyramids. As Joshua uncovered the other side, throwing the branches that would fit into the bed of the truck, I realized what we were doing.

"You're going to drive this thing? Does it work?"

"For now. Don't think you're up for walking seven miles today," He explained as he heaved the last fir branch into the bed. "Leave the tarp and get in."

I obeyed, jerking the old metal handle on the door, and cringing at the groaning sound it made. Surprisingly, the interior of the truck was clean. The leather on the bench was cracked and stray bits of stuffing were making their escape, but it was otherwise in fine condition.

"You have a truck."

"Aren't you observant?"

"Joshua, don't you sass me. When were you going to tell me about this? And the town? We could have driven to a town full of people this whole time?" I plopped my backpack at my feet and glowered at him, trying to go for anger and not hurt. Why did this revelation make me feel so betrayed?

He let the horrible grinding sound of the engine drown out anything I had to say. I was half afraid the truck was going to explode but it puttered to life after some maneuvering from Joshua. "We're only driving halfway so be ready to get out and cover the truck when I say."

"Don't think you're getting off that easy."

I wasn't convinced that driving was any faster than walking. There was no road to follow for the first mile, so we had to bump along open areas in the woods, carefully navigating trees. Thankfully we ended up on an overgrown gravel road, maybe an old logging road. I was going to hurl if we kept rolling over roots. Eventually Joshua pulled the truck into a copse of young evergreens. I had to squeeze between the door and a tree to get out.

Covering the truck with branches wasn't a bad idea. Once we were done, the rust bucket looked like it'd been there for months.

"Don't take anything for free. Everything has a price, even if you don't immediately know it." Joshua continued laying out the rules as we marched forward with packs secured on our backs. "Stay in my sight at all times. No wandering."

"What if I want to look around?" I hurried to catch up to him.

"You go where I go. No exceptions."

"What if I have to go to the bathroom?" The only response I got for that was another "stupid question" frown.

"Never disclose anything about the farm. Not location, not what we're growing, and not what we've got in storage. Don't mention weapons either."

"The farm is area 51. Got it." I wanted to start whistling the X-files theme, but I was too out of breath. "Hey, can you slow down a little?"

"I thought you said you could handle this."

"I can. You just have long legs."

"Poor excuse." Despite his grumbling, he did slow down for me. "People are going to assume that you're my woman."

"That sounds awfully proprietary." He kept his gaze forward, avoiding the accusation.

"These days it is. Women are...well not so much in town, anyway. Still, plenty of people we see today might have ties to unsavory folk. It's important that you don't disillusion them." He cleared his throat. "About you being mine, I mean."

"What were you going to say? Women are what?"

"Some folks treat them as assets. Further away from cities and camps there aren't that many women. I told you the raiders that ran out of supplies in the bigger cities have been migrating this way. They tend to have little respect for anyone outside of their groups. They prey on the most vulnerable." His attention was still fixed ahead. I knew he could feel me gaping at him.

"How can people behave like that? The power has only been out for a year and—"

"It's been more than a year," Joshua interrupted.

"Is there a certain amount of time that has to pass before people revert to barbaric behavior? We were a civilized society! Things wouldn't be nearly so bad if people just took care of each other."

He snorted. "Guess we weren't all that civilized."

"It blows my mind."

"That's because you think far too highly of people. You expect people to be instinctively good. They aren't."

"They are," I disagreed. "Most people are good. Look at the world we lived in. We were kind to each other. There was more than enough to go around."

"*You* had enough. People were nice to *you*," He pointed out, muttering under his breath, "probably because you're a pretty girl."

"Where did you learn to be so cynical?" I tugged one of his backpack straps.

"Living makes you cynical."

"You're dramatic."

Joshua finally looked at me just in time to see me roll my eyes. His eyebrows were still all crinkled up but this time because he was raising them and not because he was frowning. "Dramatic?"

"Yes. Lighten up." I laughed, which earned me an amused noise, less mocking this time. Maybe if I tried hard enough, I could even get a smile. "So, people will leave me alone just because I'm with a man. Sexist much?"

"Because you're with me."

"What makes you so special?"

"You ask a lot of questions."

"I have to understand the rules if I'm going to follow them."

"Folks 'round here know what I'm capable of. Folks that don't find out."

I considered a few more questions but Joshua was already being more forthcoming than usual. To be honest, a part of me didn't want to know. Joshua implied that he'd done things that might make me afraid of him. I didn't want to be afraid of him, so I left it alone.

We walked in silence after that. Occasionally Joshua slowed and grunted in a way that I interpreted as "keep up" but I wasn't flagging. I was distracted. Before he found me, I spent a long time alone in these woods. I was terrified, constantly on guard and for good reason. I didn't have the luxury of admiring my surroundings. I was always on the move and when I wasn't, my focus was making sure no one could catch me by surprise.

I'd never noticed how tranquil it was out here. The sporadic twitter of a bird or the rustle of dying leaves as the wind knocked them loose was meditative. Joshua felt it too, I could tell. His chin was up, nostrils flaring, eyes scanning the surroundings less in that cautious way and more to take in the painted beauty of early autumn. He seemed very at home here. His confidence and ease made me relax.

Safe. That was how I felt. It was such an easy feeling that I almost wasn't aware of it anymore. At one time I feared I would never feel safe again. I thought the rest of my life, however short it ended up being, would be spent in fear, in flight. Joshua saved me from that.

He wasn't always honest, but he *was* a good man.

I was so deep in thought that I nearly smacked into his backpack when he stopped. We'd come upon a stream, shallow but wide. Smooth rocks jutted from the water, their backs layered in lime green moss.

"This place is beautiful," I breathed.

The early morning clouds were dissipating, allowing thin beams of golden light to escape. Droplets from the morning rain still sprinkled from the trees like glistening gems. The sun splashed the surface of the water, sending a shimmering reflection on the branches stretched out above.

Joshua grunted his agreement.

We stood on the bank for a minute, silently appreciating the view. A soft breeze rattled browning leaves and added a rhythm to the sound of rushing water. Suddenly, I wanted to hold Joshua's hand. It wasn't a romantic desire, necessarily. I was overcome by the magnificence of life. Tears burned the back of my eyes.

I was alive. I wouldn't be if it wasn't for him.

The intensity of emotion had me craving closeness. I couldn't remember the last time someone held my hand—or any part of me for that matter. I'd gone months without intimate touch.

I resisted reaching for him, despite my yearning. I knew he wouldn't want me to. Instead, I shifted my weight as casually as I could until my upper arm brushed his. If he noticed, he didn't react.

When I said we stood there for a minute, I was being literal. He must have been counting in his head because as soon as sixty short seconds passed, we were on the move again.

Joshua crossed first, hopping from one stone to another with shocking nimbleness for such a big man. There was much less grace when I followed but I made it without getting wet. I failed to do the same at the next creek crossing.

At the third stream I stayed very dry because Joshua heaved me over his shoulder—without warning me that he was going to do it—and carried me across like a sack of potatoes. I intended to take my shoes off and walk barefoot through the water but apparently that took too much time.

That was our final crossing, which didn't stop me from embarrassing myself in other ways. Before this I wouldn't have considered myself agile, but I never thought myself clumsy either. Compared to Joshua, I was a mess. He seemed to glide over the forest floor, feet barely touching the earth.

Meanwhile, I was tripping over roots, running face first into stray branches, and making a general fool of myself. Joshua had to stop several times to help me untangle my boot from blackberry vines. Each time he ripped at them impatiently, seemingly immune to the tiny thorns that shredded my hands when I attempted to free myself.

"We're getting close to the road. Under no circumstances do you walk out there. We stay in the trees. If I say quiet, you shut up. If I say get down, you hit the ground or you duck behind the closest tree." He leaned close, as if we were already being watched, his voice a soft rumble in my ear. The deep timbre sent a shudder down my spine.

"Do many people travel on the road?"

"Not too many."

"What about cars? Does anyone else drive?"

"Not that I've seen. Plenty of horses. Once in a while I see a dirt bike or four wheelers. Those are much more common than cars." He tugged the strap of my backpack to draw my attention back to him. "If we see any sign of raiders we go home. Immediately."

Joshua took the lead after that, scouting ahead, slowing to let me catch up, then more scouting. The road was barely in sight when he motioned for me to get down. I dropped behind the nearest tree. He crouched next to me, balancing himself with his arms on the trunk, enclosing me between him and the rough bark.

The warmth of his body enveloped me. I was suddenly hyper aware of every little detail that made up Joshua; the thick lines that shadowed his brow, the depression beneath his beard that could be a dimple, the scar on the left corner of his lip.

The scent of cloves, sweetened with a touch of citrus and the tang of pine shavings filled my nostrils and I inhaled, sucking in more of it. I tried to ignore the way my mouth dried up, tried to turn my attention to whatever it was that had him on high alert.

My unhelpful gaze kept wandering to the inky hair that lined his jaw, my fingers itching to touch it. What would it feel like against my skin? How different would the texture of his calloused hands be if they were gentle, their touch intentional? I edged an inch closer, pretending to readjust my footing, when really, I was greedy for more of his heat.

There was something about him in the wilderness, free from the confines of the farm, that made me feel alive. Joshua was just another wild thing, another piece of the intricate system that made up the forest. It captivated me.

It distracted me.

That was the danger of Joshua, wasn't it? He kept me safely cocooned in his home, so distant from any outside threats that some days, I forgot the world we were living in. Some days I wasn't surviving, I was playing house. He had me too relaxed, too soft for our way of life.

It was so very dangerous, yet so very delightful.

Focus still on the road, Joshua's head began to tilt in my direction. He must have noticed that I was watching him. Our eyes locked, my gaze soft, his tight and intense. I held my breath, freezing the way you did when you unexpectedly encountered an animal on the trail. Would he bolt the other way or was I the one who should be afraid?

My shifting had put me closer than I realized, close enough that his breath moved the stray hairs that escaped my bun. I licked my lips, causing my eyes to flick their attention to his. The tension between us was different than the frustrated, taut binds that were usually born of an argument. It had my palms sweating, my skin feeling too hot despite the damp autumn air.

The spell was broken when a distant noise came into my awareness. Joshua tapped my ear with two fingers, pointing to the road before dropping his hand to the gun on his hip. A deep clipping noise echoed off the road, strangely familiar yet impossible to identify from within the trees.

Noises are tricky. For what felt like an eternity I kept expecting to see a small herd of goat's trot in front of us or maybe marching soldiers. Each time I was sure the sound couldn't get any louder without seeing the source of it, it did.

Finally, three chestnut horses appeared around the corner, riders on their backs. Two riders wore similar apparel to Joshua—jeans and canvas jackets. The third was wearing a camo hunting jacket, the pattern glaring against his jeans.

I felt a twinge of anxiety at the resurgence of a memory of two other men dressed the same. All three were armed, rifles slung over their shoulders or guns at their hips.

"Son of a bitch," Joshua muttered, silently jerking his gun from his holster.

"Joshua!" I hissed. Was he going to shoot those men? What if they weren't raiders?

"Quiet," He snarled, lifting his gun halfway, not quite aiming it but definitely poised to fire.

I squeezed my eyes shut, not willing to watch anyone else die. I couldn't make sense of what was happening. Joshua said raiders would send us home, not into an O.K. Corral style shootout. What was he thinking? There were three of them and one of him!

"You're not very helpful to me if you close your eyes every time you get scared." Joshua broke the edgy silence, startling me so hard I fell backward into the tree.

"You're not very helpful to me if you go around shooting people," I snapped my eyes open to glare at him.

The expression on his face unsettled me. The heat from just moments ago had suddenly evaporated, making the space between us feel chilled in its absence. "Agree to disagree."

My voice was shaking more than I cared for when I asked, "Should we go home?"

"Why would we go home?"

"Those weren't raiders?"

"Might as well be." He stood, offering me a hand. I took it, noting that even though the touch *was* intentional this time, he was very much not gentle when he yanked me from my sprawled position on the ground. "Did you see their faces?"

"Not really. I was too busy trying to not see you murder them."

"Self-defense isn't murder." He continued before I could point out that he definitely wasn't defending himself. "When you see them, remember them. That was Wheeler and his men. Plenty more where those assholes came from. They travel in packs. Even if you only see one, never to be fooled into thinking he's alone. Don't trust that fucker, no matter how friendly he seems."

"Why?"

"Don't trust him." His tone left no room for argument.

"Wheeler is your nemesis. Got it." I rolled my eyes when his back was to me.

We stepped out of the tree line just long enough for Joshua to show me around. He instructed me on how to get back to the farm from Rockham Falls if I ever got lost.

He also briefed me on the next town over, where the road led if I headed west instead. If I followed it long enough it would take me to I-5. From there I could get to major cities and the coast. It was a two or three day walk.

He was sure to add that it would be more like five or six days for me because, y'know, weakling.

The rest of the journey to Rockham Falls felt short. I'm not sure exactly how far we had to walk but I was too focused on my nerves to pay attention. Other than my new roomie, I hadn't seen other people in months. I was thrilled at the thought of seeing new faces and hearing other people's stories of survival.

Or I had been until we saw other people. Now, I was bordering on the edge of panic. The last time I saw a big group of people, it was a massacre. A literal, horrifying massacre. Would we really be safe where we were going? Joshua was putting a lot of faith in this town and its militia. What would he do if they decided they wanted to take what he had?

Joshua pointed to the first sign that we were almost in the town. It was a barricade of cars across the road. Stacked around the cars were old tires, piles of lumber, and miscellaneous heavy objects like a commercial dumpster.

I asked why the road was barricaded, got a "stupid question" frown, and a mumbled answer about raiders and so on. Further down the road was a second barricade with even more cars just in case someone showed up with a tank, which I supposed wasn't completely out of the question.

After the barricades, we came upon an impressive—and lopsided—wall pieced together with logs and lumber. Two platforms hosting armed men jutted out of the sides, reminding me of castle guard posts. There was even a narrow gate that swung outward. It was wide open.

The idea of meeting people in some cute small town seemed cozy. When Joshua described the trading post, I imagined a bustling market like that one near the water in Seattle with people selling produce, flowers, fresh seafood, and cool art.

It was a silly daydream.

Of course, there wouldn't be colorful bouquets and chatty women sampling exotic fruit. It would be hungry, untrusting people with weapons, people who looked at the world as bleakly as Joshua.

"Is there a castle behind it?" It was a joke—a lame one—but Joshua must have heard the note of anxiety in my voice. I shrank back as the guards eyed us, their hands resting confidently on rifles.

"I've got you." He squeezed my forearm so gently and quickly that I almost thought I imagined it. "This wall doesn't even surround half the town. It's mostly for show." He explained, raising a hand to one of the guards as they waved us on.

Beyond the wall, Rockham Falls looked like any other town. There was a First National bank of something or other, a church, and a strip of shops and businesses, many of which had their windows boarded up. Coming from a lifetime of city dwelling, I always romanticized small towns. Now this was as close as I would ever get to seeing one.

We had only walked about twenty five feet before the market was visible. Just past the church was a huge parking lot and a wide two lane street. Both were filled with tables, tents, wagons, wheelbarrows, and all sorts of other containers.

And people.

There had to be at least thirty or forty people buzzing about the area. If I didn't know any better, I would think I was just visiting a Saturday morning farmer's market. It wasn't Pike's Place, but it wasn't some stab-y black market for thieves and murderers either.

A few of the tables and wagons had fresh fruits and vegetables. The rest was an eclectic collection of packaged food, cosmetics, clothing, outdoor gear, and even less useful items like kid toys and books.

Joshua said most people stopped looting from stores, the competition with raiders too much of a risk. The majority of new goods taken from businesses ended up at the more unsavory trading posts and usually for a steep price. Here most items were repurposed or taken from abandoned homes.

"Remember," Joshua gripped my upper arm and turned me to face him. "Stay close, don't take anything from anyone, and don't trust them either."

"You forgot 'don't tell them about the farm' and 'pretend to be your wench,'" I added dryly.

He barely refrained from smiling. "We need corn, flour, grains, legumes, and any other pantry item like pasta. Seeds too. Anything that we can plant in the spring, we'll take. Always make sure to check for bugs before you trade. The last thing we want is a bunch of weevils in the cellar. We also need knives."

"You need *more* knives?"

"We should always get them when we see them. You need a better one than that toothpick you were carrying around. Can't kill a cougar with a pocketknife." He patted the hunting knife on his hip to demonstrate.

"What else?"

"First aid supplies. You need clothes, too."

"What's wrong with my clothes?" I demanded.

"You're going to freeze to death when winter comes, assuming all those bright colors don't draw half a hundred raiders to you first. You're swimming in that jacket. You won't be able to do anything useful if you have to wear my clothes to stay warm." Joshua tugged on the zipper of the jacket to close it up to my collar, presumably to hide the brightly colored clothes he accused me of wearing.

I looked down at my arms. My hands *were* completely lost in the sleeves of the raincoat Joshua gave me this morning. The bottom of the jacket came far enough down my thighs to pass as a dress. I suddenly felt a bit foolish, like a child in ill-fitting hand-me-downs. I started to unzip what he'd zipped up to take it off but noticed my hot pink shirt underneath and stopped myself.

Maybe he was right.

I groaned and hunched my shoulders. "Fine, but I get a say in what I wear."

"No."

"Joshua," I sucked in a breath to begin my argument.

He cut me off. "We need water bottles too. Metal, not dented. Use the water in the canteen on the outside of your pack to check for leaks."

"Joshua! I wasn't expecting to see you this week." A man with a bright smile waved to us from a folding table at the edge of the market. A loose bun of brown hair flopped atop his head when he moved. The table was covered in clothing ranging from t-shirts to winter gear as well as what looked like kitchen items. Beside the table was a kid's wagon full of vegetables.

A woman who couldn't be much older than me was seated nearby. She had the same brown hair. One of her hands rested affectionately on her pregnant belly. A little girl, maybe six or seven, squatted beside an old stereo, fiddling with it.

"Asher, good to see you," Joshua said in a tone that didn't sound like he thought it was good to see Asher at all. Then again, he never sounded like he thought anything was good. I was surprised he was even capable of that much pleasantry.

"How're you, man? It's been a long time. We were starting to worry about you up in those woods." Asher moved forward like he wanted to clap a hand on Joshua's shoulder. He must have known better because he halted the movement halfway through and offered a hand to shake instead. Joshua shook it firmly but hastily.

"Just been busy." A pointed look in my direction. If it had been anyone else, I would have felt the need to speak up and clarify that he didn't mean he was "getting busy," only occupied like someone caring for a baby bird. If this guy with the pleasant face knew Joshua well enough not to touch him then I was confident he didn't need me to explain.

"Joshua's got himself a girl." Asher noticed me hovering behind Joshua and gave me that same bright smile. He was surprisingly clean shaven and well groomed, a stark contrast to Joshua's untamed locks and thick beard.

"I'm Liv." He offered me his hand next, and I shook it eagerly. His smile got even wider and so did his eyes.

"Day-um!" This Asher guy seemed to know Joshua well, if his reaction to my presence was any indicator. A whole darn town full of people, people who Joshua was familiar with, and I was completely in the dark.

Because he thought I would put them at risk. The thought buzzed around my head like a wasp, stinging me with disappointment. *Does he still think I'm in this to gain more than my own life?*

"Liv needs clothes, and I could use more corn and flour if you've got 'em."

Asher hoisted a crate out from under the table, then another. "Maddie can get you fixed right up in the clothing department. Assuming you've got the goods."

"Mushrooms, nuts, and all the smoked meat you could ever want." Joshua took off his pack and started pulling out supplies.

I gaped at him, shocked because the way he talked with Asher was *friendly*. If I hadn't spent the last two months with him, I might not have detected the tonal shift that brushed away a layer of gravel from his voice.

So, this was Joshua with manners. Still much more stiff and rigid than the relaxed version of him I got. It made me realize that Joshua had been nicer to me than I was giving him credit for. At least there was that.

I wandered down the table to start browsing clothes, extending a hand to the pregnant woman when she noticed me. "I'm Liv, Joshua's, um..." I knew I shouldn't say friend because he'd warned me not to, but I was not about to finish that sentence by introducing myself as his "woman." What a caveman way to put it. Did girlfriends not exist anymore?

Ha! Joshua calling me his girlfriend? In what reality?

"Pleased to meet you. I'm Maddie." She pretended not to notice my stammering.

"Where did you get all these clothes?"

"People's houses, mostly. Not stolen, of course. We only take what people leave behind when they go east. I made a handful of them too."

"You *made* them?"

"Yes," She chuckled.

"Like by hand?"

"With the sewing machine when we get enough light on the portable solar panel. It's not much." Maddie shrugged, her belly lifting with her shoulders.

"Where did you learn to make clothes? How do you know what they'll look like when you're done?" Other than fashion designers, I hadn't realized people still made clothes by hand.

Maddie laughed at my enthusiasm. "My Mom taught me to sew. I used to do it for fun, make pillow covers as gifts and stuff. I never dreamed it would be such a useful skill."

"Show me which ones you made."

Maddie spent a few minutes showing me aprons and summer dresses. Since Joshua was occupied with trade talk and couldn't offer his opinion, I picked one of Maddie's dresses. It was a navy blue sundress decorated with bright yellow sunflowers. Oversized buttons climbed from the waist up to the bust.

I picked out a few thermal shirts too. There weren't many small enough that were also the brown, black, or dark green that Joshua insisted I should be wearing but I took the smallest I could find. Maddie offered me a waterproof ski jacket, which I gladly added to my growing pile.

I finished the collection with two brand new looking pairs of jeans. Since I couldn't exactly strip my pants off and try them on right there, I had no guarantee that they would fit. I would just have to hope they stayed up and made my non-existent butt look good.

I know, my end of the world priorities were awful.

Since Joshua was still busy measuring out dried food, I took some time to make small talk. It was refreshing to talk with someone who didn't grunt in place of words fifty percent of the time.

I learned that Asher was her brother. The little girl was her daughter, Mary. I asked about her due date, but I decided it would be rude to inquire about the father of her baby.

Maddie had her own questions about me. I told her the harrowing story of my journey from Seattle—with the darker details excluded. The story ended with Joshua finding me, which made her smile. Both she and her brother were weirdly fond of him for how brusque he was. The familiarity between the three of them caught me off guard.

And yeah, it added a bit of weight to the bitter disappointment I was quietly nursing. I wasn't a lifelong friend and hadn't earned Joshua's undying trust, but I was...well, I had no clue what I was to him. I lived in his house, for goodness sake. That should make me his *something*.

You're being stupid, Liv.

I snapped my head up, realizing that Maddie was still talking, and I'd been wandering through self-pitying thoughts rather than listening. She was explaining how she and her brother grew up with Joshua. It wasn't the way that most kids grow up together. They weren't quite neighbors, and they didn't go to the same school, but they played with Joshua frequently while he was waiting for his father to pick up supplies.

By the sound of it, his dad would drop him at a park and leave him there alone for hours, sometimes the bulk of the day. Maybe *that* was why Joshua never spoke about his family. I didn't get the sense that there were a lot of warm and fuzzy memories from his childhood.

I must have been making a face because she chuckled and shook her head. "I don't know if he ever considered us to be *his* friends. Ash usually strong armed him into playing with us. He's pushy."

"Hard to imagine anyone making Joshua do anything."

Maddie leaned forward, covering one side of her mouth with her hand. "I always felt like he was studying us more than playing, like we were a new species and him a biologist."

I resonated with the sentiment so thoroughly that I burst into laughter. "Or maybe like I'm an alien from another planet."

"You must be something special to put up with him."

"I don't put up with him." Why did I sound so defensive? "Joshua has a good sense of humor. He's fun." Okay, his sense of humor was a little twisted and I'd never actually heard him laugh but I always knew when he found something funny. And he *was* fun, in his very unique way.

She fixed me with a teasing look that made me feel guilty of something, but I wasn't sure what. I was about to start justifying myself when a sudden noise startled me. Mary squealed happily as music began pouring from the speakers of the old stereo. It was a Taylor Swift song.

I smiled and asked, "How in the world did you get that old thing to work?"

"Batteries." She gave a shy smile back.

"You found batteries that still had juice?"

"Uncle Ash did." She rocked back and forth on the balls of her feet.

I mirrored the motion and added in a slow sway of my hips. "When was the last time you heard music?"

"I don't know."

"Do you like this song?"

"Yeah," She admitted.

"Me too! Do you like to dance?" I added more wiggle to my step, moving closer to her with an inviting hand outstretched.

"Yes," She grinned at my antics.

I took Mary's hands and shimmied back and forth. Her grin grew wider. My movements grew wilder, less dance and more ridiculous. The more I made a fool of myself, the less self-conscious she became.

Behind me I heard Asher ask Joshua "Where the hell did you find her?"

"In my woods." Those three words were coated with regret.

"I should go out to the woods more often." Asher laughed, pointing to the surrounding market. "Not many fish in this sea."

"Don't think you'd find what you're lookin' for."

I peered over my shoulder to smirk at Joshua, expecting him to be annoyed at me for drawing attention. Instead, he seemed curious, and maybe a little confused. When I caught him watching he quickly averted his attention back to Asher. I thanked Mary for the dance, stuffed what clothes I could in my pack, and joined Joshua at the other end of the table.

"Asher, where'd you get that stereo? We need one." I jerked my chin at the boom box.

Joshua didn't give Asher a chance to respond. "We don't need one."

"Sure, we do," I told him. "Music would boost morale."

"She's right. Music is a mood maker." Asher came to my defense with a wink that was just shy of flirtatious.

"You get clothes?" Joshed asked quietly, completely ignoring the stereo discussion.

"Yes."

"No pink or yellow?"

"Nope. I'm a total Goth now."

"A useful one, I hope."

"Super useful. See? This one even has thumbholes!" I gave him a thumbs up through the thumbhole in the ski jacket. Apparently, Joshua didn't find thumbholes as cool as I did.

"You know, my offer from last time still stands." Asher folded the top of a paper bag of flour and handed it to Joshua.

"What offer?" I asked. Joshua glowered at me.

"Breeding Kuna with my dog Milo. He's nothing special but he's big and he's got good instincts."

"Oh my gosh! You should! Kuna would have adorable puppies!" I bounced on my heels and squealed. Kuna had been barred from coming with us today because she was in heat. Joshua hadn't wanted to attract the attention of any stray dogs in the area.

Joshua's answer shouldn't have surprised me. "Puppies are useless to me."

"Not everything has to be useful for you to enjoy it, Joshua." I rolled my eyes.

"Right again." Asher rang an invisible bell. With his hand cupped around his mouth, he mock whispered, "I think you'll be good for him. He's a little uptight."

"I don't have time for fun, and I don't have time for puppies." Joshua heaved a loud sigh then added, "But it is a good idea. Let's plan for early spring. I don't want to worry about a litter during the winter."

After we said our farewells to the siblings, I stood on my tiptoes and whispered as close to Joshua's ear as I could reach. "Can we trust them?"

Joshua nodded subtly. The world was ending but at least I was making friends.

The next few people we visited weren't feeling chatty. At all. I got the feeling they weren't fans of Joshua—I couldn't imagine why that would be, he was so polite and charming—but they were as courteous as could be expected given the circumstances.

I attempted conversation with just about everyone we passed but they seemed both startled and uncomfortable. To be cautious was smart. It was probably what kept most of these people alive. Unfortunately, it killed any sense of camaraderie and community in the process. Where was the solidarity?

I'm alive, you're alive, we may as well be best friends.

After watching a handful of trades, I began to notice an unusual pattern. I was sure that I had to be crazy because there was just no way that Joshua was doing what I thought he was doing.

There were dozens of people with tables and wagons, many of them offering the same items. Yet, every time we went looking for seeds, grains, and the few packaged food items we could use, Joshua first visited the tables with kids or elderly people.

And call me double crazy but he was trading for things he didn't need. How many turnip and beet seeds could one man use? I knew he used a lot of flour, but we could barely carry the amount he traded for. On top of that, I was pretty sure he gave a lady with two kids double the amount of jerky he'd previously offered another man.

Was Joshua...helping people? In a totally discreet way that neither hurt their pride or his reputation? Every second I spent with this man had me more puzzled.

Further into the market we met with Frank whose wife sewed underwear. He owned the local hardware store and still had tools tucked away for trading. Like most people, he was nervous around Joshua, eyeing him like a wild animal that might attack unprovoked. Tension slowly sapped from his shoulders when I asked him about his wife.

He and Darlene had been married for thirty seven years. They had four sons together. Frank worked the store while Darlene kept the house. They were old fashioned like that. She still preferred to stay in, sewing and tending to their animals while he attended market.

I nodded, drinking up every detail of his life. Someday Frank might be gone. Someone ought to remember him.

The conversation came to a close when Joshua's shadow loomed over us. He tugged impatiently at the strap of my backpack, but I held up a hand. "What about your sons? Where are they?"

"You met our youngest when you came through the gate." Frank smiled sadly, his thick white mustache twitching. "The twins were in Oklahoma, before the blackout. Our oldest was getting his masters in Pennsylvania." He pressed his hand over his heart. "We pray for them every day."

"Thank you," I squeezed his other hand. "I'll pray too."

Joshua wrapped his fingers around my forearm and guided me in the direction he wanted me to go. "Stop talking to people."

"No." I lifted my chin. "I might not get another chance."

"You'll get plenty of chances to chatter."

I shoved his hand away. "What's your problem?"

"Keep it down," He hissed.

"Seriously, Joshua. What gives? You're the only person I've talked to in over six months. I just found out I'm not alone."

He stopped, turning to look down at me. For a second, I *almost* regretted my words. Clearly, they bothered him. "You weren't alone before today."

But somehow you make me feel lonelier than if I was.

The distance between us was vast and in that rare moment where his dark eyes were meeting mine, it ached. I couldn't find anything to say that would ease the strain undulating in the air around us, so I opted to stay silent. That silence meant something to him because his mood darkened further—if that was even possible—and he stomped to the next table in a huff.

We met with a couple who had an abundance of squash and, oddly enough, assorted cosmetics. I couldn't believe some people were still willing to trade for makeup. Who was wearing eyeliner when the world was ending?

The couple wasn't unkind, but I got the feeling they weren't the sweet grandparents they looked to be. The woman was on the plump side and wore a pastel purple apron, but her hands told the real story of who she was. They were as calloused as Joshua's, fingers thick from years of labor.

I momentarily forgot Joshua's ire, blinking pleading eyes at him as I requested a pumpkin. They were so cute and orange, the perfect decoration for the porch this time of year. I offered to make him a pie and his lips briefly untwisted from their sour knot.

"No pumpkins," He said finally, moving on.

We traded the rest of the fruit, nuts, and mushrooms from my pack for a ten pound bag of rice, smaller bags of assorted beans, another sack of flour, and a variety of seeds.

Joshua was waved down by a man in a camo jacket on our way to the back end of the market. His skin was coppery, his black beard much longer and thinner than Joshua's. Grey flecked the scraggly hairs, making him look older than he probably was.

"Welcome back, Joshua. Folks have been asking about you. Seems your deer is in high demand these days." The man offered a polite greeting. He had one of those serious, professional voices like my father. He carried himself like a businessman too.

"There won't be much more this year." Joshua rummaged through his pack for the biggest package of jerky and handed it over.

"In that case, you should bring as much as you've got to trade. I'd like to have more than we need in the stores for winter. I'm sure we can work out a deal."

"I'll bring what I can. Now that I've got help, I should be able to pack in a little more." Joshua motioned to me. This was the first time he deliberately brought anyone's attention to me.

"Ah yes, your guest. She'll be joining you from now on?"

"Yes, I will," I cut in. I could feel Joshua's frustration with me, but I was getting pretty sick of being ignored and I was very uncomfortable being talked about as if I was some pack mule he dragged along with him. "I'm Liv."

"A pleasure." He nodded politely. "I'm Mayor Flores. Welcome to Rockham Falls."

Mayor, huh? I wondered if he was elected before or after the world ended. That must be why Joshua was giving him jerky for nothing in exchange. I assumed it was payment for entry into town, or something along those lines.

Flores turned back to Joshua. "We've heard some troubling reports of raiding groups along the interstate. Five armed men were seen at the rest stop near

River Fork Trail. Seventeen miles is a long distance on foot, but it's still closer than I like." He tugged the end of his beard. "You haven't seen any suspicious activity down your way, have you?"

Joshua's mouth tightened. "If I saw any sign of raiders in my neck of the woods, there wouldn't be anything to tell."

I frowned at him, confused and more than a little surprised that he wouldn't share that kind of information. How could he leave the whole town in the dark like that?

The mayor didn't seem perplexed at all. He nodded solemnly at Joshua, grimacing slightly. "That's what I thought. You two stay safe out there."

When the mayor walked away, I got an earful about introducing myself but eventually he answered my questions.

Mayor Flores was in charge of Rockham Falls before the blackout. He took it upon himself to keep running the town. If it wasn't for him, Rockham Falls would have been raided and the people in it left to die or worse. He organized former police officers and deputies as well as any willing resident to start a militia.

Joshua wasn't the only outsider Mayor Flores made deals with. The militia kept the town guarded but there weren't nearly enough men to uphold laws. That was where Tommy Wheeler and his men came in. On the road today we saw only two other riders with him. According to Joshua, he had a gang that was growing bigger all the time.

Wheeler recruited the men that would otherwise have become raiders, or so Joshua thought. I wasn't entirely sure why that made him a bad guy—or why Joshua spoke his name with such disgust. It kept them from ripping apart a town of innocent people, didn't it?

By the time we got to the far corner of the market, our packs had been emptied and refilled with just about everything on our list. The further back you went into the market the more we encountered shadier people, the ones with sticky fingers or those brave enough to seek out goods from other towns and cities. Ironically, they were the ones set up closest to the church.

I waited to the side, rolling back and forth between toe and heel as Joshua checked out two hunting knives, when someone offered a greeting to my right.

My gaze had been flitting curiously between the other tables and tents around us. I hadn't noticed anyone approach. I turned and immediately recognized the newcomer. Well, technically I recognized the horses tied to a bike rack behind him, but the grey hair, slight paunch, and canvas jacket clicked soon after.

"Hey, doll. Are you new in town?" Wheeler's smile was friendly, his tone conversational.

Joshua made him out like some kind of boogie man. His presence immediately put me on edge. "Nope—I mean yep. Yes. This is my first time here."

"Welcome to Rockham Falls. I'm always happy to see a new face. I'm Thomas Wheeler. You can call me Tommy." He extended a hand for me to shake.

I took it, only deciding it was a bad idea after I'd already done it. When he finished shaking my hand he lingered there, clutching my palm with both hands, and rubbing his thumb over my knuckles and wrist. I had the sudden desire to jerk my hand away, but I was too scared to be that bold.

"You have soft hands. That's rare on a woman these days."

"I moisturize," I laughed awkwardly, carefully slipping my hand away. I glanced over my shoulder as casually as I could only to realize that Joshua was gone. Suddenly I felt every ounce of confidence leak out of me, pooling uselessly at my feet. I'd become so reliant on Joshua to make me feel safe. Without him my tongue went numb, and my legs turned to lead.

For the first time in over two months, I wished I was alone again.

16

Suit of Armor

"**T**ell me a little about yourself. How did you end up in our fine town?" Tommy's voice was buttery and confident.

He reminded me of the men my father entertained, the businessmen with fake smiles, leering eyes, and if I was unlucky, roving hands. He was handsome for an older man, probably the kind of guy people called charming, but there was something about the look in his eyes that gave me a tight feeling in my gut. It was the kind of look that kicked my fight or flight instincts into gear.

"Um, I walked."

He took a step closer and fingered a stray lock of hair that was too short to stay in my bun. I flinched but either he didn't notice or didn't care. "Are you staying in Rockham Falls or just passing through? If you don't mind my asking."

"She does mind you asking." Compared to Tommy, the deep voice rumbling behind me was like gritty sandpaper. Wonderful, familiar sandpaper.

My smile was more of a grimace and my tone almost hysterical. "There you are!"

Joshua stepped up beside me, dropping his hand on my shoulder. He gripped it more like he might hold a tool than a woman, but it was the thought that counted.

I turned into his body, gripping the front of his shirt, and pressing my cheek to his chest. It probably looked more desperate than affectionate, but I didn't really care.

A crushing weight was laying on my lungs and I could scarcely take a breath. The only thing keeping me from tumbling to my knees in a gasping fit was the solid feel of Joshua surrounding me, the scent of cloves warming my throat.

His entire body went rigid when I stifled a frantic breath with the back of my hand. "I've got everything I need. Time to go."

Tommy pouted playfully. "Damn, I was looking forward to getting to know your girl, Joshua. I haven't even gotten her name."

"You're not going to. Don't let me catch you touching her again." The undiluted hatred in Joshua's tone wasn't an act.

This was personal, way more personal than a disagreement over Tommy's moral code. I freed Joshua's hand from my shoulder and laced my fingers with his. The steel of his grip told me how livid he was.

His hold on my hand was uncomfortably tight but I didn't squirm or wince. I squeezed back, letting him know how grateful I was for him. His big fist engulfing mine made me feel like I was wearing a suit of armor.

"You are your father's son, aren't you?" Tommy's charming veneer snapped away with a sneer. "You going to lock this one away like daddy, too? How long before she runs, you think?"

Okay, that was only mildly alarming. Joshua had kept me isolated but he wouldn't *literally* lock me away...right?

Joshua ignored the remarks, turning his back on Wheeler. That didn't deter him from continuing. "Joshua! Before you go, I want to ask you something. Two of my men were hunting near your woods a month or two back." Tommy knew where the farm was? Surely not. "I haven't seen or heard from them since. You wouldn't know anything about that, would you? Or maybe your girl does?"

"You know what happens to your men if I catch them in my woods, Wheeler. They should be more careful about where they're hunting." Joshua's response was unsettlingly cool. It sounded more like an explanation than a threat.

I started trembling and his fingers flexed, squeezing my hand hard enough to grind my knuckles together. It was a struggle not to wince then.

He kept that firm hold on me, guiding me past tables, crates, and wagons until we were back at the edge of town. As soon as we passed the gate, he released my hand and spun on me. "I thought I told you not to trust him."

"You didn't say not to talk to him." I crossed my arms and kept walking, half because I was upset at him for yelling at me and half because I was embarrassed by how easily frightened I was.

Joshua stalked after me. "That should have been implied."

"Whoa Joshua, you played your character so well you forgot that I'm not actually your woman and you can't tell me who I'm allowed to talk to." We were still within earshot of the militia at the gate, so I had to clench my teeth to keep from shouting.

"And for the record, if I was your *woman*, I still wouldn't let you treat me the way you have been." The anger and hurt from his deception, from the way he spoke to me today, was bubbling to the surface. I felt like exploding.

He caught my pack—because grabbing my arm would be way too much contact for one day—and stopped me. Then he stared at me, just stared at me with that oddly blank look on his face. I couldn't tell if he was frustrated or confused or maybe so done with me that he couldn't even muster up an expression.

When he finally spoke, his voice betrayed a seething anger that matched mine. "When I say don't trust someone, that means don't talk to them."

"Maybe you should be a little more blatant with your *orders* next time. Also, I didn't talk to him. He talked to me."

"You should have ignored him."

"Sorry, I guess I'm just too polite."

"Your life is more important than your manners!" His jaw was so tight I could see the muscles straining.

"It's not like the guy was about to stab me."

"No, he was only sizing you up to see if he needed to manipulate you or if he could just grab you off the road on your way out of town." Joshua ducked into the woods. I followed, powerwalking to keep pace with his pounding steps. Now he was the one running away from me.

I was completely breathless but determined to get some answers. "What are you talking about?"

"I told you Wheeler can't be trusted. He's not afraid to get his hands dirty and he has a lot of manpower."

"Why wouldn't you just tell me that? Saying 'don't trust this guy' is a lot different than saying 'this guy kidnaps women and does God knows what to them!'"

I reached out for any part of him that I could grab just to slow him down. My hand landed on his forearm. He stopped abruptly, glaring at my hand like it was a bug, before jerking away.

"If I say don't trust someone it means they're dangerous. That should be good enough."

"It's not, Joshua. You told me not trust to anyone we met today except for two people. Should I assume everyone is a kidnapper and a rapist?" I demanded.

"Yes." He started back through the woods.

"Even you?"

Joshua whipped around, eyes wide. "Of course not."

"See why I'm confused?"

"No." This was Joshua logic. It wasn't confusing because he wasn't confused. It was his rule, so it was good one.

"Next time," I panted as I rushed to catch up. "Will you please give me a little more to go on? Don't trust this guy because he's a serial killer. Or a raider. Or a puppy kicker. That's not asking a lot. You kept me totally in the dark about this whole thing until today and now you expect me to just follow your vague rules without batting an eye."

I slowed, unable to keep talking and jogging at the same time. I could hear my heart pounding in my ears. "Why am I even here?"

"What?" He stomped to a halt.

"Why am I here with you? Why are you taking me back to your home?" I rushed on before he could interrupt, lungs still burning. "I'm a burden and clearly a nuisance. And to be honest, I'm not entirely sure I'm not a prisoner. I live on your property, but I'm not allowed to leave. You don't tell me anything unless it becomes relevant to what we're doing. You bring me to a town that *I didn't know existed* but suffocate me with all these rules. Why not just leave me back there?"

My heart was pounding for an entirely different reason now. I couldn't figure out how I let those words slip out of my mouth, but I immediately regretted them. I pinched my bottom lip between my teeth, waiting for the moment he realized I was right, waiting to be dismissed and sent back to Rockham Falls to fend for myself.

Waiting to be rejected. Even in the end of the world, I was unwanted.

Joshua's tone was so cold I almost thought I could see his breath. "You want to stay in town? You'd rather be on your own?"

"That's not what I'm saying." What was I saying? Joshua had a way of mixing up my words, making me feel unclear about my own thoughts.

"Then what's the problem?"

"I just told you the problem! You treat me like I'm your enemy. I sit at your dinner table every night and you still act like you can't trust me. You're keeping things from me, *big things*. That's not going to work for us. Trust," I gestured to the space between us, "Goes both ways."

"You're not my enemy."

"And you're not actually responding to what I'm saying." I scuffed the heel of my boot into the soft earth, my voice dropping. "It won't kill you to talk to me, Joshua. If you want me to be a part of this, then I need to know what I'm getting into."

Do you want me to be a part of this? Am I anything more than your penance? I immediately scolded myself. *Don't be pathetic, Liv. Don't beg for reassurance from someone who doesn't care about you.*

"Fine."

"Fine?"

"Yes, fine. Let's go home."

I didn't follow. That response was so unsatisfactory that it made me want to grind my teeth. He was so impossible! I needed more than that.

I must have said it aloud because Joshua turned again, looking like he would rather be swallowing nails than having this conversation. "What do you need?"

"Why didn't you tell me?" I asked softly.

"Tell you what?"

"Oh my God, Joshua! That there was a whole town of people out there! After everything I've shared with you, don't you think I deserved at least that much truth? That I might want to know there were others like me?" I hadn't intended to let my hurt show, but I couldn't help it. I was trying so hard to prove myself to him but every time I thought I'd made progress, I hit a wall.

I got nothing from him for several excruciating minutes. We stood in the shade of the trees, a breeze cooling the sweat on the back of my neck, birds twittering gleefully, unperturbed by the argument happening just below them.

Finally, he said, "I didn't want you packing up and heading that way just because you found the thought of being around people more appealing than...the farm." I heard the words he didn't say. *More appealing than me.*

"But that wasn't your choice to make. And *why?* Because you thought I was raider bait, and I would give the whole town up? They have like fifty people to defend the place!"

More silence.

"Joshua, please." I swallowed, wishing I didn't have to beg him for honesty. "You owe me an explanation." I stepped closer to him, meeting his eyes. "Please."

He squeezed his eyes shut, looking pained. "I tell you not to leave because you barely know north from south! If you don't end up eaten by a cougar or walking into a ravine, you're going to run into someone much worse than me." His chest heaved. "I didn't tell you about the town because it's not safe. They're not *like you*, Liv. Everyone has an agenda and they're always looking out for themselves. Half those people you talked to today would sell you out to Wheeler if it guaranteed their next meal."

"How can you know that?"

"How can you be so naïve?" He threw his hands up. "I've seen it. I've seen women like you disappear. That's the kind of world we live in. I knew that if I told you there was a town full of people just up the road, you would have packed your bag and marched straight for it. You would have gotten yourself into more trouble than you could handle." He cleared his throat, adding as an afterthought, "I don't have time to feel guilty if something happens to you."

"Okay, hold on—" I poked a finger in his chest. Was I angry? Relieved? Confused? Yeah, I was confused. "You just said all this nice stuff and then you ruined it. Don't do that."

"I'll say whatever I want, however I want. Let's go." He swatted my finger away and steered me in the direction he wanted to walk with his hands on my pack.

"You are the most bullheaded person that ever existed." I was hurrying again, desperate to make him look at me.

He snorted. "I'm so insulted."

"I'm not trying to insult you. I'm trying to talk to you."

"We talked. Now it's time to stop talking before half the raiders in the state come find us. You're loud."

"All this time, you were protecting me. That's why you didn't tell me?" Not the people in town, not his own secrets, but *me*?

His Adam's apple bobbed but he spoke casually. "I was protecting my conscience."

"Uh huh."

Silence fell between us for half a mile, mostly because talking and walking made me feel like I was running out of oxygen.

"Joshua," I finally drew his attention when we passed our first creek crossing. He shifted to my pace but kept his eyes locked on the trail ahead. "Thank you for looking out for me."

I didn't get more than a grunt of acknowledgment.

Joshua didn't say anything else that wasn't necessary communication for the entire trip back to the truck. I wasn't sure if he was still angry or just didn't feel chatty. Not that he was ever chatty.

Not long into the hike, I started to fall behind. My pack felt like it weighed a hundred pounds, my body ached, and my head was light. Joshua slowed to wait for me three times before stopping, heaving his pack off his back, and tugging mine from my shoulders.

"What are you doing?" His answer was to unzip my bag, remove the heaviest items, and add them to his already overburdened load. "You don't have to do that."

He never responded to my protest. He also stopped walking ahead of me and tapping his foot impatiently as I trotted to catch up. The final thirty minutes of the journey we walked side by side, close enough that occasionally my hand would bump his. He didn't move away, didn't grumble, didn't even frown. Maybe he wasn't angry after all.

I dozed off the moment my butt hit the seat in the truck. Joshua insisted I get in while he removed the covering. I had no recollection of him starting the engine. When we arrived home, he sent me straight inside.

I watched him toss branches in the bed of the truck and felt a tug on my heart. I wasn't entirely sure what it meant but I knew it wasn't good. Joshua was hot and cold, as dark as a moonless night and as intense as the sunrise. He wasn't the kind of man I should be feeling warm and fuzzy toward.

How could I not when each new layer I peeled back revealed more goodness. He was so good, so quietly, secretly good.

17

Moonshine

Kuna went nuts when we walked through the door. Joshua took her to check on the animals while I unloaded our packs. When everything was on the table, I sorted through the new clothes, giving the shirts a good sniff before folding them and slipping them under the bed.

Laundry took a lot of time and effort so if I didn't need to wash something, I wasn't going to. When I got to the sundress, navy blue with big, beautiful sunflowers, I decided to try it on.

The weather was too cold for a dress, but I wasn't going to let that stop me. I slipped the soft cotton over my head, spinning so it fanned out around me. For the first time since the blackout, I felt pretty. Other than that first night with Joshua, the night I saw my reflection and wept at the frail woman in front of me, I hadn't given much thought to my appearance. As long as I was strong and capable, why should I care if I was thin?

It made a difference though, feeling good about myself. After losing such a drastic amount of weight, I feared my body resembled a little boy's. My hips were still bony and my breasts smaller and pointier than they used to be. In a dress? I was downright feminine. The built in cups actually gave me some cleavage.

Even when the world was ending, I was worried about the size of my breasts. Oh well, it was better than worrying about the scarier things.

Since I was already dressed up, I decided to go all out. Of course, "going all out" meant a lot less than it used to. I had no make up to put on, no curling iron, and no hot shower. The closest I got was a damp rag in my armpits and some chamomile oil to rub on my neck and wrists.

By the time I was done getting cleaned up I was shivering. I rushed to the fireplace and did my best to follow the steps Joshua taught me to get the fire going. I stacked the logs right but with shaking hands it was a struggle to strike a spark from the flint.

On my seventh attempt a spray of sparks came from where the metal rod struck the stone. I was holding it much closer to myself than I should have been and some of the sparks landed in my lap. I clapped them out quickly and tried again.

And again, and again and again. It had to have taken twenty tries for the kindling to catch.

Joshua returned with boots stomping heavily on the porch. When he was finished kicking the mud off—which he wouldn't admit he was doing for me—he stepped inside and slid out of his jacket. Kuna stood in the doorway, waiting per his command. He shook droplets from his coat—he hadn't mastered doing that part outside yet—then hung it on the rack by the door.

With a snap of his fingers, Kuna did the same. A mist of water flew from her thick black fur.

"You need a blow dryer, Kuna." I gave her head a gentle pat, spreading wet dog hair across my palms in the process.

Joshua locked up, kicked his boots off, then did a double take when he noticed me hovering by the table. "What's that?"

"What? Oh this?" I did another spin. "It's a dress."

"I thought you said you got useful clothes."

I grinned at him. "Don't worry, I did, but I thought this was nice too. Maddie *made* it. Can you believe that? Maybe she'll teach me to sew. Then I could fix your pants." I pointed at a tear on the knee of his jeans. "I can garden in it when the weather is warm."

"I know how to patch clothes," Joshua said. "And you can't garden in that. You'll get filthy."

"I'll wash it." I wasn't about to let his practicality spoil my good mood. "I didn't put anything away yet. I wasn't sure what belongs in the cellar."

He leaned over the table, quietly studying our haul. "It's nice."

"Hmm?"

He didn't glance up when he murmured, "the dress."

"Thanks." I propped my hand on the table across from him. "Oh, I almost forgot!"

I gently coaxed the band from the bun on top of my head. Damp hair poured over my shoulders in a cascade of amber. Usually pin straight, the bun combined with evening rain had given it a nice wave. It had gotten longer this year than I'd ever grown it in the past, reaching almost halfway down my rib cage.

Joshua's dark eyes followed my hair as it fell down my torso. He kept staring at it, slowly travelling up until his gaze met my face.

"What?" I cocked a brow.

He shook his head sharply and broke his gaze away. "Let's get these sorted so we can eat. Everything goes downstairs but the knives and the pasta. There's a shelf marked for new seeds. Put them there and I'll organize them later."

It took me five trips to carry dried goods down the ladder. I did it though. I managed to carry our entire market haul to the cellar and even heaved the bag of rice onto an upper shelf.

One of our better finds today—in my opinion, anyway—were several undamaged packages of spaghetti. With a touch of coaxing, I convinced Joshua that Italian food was the best post-hike dinner. I brought a jar of homemade tomato sauce up from the cellar and he boiled the water. I chopped up late season zucchini while he braised fresh bird from his hunt the previous day.

Somewhere between Rockham Falls and the farm, the resentment in the air around us dissipated. The quiet that fell was sturdy, smoothing out the edges of agitation brought on by the afternoon. Occasionally the deep cadence of Joshua's voice filled the kitchen as he offered instruction. Otherwise, there was tentative peace once more.

Did that mean I was forgetting about our argument earlier? Absolutely not. Whatever this was, whatever Joshua did and did not want from me, we should be on the same page. And no matter how desolate and dark a world it was out there, I had a promise to keep to myself.

I wouldn't—*couldn't*—stay where I wasn't wanted. If my welcome was worn out, I needed to know.

In the meantime, this was comfortable. Pleasant. There was something so ordinary and domesticated about us cooking dinner together, shifting around the kitchen in the way that two people who were accustomed to each other's presence did. I used to shy away from him. He used to contort his body to avoid even the slightest accidental contact.

Now, he leaned around me to pull dishes from a cabinet, his chest brushing my back. Our hands met as he wordlessly took the sauce jar from me and pried open the lid. This version of him was so starkly different than the man who fought with me in the woods earlier. How was it possible to get both in one day?

I was allowed in his space, more than a guest in his home. With someone like Joshua, that felt like intimacy. More so than touch. With touch, Joshua could be methodical. But this? Here in his kitchen, watching him work, moving in time with him, he couldn't hide himself. He didn't *try* to hide himself anymore, not fully.

Whether he would admit it or not, Joshua trusted me. If only I could get him to see that.

I finally gave up puzzling it out and distracted my brain by twirling spaghetti around my fork. "Five star Italian meals come to the end of the world. All we need is garlic bread."

"You like it?" Joshua asked with a noodle still hanging out of his mouth. "The sauce?"

"Don't talk with your mouth full." I gave him a disapproving nose wrinkle, unable to keep the reproach on my face for long. "I love it."

His broad shoulders rose and fell. "You're easily impressed."

"You're not very good at taking a compliment, are you?"

After dinner I tidied up the dishes while Joshua organized the cellar. When he came back into the kitchen there was a clink of glass on the table. The heat from his body covered me, his shadow looming over the sink as he pressed close to pull cups from the top shelf. I could smell the faint hint of cloves and citrus on his skin. His homemade soap could be an autumn themed candle.

My back was still to the table when I heard the scrape of a jar lid and the trickle of liquid. Joshua was seated, a cup in his hand. An identical cup waited expectantly in front of the seat beside him. Both were filled with an inch of a clear drink that I suspected wasn't water.

There were three jars on the table, one translucent, one amber, and one a pinkish-red.

"What are we drinking?" I slipped into the chair, my socked foot settling halfway atop his under the table.

Joshua didn't flinch. "Moonshine."

"Seriously?" I sniffed to confirm. The sharp alcohol aroma burned my nostrils. "You make your own moonshine?"

"Occasionally."

"I'm not entirely sure you're a real person."

He took a relaxed sip. "I feel real enough."

I tried to mirror his casual manner with my first taste. The moment the alcohol passed my lips I coughed. I forced myself to swallow, only making me cough harder. My throat and tongue were on fire. As the moonshine made its way into my stomach that started to burn too.

Joshua watched me suffer, my face red, wheezing desperately, and he laughed. Not a snort or even a chuckle but a deep rumble of a laugh, like southern thunder.

I felt homesick and right at home all at once.

My coughing subsided, leaving my mouth free to grin my most foolish grin. For once, he didn't look away. Amusement lingered in his eyes, making them glisten like pools of melting chocolate.

"Slow down there, Miss Moonshine," he warned. "It's strong."

"No kidding," I croaked, throat still raw. I risked another sip, a smaller one this time. I managed to stifle my cough, wiggling in an awkward shiver instead.

The burn was interesting the second time around. It felt tingly and warm, my insides filling with sparks. Joshua swirled his glass and downed the rest.

"Do you actually like the taste of that? I don't think I've met anyone who drinks something this strong without mixing it."

"It's a good burn."

"I think I get what you mean. But, no offense, it tastes awful." I covered my mouth. A wave of goosebumps came and went down my arms.

"Try the peach." He took my glass and poured the remaining contents into his, opening the amber colored jar and splashing two inches to replace what he'd taken.

"Do you grow the peaches too?"

"Yes."

The peach was still alcohol, that was for sure. There was a caramel sweetness to the aftertaste that made the burning in my mouth more enjoyable though. I also had this great fuzzy feeling tickling up my torso and lightening my head. I imagined that peaches were tumbling around in my insides.

"Good?" I nodded and watched as his lips twitched in the barest smile.

"So," I began the opening to my question now that I had tipsy bravery on my side. "Are you going to tell me why you have such a bad reputation in town? People are scared of you. Even that Wheeler guy."

"Have you seen me?"

"What's your point? They're not scared of you because you're tall." I looked him up and down and amended it to, "big."

"I'm an ugly son of a bitch. It spooks people." He stroked his fingers through his beard.

"You are not." I rolled my eyes. "What's the real reason?"

Joshua cocked his head, skepticism written plainly on his face. Maybe two months ago my opinion would have been different, though I never thought him ugly. Now that I'd gotten to know him, I saw past his hardness. When he smiled, it was friendly, even charming. His face was becoming a familiar comfort to me.

He took a long sip before saying, "I told you. Folks know what I'm capable of."

"What are you capable of?" The question came unfiltered.

His jaw worked and he was suddenly fixated on his hands. "Doing whatever it takes to survive."

"Joshua," I was approaching treacherous territory, but the drink was impairing my better judgment. "Those were Tommy Wheeler's men chasing me, weren't they?"

I didn't think he could clench his jaw any harder. I was wrong.

"Yeah." He snarled the word, anger from earlier flaring up like wildfire on dry brush. Then he stiffened, every muscle in his body tense in anticipation of the question he knew was coming next.

What did you do to those men?

Could I pretend that I didn't already know? It wasn't hard to put it together. I tossed the question back and forth in my head. What good would it do to hear him say it? I wanted more of that laughter, more of those hot chocolate eyes and the warm glitter that his smile lent them. If I asked, I might not get those again tonight.

"Uh-huh. I see it now." I squinted at him.

His tone was cautious. "See what?"

"You're the most dangerous man 'round these parts." I swallowed more drink, finishing with an exaggerated wink. "But you don't scare me."

"Maybe I should."

I snorted a laugh, catching him off guard. He watched while I finished my drink, ruminating in that quiet way of his. He finally broke his silence and his gaze by offering me another. I should have said no but I was enjoying the buzz and I didn't want the night to end.

I wouldn't go as far as to say Joshua was chatty, but the drink definitely loosened his tongue. When I asked him to tell me more about his life growing up on the farm, I knew I was probably stepping over that invisible line again. Instead of bristling, Joshua told a hilarious childhood story about chasing escaped goats as they ate their way through an entire summer's worth of broccoli.

The louder my laughter got, the more astonished he seemed. That alone had me bursting into giggles.

"Yellow and pink."

"Hmm?" He tilted a jar to pour us each another. I'd lost track of the time—not that you could easily tell time after dark when your only measurement of it was sunup and sundown—and how many drinks I'd had, too engrossed in Joshua to care.

"Those are my favorite colors. They also happen to be my favorite Starburst flavors, which happen to be my favorite candy. Besides chocolate anything. What are yours?" The drink wasn't making me shudder anymore, which I suspected meant I was a sheet or two to the wind.

"*Colors?* I don't even know if I have *one* favorite."

"Really? You don't have a favorite color? You don't have a favorite candy either. You have to have a favorite something."

"Radishes." I raised my brows in question. "That's my favorite vegetable," he explained.

"Radishes?" My braying laugh was the least charming sound I'd ever made, but it made Joshua chuckle. "Do you grow them?"

"Whenever I can."

"What's your favorite season?"

"You writing my biography?"

"I'm getting to know you."

"Spring, I guess."

"Why?" I probed.

"Startin' new plants. All the color comes back."

"Is green your favorite color then?"

He squinted at me. "Maybe so."

"What's your favorite song?"

"Don't have one of those either."

I tapped my pointer finger on the table. "Joshua who likes radishes, doesn't like colors or music, and has never eaten candy. Unless chewing a Tootsie Roll for half a minute counts."

"Sounds about right."

"So, what *do* you do for fun?"

He made his hand into a gun and mimed pulling the trigger. "Shoot things."

"Ah, how...charming. You have strange hobbies."

He swallowed his last mouthful of moonshine and pushed his chair away from the table, motioning me to follow. "Let's go."

"Where are we going?" I copied him, shooting back the rest of my drink and wondering if I should have gone a little slower.

Joshua knelt beside the fireplace and tossed in two more logs. "You're shivering, probably because you insist on wearing a dress in autumn."

"It makes me feel pretty." I plunked down on the floor beside him.

Within minutes the fire was blazing, almost too hot to sit as close as I was. I didn't think it was Joshua's intention to get me drunk but he hadn't considered that the amount of drink that would get him buzzed was enough to make me stupid.

I giggled too hard at something he said, stopping abruptly when I nearly tipped over. "I think I'm drunk."

"I think you're right."

I pressed the glass to my lips only to realize there was nothing left in it. Why was I still holding it? "I can't believe the first time I got drunk was in a shack with a man I met in the woods. My mother would be horrified."

"You've never been drunk before?"

"I've had a few sips of wine on special occasions. Where would I even get a drink? I'd have to find someone older to buy it for me."

"Someone older?" Joshua probed. "How old *are* you?"

"Twenty in December," I answered proudly. "Which isn't that far off, is it?"

"Twenty?" His eyebrows moved even further up his forehead, fully revealing his eyes. I let myself absorb into those dark irises. How had it taken me this long to realize Joshua had such pretty eyes?

"I thought you saw my birthday on my driver's license."

"I didn't look. It's not important." He cleared his throat then added, "at the time. It wasn't important at the time."

I giggled again. "I get it. You have better things to care about than birthdays."

"I do—no, I mean—I didn't realize you were so young." Maybe I wasn't the only one feeling the excess of moonshine. Joshua was *flustered.*

"*So* young? I can't be that much younger than you. How old are you?"

"Twenty four."

"See! We're only four years apart. When is your birthday?"

"Early May," he replied.

I drew on my finite knowledge of astrology. "Ah, Taurus. Dependable, sensual, *stubborn.*"

"Huh?"

"Your sign."

"You really believe that?" I couldn't tell if he was mocking or genuinely curious.

"Duh!"

He chuckled and I was tempted to leap up and wave my arms around in celebration. Tonight was the first time Joshua actually seemed human. Tonight was also the first time he talked to me, *really* talked to me. For two months I dug and dug, only receiving grains of sand for my effort. Hearing him candid felt like seeing the whole beach, stretching all the way to a sunlit horizon.

Instead of showing my elation, I yawned. The warm thrum of moonshine was energizing at first but as the night wore on, I began to feel it evaporate from my veins and rise, forming dense clouds in my brain. I yawned again, drowsiness overtaking any remaining enthusiasm.

"Time for bed." Joshua stood with a stretch, making the hem of his shirt rise and his jeans pull taut. The longer I watched him, the more appealing he became.

How did someone so big move with such easy grace? How could he be so confident without a bloated ego? And why did it take me so long to appreciate this undomesticated form of masculinity? All those preppy boys in golf shirts that I fawned over seemed vapid compared to Joshua's wildness. From where I was sitting, feral mountain man looked great.

"Really great..." I mumbled.

"What?"

My cheeks felt like sparks had jumped from the fireplace and engulfed them. "I meant to say that tonight was really great—I'm having fun! I don't want to go to bed."

Good save.

"And you won't be having fun tomorrow when you're tired and hungover."

"I've never had a hangover. Are they really that bad?" He answered with a grunt that could mean anything.

Joshua leaned down and took my hand, meaning to lift me from the floor. I brushed my fingers along his palm, feeling the rough patches toughened by years of work, before gripping his wrist and letting him heave me onto my feet.

Once upright, I immediately stumbled backward. Being drunk on the floor was one thing, being drunk and standing up was a whole different challenge. He caught my upper arms, much gentler than his normally firm grip, and steadied me.

"I guess I can't hold my moonshine." I ran my hands through my hair in an attempt to compose myself, getting my fingers tangled and having to tug them out.

"I think you'll hold it better if you have less next time."

"Yup. Good idea. Definitely less...time." I blinked rapidly. "Next time. Less next time."

I took a step toward the bed and wobbled again, knocking into Joshua's chair, and sending it across the floor with a screech. He returned his hands to my arms, guiding me through the living room and to the bedside. I turned to give him a grateful smile. The left side of his mouth curved, clearly finding my drunken state funnier than he wanted to let on. When his mouth moved his mustache wiggled.

"What's it like having so much hair on your face?" I marveled at the bristly black mat that hid his jaw.

"Feels like having hair on your face," he answered dryly.

"I want to know what it feels like." I shouldn't have thought it, much less decided to act on it. I just couldn't get the urge out of my head. Not after I saw that tiny hint of a smile.

Joshua had a great smile. I wished it wasn't so rare. His lips twitched again and suddenly I noticed how soft they looked—exactly the opposite of his coarse beard. The facial hair was only an excuse. "I bet I know how to find out."

His smile widened. "Oh?"

I grabbed the sides of his face before he could stop me, standing high on my tiptoes to kiss him. It was just a peck, not even long enough for him to kiss me back. I don't think he would have if I gave him the chance. I didn't really want to find out. I didn't want this perfect night to end in rejection.

I guess if I'd considered it for one whole second, I would have realized that kissing him out of the blue was a great way to guarantee the night ended in rejection. Of course, he wouldn't kiss me back. He wasn't interested in me, not like that. It was pretty clear, wasn't it?

Joshua tolerated me. That was all.

As soon as I told myself that I questioned it. Maybe he wasn't attracted to me, but I was his friend, wasn't I?

"Sorry, I just..." I quickly dropped my hands to my sides but didn't move away, only stood there with my mouth stupidly agape.

I was close enough that I could smell the sharp moonshine scent on his breath. He stared back at me with eyes slightly wide, but his expression schooled into that practiced neutral. I had no idea what was going on behind that stony countenance. My heart was threatening to explode, and it felt like the sun would come up before he said anything.

What was I thinking?

"You should have some water." He pivoted on his heel and strode into the kitchen, as casual and calm as always. A moment later he returned with a glass, handing it to me in a way that made it impossible for our hands not to touch. When my fingertips met his, soft skin meeting callouses in the same way they had only moments ago, Joshua jolted back.

I swallowed a mouthful that was far too big, turning to rest the glass on the nightstand so he wouldn't see me choking on water and embarrassment. My mouth fell back open with a cough, ready to blurt out anything to absorb the awkwardness from my blunder.

I finally filled the silence with a hurried, "thank you."

"For?"

"Taking me with you today."

"I needed the help."

"I wasn't exactly helpful. I know you were trying to be nice. I'm grateful." I hoped that distracting him with his least favorite sentiment, gratitude, would make him forget the kiss.

"You were helpful."

"Right up until you had to carry half my load home," I muttered, relaxing a fraction when he didn't seem offended. Though, he was being weirdly nice. I blamed it on the alcohol.

"Better than carrying it all alone." For a heartbeat I got the feeling we were talking about more than just our trip today. I was probably reading too much between the lines. Blame that on the alcohol too.

I scrunched my lips up and made eye contact with my sock covered toes. "I'm glad I could help. I'd like to do more of that."

"Careful, I'll really put you to work." His tone stayed light, playful even.

I tilted my chin up, my gaze level with his sternum. He was still unusually close. And he still smelled good. *Don't make this weirder by sniffing him.* "You should. Put me to work. I'm good at it. At work."

And stop talking, good grief.

"Tomorrow. Goodnight, Liv." Joshua's wool socks made a hissing sound as they skimmed across the wooden floor and back to the rug. The noise ended abruptly, replaced by the scrape of his chair returning to its rightful place, then a groan as he lowered himself into it. I dared a glance in his direction in time to see him shift toward the dying fire, hiding his face from view.

I could just make out his hand when he lifted two fingers and pressed them to his lips. Maybe that was one of his regular mannerisms and I simply hadn't noticed. Or maybe...maybe alcohol made me foolish in more ways than one.

He said my name. It shouldn't be a big deal. Friends said each other's names all the time, but I could probably count how many times he'd used mine on one hand. If he addressed me at all it was usually with some nickname that would be insulting if I hadn't come to recognize it as another weird Joshua affection.

"Goodnight, Joshua," I whispered before collapsing onto the bed.

I considered taking off the dress and putting on one of the winter shirts I brought home. Even with the fire going, this side of the cabin was chilly at night. When I sat back up my head was spinning, and my stomach lurched. I decided pulling the blanket up to my neck would be enough and nestled under the covers.

Just before falling asleep, I brought two fingers to my lips, touching the only memory I'd ever have of kissing Joshua.

18

Pride and Prejudice

There were no alarm clocks in the end of the world. Well, there were plenty of them, I'm sure, but none of them worked anymore. Even if they did, I doubted Joshua would use one. Every morning he was up before sunrise—which wasn't that early now that the days were getting shorter—and making a ruckus in the kitchen.

That was my alarm clock. He wanted to wake me, but he wasn't about to sit on the edge of the bed and shake me. No, he just banged pots and pans around until I bolted upright with a gasp. My gasp this morning was followed by a pained groan and fingers pressed to my throbbing temples.

So, this is a hangover.

It felt like someone stuffed cotton balls between my brain and my skull. The stuffy pain had my forehead pulsating whenever I moved. On top of that my tongue felt like it was coated in sand and my stomach was a roiling sea.

I remembered the glass of water on the nightstand and reached for it. It was empty. I must have finished it in my sleep. Maybe I didn't like drinking that much after all.

"Mornin', Miss Moonshine," Joshua rumbled from the kitchen.

I'd been so focused on my suffering that I scarcely noticed him. He stood at the stove, his broad back to me. Steam billowed up around him from a pot of boiling water as he poured it into the French press, drowning a spoonful of ground dandelion root. There was a notable lack of a frown when he glanced over his shoulder.

Huh. Joshua was in the same good mood this morning as the night before.

I thought back to yesterday; our trip to Rockham Falls, our quiet walk home, our dinner together, Joshua smiling, Joshua laughing, Joshua's lips when I—oh my God, I kissed him.

But he didn't kiss me.

What did he do? Nothing. He didn't say or do anything. I was drunk. He knew that. Was that *why* he didn't do anything? Or was it because I made an unwanted advance? Of course, that was it. Joshua and I were friends. It was an odd friendship, and he probably wouldn't introduce me to someone as his friend but that was definitely what we were. And by kissing him I crossed a very clear line.

He didn't seem upset with me though. What did that mean?

Nothing. It meant nothing and I would only drive myself crazy trying to interpret emotions that weren't there. People did dumb things when they were drunk and that was my very first time. He was giving me a pass. He was pretending that it didn't happen so we could move on with our lives and keep things from getting awkward.

Alright-y then, I could do that too. I desperately wanted to pretend it didn't happen because otherwise I had to face whatever feelings came with kissing Joshua—*wanting* to kiss Joshua—and knowing that he didn't feel the same.

Yeah, I decided I *really* didn't like drinking. It made me feel a lot worse than just a headache and nausea.

"Is it a good morning?" I groaned louder and stumbled out of bed. I was wearing the sundress from last night and the moment the covers fell away I was shivering and layered in goosebumps.

"I never said it was a *good* morning. I just said it was morning." Joshua still had his back to me, but I swear he was smiling. "It will be good once you get some water down." He was enjoying my discomfort, the jerk.

I should have warned him before stripping out of my dress. A clatter and a loud clearing of his throat told me he turned around then back again hastily enough to drop his spatula on the floor. I wasn't feeling particularly modest at the moment. He'd seen me before and though I'd probably gained five or ten pounds, it wasn't like there was much to look at.

I quickly wiggled into a pair of jeans, a thermal, and my last pair of new socks. The inside was still fuzzy and soft, an uncommon luxury after the blackout.

"I don't think I like moonshine." I pulled out the first chair within reach, plopped down into the seat, and laid my head on the table with another dramatic noise.

Joshua set a plate of food next to my face, placing his beside mine, one seat closer than we usually sat together. Not that it really made a difference. It was a small table, and he was a big man. We were closer than he probably liked no matter where I sat.

"I think you liked it just fine. You ought to go easy next time is all."

I pointed an accusatory finger in his general direction. I couldn't actually see where he was with my eye closed to the growing brightness outside the kitchen window. "You're the one that was pouring."

"I overestimated your hardiness." He settled in his chair. His heel landed on top of my toes, but he didn't recoil. A good sign.

*Wow, the end of the world has made me sad and desperate if someone **not recoiling** is as good as affection.*

"For once."

"Guess it's your turn to be grumpy." Was he teasing me now?

Joshua really was in a good mood. Not because I kissed him. Probably because he got a good haul at the market yesterday and had a chance to relax afterwards. And today was going to be a light workday for him. I would be in a good mood too.

I pushed through the stuffy headache and sat up with a wan smile. "Someday you should take me up on that help I keep offering and make me cook for you. Otherwise, you're running a free bed and breakfast."

He took a huge bite of eggs before responding. If there was food in front of him, he couldn't talk without his mouth full. "Oh, I plan to put you to work. Yesterday was a test. Now that you can carry a pack, you can dig potatoes. And harvest more from the green house, clean the chicken coop, feed the goats. I've got plenty for you to do that's more important than breakfast."

"Ah, now it's really time to pay my debt. Are you going to marry me off to one of your sons too?"

"You don't owe me a debt." He chewed thoughtfully. "Why would I marry you to my sons?"

"It was joke. You know, because last night you said your favorite book is *Pride and Prejudice*?" I waved a hunk of bread at him.

"Which you have clearly never read if that was meant as a reference."

"What? Of course, I have! There are totally arranged marriages and stuff." I lied so poorly that I felt the need to mutter, "or at least I've seen the movie...I think."

"You're going to be very busy reading this winter." He sipped his tea, lips curving over the rim of his mug.

Stop staring at his lips. God, what was wrong with me? Hopefully I wasn't being too obvious.

"Cool. Books. I love those." I cut a small roll in half and focused a little too hard on buttering it.

A few quiet bites passed before Joshua suddenly asked, "did you mean it last night?"

I stopped, full fork halfway to my face. "Did I mean what?"

Did I mean it when I kissed you? No, of course not. Silly me. I was drunk!

"About helping?"

I hoped that he didn't hear my sigh of relief. "Of course. I'll dig potatoes!"

"I've got to kick winter prep into high gear. Means I'll probably be out hunting a few times in the next two or three weeks. The more cured meat I can get prepared, the more I've got to trade before it gets too snowy to travel to town. I can't manage that and the end of season harvest. Since you offered, I was thinking I could get you set up to do most of that for me." There was a tentative note to his words.

"You're asking me?"

His browns bunched in confusion. "Yes?"

"Usually, you just thrust a tool into my hand and point." I thrust my fork at him to demonstrate. "You don't have to ask, Joshua. Helping you around the farm is the least I can do."

"You're not obligated."

"I am. It's my rent."

"Not your debt."

"Sure."

He dropped the knife he was using to butter a roll and looked me square in the face. "Liv, you don't owe me anything."

"Okay." I pursed my lips. "But if I'm going to stay, I'm going to contribute. It's only right."

His focus lingered on the bread in his grip. If I didn't know any better, I would have thought he sounded disappointed when he mumbled, "if?"

"Well, you could still kick me out and make me hibernate in a bear cave all winter." Technically he never did issue an invitation for me to stay through winter. He never really invited me at all. It was more of a command, one I was eager to follow when I'd been helpless and starving. I still couldn't really see what was in it for him, not unless he followed through with putting me to work.

He snorted and I got the feeling it wasn't because he thought the bear cave part of that remark was funny. My future on the farm, at least for now, was secure.

"I'd like to go back to town before the snow comes. It's going to be a lot of walking but it's the last chance to get more seeds and supplies before winter. Need to find some winter boots for you. You up for that?" He continued.

Joshua had taken it upon himself to make sure I was well fed and properly equipped. He wasn't the most sociable and he could use a brush up on table manners but more and more I was beginning to suspect that deep down, Joshua was a kind person. Suspicious with a heavy dose of self-preservation but that didn't mean he cared for no one. His care just didn't look like other people's. It was never going to be soft or comforting. That wasn't him.

That realization came with a rush of relief. Maybe all this time I'd been discouraged because I wanted something from Joshua that he wasn't capable of giving. I'd selfishly been expecting him to behave the way I was accustomed to, not the other way around. I was in his world now. It was me who should learn to bend.

"Really? We're going again? Yes! Count me in. That was fun. Most of it, anyway." I sipped my tea.

By now my anger at him over keeping Rockham Falls a secret had mostly subsided. We were going to have to have a chat about lying—or omitting, if you asked him—but it could wait. I wasn't keen on broaching the topic and wrecking the pleasant peace between us.

"Wheeler shouldn't bother you a second time. Not now that he knows you're mine." A hint of that unsettling coolness seeped into his tone.

"Yours?" I choked on a bite of eggs, sputtering into my cup of tea until I could manage a gulp.

Joshua scowled at my coughing, as if I was interrupting him on purpose, and continued like he hadn't just verbally claimed me like territory. "I can't promise that, though. He and his have been restless lately. Winter is on the way, and I get the feeling they aren't as prepared as they should be. And there's tension, only getting worse with the weather. Don't have to worry 'bout it yet but we can't be too careful."

"What does any of it have to do with you? Is it just because he wants what you've got on the farm?"

Joshua cleared his throat loudly and went back to speaking to his food rather than me. "There's bad blood between Wheeler and my father. That's a big part of it. But you're right. He wants the livestock, he wants me to trade them the food that I grow, and he wants me to teach his men to cure meat properly. Idiots keep making themselves sick."

"And you won't do that because of your father?"

"Because Wheeler is a piece of shit." Joshua cleared his throat again and corrected himself. "Because he's a bad person. I don't agree with what he and his men get up to and I don't agree with their presence in town."

I laughed when he felt the need to change his language for my sake. Did he transform into a gentleman overnight? "That says a lot about you."

"Should say more about him." He speared his last bite of egg with an angry jab.

"I meant it as a good thing." I forked a piece of mushroom and concentrated on it, so he didn't see the slight blush on my cheeks. We were both making more eye contact with our breakfast than we were with each other. "I misjudged you before. I thought you didn't care about what people like Tommy Wheeler did."

Joshua wasn't going to dwell on his feud with Wheeler or acknowledge my makeshift apology. "I've got to go north too. Maybe just once. I'd like to get as much ammunition as I can."

"You've got an armory downstairs. Why do you need more bullets?"

"It's not something I want to run out of. And I'll need extra so I can teach you to shoot."

"Um, no, you don't have to worry about that. I am far too easily startled to be trusted with a gun. I know the basics. My dad used to have a handgun." I shook my head so vehemently my hair almost landed in my mug.

"You're going to learn to shoot."

"I'm a pacifist and vegetarian, remember? No guns."

"You're a terrible vegetarian."

"But I'm a good pacifist. I haven't hurt anyone yet."

"You won't be so proud of that if you need to, and you can't." Joshua finally returned to that commanding tone that was standard for him, the one that left little room for argument. "I'm not leaving you alone out here without knowing how to defend yourself."

"You've done it before."

"'Cause I really needed to. When I take Kuna hunting, you're going to be on your own." He scraped his plate. "You shouldn't need me to protect you from men like Wheeler."

I immediately wanted to snap, "I don't need you to protect me," but it was both untrue and unfair. I was too timid to even pull my hand out of Tommy's grasp yesterday. If Joshua hadn't been there and I was on my own, I had no idea what could have happened to me. He was right. I should know how to defend myself.

And perhaps I shouldn't be insulted. He wasn't calling me weak; he was telling me that he wanted me to be strong. There was a big difference between the two.

"Fine but if you expect me to carry around a gun then you'll have to stop sneaking up on me."

"I never sneak up on you. You ought to be more observant."

I mock-glowered at him and reached for his plate. Our knuckles touched and he quickly dropped his hand under the table. We were back to that already. I shouldn't be disappointed.

Why did it matter if Joshua didn't want to be touched? It didn't. It might hurt my self-esteem less if he didn't shrink away from even accidental touches, but it wasn't his responsibility to care about my ego. If anything, I should be grateful for how easy and relaxed this morning was considering my mistake last night.

Now if only I could actually view it as a mistake.

19

Terminator

Kuna joined us on our trip to Rockham Falls this time, happily darting in and out of the trees with her tongue lolling out. We took a different route than we had the first time, not that I could really tell the difference. When I was standing in the forest it all looked the same to me. Joshua frequently took different trails to and from trading posts and when he was hunting, careful not to leave one that was obviously man made.

These were the type of details that would never occur to me. Days like today I was reminded just how helpless I was without Joshua. Everything I knew about survival came from him. It desperately made me want to learn more.

We hadn't been hiking for long when the scenery began to look familiar, and I wasn't entirely sure why. Until we came upon the railroad tracks, that is. They didn't lead directly to Rockham Falls but if I had continued walking along them like I planned nearly three months earlier, it stood to reason that I would have found the town.

Whether or not he had good intentions, a small part of me was still angry at Joshua for lying about it. It wasn't the actual lie that bothered me as much as the ease with which he told it. He was a good liar and that made me nervous. We needed to be able to trust each other. I was putting my wellbeing in his hands and, to a lesser extent, he was putting his in mine.

There was a chink in the safety that Joshua armored me with and I feared that small insecurity could become a breaking point.

If I was being realistic with myself, my anger had little to do with feeling unsafe. It was only a band-aid for the hurt I didn't want to acknowledge. Joshua had my back, this much I knew. Even when I was nothing more than a hopeless, starving stranger to him, he protected me.

That was the problem.

What was once infuriating behavior from Joshua had somehow become endearing. He was the furthest from charming a person could be, but it wasn't on purpose. I was beginning to understand him, to see who he was under all that gruff and grit, and with that understanding came a fragile whisper of feeling—feeling I was terrified to admit to myself because it would never be returned.

Joshua was guided by a particular set of rules and morals, ones that were crafted around the idea of survival. This meant that self-preservation was of the utmost importance to him. It wasn't because he was selfish, it was only because he'd been built that way. Somehow, taking me in fit within the code that dictated his decisions, just like trading with people who needed it most did.

I wasn't even sure if he recognized or understood this behavior. With Joshua, everything he did seemed innate. Any kindness he offered me was out of instinct, preserving the carefully organized structure of his world.

That was Joshua's greatest flaw. He was highly adaptable so long as he was in control. I don't doubt that if I'd shook things up too much, he would have found somewhere else for me to be. Maybe he would have sent me packing to Rockham Falls with a note on my back like an abandoned puppy.

Eventually, the railroad tracks led us to the first creek crossing. It didn't meet the tracks, only curved around it as the tracks headed further north than where we wanted to go. Crossing was more difficult in this spot, the water raging around the bend, splashing up against the bank like one of those dizzying waterslides.

Kuna fearlessly waded through the water, as surefooted as Joshua. He glided over mossy green rocks, barely getting a drop on the leg of his pants. I struggled over the first three slippery boulders, stalling between the third and the fourth when the distance was too far to jump. Joshua heaved an enormous sigh when he saw that I'd stopped.

"Give me your hand," he barked.

"I can make it. Just give me a sec."

"Quit fretting about your pride and come here." He boomed over the rushing current. Was it just me or had the water level risen with the autumn rain?

I carefully stretched my arm in his direction. As I did the weight of my backpack shifted. I flung my arms around like a flapping bird, trying and failing to regain my balance. My boot slipped and I lurched forward. I jutted hands out, expecting to hit stone and water, and instead found myself stumbling into Kuna as Joshua swung me onto the shore. It was an awkward move but at least I was dry.

Another quarter mile of walking passed without incident. Then I really recognized where we were and I froze in place, my feet leaden with dread.

Joshua got about twelve feet in front of me before he noticed I wasn't behind him. His impatience buffeted me like a breeze but for once I didn't care. I was too busy being utterly paralyzed.

Before us was a small clearing. Fallen leaves painted the ground in hues of red and orange but the leaning trunk of a maple and the verdant clusters of salal looked the same as they had almost three months ago. A carpet of lime green moss peeked out in patches beneath the coating of autumn colors. It should have been lovely, but I couldn't see beyond the swift and sudden anxiety that was blurring my vision.

Nothing happened. I got away. I had no reason to be this frightened. But I was suddenly aware of just how dire my situation had been, just how close I came to death or worse. It was easy to push it aside when I was back at the farm, letting it fade into a series of unwanted memories I didn't intentionally revisit.

The drumbeat of my pulse flushed all sound from my ears. I couldn't even hear my frantic panting, could only feel it when Joshua pressed a palm to my sternum. My field of view was suddenly filled with brown, uncharacteristic worry swirling in the chocolate depths of Joshua's eyes. His lips were forming words, but it was like my brain had lost all ability to comprehend. Everything he said was overridden by the fearful thoughts on repeat in my head.

They found me. Someone finally found me. Run! Never get found. Don't let anyone find you. Run!

"Olivia, breathe!" Joshua pinched my collar bone of all things, jolting me back into reality so quickly that I fell to my knees, clutching handfuls of moss and gasping in huge breaths. I belatedly realized that I had actually been running, forcing a confused Joshua and Kuna to chase after me.

Warm hands came around my cheeks. It wasn't intended to be tender, Joshua was only searching my eyes to make sure my momentary crazy spell was over, but the touch was so comforting that I gripped his wrists to hold him in place.

"Sorry," I gasped. "Sorry, sorry, sorry."

"Breathe." It was the gentlest word I'd ever heard him utter, forcing my body to obey. My diaphragm relaxed, letting a gust of cold air burn my lungs. "You're having a panic attack."

"Sorry. I didn't know. I didn't know I had panic attacks. Sorry."

"Stop it, Liv."

"Right, sorry. Not sorry." For some reason I laughed, sounding enough like a crazy person to make that unfamiliar worry crinkle his brow. "You're warm." I blurted, feeling stupid and trying to bring his focus to anything other than my ridiculous freak out.

Joshua immediately tugged his hands back, making me regret bringing his attention to the unexpected touch. He rubbed his palms up and down his thighs, wiping away the warmth he was denying me.

I blinked, taking in our surroundings to hide the longing in my eyes. I must have followed a remembered path because I'd found my way back to the railroad tracks. Joshua was kneeling on the ground in front of me, moisture darkening his denim covered knees.

Kuna stuffed her snout between us, completely oblivious to the human drama. When I turned my head to acknowledge her, she licked my chin. It was the most affection I'd ever received from the dog. Maybe she was more aware of my plight than I thought.

"Liv?" Joshua cleared his throat, swallowing the softness that coated my name. He didn't speak again until he'd masked any concern with his usual sharpness. "Can you walk?"

"Yes. Sorry. I'm fine." I chewed my bottom lip, cursing the burning at the back of my eyes. This was pathetic and we both knew it. I was surprised he hadn't asked what was wrong with me.

"Stop apologizing."

My voice was shrill with unshed tears. "But I am sorry! I've never done that before."

"It's normal."

"It's not. It's not normal. I totally malfunctioned. I didn't even know I was running!" I rubbed my face so vigorously it hurt, willing the fog of adrenaline to clear my head.

"I had you."

Of course, he had me. He always does.

That only brought on another wave of anxiety, this time triggered by uncertainty and an ache of loneliness so deep it sent a tremor through me. Why? Why did he have me? Why did I matter? Why was Joshua crouched in the mud for me when I was obviously too weak? Too needy? Too helpless?

"C'mon." I was on my feet before I could spiral into another panic attack, Joshua's firm grip on my upper arms just close enough to painful to ground me. "We can still make it from here. Kuna likes the tracks anyway."

I shifted, attempting a furtive glance only to discover him watching me. The obvious worry was gone but I could still see a hint of apprehension. He was afraid I would panic again and give away our location. Or worse, freak out in town and draw too much attention to my weakness.

I rolled my shoulders back, pretending I didn't feel like half of my soul had been drained from my body. "Why does Kuna like the tracks?"

"Rats," he answered over his shoulder, already walking ahead again. For once I was glad Joshua wasn't the kind to coddle when I was upset. Now that the initial anxiety was fading, I was overcome with embarrassment. I couldn't believe such a simple memory pushed me so far over an edge I hadn't even been aware of.

On cue, Kuna let out a yip, racing down the tracks in pursuit of a squealing rodent.

"She's not going to eat it, is she?"

"She will if she catches it."

"Gross! She just licked my face!"

Zippers jingled on Joshua's backpack when he shrugged. "Don't trust a dog near your face."

"What about you?" I asked a few minutes later, the silence making me fidgety. "Do you like it out here?"

"I don't like anything."

Relieved laughter exploded from my chest, so unexpected that it startled both of us. Joshua glowered at me as I wheezed and snorted, doubling over so I didn't stumble backwards. "You—" I started but had to pause to giggle some more and wipe a stray tear from the corner of my eye. "You would be much more convincing if you didn't try so hard. Stop acting like the Terminator and maybe I'll believe you."

"Terminator?"

"Really? No Terminator either?" He shook his head. "Okay, so the Terminator is a cyborg—"

"Cyborg?" He interrupted.

"A robot but...with feelings." I gladly jumped into a description of the movie plot. It was going to be a long one and by the end, Joshua would probably be just as confused.

For the rest of our walk, Joshua pestered me with quiet question after question. I knew he wasn't that interested in the movie. He was distracting me, and I was so grateful I could kiss him. But I wouldn't. I was mortified enough without ruining another good moment.

What Joshua was giving me now, a chance to clear my mind and redeem myself as a functioning human being, was much better than what anyone else got from him. Tentative friendship had to be enough.

It is enough, I told myself. *What we have now is enough.*

I never was a very good liar.

20

Slugfest

"That doesn't make any sense. Why would robots want to take over the world?" We were still discussing the Terminator when we arrived at the main gate leading into town.

Joshua halted the conversation to draw the guard's attention. Once we were waved in, he lowered his voice but continued his critique of a movie he hadn't even seen. Somewhere between the train tracks and here, he'd become genuinely invested in the story.

"I told you, they're sentient! They're angry that humans enslaved them, and they want freedom. And revenge." I explained, waving my hands around to make my point clearer.

"But they're robots."

"With feelings!"

"Ridiculous," he muttered, ending our discussion, and slipping on his mean face. That was my cue to stop talking.

"Liv!" Mary squealed excitedly when she noticed us approaching the table where Asher and Maddie were set up to trade.

The last time they were right on the edge of the market. Now they were situated a few rows down, surrounded by other tables and wagons. Beside them was Mary's stereo, playing a classic rock CD that seemed to have a scratch or two. A few people were gathered near Asher's tent to enjoy the music, looking surprisingly relaxed.

Hunks of wood, tangy with sap, burned in a portable firepit to Asher's right. A giant pot sat over the flames, billowing delicious smelling steam. He ladled liquid from the pot into a plastic cup and handed it to a woman, his smile charming as always. That smile stretched wider when he turned our way and waved.

Joshua nodded but couldn't be bothered to stop frowning. I barely squatted in time to keep Mary from hugging my legs out from under me. The little girl came barreling towards us, arms outstretched with an ear to ear grin.

"You're back! Do you want to dance with me? Uncle Ash found more batteries and we have apple juice," Mary rushed out.

"I'd love to dance with you. And I love apple juice." I returned her hug, waving to Asher and Maddie from my crouch.

Joshua stood beside me with his arms crossed, making all the happy people drinking from plastic cups take several steps back. A bear could have ambled in, and they would have been less nervous.

"Joshua! You made it for Thanksgiving!" Asher called over the din of conversation and music.

"Thanksgiving?" I arched a brow. "I'm not great at keeping track of the days but isn't Thanksgiving supposed to fall on a Thursday? In *November*?"

Asher shrugged. "It'll be too cold by the real Thanksgiving. We're celebrating Canadian Thanksgiving this year. Darlene and Frank harvested a couple'a turkeys, Denise's got potatoes, and I made hot cider with our extra apples. I can spike it if you want." He waggled a half full bottle of cheap whiskey at us and winked.

"Canadians have their own Thanksgiving?" I wrinkled my nose. "And thanks, but I'll pass on the whiskey. I'm still hungover from Joshua's moonshine two weeks ago."

"Oh, c'mon Tex, I know Canada is far from Dallas but surely, you're not that ignorant. Canadians got everything we got, only Canadian." Asher handed me a plastic cup. I accepted, realizing too late that I was breaking Joshua's "don't taking anything for free" rule. Maybe he could make an exception for Thanksgiving.

Joshua put a hand out to decline the cup offered to him and grunted, "Canada doesn't exist anymore."

"You should have some, Joshua. It's good." I sipped the cinnamon-y cider and smiled. "Do it for the special occasion."

"Thanksgiving also doesn't exist anymore," he said flatly.

"Spoil sport," I coughed behind my fist.

"Yeah, Scrooge, what's the big deal?" Asher cupped a hand around his mouth to ask me, "How are you not bored to death with all the party pooping?"

I was once again struck by how strange and unexpected a friendship was between Asher and Joshua. Joshua might argue that they weren't friends, but it was clear he was fond of the man. They were so different. Asher was as amicable as can be. And Joshua? He was, well, Joshua.

I laughed, nudging Joshua's arm with mine. "I like all the grumping. It's endearing."

Joshua looked down at me like a predatory bird, eyes narrowed. As usual, I had no idea what the look was supposed to mean so I winked and scurried off to talk to Maddie before he could take my cider away.

While Joshua was busy trading, I took Mary up on her offer to dance. We made it through three songs before she was distracted by refilling her drink. How many cups of cider could one kid drink?

I let my eyes wander the crowd, catching more than a few curious looks. Whenever my gaze landed on someone else's, they hurriedly found something new to stare at. I hadn't been privy to any of it but there was a lot of gossip about Joshua—apparently there always had been, even before the blackout—and I wondered if that gossip now included me. From the faces people were making, it did.

It shouldn't matter what anyone thought of me, especially not when the world was ending, but I was acutely uncomfortable with them thinking I was using Joshua. He said it would happen the first time we came to Rockham Falls. I just hadn't realized what being someone's "woman" meant.

I thought maybe they would assume I was his girlfriend, not someone manipulating him for resources and protection. I could hardly blame anyone for thinking that, I guess. I did have his resources and protection. He just wasn't getting what people thought he was getting in exchange.

Mostly, he was getting "a pain in his rear end." I was paraphrasing a little.

Someone was humming a Christmas song that was now going to be stuck in my head for eternity. Others were telling jokes over a small meal of Darlene's turkey. The market felt like a big church potluck today. Even the mayor was engaging in conversation, shaking hands, and patting backs while enjoying his hot cider. Perhaps with a wee sip of that whiskey if the rosy tint to his cheeks was any tell.

Joshua was mostly immune to the contagious glee, but every once and a while I felt his scrutinizing eyes turned on me. Whether or not he was willing to partake, the festivities interested him. He wasn't vocal about his childhood, and I'd heard enough to guess that was because it wasn't a very good one. Maybe he just needed some encouragement to learn how to enjoy times like these.

I did my best to include him in every conversation, not that he indulged me. I offered to share my drink and a bite of turkey with him too. He looked at me like I was a crazy person. At least he looked at me.

By the time our market day was winding down, I was buzzing. High on life in a way I never thought I would be again. Joshua did not feel the same. If holiday cheer wasn't enough to tick him off, our last stop to trade was.

I couldn't remember the man's name—something with a "T." Terrence? Timothy?—but I remembered his face and the two missing teeth that left gaps in his sheepish smile as he explained to Joshua that his price for tallow had changed. The price itself wasn't what set him off—Joshua had plenty to trade with—so much as it was the reason for the change.

"It's, um, not for me. I've got folks to pay too. Hired some men to help me keep the cows safe."

Tallow Terrence lived outside of town and he wasn't the only one. Most anyone raising animals, like Frank and Darlene, needed more space than what was provided in the safety of Rockham Falls. With rumors of growing raider groups, people were becoming panicked, packing up and abandoning their animals to take up residence in the church and the government buildings that had been converted into makeshift hostels.

"And they don't want your beef?" Joshua prodded.

He swallowed nervously. "Can't wait for it."

"Can't or won't?"

"I don't want trouble, Joshua. I've got to look out for myself. You understand?"

"You've got Wheeler's men camped out at your place, don't you?"

Terrence hesitated, scratching his chin. "I'm not safe out there all alone."

"You think you're safer with those bastards at your back?"

"We've all gotta do what we've gotta do to survive."

Joshua cursed under his breath. "You better sleep with one eye open."

Terrence wasn't the first to pay for protection from Wheeler and if Tommy's numbers were growing like Joshua claimed they were, he wouldn't be the last. Maybe Wheeler wasn't the most stand-up guy, but I didn't understand why Joshua took that so personally.

We bid Asher and Maddie a final farewell as we circled back—and stopped to get more cider, even if it would make me pee six times on the walk home—and had to wade through a small crowd of people. Or we would have had to if they didn't notice Joshua and give him a wide berth.

It was uncanny when people did that. Kind of creepy, even. Was there more to Joshua than I'd been made aware of? Was he known to randomly strike at people or strangle passersby? His demeanor wasn't exactly amicable and, yeah, if you weren't used to his towering, broad figure it drew the eye, but was he that intimidating? This was a man who drank chamomile tea while humming to himself, after all.

"Liv, good to see you back in town." The hair on my nape stood at attention when someone purred my name from behind us.

"Keep her name out of your damn mouth." Joshua whirled, immediately dropping what he was doing and stepping between Wheeler and I. Kuna prowled to his side, hyperalert at Joshua's unease.

Joshua's back was to me—not blocking me from Tommy's view completely, only creating a barrier. I had a sudden yearning to put my hand on him again not because I was frightened but because I wanted to feel his ferocity as he stood his ground. I wanted to touch his skin and shield myself in the same fearlessness that he wore. I wanted to take a piece of his courage.

"I asked around and learned a little about your girl. Folks like her." Tommy lifted a cup of cider and sipped casually. The other hand was holding a paper bag.

Joshua made an unhappy noise. "I've noticed."

"I felt bad for my behavior last time. I didn't mean to corner her." Another sip, his lips naturally forming a smirk.

"You mean intimidate her."

"That was never my intention."

"I don't care." Joshua jerked his chin in my direction and stepped aside. "It should be your intention to never talk to her again."

"Relax, Joshua. What have I ever done to warrant such hostility? I only want what you want; to take care of me and mine." Wheeler extended his hand, offering the brown paper bag to me. "I brought a gift. A peace offering of sorts."

Joshua reached out and snatched the bag before I could even process what was happening. An ominous cloud darkened his face as he stared at the contents of the bag.

"What the fuck is this?" He thrust the bag back at Wheeler.

Wheeler put his hands up, refusing it. "I thought she could use them. No uniforms for her type these days but we can make do."

Joshua's nostrils flared, fists clenched around the paper so tight it crumpled. "What's your game, Wheeler? Is this what *your type* does when they're bored?"

"Perhaps I've misunderstood your *arrangement*. I thought I was doing you a favor, giving you something to trade for. Quid pro quo and all that."

"Arrangement?" I mouthed, looking to Joshua for clarification.

He gave a slight shake of his head, pressing a big palm over my stomach and guiding me backward until I could barely see what was going on.

Tommy sighed dramatically. "I'm a busy man, Joshua, so I'm going to get right to the point. I'd like you to let my men hunt in your woods undisturbed. There are more than enough deer to go around but north of town has less activity to spook them. My men won't bother you and your...*girl*."

"Bullshit," Joshua said under his breath.

"I'm sure we can work something out."

"I'm sure we can't," Joshua countered.

"This is an olive branch, son. You would be wise to take it. We could use a man like you and you could use someone at your back. This agreement would be mutually beneficial."

Joshua rested his spare hand above the gun on his hip. "I'll pass. Raping and pillaging ain't really my style."

"Oh-oh, you think you can play at being self-righteous? Not when you were raised by a man like your father. I know what he was like. *We all* know what kind of man John Sutton was." He raised his voice on the last sentence and made a sweeping gesture, drawing the nearby crowd's attention.

Joshua's words snaked from his mouth in a hiss. "You know somethin' about what happened to him, Wheeler?"

"Are you still waiting for daddy to come home? What does it say about a boy when both his parents go out for ciggies and never come back? Somethin' real serious must be wrong with you. Fucking hillbilly inbred."

Joshua dropped his pack from his shoulders, and it was the most threatening action I'd ever seen. Not good. "If you've got any brains that aren't stuffed between your shriveled old balls, you'll shut the fuck up right now."

"I think I'm done being threatened by you, Joshua. You're one man against the world. Look what I've got." He pointed toward his horses, where two armed men watched the argument with beady eyes. "Y'know, back in the day, Helen—you remember your mama, boy? Well, she and I were *real* well acquainted. She told me a lot about your father. Things I didn't want to know a man was capable of doing to his own family. Whoever took him out did the world a Goddamned favor. Might be doing the world another if we end his line here."

"Try me."

"You sure you want to pick that fight? Without you around who would look out for sweet Liv here? Maybe she'd like to get well acquainted with me too."

Joshua was powerful but he was also a big man—too big to be swift. Somehow, he found that swiftness in him. One minute he was standing beside me with hate radiating off him, the next he was in front of me, his fist connecting with Wheeler's face. He lunged so fast I barely registered the movement.

A chorus of shouts rang out around us. People were calling for Flores, for the militia, and for Joshua and Tommy to break it up. Kuna was barking and snapping her teeth in Wheeler's direction. I wrapped my fingers around her collar and yanked her back. The last thing I needed was both her and Joshua in the mix.

I was having a hard time following the flurry of fists that were flying between the two men. Thankfully, neither of them were hitting each other very often.

Movement behind them dragged my attention from the fight just long enough for me to see Wheeler's men advancing. Both were gripping the handgun holster on their hip.

They were going to shoot Joshua.

Panic had my brain whirring out of control. I didn't know what to do. I needed to stop Joshua before he got himself killed but I couldn't just jump into the middle of a fist fight. I hopped back and forth on my feet, shouting Joshua's name and praying that he would snap out of whatever red haze was blinding him.

Usually, he was so controlled. I didn't know what to do with Joshua out of control.

Wheeler managed to kick Joshua back, stumbling as he did and landing awkwardly on one knee. I saw my opportunity and seized it, leaping in Joshua's path just as Wheeler's men drew their guns. It was terrifying to turn my back to a bunch of armed men, but I had to do something to keep Joshua safe. I slapped both my hands on his chest and gave him a gentle shove. He didn't even look at me, just tried to stomp past me.

"Joshua!" I snapped. "Look at me!" He rolled his shoulders in an attempt to dislodge my shaking hands. "Please, Joshua. Look at me." My voice cracked on his name. "That's enough."

With an exhale that almost sounded painful, he did. For that tiny millisecond his gaze flicked to me and softened just enough to let me know I had him. He turned his attention back to his opponent, right hand instinctively cradling the grip on his gun.

"Out!" Suddenly Flores was there with several heavily armed men at his back. "You know the rules, Sutton! I do not tolerate fighting in my town."

I turned to face the newcomers, shielding Joshua with my body. I didn't make a very good shield since he was double my width, but I still had this soul-shattering fear that someone was going to shoot him.

Oblivious to my terror, Joshua shoved me to the side and pointed an angry finger at Wheeler as he addressed Mayor Flores. "One of these days, this fucker is going to bleed you and take everything you have."

"He'll try," the Mayor agreed quietly. "But until then, this is my town, and we follow my rules. I want you out. You'll get a warning today but it's the only one you'll ever get. Are we clear?"

Joshua looked like he had a new target for his bruised fist, so I sidled up beside him, wrapped my arm around his tensed bicep, and said, "abundantly clear. We'll be on our way."

"You won't have the upper hand forever, Joshua. Things are going to change around here real soon." Tommy shouted as we shouldered our packs and rushed to obey Flores.

"You too, Wheeler! Pack up your men and leave. I don't want to see your ugly faces in my town again today!" The mayor boomed.

Joshua turned back to Tommy, a vein in his forehead bulging. "You threaten her again, it better be because you're tired of living!"

"Let's go, Joshua." I shoved his hand down, wrapping my fingers around his wrist and tugging him away from another fight.

I threw a glance back and saw Wheeler clutching his stomach. His face was bloodied and one of his eyes was swollen shut. Horrified, I gave Joshua's face another once over.

Apparently, he hit Wheeler a lot more often than Wheeler hit him. His lip was split, his eye was puffy, and there was a cut over his brow but otherwise, he looked surprisingly good for someone that just came out of a brawl.

"You shouldn't have done that. This shit's got nothing to do with you." Joshua stormed toward the gate without bothering to make sure I was following.

"I'd say it's a really good thing I did that because they were about to draw guns on you. They were going to kill you!" I covered my mouth so I could swallow the wave of nausea that came with that thought. "And, for the record, it does have to do with me. Sorry, Joshua, your problems are my problems now."

"I didn't make it your problem. I tried to keep you out of this." He readjusted his pack with far more force than was needed, making all the buckles clack together.

"I wasn't blaming you."

"Stay out of my way next time." He was moving at a pace that required me to jog to keep up with him.

"No." I stood my ground. Kuna got halfway to Joshua then realized I hadn't caught up and stopped between us, conflicted about leaving me behind but not wanting to get left behind herself.

Experience taught me that Joshua thought he was a man that wouldn't be refused—just like his father. And yet, I snubbed his commands all the time.

This was going to be one of those times. I wouldn't yield and let him think that he could drag me around town pretending that I was his...whatever I was while acting like I was completely cut off from all his dealings. As evidenced by Wheeler making threats toward me to get under Joshua's skin. We were in this together and he had to deal with the fact that I would be involved with whatever he was involved in.

"No?" He started to yell but shifted to an angry hiss when he remembered we were surrounded by people that had watched the exchange with Wheeler and continued to watch us now. "You don't get a say in the matter."

I ran in front of him and pressed a defiant hand into his chest. "Yes, I do. Now stop that. You have every right to be angry but don't yell. Not here and not at me."

I didn't give him a chance to respond, only readjusted my pack, brushed my fingers through the hair behind Kuna's ears, and carried on in the direction he'd been going. By the time he stalked after me, scowling and cursing under his breath like a dramatic teenager, I was already halfway out the gate.

Joshua didn't speak to me for the entire journey home. If he was doing that in an attempt to punish me, it was a total failure. I didn't care how mad he was because it was nothing compared to the roiling rage that was growing in my gut. With every step I took, my anger grew a little more.

How could he be so stupid? Whatever Wheeler said to him about his parents obviously touched some hidden, painful place in Joshua's heart but that didn't give him an excuse to risk his life. Over words! He could have died over words that were *intended to provoke him*.

My fury was down to a simmer when we rolled up to the farm in Joshua's sputtering truck. I wanted to show him how disappointed I was, but I was finding it harder to cling to that furious heat from earlier. I couldn't stop picturing that look in Joshua's eyes when Wheeler mentioned his mother. Helen? Was that her name?

It was so brief and so subtle, something that maybe even he didn't realize he felt, but it was there. Raw and honest heartbreak. I didn't know much about Joshua's history, and it didn't seem fair to take any information from Tommy

Wheeler as fact but I was willing to bet there was a whole lot of pain in that mysterious past of his.

Another layer to Joshua that I might never get the chance to unwrap. God, I wanted him to share those secrets with me. If he'd let me, I would shoulder some of that pain for him. I would try to ease that ache that I was all too familiar with.

I meant what I said. Whether he wanted it that way or not, Joshua's problems were my problems now.

21

Quiet Chaos

Joshua

For once, Liv was the one to stomp into the house with mud still on her boots. Though they were both angry after the events of the day, hers had been quietly simmering the whole way home, coming closer to a boil with every minute that Joshua remained silent. It pissed her off when he didn't respond to her talking. That wasn't all he'd done to piss her off, judging by the scowl that shadowed her face.

"Sit," Liv snapped, tugging his pack off his shoulders, and letting it thump to the floor when it was too heavy for her to lift. A meeker man might have been afraid of the dark look she gave him. Joshua only struggled to hold in laughter. What was she going to do? Make him?

What pissed *him* off was how easily she managed to soothe his anger. *He* was the one that got punched, that had his family history dragged out in the open for strangers to see. For *Liv* to see. What right did she have to be mad about anything? He was defending *her* as much as his ego. Sure, he was less than polite but she needed to learn not to interfere with his dealings in town.

Even if she did save his sorry ass.

"Joshua, *sit down.*" Damn woman actually bared her teeth at him.

When he crossed his arms and met her frown with his own, she yanked out one of the dining chairs, grabbed his forearms, and pushed him down onto the seat with a surprising amount of force. It was only because she caught him off guard with her unexpected manhandling that she got him to sit.

Joshua had to bite back another chuckle when she crossed her arms and did an excellent imitation of his looming. Unfortunately for Liv, she was barely taller than him when he was seated.

After a short stare down, she turned her back to him and plucked the first aid kit from one of the kitchen drawers, making a mess of it with her rifling. He refrained from telling her that she was wasting medical supplies because he knew that wouldn't make a difference. Stubborn woman would fuss about infections until he was too annoyed to say no to her.

Joshua took a long, calming breath as Liv got to work cleaning his brow. Her soft knuckles brushed his cheek, and he resisted the temptation to close his eyes and lean into the contact. That was a common reaction to her touch lately.

He quickly switched his focus to the temperature of her skin, reminding himself that he needed to find her a pair of gloves soon. When she was done sanitizing his very superficial wounds, Liv gently stretched a butterfly bandage over what must have been a cut over his left brow.

She lingered once she was finished, feathering fingers under his eye, and whispering, "you're going to have a bruise."

The tremor in her voice caused him to look up and see all the heat gone from her expression. Instead of fury in her minty eyes, he saw silent tears spilling over onto her cheeks. Dammit, why was she crying? Joshua hadn't been *that* mean to her, had he? She chewed her bottom lip, averting her gaze, but still didn't remove her fingers from their place under his eye.

"Don't cry." Joshua hated it when she cried. The unbidden words came out gruff and only seemed to upset her further.

"Sorry," she clicked her jaw shut, "I know it's so annoying when I show emotions. I'll try to be a *robot* like you." There wasn't an ounce of teasing in her voice.

Liv silently cleaned up the first aid kit, grabbed a handful of clothes from where she stored them under the bed, and shut herself in his bedroom. Ten minutes later she came out wearing his flannel over her top. A pair of his wool socks flopped loose on her feet. Why she kept stealing his socks when they were a whole foot too big for her, he had no idea.

She looked ridiculous but Joshua was smart enough not to say it.

Her mismatched outfit was so distracting that he didn't realize Liv was pouring him a drink until she set a glass of moonshine next to his fisted hand on the table. Again, her knuckles brushed him, warm this time, and he had a sudden urge to reach out for her hand.

Joshua shook the thought away and took a deep swallow of his drink. When he rose from the table he was wordlessly shooed out of the kitchen. Not wanting to let her think she could order him around, Joshua stood motionless and in her way for a solid minute, taking the time to observe her as he did.

Liv's nose was pink, and her eyes were still puffy but the tears had stopped. Any frustration was replaced with defeat as she busied herself on the opposite end of the kitchen, very determined to avoid him.

Joshua couldn't figure out what he'd done wrong this time—other than raise his voice, which wasn't exactly out of the ordinary—but that annoying, and all too familiar guilt was nibbling at him. He stepped closer, planting himself between her and the counter where she was collecting ingredients.

What his intention was, Joshua couldn't say. He only knew he couldn't stand this uncharacteristic silence from her and the sad slump of her shoulders. Liv returned to her cutting board, realizing that Joshua wasn't going to move. She locked her gaze on his chest for a few long breaths before shifting her focus to his face. Joshua forced himself to meet her eyes.

Liv glanced up for one heartbeat before her bottom lip started wobbling again. "What are you doing?" She whispered.

"Standing in my kitchen."

The tears threatening to leak began to dry up. "Oh-kay." She tried to move around him, but he blocked her. "Why are you being weird?"

"Why are *you* being weird?"

"I'm not being weird." She tapped the cutting board still clutched in her hand. "I'm making dinner."

"Quietly." *What the fuck is wrong with me?*

"Did you want me to make noise? I thought quiet was your thing."

"My thing?" He cleared his throat. "It is. I like quiet."

"Oh-kay." She repeated, drawing the word out and staring at him. He couldn't blame her. Joshua *was* being weird. "Can I...?" Liv gestured to the counter behind him.

He shifted to the side, allowing her to place her board and start cutting onions. The knock of her knife as it sliced through vegetables was the only sound beside the hiss and crackle of the fireplace. Every time she added an ingredient to the bowl in front of her, her elbow bumped his hip.

Finally, she scowled up at him and propped her hands on her hips. "You're still being weird."

Joshua lifted his cup to shield himself from her accusation and made his way to the living room, settling in his chair with a groan. His body ached and the bruise over his eye throbbed.

They didn't speak through dinner. Liv continued her careful avoidance, completely ignoring his scrutiny. Normally he was much more subtle when he studied the curves of her face or the way her lips moved when she ate but tonight, he couldn't claim subtlety. It wasn't like her to be so quiet. And why the hell wouldn't she look at him? The silence was beginning to drive him mad.

Kind of ironic, really, that the persistent chatter that had once been the bane of his daily routine was now an essential part of it. Joshua didn't know what to do without it. *He* couldn't be the one to start a conversation, not without some kind of prompt.

By the time dinner was cleaned up, he was already on his second glass of moonshine. Drinking as a result of stress was a dangerous road to go down, he knew that all too well, but he hadn't even noticed that he fixed himself another until it was already in his hands.

He let the moonshine sit on his tongue, mulling over the taste and his predicament before enjoying the sharp burn on his throat. The slight buzz from the drink was almost enough to make him say something—anything—just to get Liv talking.

That was when he *finally* had an idea. Joshua hurried to the cellar, skipped half the rungs on the ladder, and fumbled around in the dark until he found the jar he hoped was peach moonshine. There was no guarantee that anything was where it should be with blondie rearranging all his shit.

Liv eyed him curiously when he returned to the kitchen, accidentally slamming open a cabinet door in his rush to get to the glasses. Was it unfair to use alcohol to settle her mood when he knew she couldn't hold her liquor? This time he wouldn't let her have more than one. And he would be on guard in case she became overly affectionate.

A wool blanket hid her defeated posture as she curled up in the chair opposite his. The toes of his socks were the only visible part of her below the waist. A grunt of amusement escaped before he could hold it in. Liv squeaked like a startled squirrel, too lost in thought to notice his arrival.

When he thrust the glass at her she gave him a wilted smile and said, "thanks, Joshua." He almost groaned sweet relief at the sound of her voice.

I learned a long time ago that Joshua didn't apologize. What hadn't occurred to me was that it was because he didn't know how. Sure, saying the words "I'm sorry" seemed pretty simple but to someone who was never made to do it, it wasn't. Instead of using his words to make up for bad behavior, Joshua got weird. He hovered in the kitchen, his eyebrows speaking some language I had yet to learn.

I hadn't planned on accepting that as an apology, but when I saw that desperate, sad puppy expression on his face as he offered me a drink, I dropped the last handful of resentment I'd been squeezing all evening. The eggplant colored bruise around his eye gave him an unfair advantage.

"How's your face?" I asked quietly.

"Fine."

A moonshine shiver had me tingling all the way to my toes. "I don't think the other guy can say the same."

Joshua gave me the faintest of smiles and wow, how did bruises and a swollen lip make him look more handsome? "You're pretty brave for a squirrel."

"I'm not the one that punched a man that had armed friends standing behind him."

"You did more than that and you know it. You meant business." That was probably as close to acknowledging that I saved him from trigger happy psychos as Joshua was going to get.

"My dad always said I had a knack for business. I think he was bummed I didn't want to go for an MBA like he did. I guess it wouldn't matter now."

"You would've been bored." He knew me better than I thought he did.

"What was in that bag, anyway?" Based on his reaction today, I almost didn't want to know. What if it was a cat head or something equally creepy?

Shadows shaped his anger into a terrifying expression. When he said, "lace panties," I burst out laughing. *That* was what had him fuming? Joshua didn't laugh. If anything, his features hardened even more. "Nothing funny about what he did today."

"I don't understand why it makes you so angry." I swirled my glass around, watching the firelight warp in the reflection. "It's just underwear."

"It's not. He was insulting you."

"By assuming I'm your 'woman,' the same way everyone else does?" I made air quotes.

Whatever words Joshua wanted to say, he chewed them back down. God, I was so sick of not getting answers from him.

"Joshua? Don't ignore me," I demanded.

"He was calling you a whore!" He blurted.

My cheeks heated, the drink pooling uncomfortably in my stomach. "He—what?"

"I told you he was insulting you. Wheeler likes to rile people up." He leaned forward in his chair, rubbing his face aggressively then wincing. "I don't want to talk about it anymore."

"I don't think I want to either."

He flopped back into the chair, eager to change the topic. "Why were you going to school if not for business?"

"I was going because my parents gave me money, put my stuff in a box, and said, 'see ya, kid!'" I snorted. "Isn't that why most people go to college?"

"No."

"I was kidding."

"No, you weren't." Joshua shook his head, the last of his drink gliding down his throat with ease. "You didn't want to go?"

"I didn't not want to."

"But?"

"I didn't want to go for any of the degrees my parents wanted me to get. They were practical and maybe wiser than me but why waste my life in marketing if it's not what I want? I craved satisfaction, not success. I mean, maybe I could have had both. It didn't really feel that way at the time."

"What did you want?"

"And you say I ask a lot of questions." My lips teased the edge of the glass, preparing myself for another shuddering sip. "You're going to think it's dumb. I didn't exactly want to do something useful."

His brows formed an expectant line. "Will I?"

"I wanted to be an interior decorator." I waited for his mocking noise. There wasn't one. Instead, he went silent for so long that I started to worry I'd said something wrong. "Joshua?"

"Hmm?"

"See? I knew it! You think it's stupid."

"No," he disagreed sharply.

"That's why you stopped talking."

"Obviously someone has a use for it if it exists."

"Wow, you're really trying, aren't you?" That was new. "I would have wanted to do it whether or not anyone else thought it was a good idea. But what does it matter now? I'm a farmer in training. That's my career of choice."

A derisive sound reverberated in his throat. "Hardly a career."

"What else am I going to do with myself?"

Joshua stiffened. "World won't be this way forever. You'll have plenty of opportunities for a good life."

"Don't you think this life is good?" That question didn't make him relax at all. His jaw worked, hard muscles swelling under inky sideburns.

"Do you?"

"Yeah, totally. My glass is full," I said, finishing the last of my drink with a smirk.

"Your glass is empty," he replied dryly, his tension leaving as quickly as it came.

I wrinkled my nose. "My metaphorical glass, silly."

He finally let that little twitch of a smile curve his lips unrestrained. "Nothing discourages you."

"Plenty of things discourage me. I was discouraged when Firefly was cancelled."

"It doesn't count if it has to do with television."

I waggled my pointer finger at him. "You're just grumpy because you never got to watch Dexter."

"Dexter?"

"The one about the serial killer, remember?"

"Right. I'm heartbroken I missed that. So many hours wasted reading books and working in the sun when I could have been watching movies about robots with feelings."

My laughter sent the blanket sliding off my lap. Today was an uncomfortable reminder of how fragile life and safety were after the blackout, but it was hard to remember any of that now that we were home. Funny how quickly a stranger's house could feel like home to me.

Even funnier how that stranger didn't feel very strange to me anymore.

Was it the house that felt like home, or was it Joshua?

22

Optimist

Joshua glanced at the chair across from his, watching carefully as Liv's sleeping form moved with every breath. He knew he should wake her. The last time she fell asleep in that chair she woke the next morning complaining. The problem with waking her was that it required touching her.

What used to be innocuous and sometimes necessary was now increasingly dangerous—dangerous because he liked it more than he should. Not the kind of thing he needed to get accustomed to. The safest route was to avoid it altogether.

He repeated her name, increasing his volume until he was practically shouting, "Livvy!"

She stirred a little, shifting in the chair, but didn't wake. Joshua crept across the room. Her slender fingers were still wrapped tight around her empty glass. He couldn't easily free it without skin contact.

With a heavy sigh he pinched the edge of the glass and slid it out of her hand. Leaning over the sink, he contemplated his excuse for not waking her. The floor creaked behind him, and he whirled, almost shattering the glass as he did.

"Oh, sorry," Liv apologized hoarsely. "I thought you heard me get up."

"No." Despite his brusque response she offered him a sleepy smile.

"Thanks for the drink." She trudged over to the bed, rubbing her eyes and covering a yawn.

"You—" That was the only word he got out before snipping the sentence off.

"Hmm?"

"Ugh."

"Words, Joshua. I don't speak caveman, remember?" She turned to face him, deftly twirling her hair into a knot at the top of her head.

"You did good."

"I know you haven't seen any of the Rocky movies and even if you had, I wouldn't understand why you would be quoting one in the middle of the night."

"Today." Joshua frowned at her. Why did she always make this so hard?

"Um, when?"

He stifled a frustrated noise. "When you stopped me. With Wheeler. You shouldn't have put yourself in the middle of that, but it was good that you stopped me."

Her words were barely a whisper, eyes dipping to her toes. "You were going to get yourself killed."

"Doesn't matter. Don't do it again." Before she could argue with him, he said, "things with Wheeler are going to get worse."

"So, you just like, have to punch him?" She finished tightening the tie around her bun and scuffled back into the kitchen. The loosely wound hair flopped back and forth on top of her head. When her clumsy hand met the back of one of the dining room chairs, she stopped and fixed her attention on him.

He was looking at her fingers, not her face, but he could feel her eyes on his.

Liv was a very direct person. Joshua found it hard to make eye contact with her. He only met another person's eyes in challenge or defiance so when she looked at him with that gentle expression, he avoided it. But he was getting better at directness every day and he successfully let his gaze flick to hers twice.

"Maybe I'll have to do worse than punch him."

She looked like she wanted to cry again. "They have guns."

"I have guns."

"We can ignore him."

"For now."

Liv's voice cracked when she said, "you could get hurt."

Ah, so that was why she was upset. "You'll find someone to take care of you if something happens to me."

Okay, apparently that wasn't why she was upset. Her jaw dropped and she glared at him so hotly that his face felt warm.

"I'm not worried about who's going to *take care of me*, Joshua." She bit out every word. "I'm worried about *you.*" He could have sworn he heard her mutter "doofus" at the end of that sentence.

*She's worried about **me**?* Oh. Damn. Well, that explained a thing or two.

"Is *that* why you're crying?"

"Duh!" She angrily wiped under her eyes. Joshua was suddenly frustrated by the table separating them. He couldn't move closer to her without being obvious about it. "Look at you! Your eye is the color of an eggplant. They could have hurt you, Joshua. *Really* hurt you."

The slight tremble of her bottom lip shot an uncomfortable pain through his heart. Though he desperately wanted to look away and avoid the sight of her tears, he couldn't. He was totally transfixed by the genuine fear on her face. Fear for *him.*

Why did she care so much if he got hurt? As long as she was in town, she could seek out Flores and the militia could get her settled there. It wasn't the safest option for her, but it would protect her from Wheeler, for a time.

"I'm fine." Joshua wanted to slap himself for such a stupid response. He didn't know what else to say.

Unlike him, Liv had no qualms about coming around the table to get closer to him. She ignored his last statement and the way he flinched away from her hand when she reached out for his face. Her thumb barely touched the skin under his eye as she traced his bruise. Her fingers dropped from his eye to his chin. His hand shot up to grip her wrist when she tried to lower it, her pulse thrumming beneath his thumb.

Everywhere she touched tingled warmly. He wasn't ready for her to stop. Not yet.

But he couldn't read the way her eyes widened or the parting of her lips. Was he crossing a line? Could she touch him but not the other way around? Did he scare her? Was he being too rough? The insecurities swirled into a frenzy of questions, forcing him to release her, his fingers flexing in protest.

"What's going to happen with Wheeler?" she asked softly, saving him from floundering in his own head.

Joshua gritted his teeth. "He wants the farm. You know that part. He wants the town too. That's what he meant when he said I won't always have the upper hand. He's got a lot of men these days and if they could take the militia, they might. Flores is an ally, but I don't know how long he'll be around."

"If Wheeler has so much manpower, why doesn't he just come after the farm? It's a lot of land to cover but they could find it eventually, couldn't they?"

"Eventually. They don't have time for eventually right now. A lot of men need a lot of food. And winter means they'll need shelter too. Next year is when it'll get interesting. We've got to be on our toes," he explained.

"But he won't leave you alone."

No, he wouldn't, especially not now that Joshua revealed his soft spot. Wheeler was looking for leverage today and he found it. Fuck, Joshua was so stupid. He should have seen what was happening. His mistake put Liv in an even more dangerous position than she was already in.

Punching Wheeler was deserved and a long time coming, but it was a rookie move. Now it was obvious that Liv was more than an *arrangement*, as Wheeler put it. Joshua hated the idea of letting such a degrading image of her be the one people saw but it was probably safer for her that way.

Or maybe it wasn't. Not if it gave men like the kind Wheeler associated with the wrong impression. It was hard to know the right way to handle their relationship. She complicated everything.

"He's not going to stop now. He's getting desperate. He wants men who can bolster his winter stores. And he wants men who are well armed and well trained."

"He was serious about you guys being a dream team?"

"If I'd follow his rules, yeah. He knows Pops gave me some tactical training. He might even know what I've got hidden away in the cellar." Just thinking about that had him seething all over again. If Wheeler was telling the truth about Helen, then he knew the farm was a treasure trove for a raider group.

She nodded, covering a yawn. He shouldn't have started this conversation now. Liv would have questions and wouldn't go to bed until they were answered. "If he had something you wanted, would you have joined him?"

"Never. Even if my Pops didn't hate his guts. I don't want anything." That made Liv laugh, probably because she didn't believe it for a second. She had a delicate tinkle of a laugh but somehow it managed to carry across the cabin and fill the whole space with warmth.

"Well good, I don't have to get you a Christmas gift then." The smile slipped from her lips as her countenance shifted.

"I won't let Wheeler dictate what I do." He ran fingers through his beard to compose himself and added, "or what you do."

Joshua met her eyes. Liv was smiling again, and he wasn't entirely sure why, but he was pleased to have earned that smile. It meant he'd done or said something right, finally. She started to ask another question, but her words were lost in a yawn.

"Go to bed."

"But I want to know our plan. What do we do if they take the town?"

Our plan? What do we do? He did his best to ignore the way that made him feel but he couldn't stop hearing her words from earlier. *Your problems are my problems now.*

"It's not happening tonight. We can worry about it later."

I can worry about it later. You don't have to worry about it at all.

Liv turned and took a few steps toward the bed, then paused. "Do you think people like Wheeler will ever get better? Or did they just break when the world ended? There are still good people, but what if that's not enough to make the world good again?"

"Folks like Wheeler were always broken. They just couldn't do much damage when there was enough authority to keep 'em in check," he replied. "Maybe the world was never that good."

"I think you're wrong, Joshua. The world was always good. Well, I guess there was evil, but I think the world always had *more* good." She hesitated. "Or maybe I'm the one that's wrong. Maybe I just wanted to see good."

Liv shrugged her shoulders in subtle defeat, finishing her journey to the bed. Joshua was disappointed in his answer. It didn't seem to be what she wanted to hear. He wasn't in the habit of telling people what they wanted to hear but he could make an exception for her, couldn't he?

"If you're looking for good, I reckon you'll find it."

As she slipped under the covers, she said, "I knew you weren't as pessimistic as you pretend to be."

Only when it comes to you.

23

Stolen Moments

"Joshua, I can't." I squeezed my eyes shut so hard I saw stars.

"You can."

"I really can't."

"Put your damn finger on the trigger, Olivia." Ooh, I was Olivia. Joshua was really getting impatient with me now. I warned him this wouldn't go well.

After his brawl with Tommy Wheeler, he was adamant that I finally get those shooting lessons he kept promising. If something happened in town, I needed to know how to protect myself. Not a pleasant thought. It implied that Joshua would be injured. Or worse.

I readjusted my grip on the handgun and cracked my lids to peek at him. "I'm scared."

Joshua stomped over to me, his palm engulfing my hands as he readjusted my hold. He used his free hand to pry my curled pointer finger open and slip it onto the trigger. Then he moved it to my shoulder, bracing me for the kickback. "Squeeze slowly, feel for the click. Just like we talked about."

"Okay." I exhaled a shaky breath, letting the warmth of Joshua's skin soothe my nerves.

"Liv—" Whatever admonishment he was about to give me was cut off by the loud crack of the Glock. I tried to remove my finger from the trigger and let go but he held firm, keeping me in place. "Good. Again."

"Joshua."

"No whining. Do it again."

I squeezed the trigger. My whole upper body jolted back into Joshua's chest. He removed his hand from beneath mine and put both on my shoulders, urging me to continue. This time I actually aimed the way he showed me. I didn't hit anything. Even when I'd used every bullet in the gun, I didn't hit anything.

"What's the point of this? I couldn't hit someone if they were standing five feet in front of me. I'm just wasting your bullets." I set the gun on the wooden table beside me and wiped clammy palms on my jeans.

"Your aim is never going to get better if you don't practice." Joshua stepped around me and opened a box of ammo. "Reload."

I wanted to complain about how hard it was to shove the bullets in the stupid magazine, but I was already on Joshua's last nerve and not eager to push it. Halfway through my failed attempt with bullet number one, he took the magazine from me and demonstrated how to do it. Again.

It wasn't that I hadn't been paying attention. It was difficult. All of this was hard, and it made me feel nervous and I didn't want to do it.

"We're not going in until you hit something, so don't even start," he said, reading my thoughts and cutting me off before I had a chance to try talking my way out of this for the five hundredth time.

"It'll be dark before then."

Joshua clenched and unclenched his jaw. For how frustrated he was, he was doing a remarkably good job of keeping his tone even. "It won't be if you get your skinny ass over here and aim that gun."

"Will I be excused if I shoot myself in the foot?" I asked sweetly as I took the gun and fiddled with my hand positioning.

"No." He was behind me again, wrapping his arms around mine to fix my hold.

Maybe shooting lessons weren't all bad. Joshua's hands were on mine, his arms draped easily over my shoulders as if this was our normal and he didn't act like he'd been electrocuted every time I touched him. He stood so close that I could feel his breath ruffling my hair. I was tempted to keep sucking at shooting so he would keep holding me.

These are the kinds of thoughts that end in heartbreak. My heart wasn't keen on heeding my head's warning. The war between the two was one as old as time and much to my dismay, my head was losing.

Of course, what I felt was only a teeny tiny, itty bitty crush. The stupid kind that made butterflies take flight in my stomach when he was close to me, even though we'd spent weeks standing close to each other before. Nothing more. Nothing *serious.* Didn't a girl have the right to entertain a crush in the end of the world?

How could I not when every day I saw flashes of a man much kinder and more understanding than who he pretended to be? Glimpses of someone who was hurt when he was vulnerable, someone that lost his way because of it.

Anyway, it didn't matter how I felt because it would amount to nothing. It wasn't as if Joshua was going to reciprocate those feelings. Was he even capable? He probably viewed it as too frivolous. Emotions were useless, after all.

As far as I was concerned, that made my infatuation perfectly innocent. I'd grown to enjoy his company. And yeah, he was attractive. I didn't normally go for tall and muscly, but Joshua wasn't a gym rat. He was just strong enough to do the things he had to, like chop wood and work the land. He had a nice butt too.

Sure, I noticed. I noticed a few times. It was hard not to notice a guy when you shared six hundred square feet of cabin with him. Not much room to avoid him.

"You remember how to aim?"

"Yup." I swallowed dryly.

"Keep your eyes open. Don't you drop that damn gun after you pull the trigger." His hands retreated, one of them taking place on my shoulder to help with recoil.

"Got it. Eyes open, no dropping." I exhaled slowly, centered my feet, and aimed.

I went through another magazine without hitting anything. The sun was already behind the trees and the evening was quickly growing dim. I was hungry and grumpy, and Joshua wasn't far behind. Stubborn as he was, he wouldn't let hunger, or a bad mood break his rule. No going inside until I hit something.

Fine. It was going to be a long night for both of us.

Or so I thought until I carefully aimed on my next try and successfully hit the wooden target directly in front of me. Then I felt like I was the one taking the bullet, haphazardly dropping the gun on the table, and doubling over with a familiar sensation of panic.

My head swam with images of all the ways I'd seen people die. Bullets weren't such a bad way to go compared to machetes and fists, but they still killed people. Innocent, helpless people. People that just wanted to survive. The stutter in my heart quickly became a tremble in my hands and I couldn't get away from the sight of that target fast enough.

I wrenched the noise-cancelling earmuffs from my head and whirled out of Joshua's reach, unable to hear whatever praise was coming from his mouth. Tears stung my eyes, making twin waterfalls of my face before I could stop them. I gave Joshua my back, hugging myself and desperately trying to catch my breath.

If I was aiming that gun when I truly needed to use it, I wouldn't be shooting at wood and aluminum. I would be shooting at another person.

"Where are you going?" Joshua boomed when I scurried away from him. "What the hell are you doing?"

"I need a minute." I managed to gasp out. "Please, just give me a minute."

Of course, he didn't.

Joshua stalked after me, cutting off my retreat and standing so close that I was eye level with his chest. I braced myself for the inevitable, "what's wrong with you?" It didn't come. He just stared, helpless. That wasn't much better. I had no interest in being a spectacle right now.

"What's going on?" His voice was surprisingly gentle.

I covered my face with my hands, muffling the words, "I can't."

"You can't what? You hit the target. What's the problem?"

I risked a glance up at him. "I can't shoot someone, Joshua."

"You might have to." Not exactly comforting but I didn't expect him to comfort me. "I need you to know how to do this, Liv."

"I couldn't live with myself. I—" I choked back a sob. "I hate this. I hate this world. I hate how we have to live. I hate the idea of hurting someone."

He stood over me through every one of my halting breaths, scowling and uncertain. I had to resist the urge to reach out for him. I wished he would just hug me like a normal person. I needed some way to distance myself from this...whatever it was. Another anxiety attack? Did I have PTSD? How would I know? How would I fix it? A hug really felt like it would fix it.

"I didn't yell at you." Joshua finally spoke. I gave him a teary, stupid look, clearly not following. "You still going to make me that casserole?"

Was he really thinking about food right now? I *did* promise to make dinner if he promised not to get snippy during our shooting lesson. He must have been really excited about that chicken-whatever casserole because he was unusually patient today.

"Got some blackberry wine in the cellar. Back of the shelf where I keep the canned fruit, to the right. Go grab it. I'll get this cleaned up." So, this was how he was going to react? Joshua was just going to ignore my feelings.

I harrumphed to myself, deliberately stomping up the porch steps. By the time I climbed off the last ladder rung in the cellar, I was barely sniffling. I pulled what I hoped was the right bottle of wine—Joshua didn't label any of his homemade alcohol concoctions—off the shelf, realizing that perhaps he wasn't being as insensitive as I assumed.

Joshua wasn't the nurturing type. He wouldn't coddle me when I was upset. Since he didn't know how to fix the problem, he did the next best thing: averted my attention. I enjoyed making dinner and he rarely ceded control of the kitchen enough to let me cook any dish on my own. I'd begged him to let me try this recipe even though he only had a few chicken breasts to spare.

Once again, he was being nice. Gentle in his own unusual way. Aw shoot, why did he have to be nice to me? It wasn't going to help the whole catching feelings thing one bit.

We didn't talk much over dinner. Joshua seemed to be lost in his thoughts, sipping wine more often than he took a bite of food. I wasn't much better, though I barely touched the wine. It was clearly one of those acquired tastes.

By the time we were clearing the table, I felt exhausted in a way that had nothing to do with any work I'd done today. My heart was heavy and my whole person felt shaky. I just wanted to curl up under a blanket and stay there indefinitely.

Joshua didn't say anything when I quietly retreated to the bed and pulled the quilt all the way up to my cheek.

Joshua

Joshua was sick of feeling guilty. How the hell was he supposed to know shooting a gun would give Liv a meltdown? And why the hell did he feel so bad about it? The whole thing was a mess. He had no clue how he could have done it differently, but he needed to figure it out because she *had* to know how to shoot.

Leaving her unprotected and unable to defend herself was not an option. Not after what happened in town.

Liv understood the basics of gun safety but had clearly never actually held one before. Her form was terrible, which left him needing to correct her.

Forced him to touch her.

There had to be a more hands off way to instruct her. Joshua would never let someone in his personal space like that and for good reason. It made him notice weird details about Liv that shouldn't matter to him. Like how her hair smelled faintly of strawberries. Or how she fit between his arms. He was noticing those types of things a little too often lately.

Even worse, Joshua kept catching himself making excuses. He was not the type of man to make excuses and yet he did exactly that this evening. Shooting instructions were supposed to be about equipping Liv to be a safe companion to keep by his side. He couldn't protect her twenty four-seven.

Of course, shooting instructions also gave him justification for all the ways he wanted to touch her. The perfect out for his behavior.

It was only curiosity that made him do it, he insisted quietly to himself. Curiosity about what, he wasn't sure. How Liv's hair smelled? How her hands felt in his? Those were not the types of thoughts he'd ever given himself permission to think about a woman. It was a waste of time, and it would lead him to nothing good.

Liv suddenly made a startled noise from the corner where the bed was shrouded in shadows. Joshua tilted his head, listening for what he knew was the sound of a nightmare. She had them less frequently than she used to but given her dramatic reaction to something as simple as firing a gun, it was safe to assume he'd dredged up a memory that was best kept untouched in her mind. Cue the second round of guilt.

There shouldn't be any guilt. He wasn't happy that he'd upset her, but it had to be done. The world was ending, and life wasn't going to get any easier from here on out. Sooner or later Liv was going to see or hear something that set her off. She'd have to be able to deal with it or risk freezing up in a situation that required action. Better for her to face that now, with him, than when someone was trying to hurt her. At least with Joshua she would be safe.

The noises from the bed stopped abruptly. Sheets rustled as Liv sat up. Joshua quickly averted his eyes, pretending that he hadn't been watching her toss and turn in her sleep. After a stretch of quiet, he heard her feet shuffling along the wood floor. She stepped over to his chair and slid down to the rug without a word. Her back rested against one of the arms, her shoulder lightly leaned into his thigh. Though the room was dim as the fire died down, he could easily see how violently she was shaking.

When she didn't speak or move for more than five minutes, Joshua leaned forward in his chair and whispered, "Liv?" It always disturbed him when she got quiet.

"I'm just cold," she rushed out. Her tremulous tone said otherwise.

"Right."

Joshua waited a beat before climbing from his chair to kneel in front of the fire. He added two more logs, stoking the flames until they were blazing and bright. Then he settled on the floor next to Liv, adjusting his position so he could sit shoulder to shoulder with her—or as close as possible with their height difference. She didn't even look up at him. Her gaze fixed on a spot on the floor, unfocused as she replayed whatever images were haunting her.

Desperate to bring her back to the present, Joshua reached for her hands. She blinked confused green eyes at him but didn't stop him. Joshua cupped his palms around hers, brought them to his lips, and blew hot breath onto her fingers. They really were freezing.

He traded off between blowing on them and using his thumbs to rub the pressure points between her fingers and wrists. The barest smile touched her lips, and she scooted close enough that their hips touched. He didn't let her go, even when she stopped shaking.

"Better?" he asked softly.

She nodded, her smile widening a fraction. "Much better."

They sat in silence until the fire had almost completely devoured the bottom log, her hands a notable weight in his lap, head slowly easing onto his shoulder. It felt...comfortable. It felt normal, which was strange because this was so far outside of what was normal for him.

"How come you're so good at that?" Her quiet question startled him.

"Good at what?"

"Making the panic go away."

Joshua stilled, his tongue paralyzed. He debated with himself until the silence felt awkward, finally blurting, "I used to have them. Panic attacks, I mean."

"Really?" She was incredulous. "I can't imagine you being afraid of anything."

"Plenty of things scared me when I was younger." And John was at the center of all of them.

"What made you panic?"

"The dark."

"Because you have no lights in your house?" Liv lifted her head from his shoulder, her eyes jumping back and forth between his.

"Because I was alone in the dark. Sometimes for twenty four hours." Sometimes longer if John was feeling particularly vindictive. As a boy Joshua paid for his own sins and those of both his parents.

"*What?* Why?"

"Punishment." His throat worked. Why the fuck was he telling her this? Why was he willingly giving her memories that he himself couldn't even stomach?

Joshua forced himself to look at her, expecting pity on her sweet face. What he got instead was fire. "I think I hate your father." Her brow creased, lips pinched into an angry line.

It felt like the wrong time to smile but he couldn't hold it in. She was so unpredictable. "You've never met him."

"Yes, and I'm glad. He sounds cruel. I can't believe anyone would compare you to him." She slipped her bottom lip between her teeth, softly adding, "Sorry. Only a little, but I am."

I can't believe anyone would compare you to him. Did she know what she was saying? What it meant to hear that, albeit from someone who didn't know John?

Since Liv arrived more than three months earlier, Joshua had been in an almost constant state of frustration because she made him feel like John. The way she cowered away from him in the beginning, the way he made her cry with his inability to be gentle, to be understanding.

He'd seen that image before, a sweet, frail woman sitting on the edge of that same bed, shoulders shaking with silent tears. He'd done that to her the way his father did it to Helen all those years ago.

Not on purpose. Never on purpose. For reasons he couldn't explain, Joshua made an effort for her. He tried to be better, to be just a little softer, he really did. Problem was, he did it terribly. The first thing in years that he wasn't good at. He hated it. Joshua didn't fail. Not at anything but this.

For once, his failure didn't matter. He wouldn't be punished for it, ridiculed, or even pitied. Liv saw that he tried and that was enough for her. It made him feel like he was enough.

I can't believe anyone would compare you to him.

Eventually he caught Liv in a glance, ready to ask her if she thought she should go back to sleep. Morning would come too soon, and they would both be exhausted. She was way ahead of him, her eyes closed, lips parted to release soft breaths.

"Liv?" he whispered.

He wiggled his arm away from her head, hoping the movement would wake her. All it did was pin it awkwardly between them. He rested it on his thigh, then raised it over his head with the intention of setting it on the chair, then was finally going to give up and shake Liv awake when she shifted on her own.

It was like she became a liquid, melting into him. Her hips swiveled to drop her thigh over his, her arms constricting around his ribs. The movement rocked her head forward until it was nestled into his chest, the tip of her nose teasing his collar bone.

She certainly wasn't cold now. Even through his shirt, he could feel the searing heat of her palm on his stomach. Her breath was warm in the crook of his neck. A heady rush tickled up his body, an electric current jolting through him.

Liv was like moonshine, burning and soothing all at once. She heated him, intoxicated him, swirled his mind until clarity was a distant memory. She was thrilling and she was dangerous, the most dangerous thing under the small roof of his cabin.

That comfortable feeling evaporated, leaving him in a sudden state of panic. Joshua desperately needed to get away from her, to find some balance again.

Only, he couldn't get himself to move. Not when she stirred, rearranging herself for a third time, brushing her nose along his collar bone and murmuring his name in the softest sigh. Something inside of him broke at that sound, something that had been teetering on the edge for months. Was it his willpower? The wall that kept him safely isolated and his emotions in check?

Joshua warred with himself. He needed to send Liv to bed, to put space between them. That safe five feet of space he was always working so hard to keep. That space he shattered today with the excuse of teaching her how to protect herself.

That was only half his motivation for shooting lessons. He was being selfish. Secretly, quietly selfish. He was doing it again right now. Every second that he sat there holding Liv, refusing to let her go even though his sanity and all their established normalcy depended on it, he was being selfish.

When in his life had he ever allowed himself anything? When did he ever get to be selfish if not now, when it felt so important?

Joshua sank further against his chair, settling his arm over Liv and resting his hand on the small of her back. With every minute that ticked by he expected her to shoot awake, accusation and confusion marring her pale face. His thoughts felt so loud and clumsy that he feared they would wake her. They didn't. Nothing did. Liv stayed right where she was, comfortably tucked against him.

Comfortable. Such an unfamiliar sensation. It wasn't at all what he'd anticipated intimacy to be like. Quite the opposite. Discomfort was almost always what he got from touch. He hadn't been hardened off to affection like everyone else. Then again, he'd never really tried touching anyone like this. Tenderly. He'd never let anyone close enough for it.

Joshua felt the gentle rise and fall of Liv's chest on his and for one breath let himself admit that he was enjoying this. That he *wanted* it, wanted to close that manufactured distance between them. Those thoughts were shuttered before they had a chance to become substantial. She'd made it clear what she thought of his character—harsh, insensitive, and too rough—and being nice to him didn't mean those opinions had changed.

Liv was nice to everyone.

There wasn't really much he could give her, anyway. Joshua was good for taking care of her most basic needs but not her emotional ones. Liv liked sweet words and kind gestures. He could do neither on purpose. Joshua wasn't built for stolen moments in the dead of night. He didn't deserve them. Maybe he helped Liv when she needed it most but beyond that, he wasn't a good person. Not like what she wanted him to be.

And why should he change simply to be what she wanted? If he wasn't enough as he was, it didn't matter. There was no use even pursuing that quiet craving. Not if it was destined for failure. Joshua could live with unfulfilled desires. That was nothing new for him.

What about this, though? Had she not sought him out? To soothe the fear of nightmares?

Sure, in a moment of terror, in the middle of the night, when she was sleep-dazed and adrenalized all at once. Liv was accustomed to tactile inter-action, regular affection from people that she trusted. This was an instinctive response to a deficit of physical contact. In sleep she wasn't conscious of her actions or who it was that she wrapped her body around.

But she said my name.

Sleep was as intoxicating as alcohol. If he was going to discount her kiss that night she had her first drink, he would have to discount this too.

That didn't mean it had to end just yet. Liv was curled in his lap, palm resting over his heart as if this was always how she slept. An odd wispy sensation flickered inside of him, one he almost dared call satisfaction.

"What the hell are you doin', boy?" Joshua squeezed his eyes shut. His father's words were not welcome in his head, yet he rarely succeeded in pushing them out. As the hour grew late and the fire dimmed, he would hear that hoarse, alcohol-laden voice echo as if he was still in that adjacent chair. Pops was dead though and there was someone very much unlike him sitting with Joshua now.

Liv's breath breezed in that steady rhythm Joshua had grown accustomed to hearing in the quiet hours of darkness. Her face was veiled by a curtain of blonde hair, but he knew that her eyes were closed. He could just barely see the dip of her brow as she frowned at something in her dreams.

Some nights she looked so serious when she slept. Not that he was in the habit of watching her sleep. Then again, how often did one have to do something for it to be considered a habit?

*What the hell **am** I doing?*

Joshua had asked himself that question too many times to count over the last three months. Even as he carried her back to his home on that very first day, the question was playing on repeat in his mind until it nearly drove him mad. He didn't know what he was doing or why.

That would have made his father furious. Pops was careful to teach him not to be impulsive. "Impulsive gets you killed. You better think before you act, boy. Every move could be your last when you're surviving."

Pops never was very good at living his own lessons though. John Sutton only possessed a modicum of prudence and that was when he was sober. If he'd been in the bottle, anything was possible. The man was cruel at his best, downright evil at his worst.

Folks might not see it, but father and son had their differences. Pops would have left Liv to die. Learning that Joshua didn't would make him livid.

I can't believe anyone would compare you to him.

She saw it.

Just because he wasn't his father didn't mean there weren't remnants of him embedded deep in Joshua's psyche. He remembered looking down at her prone form in his arms, analyzing her objectively, the way he'd been taught.

No, he was being more than objective. It was a brief moment of weakness, the kind that could have been lethal. Joshua stared at her thin, dirty face and he saw redemption. The men he killed to save her weren't the first lives he took. They might not be the last. Doing what it took to survive came with a price, the kind that weighed heavily on a soul.

It wasn't guilt that Joshua felt. Rather it was the absence of guilt that kept him awake most nights. What reason did he have to feel guilty if he was defending himself? He knew he should, though. The minuscule part of himself that was still that young boy, raised obedient and devout, felt like God was judging him.

Then out of nowhere came Liv, asking for his help when everyone else shunned him or tried to take from him. She was innocent, maybe the very last innocent person left. He saw her as an opportunity to do something good, to balance the scales and pay for his sins.

Liv was one life in exchange for many others, but she *deserved* to live. The world would have been a worse place without her.

But she was so weak and defenseless. Useful for only two purposes, John would say. If she couldn't survive on her own, then she didn't deserve to live. She would only be a burden. That word lingered in Joshua's thoughts during those first weeks with her. It was because of his father that Joshua treated her as one. That was how John taught him to care for others.

What did it matter to him if he had a burden on his shoulders though? Survival was already a burden. Joshua had nothing to lose.

There wasn't a good explanation for the way he treated her during that first month, other than the persistent poison that was John's influence still filling his veins.

It wasn't fair to blame it *all* on that. Joshua was mean and suspicious simply because she made him uncomfortable. That had to be a reason not to trust someone, right?

That confusing weightless feeling in his chest was instinct telling him to be wary. Joshua trusted his instincts. Only now, he was realizing he'd thoroughly misinterpreted them. It wasn't because she was after anything that Liv made him nervous.

It should have been obvious when it bothered him that he made her nervous too.

Then again, he made everyone nervous. He always had. As a boy, long before he grew to be unusually tall and unapproachable, people disliked him. Some of it was his father's reputation, but the other children saw it too. Joshua was different in some indefinable way. It must have carried on his scent. It made people avoid eye contact and hurry past him, like he was a predator that might decide he was hungry.

That was the real reason he was alone. And that was the reason he was alive.

Until Liv, that had been fine. Being intimidating was important to his survival. But it started to rankle when he made *her* shy away from him. Joshua viewed Liv differently than most people, maybe because he knew she wasn't capable of doing him any real harm. He didn't need to be liked by her, but he wasn't keen on being disliked by her either. He didn't want her to see him as *other*, though he knew he was.

Joshua hadn't been made like normal people and when he was with Liv, it showed.

Just then, it didn't matter. In the light of morning, she might shrink away from the memory or her hands in his but here, in the perpetual darkness, there were no barriers left between them.

A little longer, he told himself. A little more time in this moment that he wasn't supposed to have. A truly stolen moment, taken from an alternate world where Joshua hadn't been raised to be cold and empty, where Liv didn't long for a clamorous city street and bright lights. For people.

Just a little longer. He rested his chin on top of her head and closed his eyes.

Cold and Confused

The moment I had the urge to open my eyes, I knew I wasn't in bed. I shouldn't have been surprised. Not long after falling asleep I was tossing and turning, haunted by some terrible nightmare I couldn't shake. The worst part about nightmares was closing my eyes and falling right back into them, which was why I decided to stay awake rather than lying there and hoping it passed.

I expected to sit up from a heap on the rug in front of the hearth or find myself crammed into the least-loved recliner. I expected to wake up just about anywhere except *on top of Joshua*. I carefully readjusted my head and yup, that was a muscly chest under me. My arms were hugged around him like he was a giant, firm body pillow.

I must have woken in some alternate universe because he had his arms around me too. His cheek was resting on my forehead and by all appearances, he was asleep. I'd never actually seen Joshua sleep, but I knew he had to at some point. No matter what he claimed, no one was awake forever.

In sleep he was uncharacteristically peaceful. All that tension was finally gone from his body, the alert and wary expression that lingered on his face faded. I never would have thought the word cozy could apply to Joshua, but he was exactly that. Cozy and so warm beneath me. I twisted my head to get a better look at him. He was handsome when he wasn't scowling.

I settled my head back onto his chest with a sigh, then immediately jolted back to reality.

How did I end up here? As much as I wanted to just lie back down and enjoy this, I was being pretty ridiculous. Joshua wasn't a cuddler. Joshua wasn't a *toucher*. He didn't even like shaking hands, so why in the world would he suddenly be okay with me sleeping in his lap? Did I sleepwalk here? Did I get up from the floor, half asleep and confused, and flop on top of him?

Yeah, sure, and then Joshua, who barely slept a wink because he was so on edge, just didn't wake up.

I wished that I could freeze time and hold onto this moment because I knew it might be the only one I would ever get with him, but I couldn't. It had to end. I had no idea what was going on, but I was reasonably worried that Joshua would wake up, find me latched onto him like a barnacle, and freak out. Maybe he'd send me away for violating his personal space so thoroughly.

The problem was that extricating myself from his arms and tip toeing back to the bed would require ninja skills. I slowly—very, very slowly—eased into an upright position. His head lolled to the side, resting against the arm of the chair instead. When I tried to lift one of his arms from around my hip he groaned and tightened his hold, dragging me right back to where I started.

Any attempt to loosen his arms only made him cling to me tighter. By the fourth try I was almost having a difficulty breathing because of how hard he was squeezing me. This was getting ridiculous. I might as well wake him and face the firing squad.

I sat up again, pulling against him as hard as I could. "Joshua?"

His dark eyes snapped open. In one breath he was upright, pinning my head to his chest with one hand, and thrusting the other in front of him. My gaze trailed down his outstretched arm to realize he was pointing a *gun* at the darkness in front of us. I hadn't expected a *literal* firing squad. Where did he even pull that from?

"What are you doing?" I squirmed, trying to sit up.

Joshua's eyes were wild, his breath coming too rapidly. He didn't respond, just scanned the room, his gun hand tracking his gaze.

"Joshua!" I said louder because he was gripping me too hard, and it was starting to hurt. "There's no one here. You were asleep."

"Fuck!" He muttered, releasing me, and dragging his other arm back to return the gun to wherever it came from. I moved with his diaphragm when he sucked in a ragged breath.

"Are you okay?" I twisted to look at him. "Jeez, remind me never to sneak up on you when you're sleeping."

Joshua's eyes still had that deer in the headlights look. In the dim light of the living room, with the fire casting shadows onto his face, they looked closer to black than brown. He frowned at me, then at his hand which was loosely resting on the back of my neck, then back at me.

Joshua practically leapt away. He shifted out from under me, dumping me unceremoniously onto the floor and backing up until his shoulder hit the fireplace mantle. He rubbed his palms over his tired face and muttered another curse.

"You were cold," he said stiffly.

"I remember." I scooted upright and put my hands up like I was placating a scared animal.

"You were cold, and you fell asleep." His voice was extra gruff and now he was refusing to look at me. "I tried to wake you."

"Okay," I was trying to urge him to keep talking but he only dipped his chin to his chest then gave me his back.

Joshua braced himself against the fireplace with one arm and let out a frustrated sound. I rose from the floor, approaching him cautiously. I thought he would be upset with me. He seemed more upset with himself.

"Are you okay?" I risked resting a gentle hand on his arm. Bad idea. Joshua flinched away like I'd burned him. I quickly retracted my hand. "Sorry, I didn't mean to—"

He whirled, startling a small squeak out of me. Warm hands travelled up my neck to cup my face, his eyes blazing in that delicious chocolate color. So soft and vulnerable. So not like Joshua. For a hopeful second, I thought he was going to kiss me. Then he leveled his gaze to mine and ground out, "I don't want you to be sorry."

I gaped at him, not sure if I should touch him back. Not sure of anything anymore. Before gathering myself enough to respond, Joshua was jerking away from me and stomping toward the door.

"Where are you going?" I asked as he yanked his jacket on like it had personally offended him.

"To get firewood," he grunted, stuffing sockless feet into his boots.

I looked between the front door and the almost full pile of firewood by the hearth. "But you have more than enough..." my sentence trailed off as he stormed out the door and disappeared into the night.

I stood stunned in the living room for almost two minutes. When there was no sign that Joshua would be back anytime soon, I sank down into his chair to wait. Kuna, who had started pacing in front of the door as soon as Joshua left, came to rest her chin on my lap and whined softly.

I ran my fingers over the soft fur around her ears and said, "your guess is as good as mine."

No matter how late it got, I wasn't ready to go back to bed before I had a chance to talk to Joshua. Whatever happened between us felt significant. Until tonight, I'd never seen him look panicked before. Did I do something wrong? Did he think he did something wrong? I wanted to know how he felt. Was there a chance that I was totally off this whole time and Joshua might feel something for me?

Without a clock it was hard to keep track of the time but at least thirty minutes had to have ticked by without Joshua returning. The woodshed was a four minute walk at most. Not that I believed he was actually getting firewood.

I was hoping he would take whatever time he needed to cool off then come back and talk to me. Silly, I know. Joshua clearly didn't want to talk about this. He was avoiding me and this conversation.

I tried to ignore the sting of that as I made my way back to bed and wrapped myself in a quilt. For a tiny moment I thought things might be changing between us, but as quickly as that spark ignited, Joshua snuffed it out. I risked one more glance at the door. He was gone.

I recognized a long time ago that I would probably never understand him, I just hadn't realized that confusion could be painful. I could live with it if Joshua never took an interest in me. Being his friend felt like a huge accomplishment. I only wished that friendship with him made more sense. One minute he was cold as ice and the next he was holding me while we slept.

That felt like more than friends. But who was I kidding? Joshua probably didn't even consider me his friend.

Tortured Silence

"Wow, a few months ago you wouldn't trust me with my own tampons and now you're letting me hold scissors an inch from your neck." I gave Joshua my best attempt at a grin, desperately trying to keep my tone casual as I ran fingers through the front of his hair.

"Should I be worried?" He raised his eyebrows in mock alarm.

"Oh yes. This was my plan all along: spend months convincing you I'm trustworthy enough to cut your hair so I can kill you with dull scissors and take your stuff."

"Those scissors aren't dull."

Some of my tension eased and I managed a real laugh. "Okay, don't make me laugh or I might actually stab you."

"So, I should be worried."

"Only if you care about how even your hair is in the back."

"Lucky for you, I can't see the back."

Joshua was torturing me. That was the only way I could make sense of this downright cheerful behavior from him.

Almost two weeks had passed with barely a word exchanged between us. For a brief time, I thought I was going to go mad. The morning after Joshua disappeared to "get firewood" and never came back, I woke to find a note on the table that read "went hunting." There were a few scribbled tasks for me to look after while he was gone.

That day dragged on into a dark and empty evening. I had no concept of how long hunting a deer would take and when the evening faded to night with no sign of him, I began to worry. That entire night I sat awake in his chair, watching the fire like he usually did. The next morning, I almost screamed when I stepped out with Kuna to see Joshua approaching the outdoor well pump with blood staining his arms and dotting his white shirt.

"Not mine." Those were the only two words he grunted to me the entire day.

It continued like that. Joshua avoiding eye contact, avoiding conversation, even avoiding sitting at the table with me to eat. He had the excuse of being busy processing and storing meat for those firsts few days but when more than a week passed in silence, the message he was trying to communicate was clear; he wanted me to leave him alone and forget about whatever happened before he left.

Then this morning, everything returned to normal. The clanging of cast iron and the cracking of eggs went off like my alarm clock. Joshua and I had breakfast together and he talked to me about what needed to happen to put the garden to rest for winter. And the cherry on top? As we were clearing the table, he casually asked me to cut his hair.

I should have been mad at him for giving me a ten day silent treatment but I didn't have it in me to be angry. More than anything, I felt defeated. I'd foolishly let myself believe that there could be something more between us. Joshua was hot and cold, short tempered and emotionally unavailable. We just happened to be going through one of his longer heat waves when that unexpected cold front blew in and destroyed any notion, I had of connecting with him.

It was time to let all that go. He kept me fed and sheltered, asking nothing in return. That alone was an amazing gift, and I should be grateful.

"The second worst time I ever got grounded was when I cut my own hair." I reminisced aloud as I made my first snip.

"You got in trouble for cutting your hair?" He scoffed.

"I made it ugly. My mother hated ugly."

"She called you ugly?"

"No, she called my hair ugly. I did it a week before this big dinner party she was throwing, and she was mortified. All her friends were going to judge her."

"Why would she be embarrassed if *your* hair looked bad?"

"My bad behavior reflected poorly on her. Anyway, I tried to cut my bangs and ended up looking like a space alien with a giant forehead. She paid fifty bucks for her stylist to fix it and that barely helped, so she grounded me for a month."

"They punished you for being independent? They should have encouraged you." Joshua would not get along with my parents.

I paused my cutting to entertain that daydream. I couldn't even picture him standing in the foyer of my parent's ostentatious house. It would be hilarious to see the way my mother's face scrunched up as she took in Joshua's appearance. He was the kind of man she would call "rural" with more than a drop of venom on her tongue.

I snickered to myself. He'd probably track mud all over her marble floors.

"Independent? That was a bad word in my parent's household. All they wanted was obedient."

"You must have been grounded a lot then." He chuckled, actually chuckled!

I smiled at the unexpected sound and pinched a lock of hair between my fingers before clipping an inch off. "Nope. I rarely got in trouble."

"Yeah, right."

"It's true. I was docile and well-trained." He twisted to look back at me. "Hey, hold still. I've got sharp blades pointed at your head, remember?"

"Sounds boring." Joshua grumbled then added, "sounds like you're lying to me too because obedient is not a word I would use to describe you."

"Oh, come on. I do what I'm told."

"Only after arguing about, it for twenty minutes," he accused.

I threw the accusation right back at him. "You bring that out. I don't argue with anyone else."

And I never enjoyed arguing until I started doing it with you.

"So, it's my fault you're surly?"

"I am *not* surly. You must be talking about yourself." I scoffed. "Besides, you need someone to disagree with you. I'm doing you a favor. It wouldn't be good for you to walk around thinking you run the world."

I'd finished the back of his hair and moved in front of him. He looked up at me, chocolate brown eyes fixed intently on mine. Joshua never met my gaze, with the exception of when he was fuming. This was so unlike him and after two weeks of apathy from him it caught me completely off guard. The intensity in his expression gave me chills.

My lips parted for quick, shallow breaths. I couldn't explain what happened in that short moment, but I might never forget it. Something passed between us, some feeling or vibe or I don't what. Joshua was so intensely serious. There seemed to be words he was trying to say without speaking. My thumb moved without my consent, brushing along his cheekbone until it met the curled hair of his sideburns.

I caught myself doing it and quickly lowered my hand, staring at it like it was a foreign object. "I'm going to miss a spot if you keep moving your head."

"I won't mind." His voice was quiet and gruff.

"Do you want me to trim your beard too?" I still had my eyes down, but I ran my free hand through the coarse hair on his face. I shouldn't have. I couldn't stop myself. I wanted to touch him again. I wanted to feel that strange fluttering in my chest that came only when my skin met his.

"Nah, it's good winter insulation. Anyway, I can see that part."

"Right." I nodded much more rapidly than before and finished up on the left side of his head. "Okay, let's see you."

I pulled each side of his hair down to make sure it was even. I chewed my lip in concentration, snipped some more on the left, chewed more, snipped more, and then finally set the scissors on the folding table and clapped my hands together.

"Hey, it doesn't look half bad."

"Only half bad, huh?" A teasing grin curved one side of his mouth; something I thought this man's face wasn't capable of making.

"You think you're pretty funny, do you?" I crossed my arms and stuck my tongue out at him.

"You laughed so I'd say you do too."

"I think I did okay. Go see for yourself." I pointed to Joshua's old room where he kept the full length mirror.

He shook clippings loose from his hair. "I trust you."

"You do?" I hadn't intended to doubt the statement out loud, but I blurted the question before I could stop myself.

"'Course." He shrugged, as if I should have known he had unequivocal faith in me and yanked his shirt up over his head.

Now I was the one staring at him. He marched off the porch and into the yard, snapping the shirt into the air to shake the hair off. I hovered in the doorway, watched the muscles on his shoulders flex with the movement, and did my best not to drool. I broke from my trance and busied myself cleaning off the chair and collecting my tools before he noticed me. If I was going to fawn over him, it should at least be in secret.

When Joshua came back up the stairs, he had his shirt slung over his shoulder. I swallowed dryly with another glance at him from the front. The contours of Joshua's chest were outlined by hair as coarse and dark as the locks that decorated his head. The patches of fuzz were like a blank connect-the-dots puzzle, highlighting all the places I wanted to touch and all the places in between that I would draw lines to with my fingertips.

Good grief, I need to find a hobby.

"Nice job, Squirrel," Joshua said, facing the stove.

I swallowed again—apparently, he had no intention of putting his shirt back on—and dragged the chair back into the kitchen. "Glad you approve."

When I made no move to serve myself lunch, he twisted to glance at me. "You just gonna stand there?"

"Huh? No. Sorry." I shook my head.

"Stop that."

"Right. Not sorry."

"Liv?" Joshua set his bowl on the table and took a half step in my direction.

"Aren't you cold?" I asked, failing at nonchalance.

"Is that what you're worried about?"

Well, at least I looked worried and not—I don't know, wanton?

"Better?" I almost jumped when I realized how close he'd gotten. I blinked at the half-buttoned flannel, at the still visible hair between his pecs, then up at his face. His dark brows knitted together. "Livvy?"

"Yes. Better. Sorry." God, I was starting to sound like him.

"Stop apologizing," he gritted out.

I forced a small chuckle and brushed past him, steeling myself so that my fluttering heart would calm down before my cheeks flushed pink. "Sorr—Nope. Not sorry. I guess I need to eat. My brain is all scrambled."

Joshua tracked me with a penetrating gaze. "You sick or somethin'?"

"Nah, just hungry. Don't worry about me. Eat your soup before it gets cold."

He narrowed his eyes at me. "Fine."

I thought I was in the clear when his palm came out of nowhere and slapped a little too hard onto my forehead. Joshua left it there for thirty seconds before nodding and refocusing on his monstrous serving of soup.

The smack to my head seemed to be just what I needed to snap myself out of a muscle induced stupor. I still did my best to avoid looking at Joshua during lunch. I was afraid that if I did, he might see whatever emotions I was juggling in my brain. My avoidance was clearly making him suspicious because he spent the entire meal studying me, which didn't help matters.

How long did I plan to stay in this little cabin with him? A few months ago, my answer would have been "until he makes me leave." But Joshua had made it clear that I wasn't wearing out my welcome, even when I irritated him. Even after our weird stretch of silence.

What did that mean? Why did he panic so much that night by the fire if he felt nothing that wasn't platonic? Was I reading too much into it? I *needed* to know.

I needed to know because I was coming to recognize just how impossible it would be to live with Joshua and ignore my blossoming feelings for him. The last two weeks were spent on the cusp of something that felt like heartbreak. All because he was ignoring me.

My attraction to him wasn't strictly physical, otherwise it might not be a problem. I could blame the allure on hormones and curiosity and inexperience. I'd seen a man's body only a handful of times and never in a particularly intimate way.

My growing sexual awareness was just the icing on this emotional cake. I liked Joshua. *Really* liked him. Even when he was too quiet or unnecessarily grumpy, I was happy to be around him.

When he did speak, he was intelligent and perceptive. When his mood was lighthearted—or as close as Joshua got—he was downright charming. Maybe I was the only person in the world who could see that charisma, but it was there. And I was hooked on it.

I'd spent the last two weeks trying to convince myself that I cared for Joshua because he rescued me. Or that it was simply friendship and it only felt different because we lived together. I'd also tried to persuade myself to believe that I was fine with how things were going between the two of us. There was no need to share my heart. Nothing would come of it so why bother?

But what if something could come of it? Joshua didn't flirt or seek out my affection but that didn't mean there couldn't be more there. In a gradual and subtle way, he'd stopped bristling at my closeness. Today he didn't even flinch when I put my hands on his face.

Jeez, no sane person would view that as a sign that someone was interested in them.

If I admitted my feelings to Joshua it could change everything, not necessarily for the better.

This was going to require some serious thought. We'd only just recovered from whatever unspoken words were clouding the air between us for the last two weeks. If I said something now, I wasn't just ruining that recovery.

I might be ruining everything.

26

Misery Loves Company

Joshua

"**C**an I come with you?" Liv asked, big green eyes glittering with excitement.

Joshua was hoping that she would.

He'd given up pretending he didn't want her around. He wasted two weeks trying to remanufacture that space between them and failed miserably. All it did was make her walk around with this sad pout on her face and make him feel empty, like every ounce of life that was flourishing inside of him came from her. The dejected sink of her shoulders, growing deeper with each day that passed, gave him an acute pain in his chest.

Worse, no matter how much he tried to act the way he had before *that night*, nothing felt the same. He couldn't pretend to be disconnected from her like she was just anyone. Every time he watched her delicate hands working at a task, he remembered the feel of them. It made his skin prickly and hot. It had him swallowing down a yearning so fierce he thought he would choke on it.

"'Course." For Joshua, that was an enthusiastic answer. He wanted her to know that she was welcome. They could at least be friendly, couldn't they? Friendship was safe. He would let himself reach that point and stay there.

"Really?" She beamed up at him. "I'll get my jacket!" And with that Liv was bolting back inside, boots clunking inelegantly on the steps and nearly tripping her in the entryway. She was so damn clumsy.

Joshua tried to walk the perimeter of the fence twice weekly. In total it was a little less than three miles round trip. On busier days, during the abundance of spring and summer or when he spent the morning hunting, he wouldn't have time to check the whole thing before the sun went down.

The work load out on the farm was lightening with winter on the way. And with Liv helping, Joshua managed to finish the daily chores before the sun completed a languid journey behind the trees. The light was only now shifting to the rich gold color that accompanied evening in autumn.

It was an exception to witness the show the sunset put on at this time of year. Most days the sky darkened to a dull grey, dampening them with a perpetual drizzle. Today they were treated to one of those rare days where the clouds were gone, and the breeze was crisp and cool.

Liv bounced back outside with her jacket and one of his knitted wool hats. The hat was too big. Joshua liked the way it made her scowl when it slid down her forehead.

Her hair was braided into two shimmery gold ropes that hung from either side of her head. It was tempting to run his hand down each braid from root to tip. Liv's hair, like most of her, was incredibly soft to the touch.

"Ready when you are," she said, folding the front of the hat in yet another attempt to keep it out of her eyes. An annoyed huff ruffled the loose blonde hairs that framed her cheeks when the chunky wool accessory defiantly flopped back down.

They started toward the gate. Kuna took the lead, trotting ahead and occasionally returning to nuzzle Liv's hand. Damn dog was becoming a love drunk dope around her.

Joshua and Liv strolled at a leisurely pace, the only noise between them the whisper of the wind. Silent was not typically a word he would use to describe Liv, but she'd been unusually quiet today.

She was probably hesitant to speak after how he'd behaved. He would just have to live with the consequences of his own stupidity and suffer through her quiet spells until she felt he deserved her chatter.

At one time he might not have considered a walk pleasant. Liv's stride was short and if he intended to keep pace with her, he had to take half steps. There was no reason to hurry today, and he'd come to realize that a walk could be satisfying without being productive.

When had Joshua started enjoying mundane tasks?

A better question would be *why* had he started enjoying such things?

The answer was leaning into his shoulder as she twisted to look up at the barren branches of a maple tree. The back of her hand brushed his, making him aware of how easily he could hold it.

Such behavior was so far out of the realm of what was known to him that Joshua felt ill with anxiety just thinking about. Besides, that would encourage the change in their relationship that he'd been desperately trying to avoid. Friends didn't hold hands, as far as he knew.

Yet, things had already changed between them. He couldn't say precisely when the shift happened, but it came long before that awkward night two weeks ago. Maybe it started that first day he brought her to town and realized how furious it made him to see her frightened. It could have happened later that evening when she'd unexpectedly kissed him. Falling asleep in his arms only solidified the fragile roots of an emerging shoot.

Or perhaps the change started from something less significant. One of those simple evenings where Liv was perched on the counter by the sink and he was leaning on the cabinet adjacent to her, both of them brushing their teeth. She could never keep her toothbrush in her mouth because she was always giggling at his frothy mustache.

There were so many moments like that. They cooked dinner together, talked by the fire until Liv couldn't keep her eyes open, and even folded laundry together. That alone was a sign that he was different. Joshua despised laundry and rarely folded anything if he could fit it in the drawer without doing so. But for Liv? He sorted fucking socks.

Whatever the catalyst for this evolution in their relationship was didn't really matter now. It was already done, and Joshua had solidified it further this afternoon, at least in his mind. He knew he wasn't seeking affection in any ordinary way by asking Liv to cut his hair but to him, it was another step down that path. It was him selfishly giving in to that need to be touched by her and carefully giving up his attempt at distance.

Did she realize that was as close as he'd ever come to being vulnerable with another person?

Joshua cared about Liv. There it was, out in the open—well, out in the open in his head. Liv might be good at reading him, but she couldn't possibly understand the unspoken desires he'd been entertaining.

That little step had to be as far as it went, though. What they had right now was good. It was easy. By some miracle Joshua still hadn't sabotaged it, even after his vanishing act. He needed to keep it that way. Keep it steady. Liv was happy enough and Joshua was satisfied by that.

The rest could simply be ignored. Never mind that when she touched him today, he wanted to rub his chin up and down her fingers like a purring cat. Forget how often he "accidentally" caged her between the counter and his chest while reaching for the top shelf just to have an excuse to be near her. Even now he was walking close enough for their arms to touch because he couldn't help but gravitate towards her. And he was having a hell of a time forgetting just how good her sleeping breaths felt on his skin.

"Did it ever make you feel like you were in a prison?" Liv stopped walking and pointed to the barbed wire at the top of the fence.

"Nah." It was never the fence that made him feel trapped.

She studied his face, considering his answer as if it had been much more than one grunted sound. "Was the fence there when you were a kid?"

"Been there as long as I can remember." He nudged her elbow with his. "C'mon, Squirrel. We'll never make it home at this pace."

She took a few quick steps to catch up with him. "Were you happy?"

"Huh?"

"When you were a kid. Did you like living here?"

He shrugged. "Never had anywhere else to compare it to."

"I bet it was fun, spending all that time outside." She fidgeted with her hat, finally giving up and taking it off when it wouldn't stay out of her face. "Maybe you'll tell me more about it someday."

Liv only knew as much about his young life as he'd told her and that wasn't much. Still, she was a perceptive one and she'd gleaned that not all of it had been pleasant. So why was she asking about it now? What could she hope to learn?

She probably wanted a nice story, some reassurance that even Joshua's small world had been more good than bad. No matter how much he wanted to offer her that reassurance, it would be dishonest, and he didn't like to lie to her.

"Maybe." Apparently, that answer was enough because she nodded and went back to her quiet contemplation. A few minutes ticked by before Joshua found he couldn't hold back his own question. "Does the fence make *you* feel like you're in a prison?"

She looked like there was something that immediately came to mind but she held back, worrying her bottom lip. "No." That was it? Why did she sound so reluctant? "But...oh, never mind."

"What?"

"You'll think it's silly." More lip biting.

"So?"

Liv gave him that pouty look. "It makes me sad sometimes."

"The fence makes you...sad?"

"I don't like that we have to isolate ourselves. I hate that we're really only safe behind a wall." She stopped walking again and craned her neck to meet his gaze. It was a struggle not to look away. When she spoke, her voice was barely above a whisper. "And I guess it makes me sad that you spent so much of your life alone behind a wall. Don't you get lonely out here?"

It wasn't the first time she'd asked that question. And just like the last time the question came up, his only response was a snort. Joshua tried not to lie, but he wasn't interested in being that honest either. Admitting loneliness was admitting weakness.

If he was lonely, it meant that in a way, he needed someone else. Joshua had never and would never *need* anyone. Even as a child he didn't need his parents. He learned not to at a very early age.

Still, the now familiar spark behind his sternum grew a little brighter at her concern. Liv might be the only person in the world who'd ever been sad for him. It was much different than the pity folks in town offered him when he was a kid. There was no judgment in her tone. That was just the type of person she was.

"Right, I forget you're a robot." She imitated his snort.

Though Joshua was concerned with her unusual behavior, he did his best not to let it eat at him. Despite her quietness and odd questions, Liv was smiling at all the things that would regularly make her smile—like Kuna's frisky excitement at the cold weather—and her body language dictated that she was mostly at ease. There was a slight tension in her shoulders but that could easily be tight muscles from the daily chores she did around the farm.

"Cold?" He halted his trailing thoughts when he noticed Liv shivering. They were two thirds of the way through their walk, but he wouldn't hesitate to send her home if she couldn't handle the dropping temperature. Damn woman needed to put more meat on her bones before winter.

"A little, but it's a good cold," she answered through chattering teeth.

"Didn't realize cold could be good."

"It's like when you say moonshine has a good burn. It's invigorating. Plus, it will be that much better when we go inside and start the fire. It's easier to appreciate warmth and shelter when you've gone without." And she would know.

"Your lips start turning blue, I'm sending you home."

The only response to that was a smirk that Joshua interpreted as "like hell you will." Stubborn woman had yet to learn that he was not a man to be tested. Joshua would sling her over his shoulder and haul her ass back to the cabin simply because she implied that he couldn't make her go. His brain was not wired to allow him to back down from a challenge.

The perimeter check went off without a hitch, as did dinner. When they'd finished eating and tidying up the kitchen Joshua sent Liv to fetch a blanket and meet him on the porch. By the time he stepped outside with two mugs of tea she was nestled in the far corner of the wood bench, tightly wrapped in a crochet blanket. There was still a hint of inexplicable uncertainty in her expression. All of it faded when she caught sight of him and beamed a honey sweet smile. What did he do to deserve that?

"How was your day?" She asked as he handed her a mug.

It was terribly tempting to take the spot next to her. The way she sat curled in the corner left the perfect place for him, almost as if she wanted him there. That would put them so close together that no position or posture would keep them from touching. And if he was going to claim he didn't want anything from her beyond friendship, he couldn't take that seat.

Because if Joshua let himself spend that much uninterrupted time beside her, he couldn't predict how he might react. He was not about to risk giving her the impression that he *did* want something. Even if—oh, for fuck's sake—he did. Damn, when she smiled at him like that it made his insides feel like they were made out of feathers.

And to admit to himself what he *really* wanted? Even thinking it opened a well of fear so deep it seemed fathomless. Since the day he became a young man, too broad and tall to be the victim of John's wrath, Joshua hadn't been afraid of anything. Until Liv. She terrified him because she made him hope. She made him want. Both could be deadly to a man in the end of the world.

Both could be deadly to a man, period.

Joshua took the cedar Adirondack furthest from her, but when she turned to him to say, "Beautiful view you've got out here," he was looking directly at her when he responded with a firm, "yes, it's beautiful."

27
Captivating Cruelty

After a rough few weeks, today felt absolutely perfect. The weather was perfect, the walk before dinner was perfect, and spending time with Joshua was—yes, believe it—perfect.

Today he'd been so—what was the right word?—docile. Friendly. Happy, even. There was an uncharacteristic lightheartedness to him that completely caught me off guard. That dark and churlish man from the last two weeks had vanished as quickly as he'd come.

I couldn't make sense of it.

What was it about Joshua that had me so enthralled? I'd been mulling it over all day, and I had yet to work out how I ended up moonstruck. *We were so different.* If he was black coffee, I was a white chocolate mocha. Some days I almost felt as if he was an entirely different species.

That was what made him so exciting. He was a puzzle for me to solve, a new terrain to explore. He was challenging and bewildering, and he opened the world up to me. He taught me to be brave—no, he showed me that I already was. *That* was why he had me captivated.

How could I leave life with Joshua as it was after realizing that? How could I let such precious feelings go unsaid in a time where our days were numbered, where everything was fleeting? We never knew if there was a tomorrow for us. I was acutely aware that the end could come at any moment.

What if it came without him ever knowing that he was cared for? That someone treasured him for exactly who he was?

Joshua set his mug at the base of his chair and rose abruptly. Just when I thought I'd unexpectedly lost my chance to say anything, he returned with the mystical guitar that sat dusty and untouched in the corner of the cabin for the entire three months I'd been there.

Deft fingers plucked each string, bringing them back to tune like it was habitual. I never dreamed he knew how to play. It seemed more like a decorative prop to add to the rustic cowboy aesthetic of the house. I should have known better. Not a bone in Joshua's body was concerned with aesthetics.

I scooted to the edge of my seat, careful to keep my gaze forward in case he felt me watching him and withdrew back into himself. His eyes were shuttered, lips pressed together in concentration. Then those lips were moving, and a deep hum buzzed from his throat, gradually rising in pitch until it turned into words.

The song was one I recognized, only vaguely. Willie Nelson, or maybe Johnny Cash? The music softened the edges of his gruff voice, turning it to a rich basso vibration that seemed to make the entire world go quiet. Every groaning tree, late autumn bird, even the wind, went still in silent awe. His music was so unexpectedly beautiful that it threaded my arms in goosebumps and left my eyes sparkling with unshed tears.

This.

This was what I loved about Joshua. Every time I thought I had the man figured out I discovered a new dimension, a version of him hidden away under that ridiculous boorish attitude. From the very beginning he made it clear to me that he was not some altruistic, gentle giant that just needed to be coaxed out of his shell. He was selfish and he was mean.

And that was true sometimes, but that narrative didn't tell his complete story. Even Joshua himself didn't see the full portrait of the man he was.

There was so much about him that was good. He was decent and principled and insightful. And yeah, maybe he wasn't gentle and even tempered—I'd watched him nearly rip Wheeler to shreds over petty comments—but he'd never raised a hand to hurt me.

In fact, he'd gone out of his way to protect me—arguably gone against his nature to do so, if he was to be believed. Joshua cared about me, which was not something I ever imagined I could say with confidence until now.

I'm in love with him.

The feeling was so intense that I felt punched in the heart. I was in love with Joshua. My stomach fluttered like I was about to ride the first drop of a rollercoaster and for a moment I almost thought I would be sick.

It was one thing to ignore my feelings for him when it was mere infatuation, but this was huge, too huge to silently live with. Love was magic. That was the stuff that made the end of the world worth living through. Love was worth taking a chance on. My mind was racing, heart thudding an anxious, excited rhythm behind my sternum.

"Joshua," I exhaled sharply.

His eyes snapped open, alarm drawing creases around them. The guitar strings vibrated as his hand whipped away from the instrument. That action-ready expression on his face was almost enough to make me lose my nerve.

"What is it?" He started to rise, frantically scanning the garden in front of us. I must have looked afraid because he took a side-step toward me, still eyeing the property for whatever had me frightened. "Liv, *what is it?*"

Okay, I hadn't meant to put him in survival mode, but I was freaking out. Now that he was freaking out, I only felt more panicked.

"I'm in love with you," I blurted.

Joshua swiveled on his heel, the motion so painfully slow that it seemed the sun dipped further below the horizon before he was fully facing me. "What?"

"I'm in love with you," I repeated in a whisper.

His mouth dropped open before immediately clicking shut again. One of those familiar frowns darkened his face, this time showing anger and something unidentifiable but equally unexpected. "No, you're not."

Now I was the one standing, frowning, asking, "What?"

"You're not in love with me." His words were clipped. Before I could defend myself, he was storming back into the house. I heard the guitar strings vibrate when he thumped the instrument back in place, hopefully not hard enough to break it.

"Joshua," I followed him inside. "It's okay if you don't feel the same. I just thought I should tell you. What if I never get another chance? The world is ending! I needed to say it at least once."

"Stop it!" he snarled.

"Stop what?"

Joshua started pacing the space between the bed and the kitchen. "Stop saying that!"

"Why does that make you angry?" I hated how small that question made me sound.

"I'm angry because I have some foolish woman wasting my time, pretending like we're in a fairytale. It's the end of the fucking world! You don't get to love."

Any surprised hurt I was nursing flared into anger of my own. "Oh, trust me, I know this isn't a fairytale. You're definitely not prince charming!" I shouldered past him to the bed, which really only served to bounce me off of him because he was so hard and unyielding.

"What do you think you're doing?"

What was I doing? I had my backpack in my hand, kicking my belongings out from under the bed with my feet. Whatever I was doing, it was rash.

"It's none of your business what I'm doing. Last time I checked, I still have autonomy. You don't get to tell me what I can and cannot do, Joshua." I slammed my pack on the bed, taking indiscriminate handfuls of clothes and shoving them inside. When Joshua grew quiet, I paused to look back at him. "I realize that I'm the bane of your existence and you can barely stand my presence, but you don't have to be so cruel."

"I told you I was mean." His voice was frigid, so completely void of emotion that I couldn't believe I'd ever thought him capable of it.

"You did." And I was the one who ignored it. I had no right to be angry with him. He warned me from the start that this was who he was, and he was completely unchanging in it.

Joshua was right. I was foolish. I'd spent the entire time treating him like a normal person and imagining that his behavior meant something more, as it might have with anyone else. He wasn't anyone else, though. He never would be, and I couldn't expect him to change. Shouldn't expect it. That wasn't fair.

It didn't make the rejection hurt any less.

I hesitated, one strap of my backpack slung over my shoulder. "What happened to them?" I wasn't sure why the question surfaced now of all times. I thought maybe if I heard the answer from him, heard the truth of the one bad thing I knew for certain he'd done, it would steel my heart against him. I could walk away from Joshua only if I could erase the good, I saw in him. "To Wheeler's men?"

Joshua must have realized why I was asking. The frost spread from his voice to his expression, turning him rigid. "Shot 'em in the head and left 'em for the animals."

"You killed them?" The next sentence out of my mouth surprised us both, a justification. "They were bad people."

"I'm a bad person! I didn't *rescue* you. You want to know why I stopped them? Why I brought you back here?" Joshua loomed over me, his icy demeanor suddenly melting with a livid heat.

"No," I whispered.

"You're a woman. Thought you'd be useful." Useful for what? It didn't matter. Whatever use he thought I might have, he never sought it out.

"I don't believe you."

"Because you're naïve. You're just a resource to me." Joshua shrugged. He lifted his shoulders and shrugged off me and my feelings.

"Liar!" I shouted. "If you want to lie to yourself, fine! Whatever keeps you comfortable in your isolated little world. But don't you dare lie to me, Joshua. Not again. I deserve better."

"What are you doing?" Joshua repeated when I finished tugging my pack on, skirting around the kitchen table to avoid him. "Olivia, where are you going?"

"Away from here. I won't stay where I'm not wanted."

His silence said everything that I needed to know. Now I just had to make it out the gate without him seeing me cry. I wouldn't let him. I already felt pathetic enough.

What was I thinking? Maybe I wasn't.

"You're leaving?"

I answered sharply, not giving myself room to change my mind, no matter how stupid I was being. "Yes."

"Maybe you should," he mumbled, like even annunciating the words took more effort than he cared to exert.

I could feel his eyes on me when I pushed the front door open, but I wouldn't let myself look over my shoulder. He was cold, crueler than I thought him capable of. I couldn't stand to see him anymore, couldn't bear to be within a hundred feet of him. Or even on the same continent as him.

"You can't go out there." I was almost to the gate when Joshua's booming voice made my steps stutter.

"No?" I whipped around, catching him off guard. He almost barreled into me. "You want me to leave the house but not the yard? Am I no different than the dog to you?"

"I didn't say I wanted you to leave."

"Yeah, you kind of did!" I yelled. "Go home and sit in your stupid chair. You obviously don't want me around unless I serve a purpose."

"Liv, don't you dare open that gate!" I did. "Do not walk into those woods!" I did that too.

Joshua was still standing where I'd left him when I swung the gate shut. He jumped to catch it, but it closed with a thud, almost crushing his fingers. Kuna whimpered on the other side, and I resisted the urge to turn back, maybe murmur something apologetic or reassuring. Dogs couldn't understand reassurance anyway.

"Olivia! Come back here," he snarled, flinging the gate open wildly. Talk about mixed signals.

"Go away!" I called back. "You've made yourself clear. I won't be a burden or a resource."

Joshua didn't go away. I marched straight from the gate to the woods, and he followed. At a distance, I might add, like he couldn't make up his mind about what he was doing. Confusing, mean man.

I had no clue where I was going. Even when it wasn't dark, I couldn't tell one path from another out here. The only vague sense of direction I got came when, after twenty long minutes of walking, I found the railroad tracks. That was also when the crashing of undergrowth behind me ceased. If Joshua and Kuna were still with me, I couldn't hear either of them.

He was gone. And it was dark.

No, it was dim not dark. The forest thinned on the other side of the railroad tracks and the few stray beams of sun that peeked over the horizon provided an eerie glow.

Fifteen minutes later that last touch of light disappeared, and it was dark. Scary dark. Can't-see-where-I'm-going dark. And in my rush to leave the cabin I didn't think to steal a flashlight. I only got a few steps before nearly smacking into a tree.

What in the world am I doing out here? I'm going to get lost or fall down a cliff or get eaten by wolves. I was fairly certain Joshua said there weren't wolves in this part of the country, but I could imagine a pack of them stalking me anyway.

Grudgingly, I turned back the way I came. I would return to the farm and storm out again in the light of day, make a proper exit when I knew where I was going.

I expected to see the railroad tracks twenty five feet or so behind me. They weren't there. All I saw was darkness. I swiveled slowly on my heel and saw the faint outline of trees and nothing more. Now that I'd turned in a full circle, I wasn't positive which direction I'd been heading or which direction I came from. Panic welled in my chest, and I started to pant.

I'm lost in the woods. In the effing dark! After everything I've survived, I'm going to die out here, alone.

"I'm not going to die," I insisted aloud. "Calm down, Liv."

I couldn't calm down, though. I didn't even have a compass, not that it would do any good. My brain whizzed through thoughts, desperate to remember anything Joshua told me about finding your way in the forest. Any detail I could recall required—you guessed it—a compass and light. Otherwise, I could be heading straight for the gorge.

So, I would wait until the sun came back up. I could lean against a tree to make sure an animal didn't ambush me and make it through the night before continuing. Great plan, assuming it didn't get cold enough for me to freeze to death.

I want to go home.

Where was home, exactly? With Joshua in that weathered old cabin. I don't know when it became home, but as my fear ballooned and I sought a comforting thought, that was what my mind conjured. I'd never had a strong sense of home before. Home was a place to sleep and shower. It was nice to have one and I liked decorating mine but that was it. Home was a building.

Now home was a place with a person that hated my guts because I *loved* him. That wasn't the kind of home I wanted. That was dysfunctional. I swallowed a hard lump in my throat and pushed away the tears that came back for round two. I wouldn't cry over him. Not anymore.

What did I do wrong?

Nothing. I didn't do anything that warranted that kind of response. I knew that having feelings for Joshua could complicate things, I just hadn't realized that dropping a bomb on his house would be met with less hostility than admitting love.

A twig snapped behind me and in that exact moment I remembered the cougar, coming at me with every intention of eating me. I scrambled to the nearest tree, my pack scraping bark as I frantically pressed my back to it. I knew that was the wrong move. I should be slower, more confident. Joshua told me that running would only make a cougar chase, but I wasn't waiting around for it to sneak up on me and break my neck.

There was another noise, this time right in front of me. I opened my eyes wider, still seeing nothing. "Holy crap."

Something cold and wet brushed my fingers. I shrieked and leapt away. A hand wrapped tight around my upper arm, and I shrieked again. Another hand clapped over my mouth, followed by an indistinct curse.

"Joshua?" The sound was muffled beneath the palm covering the lower half of my face.

For one terrifying second, I had no idea whose hands were on me. I should have fought. I should have kicked and screamed and run. Instead, I froze, utterly paralyzed with fear. A deep voice, rough as gravel, ordered, "be quiet. C'mon," and I exhaled a quaking breath.

Apparently, Joshua didn't stop following me, only made himself more discreet.

Kuna nuzzled me again. That was the cold and wet feeling. She must have been the one snapping twigs, too. I gave her head a quick pat and she leaned into my leg. I was getting more reassurance from the dog than Joshua.

His thick fingers laced through mine, gently tugging me in his direction. No, he wasn't holding my hand. Fine, he was *literally* holding my hand, but it wasn't some nice gesture. He just didn't want to lose me in the dark. He didn't want me to bolt again and inconvenience him by making him come after me.

I had you. And he had me still. His actions and his words told two distinctly different stories.

Somehow Joshua knew the way home without a compass or a light. The going was slow, trudging through the woods for what felt like an hour before even reaching the railroad tracks. The quiet between us was painful, adding to the weighty sadness that made my insides feel chilled.

As soon as we stepped back through the gate Joshua dropped my hand, locking up and stomping up the porch steps without checking to see if I followed.

I counted out two miserable minutes, shivering more violently with each second that passed. In addition to a light and a compass, I'd also forgotten to take my jacket off the coat rack. Some survivalist I was. I could have gotten myself killed all because my heart was bruised.

Broken, I corrected. It felt utterly broken.

Joshua was already in his chair when I came through the door, his jar of moonshine turning into crystalline shades of red in the firelight. He didn't offer so much as a glance when I snatched the jar from his hand, took a long, burning swig, and set it on the mantel. I wobbled back to the bed, chucked my bag on the floor, and sank down onto the aged mattress.

The recliner let out a familiar groan and a floorboard squeaked. Then the mattress shifted as Joshua sat on the other side of the bed, his back to me.

"I do," he murmured so quietly I barely understood the words.

I twisted to look at him. His shoulders were slumped, his head bowed, face hidden in shadows. "You do what?"

"Get lonely out here. Some days I feel like I'm suffocating on it."

The dam finally broke, tears spilling down my face, making him into a watery blur. I turned to hide, feeling confused and ashamed and certain it would make him angry to think I was pitying him. I heard Joshua swallow, then thump the jar of moonshine on the nightstand. There was a touch on my shoulder, so tentative and soft that it could have been a puff of air instead of the brush of fingers.

I slowly eased around, steeling myself to face him. Those dark eyes were fixed on me, swirling like melted chocolate. Sad chocolate.

I went from quiet tears to blubbering, "I'm sorry."

"Never, Liv. Never apologize to me. You have nothing to be sorry for." He raised his hand from my shoulder, cupping my face and wiping tears away with his thumbs. "Don't do that. I hate it when you do that."

It occurred to me that Joshua hadn't been saying that out of irritation. Another of our many miscommunications. My tears made him uncomfortable but not for the reason I thought.

"How do I make it right?" His rough voice was dripping with desperation. "Tell me how to make it right."

"Hold me." I didn't know why I said it. For once I just wanted him to comfort me. I didn't really think he would do it.

But he did. He slid across the bed and towed me into his lap, hugging me tight against him. And God, did it feel good. The heat of his skin and the shelter of his arms were exactly what I needed. Not just tonight. I'd needed this for months. I was starved for it.

Joshua's fingers splayed in my hair, cradling my head so gently. I closed my senses to everything but his arms firm around me and the pounding of his heart in my ear, doing my best to memorize the sound. It moved wildly beneath my palm, thrumming with feelings he couldn't deny. Feelings I wouldn't let him deny.

He finally spoke. "I didn't mean it."

"Then why did you say it?"

"I told you I was mean."

"You're not," I whispered. "You should stop pretending to be."

"I'm not what you think I am."

"You don't even know what I think you are."

Joshua went still. His heartbeat quickened. "What do you think I am?"

"Confusing." I sat up to look at him. "Short tempered. Impatient." He sat up too. "You're rough around the edges. Really rough." I continued before he could interrupt. "You're also smart, resourceful, considerate. You take care of people in the subtlest ways. I don't think you know how good you are."

His face sunk. "I'll only disappoint you if you walk around thinking I'm a good person."

"You're the cougar."

"Huh?"

"I ran and you chased me. You're a territorial predator."

Despite his best efforts to contain it, a twitch of a smile danced on his lips. "I guess you could put it like that."

"You really did kill those men." It wasn't a question. I knew he did.

"Yes." His answer came sharp and quick, ripping off the band aid.

"Do you think they deserved it?"

"Does that make it better?" The question was searching, cautiously hopeful.

"I don't know. The rules of the world have changed. Maybe there isn't right and wrong anymore. There's only survival."

"I don't think people can live without some concept of morality." That surprised me coming from him. He had principles, sure, but it mostly seemed like they determined what was beneficial to him or damaging, not what was moral and immoral.

"You have to redefine it then."

He swallowed. "So that it's okay to kill people?"

"To kill people who intend to hurt you." My answer was as careful as his question.

"To kill people who want to hurt *you*," he added firmly.

I mulled that over for a minute, then asked, "it's more than just those two, isn't it?"

Joshua took his drink from the nightstand, swallowed a sip, then another, and hesitantly answered, "yes."

"How many?"

"Six."

"Would you have done it if the blackout never happened?"

"Of course not."

"Do you feel bad about it?"

"Not usually."

"Why did you kill them?" It felt strange to ask so casually, as if we were talking about why he decided to switch majors.

"They wanted to kill me or take my stuff. Or both."

I laughed. It was the wrong reaction. It was such a horrible, heartless response but I couldn't hold it in. This was the world we lived in now. We killed people who tried to take our stuff, like toddlers with guns.

"Are you okay?" Joshua straightened, bewildered alarm clouding his features. I suspected he thought I was in such shock about his confession that I suffered a mental break.

"I have no idea," I chortled, wiping tears from the corners of my eyes.

He subtly shifted away from me, fingers moving nervously up and down the side of the glass jar in his hand. "Does that make you look at me different?"

"Yes. Now I'll be more careful about making you angry."

"I would *never* hurt you."

"But you did," I whispered into the space between us.

"Dammit." Joshua set his drink down with a clack. He inched closer, gripping my chin and bringing my attention to his face. The softness there was so different from his usual countenance, so vulnerable. "I wish I didn't. I wish I could take it all back. Not just today. Two weeks ago. Two months ago. All of it." He squeezed his eyes shut. I took his free hand and caressed his knuckles with my thumb. "I don't mean to. I don't mean to be this way."

"I know."

His lids slowly lifted, eyes dull with defeat. "I don't know how to be any different."

"I know." I nodded again.

"What do I do?" His voice broke, provoking a fresh wave of tears from me. This was the real Joshua. The secret Joshua. The part of Joshua that was only mine.

"Tonight, just hold me." I tugged him down onto the bed, draping my body over his chest because I wasn't the only one that needed to be held.

I managed to lie there for almost ten minutes before I couldn't hold it in any longer, finally asking, "Why them and not me?"

"Not you?"

"Why did you kill them but help me?"

I expected an excuse, a non-answer like, "because you're a woman." What I got surprised me. "I thought finding you was a sign."

"Why?"

"Exactly. Why was I doing anything I was doing? Pops was gone and I was surviving but *why?* My whole life was on autopilot. I'd never lived outside the farm, never done any good outside that stupid wall. I was alive and it was pointless." I swallowed back my interruption. "The path I found you on? I never take it. I never go west when I'm hunting. But that day? I just...I don't know. I woke up, took my rifle, and left. Didn't question where I was going or what I was doing, I just left. Then there you were, asking for my help. No one had ever done that before."

"So, you think it was fate that we met?"

"I don't believe in fate."

"God then?"

"Maybe."

The silence that fell wasn't comfortable or easy. Threads of anguish and confusion were taut between us, uncertainty strumming along them like his fingers on the guitar earlier tonight. Woven into that song of heartbreak were notes of hope, just enough to keep me steady. Just enough to keep my faith in whatever this was.

Joshua could be many things, sometimes terrible things, but I loved him. I trusted him. I was determined to fight for him, even if that meant fighting *with* him.

Carefully, even more tentatively than before, Joshua's fingers danced along the curve above my hip, tracing goosebumps into my skin. I fell asleep in his arms, lulled by that delicate touch from a man that was anything but delicate.

28

Legacy of Poison

Joshua

Joshua was sure of two things: he absolutely did not deserve Liv and he would do absolutely anything to have her anyway.

She was deeply asleep. Her lips parted, her brow relaxed. Nothing was quite as peaceful as Liv when she slept. How she managed to get in that state after being so upset just an hour earlier, Joshua had no idea. Damn woman was resilient, he had to give her that. Yeah, he had to give her a lot of credit. She put up with him, hadn't she?

Joshua was everything Liv had ever accused him of being and more. He was a selfish, arrogant, overbearing ass and what he'd done tonight was inexcusable. Had he really expected her to just stand there and take that, then go to bed like nothing had changed?

Unfortunately, he had. Joshua was just that dumb. And he'd gotten comfortable, too comfortable. For a minute he forgot there was a possibility she would leave.

The problem was that her words sent him into a state of panic. When Joshua's fight or flight instinct was activated, he always chose fight. It was in his nature to be brutal, to survive. He was born and bred that way. And for some senseless reason, Liv expressing love to him felt like a threat.

Which only verified what he'd known his whole life.

Something was wrong with him that made him incompatible for relationships. He sorted people by usefulness and threat level, dehumanizing them so that they could be placed in categories and handled accordingly. Liv didn't fit into any of his categories and when he tried to make her, it made them both miserable. He hated that misery more than he'd ever hated anything.

And yet, there he went again, snarling at her like he was some rabid animal. How dare she threaten him with...adoration? Yeah, he sure showed her. Joshua went out of his way to be all the worst things she saw in him.

You wanna love me? This is what I am. This is who I am. Can you still love that?

John used to snarl at affection too. He met all of Joshua's soft spots with hardness. Liv was one big soft spot. She was gentle and far too forgiving for her own good. Joshua didn't want to be hard on her and he didn't want to harden her. She was honey and sunshine and that, he knew, was very precious.

Joshua almost ruined it. He knew that. Watching Liv pack her stuff made him feel like there was a viper writhing in his belly. It was a snake of his own making, one whose venom seeped out onto his tongue, almost poisoning all the good they had between them.

Why did he do it? Why did he strike at her when she got too close?

Liv threw that bag over her shoulder and his insides tied in so many knots it would take him weeks to untangle them all. That sick feeling in his gut was so foreign to him that he couldn't immediately name it.

Fear.

Joshua was experiencing fear.

She's the only thing that truly scares me.

It wasn't just fear for Liv, though he was terrified at the prospect of her stumbling through the dark, encountering God knew what—or who. It was fear for himself. He dragged her through the woods to bring her home not only to protect her but because he selfishly couldn't let her go. He was afraid to be alone again.

Fuck, even if she wanted to leave, he didn't know if he could accept that. Joshua stormed after her tonight with the intention of following her as far as she went. Maybe Liv was right. He was a territorial predator. In his mind, she was his. She had been for a long time.

Suddenly Joshua understood what the feeling was that had been clawing him up for weeks. The feeling that caused an inexplicable burning in his fingertips when she was near, that heavy dread which sunk from his chest all the way to his toes whenever she was upset, the relief at the sound of her laughter—all his suffering and joy.

The explanation was so clear, so obvious. He'd ignored and dismissed it as some bizarre illness of the mind caused by weariness because until now, he didn't know how to identify it.

Longing.

Liv rolled with a quiet moan, giving him her back and leaving cold, empty space where she'd rested atop him. Even those two inches was too much distance. He was afraid that if he let her go now, she would somehow slip away in the night, disappear out of his grasp forever. Joshua carefully snaked his arm underneath her and drew her back to him, pressing her spine to his stomach.

Liv tilted her head back and murmured his name.

God, how could a name be so thrilling on her lips? Somehow Liv managed to make it sound beautiful. Joshua wanted to hear his drowsy name muttered into her pillow every evening as she dozed. He wanted to hear it in that husky tone when she stretched sleep from her muscles in the morning. He wanted to hear her say it like a reprimand, trying to hide her smile because she secretly thought it was funny when he was vulgar.

Joshua wanted his name to sound like pleasure purring from her throat. He wanted his name to be a plea on her tongue, hungry and desperate. Could he earn that from her? Could he give her a reason to stay? Maybe not, but he would try his damnedest.

His greatest fear was that she would see him in the light of day and remember what he was, what he showed her he could be, and then she would leave again. Liv would get a lot further when the sun was out.

Not if he got his way. Joshua would do anything to fix this. He needed her to stay.

Yes, there it was. He needed her. He *wanted* her. He wanted this—her skin on his, taking comfort in her closeness, in finally sharing his space with someone.

Liv let out a long, contented sigh and he echoed it into the night.

29

Habits

$\mathbf{A}$ languorous stretch found the other side of the bed cold and empty. I failed to swallow down my disappointment when I sat up and learned I was alone not just in bed, but in the house. The crackling heat of the wood-burning stove warmed the air, and the smell of food permeated the small space, so Joshua hadn't been gone long.

It shouldn't surprise me that he left. I was terrified he would disappear for days, coming back to pretend like nothing had happened between us once again. I couldn't live that way anymore. Surely Joshua realized that.

Unless he assumed my escape last night was a dramatic show and nothing more. It might as well have been. If he hadn't come after me, I would have been frozen to death, eaten by a predator, or starving again within three days.

Mingling with the scent of food was a familiar aroma I hadn't initially detected. I slipped from bed, following my nose to the table, where I found a full plate, a hot mug, and a note. Curiosity wavered between the note and the mug of rich, brown liquid. Steam curled off it invitingly. Couldn't be. There was no way.

I lifted it to my lips and took a tentative sip. "Holy coffee!" And it was. The real deal. Joshua made me coffee. It was a little stale and watery, probably instant, but I would take what I could get.

I scanned the note while I fixed up my coffee with goat milk and honey. It was short and to the point, very Joshua.

I'm sorry. Don't leave. Dinner?

Beneath the note was a small list of tasks for me to complete, mostly harvesting the last vegetables before an expected freeze. I was too focused on the first two words to care.

I'm sorry.

From Joshua, that was one of the most meaningful sentiments I could ever receive. I had never once heard the word sorry on his lips. It didn't fix everything, not by a long shot, but it was a good start.

Not wanting to wait until dinner, I threw on my jacket and boots, grabbed my mug of coffee, and stumbled down the steps. The farm was big, but not big enough that Joshua could avoid me all day. When I couldn't find him in the goat house, the woodshed, or any other place I thought, I began to worry that he left the property just to avoid me. Why hide?

It was only when I was back inside and seated at the table that I remembered Joshua mentioning wood collection yesterday. He had plans to break down a dead tree a quarter mile off the farm and bring it back for more firewood. Hope sparked in the chambers of my heart, a fragile, flickering ember. It was a reckless heat, too easily snuffed out, but I intended to feed it.

I was an optimist, after all.

The rhythmic thumps on the porch step matched the pounding of my heart. For nearly three and a half months I lived with Joshua. He'd seen me at my very worst, literally at death's door, and I had only been half as nervous then as I was now. I went back to slicing apples for the sweet cinnamon bread I was attempting, busying myself so I had the excuse of not noticing his return.

I'd seen him out the window an hour earlier, dragging a collection of logs with a thick rope. He was shirtless, mist collecting in dew drops on his beard, steam rising from his heated skin in the brisk air. I watched him until he disappeared around the side of the house, appreciating the candid moment.

The natural grace infused in his movement always surprised me. His feet should have thundered against the ground, his broad body lumbering inelegantly. Every step he took seemed to be practiced, the tautness of his arms precise and planned, his long legs dancing more than shuffling, even with the load he hauled.

I couldn't help but wonder if he'd have that same grace when he touched me, tough hands sweeping carefully across my hips. Would he be as meticulous with his lips if they explored the column of my throat?

By the time I heard the rustle of Joshua's coat hanging on the rack, I was frantic. The warmth that flushed my cheeks spread down my neck and into my stomach, tightening it with nervous anticipation. One thud followed another as his boots hit the ground, then nothing. The cabin was painfully quiet but for the muted hiss and crackle of the fire and the crunch of the blade cutting through apple flesh.

The harsh gaze boring into my back was tangible, raising the hairs on my neck and sending a cluster of soft winged butterflies into flight in my belly. I waited. I waited until I'd run out of apples and my hand was unnecessarily running a rag over the knife blade. The rest of my ingredients perched on the table, ready to be assembled. Then I would have to turn around and I wasn't brave enough.

And somehow, it felt like capitulating to him. Not tonight. It was his turn to surrender.

"I didn't mean you had to make me dinner." I dropped the knife onto the cutting board a little too hard, almost sending it off the counter and towards my helplessly bare toes.

"I should. You do all the cooking."

And there it was. A recycled conversation, one we played out at least once a week like we were already a couple with a history and a routine.

Because we were.

Maybe it was never spoken aloud and maybe the definition of our relationship wasn't as clearly marked as some, but we'd become *more* long before my ill-received confession. I knew it with utter certainty.

I had you. He did. He always did because Joshua cared about me enough to bring me home.

Home.

I turned then, preparing myself for whatever I might see on his face. He held my gaze, unblinking and intense. I wished I could read what was going on in his head. His eyes churned like a river swelling with snow melt. Nothing was visible through those dark rapids.

Joshua reached into his pocket and removed a piece of paper with painstaking care. This one was discolored and wrinkled. One corner even looked as if someone had started burning it but then changed their mind. It wasn't a note he scribbled out on scrap paper from the junk drawer this morning.

"Are you writing me love letters now?" I wanted to cringe when I saw his reaction to that question. Where I'd hoped for a smile, I received a grimace instead. My fingers skirted around the bag of flour, spices, and mixing bowl, brushing the paper cautiously.

I couldn't tell if it was reverence or something darker that made Joshua handle it with such care, so I treated it the same, gently unfolding it and flattening it on the table.

John, I thought if I loved you hard enough, I could thaw your cold heart. I was wrong. I can't live like this anymore. Tell Joshua I love him. -Helen

If I hadn't already heard Tommy Wheeler throw their names around like barbs intended to prick Joshua's skin, it would be obvious now who Helen and John were. This was a note from his mother.

I studied him in my peripherals, trying to imagine how old he was when those words were written. I pictured a little boy, unkempt black hair falling in his eyes.

He was probably mistaken for an older kid, unusually tall for his age, leggy, but in my mind he was young. Too young to be motherless. Too young to be left alone with a half-crazed father hellbent on isolating them from the world.

No wonder he was rough around the edges. He was already destined to grow up different living the way he did. He had no friends, no siblings, no support except his parents.

And he *didn't* have their support, apparently. I thought back to the way he described his loneliness. When I looked at the words on that note, saw every crease from where he'd read them over and over, I felt his ache. I felt the emptiness. It hurt.

"Joshua," I said softly.

He flinched at my gentle tone. "Love doesn't guarantee anything."

I set the note down and stepped around the table, close enough to touch him, if he'd let me. I could tell that he wanted to retreat, eyeing his potential exits like a cornered animal, but he held his ground. "What is guaranteed?"

He looked at his hands, taking so long with his single word response that I thought he might not give me one. "Nothing."

"Nothing is guaranteed," I agreed. "Look at the world around us. Did you ever expect to be living like this?" I glanced to the woodburning stove beside me and shifted the question. "Okay, did any other person expect the blackout? Of course not. We thought driving cars and taking selfies and Game of Thrones were going to go on forever."

"Selfies?" Confusion lightened his words.

"It's a picture. Of yourself. Self-ie? Never mind." I waved at his increasingly puzzled expression. "My point is that there is no certainty. Not before the world ended and not now. Love isn't a guarantee, not of happiness or safety, but it does add a little light to a dark world." I slid the note across the table, rejecting whatever fear he was projecting onto me.

Joshua shoved it into his pocket, his fist lingering there, trying not to fidget. "What are the apples for?"

"Apples?" We veered away from the heavy topic so quickly my head was spinning. "Oh. Apples. For the bread." I held up the book full of dessert breads and muffin recipes.

"You didn't have to..." His hand was still fisted in his pocket, head down, shoulders so taut I could hear his muscles straining.

I reached for his free hand, squeezing it before he could pull away. "Thank you. That's all you have to say."

His mouth moved, chewing the foreign word until he knew the taste. "Thank you."

I smiled my first real smile that day. "You're welcome."

Our conversation over dinner was a well-practiced dance, artfully sidestepping all the discomfort brought on by unspoken words. Potent emotions took the empty chairs at the table, watching us with growing impatience, waiting for their turn to be heard. More than once I turned to them and more than once I hesitated. Not yet.

Then when? I wanted to shout. ***When is he going to stop pretending?***

An hour later I was crossed legged in front of the hearth, licking sticky apple bread from my fingers. Joshua eased down beside me, shifting uncomfortably. I wasn't sure if it was nerves or because he struggled to find a good position for his long legs. He eventually ended up with his legs crooked, leaning forward to rest his elbows on his knees. The fire reflected vibrantly in his eyes. Eyes that were not looking at me.

"My parents didn't want me," I blurted when the silence became too much. He shared his pain so I would share mine. Then maybe we could understand each other better, maybe he would feel less exposed.

"How can you know that?"

"I mean my real parents. My birth parents. I was four when they put me up for adoption. If I'm being perfectly honest, I don't think my adoptive parents really wanted me either. They only wanted a prim doll that would sit pretty at their dinner table. I always got the feeling they weren't happy with how I turned out." Wow, this was much harder than I'd anticipated.

No wonder Joshua was uneasy. It hurt to bear your already raw heart to someone else.

My voice was shaking on the next sentence. "That's why I left last night. I spent so much of my life desperately chasing love from people who didn't really care about me. When I left for college, I promised myself I was done with that. I won't stay somewhere I'm not wanted. Never again.

"I don't remember life with my birth parents, and I don't want to care about them but some days, I really do. If I think about it long enough, I feel rejected. I feel like I'm not lovable. Or that maybe I'm broken somehow and that's why they didn't want me."

Joshua shifted closer, our shoulders almost touching. "You're not broken."

"Neither are you."

"I never said—" He bit the harsh words off and inhaled deliberately. "I'm not like you."

"No, you're not."

"I can't pretend it didn't happen."

"I don't pretend. I just decided that the problem was never with me. It was them. And it was their loss when they let me go." I rested my palm on his bicep, watching for a reaction. He tilted his head my way and I took it as permission, sliding my hand further down until it could rest in his. "I don't want to leave."

"I don't want you to." I held my breath through the pause that followed. "You are...unexpected."

"Okay," I nodded, encouraging him to say more.

"You mess me up."

"That doesn't sound like a good thing."

"It's not. I meant—fuck, I can't talk to you." He jerked his hands up and rubbed his face.

"Try," I pushed. "I need to hear it."

"There are things I want to say to you and when I try to say them, they come out wrong. Then I try to correct it and you misunderstand me and you think I'm being mean to you, and it all goes to hell. I don't know what to do with you. You always do unexpected things. You say unexpected things. You aren't what I expect you to be." Joshua heaved in air, the admission leaving him breathless.

"And that's bad?"

"No. It's good. I mean, yes, it's bad too, because I think you'll be a way and then you're not and I've been acting like you will be and..."

"How do you expect me to act?"

His eyes got this wide, deer-in-the-headlights look, and I almost wanted to revoke the question. "Manipulative. I expect you to want something from me and that's why you're nice. But it's not. You're nice for no good reason. I don't know what to do with that."

I faced him, not giving him an opportunity to avoid me anymore. "I'm grateful for what you've done for me but that's not why I like you, Joshua. I like the way you think. I like your stories. Sometimes I even like your grumbling."

Joshua was genuinely bewildered, staring at me like I'd grown two heads. "I don't have anything to give you. My world is black and white, always has been. You're not even grey, you're colors. Bright shit, like purple and yellow. I don't know where that fits."

I laughed. "I've fit pretty well so far, haven't I?"

"You took a hammer to a bunch of screws."

"I have absolutely no idea what that means."

"Means you're a damn stubborn woman." Joshua dropped onto his knees, taking my face in his hands. "Damn stubborn, beautiful woman." Then he kissed me, quick and unexpected. I understood how he must have felt that night I slapped him with a drunken peck.

"You think I'm beautiful?" I grinned, wrapping arms around his shoulders so he couldn't escape.

"Was that the only part you heard?"

"It was the only important part." I rose to meet him, chin tilted so I could reach his face. "You owe me more than that."

"More than what?" I inhaled his breathy question, our lips so close that my mouth moved when his did.

"More than one rushed kiss."

Joshua pulled away, mischief sparkling in his eyes. "You kissed me first, so it seems like maybe you owe me."

I tackled him to the rug, wrapping my thighs around his hips. Joshua let me pretend I had the upper hand, his arms lying limp where I held them over his head. "You haven't asked me yet."

He scowled. "Asked you?"

"To stay," I whispered, barely swallowing the emotion that threatened to break me open again.

He propped up on his elbows, drowning me in the headiness of his heavy gaze. "Stay. Stay here with me, Liv." It wasn't a question so much as a demand. I expected nothing less of him.

I answered with my lips pressed to his, tasting the cinnamon and honey on his tongue. There were a hundred promises in that kiss, a hundred more days, and nights, if we were lucky enough to get them.

"Yes," I breathed.

30

Lost Time

Many nights ago, buzzing with moonshine and the joy of being alive, I wanted to kiss Joshua. That desire hadn't been quelled by one drunken press of lips. I wanted to devour him.

Or maybe I wanted him to devour me.

I'm not sure how long we stayed on the floor, drinking each other in. My worldview had narrowed to nothing but the feel of Joshua's lips, the textured calluses at the apex of his fingers as they became bold enough to slip beneath my shirt and caress my lower back. The fire crackled lazily beside us but the heat of it was nothing compared to what was rising between us.

He didn't stop me when I pressed him onto his back, returning to my place on his lap and leaning over him to kiss all the exposed patches of his face that weren't coated in thick hair. His beard rasped against my cheek when I turned his head to press my lips beneath his ear.

"Olivia." The gravel of his voice sent chills up my arms, like it too was a touch that was both rough and tender. For once I wasn't tempted to chide him for using my full name. It was a name only he knew me by, an intimacy that we'd shared long before this.

I eased away, staring down at Joshua with palms on his chest. His eyes were half-lidded, swirling in that delicious dark chocolate way. More light sparked in them as I adjusted my hips atop his, making both of us aware that he was enjoying my affection. A lot. My own sense of boldness grew with that awareness until I was tickling my fingers through his beard, moving lower, plucking buttons on his flannel, moving lower still.

My first layer went too. Another followed and another until his chest was bare and I wore nothing but my discolored pink bra. I was more embarrassed by the state of the tattered piece than I was shy about him seeing me undressed. For a selfish moment I wished for the world to be right only so that I could make myself beautiful for him.

Then I remembered that he already thought I was beautiful, tattered clothes, unplucked eyebrows, and all. Joshua's first and only impression of me was real. Raw. Honest. That was the gift of the blackout. No one could hide themselves anymore, not really.

Joshua shuddered as I ran two fingers down his sternum, finally tracing every line of muscle I'd so desperately wanted to touch. He was letting me explore, giving me complete freedom to touch him as I wished. I'd finally captured his surrender and I intended to celebrate my victory.

I tasted his skin from neck to navel, touched every fine scar—he had quite a few. When his breath was ragged and the grip of his hands felt feverish on my thighs, I moved to the final button keeping him from being fully exposed to me. The rough zipper of his jeans filled the suddenly quiet cabin. Joshua sat up on his elbows, studying my face with an unreadable expression.

I didn't want him to stop me. Not until I'd taken everything he had to give. Not until he'd been mine, at least once. If he would let me in, pry open those steel doors that kept him so carefully in check, I knew he couldn't take it back. He couldn't run from me anymore than I could run from him. Joshua would belong to me in a way that no one else could have.

But he was hesitating, and I was suddenly afraid he wasn't ready to share that much of himself, that maybe he never would be, and I would always be just one foot closer than everyone else.

"Liv?" I froze, waiting for him to tell me that I'd misinterpreted everything, and he didn't want me, not like I wanted him. Instead, he asked, "are you sure you want to do this?"

I wasn't sure what *this* was yet, but I knew I wanted it. Whatever he would allow, I wanted it. "Yes," I exhaled. "Can I touch you?"

"Yes." The word was a groan as my roving fingers continued their exploration, barely waiting for his permission. The way he followed my touch, arching his back to move closer, seemed permission enough.

I quickly learned from Joshua's reaction when I did something right. It must have been really right because after only a few minutes he was panting, his eyes rolling shut.

With a growl he shot upright, taking my wrists to still my hands. "Stop," he breathed.

I studied his flushed face with a confused pout. "Did I do something wrong?"

"Fuck no." He chuckled. "But it's my turn."

I was on my back, my bra flying across the carpet and my jeans slipping past my knees before I grasped what he meant.

Joshua chuckled again, his deep laughter a delicious vibration that hummed along my skin. Only when the coarse hair on his chest brushed against my skin, sending a strange shiver down my spine, did I realize that we were both naked. And he was on top of me.

Trepidation suddenly had me shivering for a whole different reason. This was what I intended, wasn't it? At this point I wasn't entirely sure who started what anymore, only that I had been determined to finish it.

And now?

I lost my train of thought when Joshua brought his lips to the spot just above my collar bone. He withdrew but only long enough to repeat the question I'd asked him. "Can I touch you?" My eyes met his, wholly focused on me, completely open in a way I'd never seen them before. I nodded gently, but that didn't satisfy him. "Say it."

I answered his demand with a shy, "yes."

Joshua settled on the rug beside me, his body pressing against mine as he used one hand to explore from my neck, stroking the crescent of flesh beneath my breasts, tickling along my stomach, and skimming work roughened fingertips down to my thighs. His exploration was slower than mine, more confident, and I began to wonder how many times he'd done this.

My nervous thoughts were once again disrupted when his fingers finally found the spot where all the heat from his kisses seemed to migrate. It was almost an ache, thrilling yet uncomfortable, but it was immediately eased by his touch. More than eased. I felt as if my body matched his eyes, melting like chocolate until I was soft and pliable on the floor.

I let him continue, knowing those eyes were on me but feeling too afraid to look up and meet them. I couldn't see his expression if I was going to muster up the courage for my next request.

"Joshua?" I inhaled a shaky breath.

I squeezed my eyes shut but his breath on my cheek and his quiet command forced me to open them. "Look at me." What was that expression he wore? It was intense and a little wild. "Tell me what you want."

Maybe he was feeling exactly what I was. "I want you to make love to me."

His pupils warped into black pools, his Adam's apple bobbing. "Make love to you?"

"Yes." I snaked my arms around his neck, arching my back and wrapping my legs around him. "Make love to me."

Joshua shifted, a subtle smile playing on his lips.

"Wait!" I put a hand on his chest, and he froze.

"It's okay if you change your mind," he said softly.

"No, it's not that." I blushed. "I've never done this before."

"I know."

My blush deepened. "Is it that obvious?"

"No." He brushed his thumb along my bottom lip. "But it's not something you take lightly."

"It's not." I laid back beneath him.

"It's okay." His whisper caressed the side of my ear. "I've never done this either." A kiss landed beneath my ear, another lower down my throat.

We came together on a hiss of breath. I felt too full and yet it felt like some missing part of me had finally been returned. Joshua made me whole in a way I didn't know I could be, in a way I didn't know I wanted to be.

His gaze was fixed so intently on me. I was all that existed to him and he all that existed to me. The faster we moved, the more I felt I was reaching for something. I couldn't quite put my finger on it, but I knew there was something I wanted, a sensation I was seeking that only he could give me.

That warming pleasure increased with every movement, every touch, every brush of his chest along my breasts. Each muscle in my body was tightening, tension winding me tighter and tighter until I was like a string pulled too taut. When I let out an unexpected moan, Joshua stilled, cupping my cheek with an expression of concern that was so unlike him I almost wanted to laugh.

"Am I hurting you?"

"No," I panted. "You're definitely not hurting me."

A smug smile spread his lips. I couldn't fathom how I'd ever thought him anything but beautiful. The way his eyes settled on me had butterflies coming to life in my stomach all over again.

The more fervent Joshua became, the tighter I felt pulled until, finally, unexpectedly, I snapped. At first it felt as if my entire body went rigid, back arching up, legs tightening around his hips. Then everything softened and again, I was melting. Heat pulsed through my veins and a series of moans came unbidden from my throat until I was absolutely breathless.

Joshua slipped his arm beneath my back and pulled me closer. I was utterly lost in the feel of his hands pressing into my hips, the place where we connected. The tendons on his neck strained and he let out a gravelly breath, collapsing over me like every ounce of energy he had was spent.

I curled my limbs around him, feeling his labored breathing match my own. We stayed that way for a small eternity, sweat slicking our skin, his face warming my neck. Joshua finally rolled away with a lazy stretch, reminding me of a very large cat.

As I watched him relax on his back, staring up at the flicker of firelight that danced across the ceiling, I felt a quiet dread slithering through me. There was so much I wanted to say to him, so many questions I had about how he felt, but I knew there was no better way to make him retreat than to speak any of those words.

He would disappear, maybe not physically but into himself. Like the cougar, Joshua quietly slipped away from every perceived threat to watch it pass from his hidden perch.

And this? This budding relationship between us—if it could even be called that—was as dangerous as it got for Joshua. I knew him well enough to understand that he didn't want attachment. I would have to be still, crouching with my hand out to feed him morsels of affection until he was sure they weren't poisoned, that none of this was a trick. Loving Joshua meant being patient.

I didn't have much patience left in me.

I shifted onto my side so I could rest a palm on his chest. "That was..." I let the sentence trail off, unable to find the words to describe that particular brand of pleasure.

"It wasn't bad, was it?"

I shot upright with a scowl. "It *wasn't bad?*" I hissed, trying to channel frustration so he wouldn't see the hurt at those flippant words.

I turned to the fire, hiding my face from him. Quiet laughter from behind me made me wince. Apparently, I was amusing. Had I really expected this to be special for him?

God, I was such an idiot. I kept hoping that I just had to coax Joshua out more when in reality, there wasn't anything more for him to give. This was what he could offer, and I couldn't ask for more because I'd come into this knowing who he was.

I came back into focus, realizing that Joshua had been saying my name. "*Liv?*" He tugged my shoulder, forcing me to meet his eyes. "What is it you're always telling me to do? *Lighten up.*" I nodded meekly and let him tug me back down onto the rug beside him. "Do you want to know what I really thought of that?"

"Yes."

He propped his hands under his head. "For a minute there, I thought for sure I was dead."

"Dead?"

"How else did I end up in heaven?"

My lips formed into a tight line as I desperately tried to contain my reaction. I failed miserably and laughter tumbled from me so hard I snorted. "That is the cheesiest line I've ever heard."

Joshua sat up to stoke the fire. He was quiet as he added another log and encouraged the flame to catch. For a second, I was worried that I'd offended him but when he looked back at me, he was grinning. *Joshua was actually grinning.* "You liked it though."

I returned his smile. "I did."

We both flopped onto our backs, enjoying the heat of the growing fire and the sleepy, sated feeling that accompanied making love. Peace filled the air, replacing the agitating tension that had coiled around us both all day. I let the silence linger for a long stretch before I decided to be brave again.

We were naked before each other—literally. It couldn't get any more vulnerable than that, right?

"Joshua?"

"Hmm?" He hummed sleepily.

"I don't want that to be a one-time thing."

He cocked his head to meet my gaze. "You want to do it again? I thought you might want a little break."

"No—I mean yes! Not right now." I hooked my pointer fingers together and fixated on them as I fidgeted. "I don't just mean sex. I mean *this*." I gestured between us. "I don't want to wake up tomorrow and act like none of this happened. I know this isn't really your thing—relationships, I mean—but maybe you haven't given it a chance? Maybe we can...try?"

"Liv," I let out a startled yelp when Joshua yanked me on top of him. "I'm an idiot but I'm not *that much* of an idiot." I yelped again when he flipped us, gently pinning me beneath him. "I know I've done a lot of things wrong. I've made a lot of mistakes. What I can't figure out is what the hell I did right to make you *want* to stay."

I opened my mouth to respond but he cut me off with a kiss. "You're mine. You've been mine, I just didn't know what to do about it." He wrapped a big hand around my jaw. "I wasted so much time pretending like you didn't matter to me. I don't intend to waste any more."

Twin tears escaped the corners of my eyes before I could blink them back. Joshua caught one on the tip of his finger and scowled at it. "Is this one of those times where crying is a good thing?"

"Yes," I giggled. "Definitely happy tears."

The silence that resettled between us was a comfortable, sweet quiet. Our limbs became a tangled mess as I attempted to get as close to him as possible, soaking in his warmth and feeling elated that I had the freedom to touch him. My fingers were following a lazy path between his ribs when I drifted off to sleep.

I roused later to Joshua carefully placing me on the mattress. I choked back the disappointment that tried to set in my chest when I felt his looming presence vanish from the side of the bed. A moment later the opposing side lurched under his weight, then a warm chest came against my back.

I turned in his arms, catching his face between my palms. He blinked heavily, another part of himself he usually wouldn't let me see. I laid a soft kiss on his lips, then another on his cheek, before quietly whispering, "you're mine too."

31

Canyon Heart

Joshua

Joshua jerked awake, adrenaline punching him in the chest and making his heart race. A tangle of quilt wrapped his legs like a bug in a spider's web, nearly sending him toppling to the floor when he tried to get up. Where the hell was he?

Oh. Damn. Right. In bed. In bed with Liv after stripping her down in front of the fire and making love to her until she was drowsy and limp in his arms. *Making love to her.*

Instinctively his hand traveled to the pillow next to him, though he knew he would find it cold. Off key humming drew his attention to the kitchen, where Liv was cracking eggs and swaying her hips to whatever song played in her head. Her long, pale legs were bare, the rest of her draped in nothing but one of his flannels.

The shirt was far too big—she'd rolled the sleeves up half a hundred times to free her hands—but rather than finding it unflattering, Joshua was pleased with the sight of her in his clothes. It fed his ego with a pride that was close enough to proprietary that he thought it best to keep to himself.

The jolt of panic that initially woke him receded on a heavy sigh. Joshua reclined with his head propped on his arms, enjoying the view. So much of their time together had been wasted on cowardice, on him acting like he was made of stone.

If he was made of stone, she was water, washing over him continuously, drawing away little bits of his hard exterior day by day until there was a gaping canyon inside of him. All that wide open space and she was flowing easily through it, sinking deeper and deeper into his soul with every rapid.

Joshua quietly untangled himself from the blankets and crept into the kitchen. Liv yelped, dropping an eggshell when he snaked his arms around her waist and yanked her back until she pressed against his chest.

"Holy cow!" she panted. "You scared me."

He couldn't hold back his chuckle. "Holy cow? What self-respecting person over the age of five says holy cow?"

She flicked a glare over her shoulder and wrinkled her nose. "Maybe I say it *because* I respect myself. What kind of person would I be if I went around spewing curse words?" She waved her hand dismissively, chin jutted up with an air of superiority.

"You'd be a normal fucking person."

"Joshua!"

He tugged her even closer and pressed his lips to the shell of her ear. "I think I like hearing my name on your tongue." His hands drifted down to her hips and squeezed. "I'd like to hear it again."

"Oh?" It was more a breath than a word. "How do you intend to make me say it?"

That was a challenge if he'd ever heard one. Joshua whirled her around, used one arm to push aside the fixings for breakfast, and hoisted her up onto the counter. Several items clattered to the floor and what was probably an egg rolled into the sink.

"Wait, wait, wait!" She giggled. "We'll burn breakfast."

"Fuck breakfast."

Joshua silenced her protest with his lips. Her mouth tasted like the tart blackberry jam she'd been liberally spreading on hunks of bread while she cooked. At first, he kept his hands at her back, anchoring her to him and preventing any attempt at escape. When Liv finally gave in, her delicate fingers tickling through his beard and threading into his hair, Joshua relinquished his hold to swiftly unbutton her shirt.

The loose fabric glided down her shoulders to reveal bare breasts. He unhooked the final button with a satisfied groan. Liv wasn't wearing *anything* but his shirt.

A beautiful blush spread from her cheeks all the way down to her chest when he stepped back to admire her. Honey blonde hair, tousled and soft from sleep, shimmered in the firelight. It fell nearly to her stomach, slipping over her shoulder to hide one breast behind a curtain of gold.

Her hips were plush and seductive, quite a difference from the waifish woman he brought home earlier that summer. The grey and black flannel draped halfway down her arms, framing her figure but hiding nothing. He'd originally intended to remove it but the sight of her changed his mind. She looked damn beautiful.

The longer he studied her, the more Liv began to squirm. She'd been so bold the night before. Now, in the light of day, she was shy. For some reason that spurred him on. He liked making her feel off kilter. It was only fair. His entire world was turned upside down thanks to her.

"No." The word came out sharply when Liv started slipping the shirt from her body. "Keep it on."

She frowned, her confused gaze travelling from his face and down his torso. She took a very long pause when she reached the place between his legs, her eyes widening with a hint of trepidation. Joshua hadn't bothered dressing when he got out of bed, knowing what he intended to do would warm him up faster than a pair of jeans and a sweater.

"Don't you think...um," Liv cleared her throat and forced her chin back up to find him smirking. "Don't you think I'm a little overdressed?"

Joshua gripped her thighs and slid her to the very edge of the counter until she was held up more by the pressure of his body against hers than the surface beneath her. Her arms tightened around his neck, and she let out a surprised squeak. The sound melted into a quiet moan when he pressed into her.

"I like you like this," he answered with a gentle thrust.

Liv wriggled to follow him when he retreated, losing even more purchase on the counter. She quickly wrapped her legs around his hips to keep herself steady, successfully locking him in where she wanted him.

Joshua gave her more of the same, slow and gentle. She made an impatient noise and squeezed him with her thighs. He ignored her, continuing at his languid pace until he'd worked her into a frustrated frenzy.

In most of their relationship, Liv had the power. He liked to think it was the other way around, that he was in control, but the truth was that Joshua was at her mercy. Except, he was finding, when it came to desire. Desire softened her will until she was supple and ready to do anything to get what she wanted from him.

"Joshua," her voice trembled, as did her body.

"Olivia," he echoed her tone. "You know what I want."

Fire burned in her green eyes when she lifted them to his. That fire was burning for *him.* He was never going to get used to that. With one hand Joshua gripped the nape of her neck. The other kneaded the flesh of her hip, using it as leverage when he finally gave in. Her lips parted in a silent cry, and she shuddered.

So much wasted time. Joshua could have had his hands on her every day. Every minute of every day if he had his way. He thought intimacy was a nuisance, a biological function and nothing more. He was so wrong.

Each time he touched her was thrilling, invigorating in an indescribable way. All the poetry he'd spent his youth reading suddenly made sense. Who wouldn't want to write artful words about the weight of her breast in his palm? The peachy blush of her nipples? The strawberry taste of her kiss?

"Joshua!" It was guttural and a little wild. He liked it when she came undone.

Why had he ever lied to himself about wanting this? It was worth the risk. It was worth it if he had to chase her down in the dark every night. Joshua had heaven between his arms, and he was going to worship her. Especially when his name spilled from her mouth again. And again, and again until they were both at a desperate edge, then frozen in wordless pleasure.

Liv pressed her forehead over his heart. "I love you." She breathed it so quietly he wasn't certain it was meant for his ears.

Joshua held her to him, trembling from exertion and cold and satisfaction. He couldn't say it back. Did he even know what it felt like to love someone? Whatever he felt for Liv was as close as he'd ever come, but it wasn't a sentiment to be thrown around if he didn't mean it. To Liv, love was sacred. She cradled that word on her tongue like a prayer.

If he was ever to share that with her, to give her what she wanted to hear, it could only be genuine. Otherwise, he was breaking her heart all over again.

32

Everything Good

It was an early snow and though it was light, Joshua assured me that it was a sign winter would be early too. This would be our very last trip to market until the spring thaw. Even then, our trips were likely to become scarcer. Joshua was a decent mechanic but there was only so much he could do to keep that old Chevy running. The supply of motor oil and other necessary parts was dwindling, even in the seediest trading posts. Not to mention, gasoline was becoming scarce.

Today I was hoping for a peaceful trip. I wanted to enjoy my last visit with the people that were quickly becoming my friends. I enjoyed my time with Joshua, but it was nice to be out in the world. Going to town made me feel normal. It wasn't quite a trip to the mall or going out for brunch with friends, but it was the closest we could get in these desperate times.

The fit of my pack was more awkward sitting atop my jacket and all my other layers. Still, I was impressed with myself. Several months ago, I could barely carry a backpack full of clothing and empty food wrappers. I'd come a long way. I shot a furtive of glance in Joshua's direction and smiled to myself. We'd both come a long way.

We walked in silence. The gentle drift of snow around us seemed to mute the world. Even our foot falls on dead leaves sounded softer. It was going to be a cold winter. By the end I was sure I would really miss hot showers and central heating, but I couldn't wait for the beauty of snow. The delicate flakes were ethereal, dusting the forest in glittering white.

The road was almost in sight when Joshua froze. He lifted his face, nostrils flaring as he scented the wind. His head tilted like a curious animal and once again I found myself imagining him as a large cat. I knew better than to ask what had him on alert. Whatever it was, it was close.

With careful precision, Joshua removed his pack and leaned it against a tree. He pressed a pointer finger to his lips and urged me to do the same. Once my bag was on the ground, he took my hand, crouching and slowly trailing us between trees. We only moved another ten feet before I smelled it.

Smoke.

Then there were the voices. I couldn't say how many men were talking, their conversation interspersed with boisterous laughter and the clattering of gear. People were cautious these days. If they were making this much noise, then they had a big enough group that they weren't afraid of being found.

Joshua's grip on my hand tightened. He drew us just a little closer, his breath shallow. There had to be at least thirty of them. Well-equipped men, some of them in hunting gear and camouflage. There was a rifle or two slung over shoulders and a handful of handguns on hips but most sported hunting knives and machetes. My gut twisted at the site and a shiver took my body that had nothing to do with the cold.

We were looking at a camp of raiders and they were barely more than a mile from town. By the looks of it, they would be arriving by dark.

I had to stifle a gasp when suddenly Joshua jerked my arm, tugging me quietly but frantically back to our packs. He didn't give me a chance to put my pack back on, yanking both up off the ground and precariously throwing one over each shoulder. The silence, which had moments ago been beautiful and peaceful, was deafening as he marched back the way we came.

"Joshua!" I hissed.

He ignored me.

Panting from my rush to keep up with his long stride, I hurried in front of him and put out a hand. We had to have walked half a mile in less than five minutes at this pace. By now, we were hopefully far enough away that no one would hear us. "Where are you going?"

"Home," he grunted, skirting around me.

I planted my feet and lifted my chin, refusing to take another step. Joshua got several paces ahead before he turned around and realized I wasn't with him.

"The hell are you doing?"

"We can't go home." I gestured behind us. "They're going to Rockham Falls. We have to warn them!"

"They have walls and guns. The militia can handle raiders." He dismissed me and turned back onto his trail.

"They don't know what's coming. They're unprepared! I've seen what happens when raiders catch people off guard. I can't let that happen. I won't run, not again."

That was what I was always doing. I ran from Seattle, I ran when raiders attacked my group, I ran from Wheeler's men—I even ran from Joshua! When things got rough, I fled like a coward.

Not this time.

"We go to town now, there's no getting out before those raiders show up. For all we know, they're already on their way there. Did you see that camp? They have four wheelers, horses, everything they need to get to Rockham Falls in two minutes." He rocked on his feet, the only visible sign of his anxiety. "We could end up between them and town. I'm not taking that risk."

"I am."

Joshua pivoted, his face full of thunder. "You get your skinny ass on this trail, or I will haul you home."

I matched his steely gaze. "Joshua, I'm doing this. I won't let innocent people die." My voice rose to a hysterical note, but I didn't care. He was wasting precious time.

He dropped both packs and marched toward me, fully intending to throw me over his shoulder and carry me back to the cabin if that was what it took. "Olivia," he growled.

I pressed my palms to his chest. "Don't you dare."

Anger puffed from his nostrils in a steamy cloud. I met his eyes. There was familiar rage swirling in that dark umber but there was something else too, something I was sure that only I would recognize: fear. I didn't blame him. I was afraid too, absolutely and utterly terrified.

That wasn't going to stop me from doing the right thing.

I had to be brave for all the innocent people trying to rebuild. I had to be brave for the bank teller turned farmer, the hardware store owner sewing clothes for women and children, for the people that took up arms to defend their families. I had to be brave for little girls that liked hot cider and Taylor Swift. If I wasn't, they would die.

Or worse.

"Liv," Joshua gentled his voice, wrapping his hands around mine. They were warm despite the frigid air. "I can't let you risk your life over this." He squeezed his eyes shut and whispered, "I can't."

I brought one hand to my face and pressed my lips to his knuckles. "It's not your choice to make. I have to do this. Otherwise, what's the point? What's the point of living if there's nothing left to live for? Why survive if everything good is gone?"

Joshua inhaled, his gaze tracing my face, undefinable emotions drawing tight lines across his features. With each passing moment his scowl grew deeper until his eyes were so shadowed, they almost matched the black of his hair.

"Liv, I—" whatever it was that he planned to say, Joshua cut it off so abruptly that his teeth clipped together. He removed his hands from mine and rub them vigorously over his face. "I won't let you die for strangers."

"They're not strangers, Joshua!" I pushed past him and grabbed my pack, unzipping it and pulling out the gun he had me carry. Unfortunately, those shooting lessons were probably going to come in handy.

"Olivia, please." It was the please that gave me pause. The words that left his mouth next were quiet and fragile, almost lost to the wind. "You're everything good I have."

I smiled softly at him. "Then come with me. We can do this together."

Then I shouldered my pack and took off at a jog toward Rockham Falls before he could stop me. No more running away.

33

The Enemy of My Enemy

Joshua

"Close the gate!" Liv shouted to the militia stationed on the makeshift watch towers that guarded the road into town. Joshua rushed behind her, trying to clap a hand over her mouth to quiet her. The last thing they needed was the raiders to know they'd been spotted.

Liv dodged Joshua's hand and rushed through the gate. He barely managed to catch her around the waist before she began ascending the ladder that led to the watchtowers. Both militia, bewildered and obviously cowards if they felt threatened by the slip of a woman, had shifted, weapons pointed directly down at her.

"You have to close the gate!" she panted, struggling against Joshua's hold. "There are raiders coming."

"Raiders?" One militia, a young man around his age—James maybe?—turned to glance back at the road. The snow had ceased but there was a thin layer of white coating the asphalt. A quarter mile down the road, the collection of cars that made up the roadblock was just in sight. There was no sign of anyone approaching—yet.

"Where? How many? Are you sure they're headed this way?" The other militia asked, his gun still trained on Liv.

Joshua stepped in front of her and glowered at the man. "You're going to fucking kill someone. Point that shit somewhere else!"

The man returned Joshua's glare and lowered the barrel of his rifle, but not enough that he couldn't still hit them. "Where the hell do you think you saw raiders?"

"Oh, for fudge sake!"

While the men were distracted by their standoff, Liv dropped her pack and began tugging on one side of the heavy wooden gate. Each side was constructed from eight massive logs, requiring at least two strong men to move them. There was no way in hell she had a chance of shutting it on her own but damn if she wasn't determined.

As she should be. They could be under attack any minute and all three men were wasting their time with posturing.

Joshua was still convinced they were wasting their lives even being here.

He hurried over to help her regardless of his reservations. "Get your ass down here and close this gate!" He grunted at the militia. "You've got almost three dozen raiders on your doorstep and they're gearing up for a fight." Going against every screaming instinct to keep Liv in sight, the next words had to be choked out. "Liv, take your pack and go tell the Flores."

She studied him, her face pink from effort and cold. "Are you sure?"

"Go!" He boomed.

"Find me!" She called over her shoulder as she trotted off.

Joshua did exactly that five minutes later. A small crowd had gathered around Liv as she frantically waved her hands in front of Flores. Wheeler and two of his men stood beside the mayor, their expressions varying shades of disbelief. Flores looked like he was only taking her slightly more seriously.

Why weren't they alarmed? Militia or not, this town was not prepared for a raid in its current state.

The market was packed today, filled with people anxious to get as many supplies as they could before winter barred most of the outside traders from returning until spring. Joshua spotted children, unarmed women, and several older folks. These were the people Liv wanted to protect and they were staring at her like she was crazy.

Her frantic chattering paused when Joshua came up behind her and rested a gentle hand on her shoulder. Green eyes found his, swimming with frustrated tears and beseeching him to help her.

"Are you sure they were raiders? Not travelers seeking shelter from the snow?" Flores asked Joshua. Liv bristled beside him but kept her mouth shut.

"Oh, I'm sure they're seeking shelter from the snow. All thirty of 'em, with ATVs and enough weapons to kill half the people in this town before you've pulled your pistol. Harmless." He loomed over the mayor and watched with a little too much satisfaction as the man paled. "Do I look like I'd risk my fucking life to warn you about some grannies in covered wagons bumping along the Oregon trail?"

"You're not exactly the most altruistic neighbor we have, *son.*" It was Wheeler who responded. "We just had to make sure you two weren't stirring up trouble for the hell of it."

The crowd around them, which had grown considerably, rumbled with murmurs of uncertainty and fear. Several people began packing up bags and wagons, preparing to make a swift exit.

"Gate's already closed." Joshua warned them. "Best thing to do is ready your weapons and find somewhere to wait it out. You've got about four hours before sundown. I reckon you'll have raiders on your doorstep by then."

He wasn't surprised by some of the strange looks thrown his way. Wheeler was right about Joshua. There was scarcely an altruistic bone in his body. On his own, Joshua probably wouldn't have wasted his breath trying to save these fools. It was only because of Liv that he was here, only because of her that he'd done any good in his life. She was his moral compass and according to her, this was north.

The chaos was slow building. It started with a handful of people quietly slipping off toward the other side of town. There were plenty of ways in and out. Rockham Falls wasn't completely walled in. Joshua could almost smell the sour stench of fear in the air. It carried on the wind, alerting some animal instinct until the whole market was abuzz with anxious people scurrying to make their escape.

Voices rose above the frantic crowd, shouting orders and trying to keep people from trampling each other. It took fifteen minutes and several armed militia to quiet the residents who had nowhere else to go but eventually the scene calmed enough for Flores to start organizing.

The men that weren't guarding the wall made a half circle around the mayor. Some of them were twice Joshua's age, some of them not yet old enough to shave. He didn't doubt that they were skilled with their weapons—using a hunting rifle was second nature to most country folks—but he wasn't confident they'd survive in close combat. Hopefully they were stocked with ammo, or else they might not be as evenly matched with raiders as Joshua assumed.

For once, he had to acknowledge the value of Wheeler and his men. They were well equipped and eager for a fight. He would just have to be careful not to turn his back to any of them. Not-so-friendly fire was not how he planned to go.

"Joshua," Flores pulled him aside and lowered his voice. "We could really use you."

He couldn't hide the irritation in his voice when he muttered, "I'm here until this is done."

Flores's eyes skirted over Liv, who was watching them curiously. "The church is equipped to be a safehouse. I've got six men stationed there to protect families and anyone who isn't prepared to fight."

Joshua gave a grateful nod, understanding precisely what the mayor was telling him without outright saying it. He took Liv's hand and silently began leading her through the throngs of people. They slowed enough to let people pass in front of them. It was his hope that they could be the last to arrive. Harder for her to make a scene then.

If she wouldn't forgive him for dragging her back home, she wouldn't be too forgiving of this either. That was fine. He could live with her resentment so long as she was still living.

"Where are we going?" Joshua didn't answer. "Shouldn't we stay close to the wall?" Damn woman thought she was going to fight off raiders. There was brave and then there was reckless. Liv was walking the line.

They stalled outside the double doors. The sky, already overcast and dim, was quickly greying. There were a few hours before sunset but this time of year the days were dark. Men raced to light fires along the wall and in the town center. They would improve visibility but not by much. Even in the best case scenario, Joshua knew there would be a lot of bloodshed when those raiders arrived.

"Joshua? What's going on?" Liv tugged his attention back to her.

"Show me your gun." She dutifully reached around her back and pulled out the handgun from her concealed holster. "Good. Keep it on your person. Anyone you don't recognize comes at you, shoot them."

"Anyone? Joshua, I only know half the people in this town!"

Joshua gripped her shoulders, probably too hard, and trapped her in his steely gaze. "You want to save people? That means *killing* people, Olivia. That's what those raiders are coming to do. I know you know that. Don't get squeamish on me, Squirrel."

Shock widened those beautiful green eyes before reality registered with a quick sheen of tears. She blinked them away and nodded resolutely. "People are going to die."

"They are. It's us or it's them. That's what we walked into. That's the choice we made by coming here."

"I hate it," she whispered. "But I'll live with the guilt if it means we save innocent people."

Joshua pressed his lips to her forehead. He paused to soak up the feel of her skin, to inhale the faint strawberry scent of her hair, to wonder at the feathery, soft feeling that puffed up in his chest when she returned his affection. Never in this life would he understand why she wanted him. Joshua didn't deserve Liv. It was obvious to him and everyone that looked at them.

There had to be a reason for this. He'd thought as much the moment he found her in those woods. Joshua didn't often think of a higher power anymore. As a child he couldn't stomach the thought of an all knowing father who would allow his misery, so he imagined that God was a myth. Only, he'd never truly convinced himself of that.

When he found Liv all those months ago, he thought it was God giving him a chance to do some good. Now he understood that taking care of her wasn't the sole good he was meant to do. Joshua didn't want to be here sticking his neck out for other people, but he was.

Just like he'd made more trips to town than he really needed and traded with folks because he knew they could use his supplies and not because they had anything for him.

None of it was out of the goodness of his heart, though it was driven by the heart. Every sacrifice he made, every uncharacteristic kindness he offered, was for her. Liv was his redemption. He wasn't a good man, but Liv made him *want* to be one.

So, there he was, doing the right thing. He could only do it if he knew she was safe.

"Why are we here?" Liv's brow was still crinkled, her confusion only heightened by his unusual display of affection.

"Safety," he grunted, taking her hand, and nearly dragging her through the church doors.

"Safety? Joshua, we need to be out there! You know how to protect yourself."

"And you don't."

Liv stumbled down the basement stairs, so he lifted her and carried her the rest of the way. By that point she began to realize what he intended to do and kicked her legs wildly. Joshua took a good hit in the shin but didn't stop until she was in the doorway of one of the meeting rooms.

Huddles of families, old folks, and men unequipped to fight stared wide-eyed at the scene. Normally Joshua would have balked at drawing so much attention. He couldn't be bothered to care right now.

Several militia were stationed outside the door. One man, clad in worn jeans and a black leather jacket with club patches that belied his history, cleared his throat, and gave Joshua a disapproving scowl. As much as Joshua wanted to deck the man, he had to concede that the situation looked bad. Damn woman flailed in his arms, yelling, and pointing angrily at the room.

Whatever she was saying, Joshua didn't hear it. Liv froze when he covered her downturned mouth with his, giving her a final, forceful kiss before shoving her into the meeting room and slamming the door. She was still shouting from the other side, her tiny fists pounding uselessly against the door when she found she couldn't turn the handle.

"You let her out, I'm coming for you when this is done." Joshua turned a scowl on the six men lingering in the hall. They bore wary expressions as they watched him hold the door shut. He narrowed his eyes, daring them to defy him.

"Keys?" Unless the raiders managed to set a brick building on fire, the room would be better protected if it was locked.

The man in the leather jacket handed Joshua a hefty key ring. He had to try three keys before he found one that fit, twisting until he felt a click. He wasn't foolish enough to believe a door could keep a motivated group of raiders out, but he was determined to make sure not a single one of them made it that far.

A thick fog of tension shrouded the air in the town center. The sun had set hours earlier, leaving no light but the barrel fires and the faint shimmer of stars through the clouds. It was a good night for a raid, assuming the town was unprepared.

Thanks to Liv, they wouldn't be.

When dusk had come and gone with no sign of raiders, the militia became cagey. What reason Joshua would have to lie about an impending raid, he couldn't say. That didn't stop the accusations from flying. They lasted a few short minutes before Flores's scout returned, pale and breathless.

One cue, there was a shout from the main gate. Raiders had arrived, but not where and how they were expected.

The armed men that presented themselves to the guards at the gate were clearly familiar with the defenses. They approached with their weapons holstered and sheathed, hands high in the air. Joshua couldn't hear what was being said but it was clear that they were claiming innocence and begging entrance.

The first shot came from the east end of town, where the woods were thickest at the perimeter and the wall ended in the trees. There was a painful stretch of silence following the single echoing boom before the tightly strung men exploded into action. One of the militia stationed over the gate fell to Joshua's right. Several more shots rang out and the distinct sound of scuffling on concrete drew his attention.

Smoke and darkness made for poor visibility. The dark colors and camo donned by the raiders didn't help. They easily made it past the perimeter guard. One look at the large swell of men and Joshua realized this wouldn't be a raid. This would be a battle.

And he realized with a stomach churning chill, he might be on the losing side.

The group Joshua scouted on the outskirts was incomplete. Far more than thirty men were violently making their way through the town. It was common knowledge that raiders were forming packs and becoming more organized as resources became scarce. A raid was always anticipated, which was why the mayor formed the militia. What wasn't anticipated was that the men doing the raiding would have amassed a small army.

Fortunately, waging war during the end of the world meant ammunition was finite, making it harder for men to drop each other from the shadows. Unfortunately, the militia were far more trigger happy than the raiders and were quickly running out of bullets. Joshua was careful and precise when he took his first shot. In the dark it was difficult to discern friend from foe. The militia wore black and red patches on their arms but even those were nearly invisible in the moonless night.

Wheeler's men were impossible to tell apart from raiders, except that most of them weren't wielding the machetes that raiders had adopted as their signature weapon. When Joshua fired his second shot, he wasn't entirely sure it was a raider he clipped. He didn't really care, either. If the world was short one more raping, thieving, murdering asshole, no one would be grieving.

The longer the fighting went on, the more chaotic the square became. The occasional flash of a gun muzzle lit up the shadows but otherwise, he could scarcely see who was doing what anymore. Careful to keep to the edge of the wall, Joshua backpedaled closer and closer to the church.

There was no way to tell who was winning and who was dying. There were bodies on the ground everywhere, half of them groaning in pain as they desperately tried to drag themselves to the safety of a building or to lean up against a wall.

No matter how this ended, the aftermath would be tragic.

Joshua had killed men before, but never like this. He was a hunter, swift, silent, and lethal. Every man he'd kill hadn't seen it coming until it was far too late for them to act. This situation required his focus to be in five places at once, his gaze darting back and forth, the hairs on the back of his neck prickling as he felt the potential for an ambush constantly growing. John might have trained him, prepared him with all the tactical skills a young man could need for the end of days, but he could never have been mentally prepared.

The stress of it was wearing on him, his adrenaline quickly dissipating and leaving him disoriented. He wasn't unfazed by the death either. Though he had grown up witnessing death, had seen it at his own hand, this was different. This was horrific. This made him finally understand the hatred Liv had for the new order of the world.

So many unnecessary deaths. So many people gone in an instant because every man was fighting for his own instead of fighting for each other. Joshua would never erase the images seared into his mind. The only way out of this was to harden himself. It proved more difficult than it should have. He had exposed that soft spot, opened a vulnerability, and he was struggling to cover it again.

A sudden weight struck him in the shoulder, knocking his rifle from his hold and nearly toppling him. The man that hit him was smaller and leaner, but he had the element of surprise. Too late, Joshua remembered why John raised him to be cold. To feel was a weakness and it just might be the death of him.

The rifle skittered across the concrete, just out of reach. His next move was swift and practiced, his left hand sweeping to his lower back and reaching for the handgun he kept strapped there. Unfortunately, practice didn't mean success in a real fight. The man, who Joshua recognized in a fleeting glance as one of Wheeler's boys, slammed into him. They both went down, pinning the gun behind Joshua's back.

A fist clipped his chin as he rolled, narrowly avoiding smashing his head into the concrete and instead taking the impact on his shoulder. The move put him under Wheeler's man, still heavy even if Joshua did have the size advantage, but he was almost close enough to reach the rifle now.

He twisted and bucked sideways, throwing his opponent off just enough to bellycrawl forward toward the rifle. His other arm, which instinctively reached for his handgun again, was pinned under the other man's knee. A booted foot crunched down on Joshua's forearm and followed the move with a kick to his jaw. Joshua's head flipped sideways with a sick snap, and he flopped limply onto his back, vision dotting with stars.

His reaction to the next attack was slow but not so slow that he ended up with a cracked nose or putty for brains. Joshua yanked the other man's ankle just as a foot came down over his face.

"Son of a bitch!" He grunted when he tumbled forward, landing with his knee in Joshua's gut.

Breathless, bleeding, and throbbing with pain in rather important places, Joshua used his fading stamina to swing his elbow toward the other man's nose. Wheeler's man was leaning back, reaching for some weapon on his belt, and only caught the elbow in a glancing blow. Seconds later a hunting knife was flying toward his chest.

John taught Joshua that a knife should be his last resort weapon in close combat. It was too easy for your opponent to turn it on you or to cut yourself "like a damn fool." They'd spent many mornings wrestling in the grass when Joshua was a boy. John bested him every time until he was thirteen and could match his father in strength and size. By the time he was fifteen, John had ceased lessons that required too much contact, aware that his son towered over him and would likely crush him.

In the years leading up to that, Joshua had earned many scars. John always insisted they train with real weapons to put Joshua in survival mode. He'd once thought his father cruel. Now, he had to wonder if there was a method to the man's madness.

Joshua wrapped his thick hands around the other man's wrist and pushed down with all the strength he had left. They were both quickly growing tired, but Wheeler's man showed impressive resistance. With a grunt, his arms gave, and the knife sank into the side of his thigh. It was a painful wound but probably not fatal.

Out of the corner of his eye Joshua caught sight of a second man approaching. Light from the nearest barrel fire flickered across his face, which was filthy and spattered with blood. The machete in his hand sported matching red stains. The world seemed to slow, every flex of muscle on the raider's arms notable, the tendons rippling in the neck of the man atop him as they strained in pain.

Joshua had heard this was what it was like, that final moment before it was over. Life whizzed by like a truck at ninety miles an hour until suddenly, with no warning, it lurched to a halt. He knew this was a potential outcome tonight, maybe understood that it was definite. That was why he'd done his best to keep Liv out of it. Damn stubborn woman would have gotten herself killed.

And she didn't deserve to watch him die.

That thought was a hundred pounds of sickening dread on his chest, making his stomach churn and his body go cold. Were the raiders overpowering them? Was this the end for them all? What would happen to Liv when he was gone? Who would look out for her? Joshua couldn't bear to think of the outcome if raiders got ahold of her.

Please God, don't let them have her.

Then there was another brief thought, one he never would have entertained if not for his predicament. Why was life so unfair? Why was it always *so unfair*? He'd suffered through John's reign for more than twenty years and finally, *finally*, found something good. Now it was over when it had only just begun. A curse as foul as they came left his lips, a curse for a God above that must be sadistic and hateful.

The sound barely escaped him when a real weight came down on his chest. His ears were ringing as the next shot rang out. A machete clattered to the ground, the noise distant and muffled. There was another shot, then another and another until whoever was shooting had emptied their magazine.

Just about every part of him hurt. More stars danced in his eyes, blurring his vision, and, as his consciousness faded, he briefly wondered if he'd been shot.

34

Sacrifices

"**S**tupid, stupid man." A familiar voice sobbed as a weight left Joshua's chest, making his lungs inflate like balloons.

He blinked rapidly, momentarily unsure of where he was and how long he'd been there. Tiny, warm hands were tugging his forearm, trying to move him with absolutely no success. The feel of those hands was the only proof that he was even alive.

Unless this was heaven. Though, if it were, he was pretty sure Liv would be much more naked and she would be using words much worse than "stupid." It was possible he was in hell—that would explain the pain. Hell would be a well-deserved sentence for him.

"Son of bunny, you are so flipping heavy, Joshua."

Yup, definitely hell.

He must have said it aloud because a tearful Liv snapped back, "you shut your mouth! You are not in hell because you're not dead!" She ceased tugging on his arm and kneeled beside him. It was cold out but not nearly cold enough for her to be shaking as violently as she was. "Can you hear me? Where are you hurt? Can you move? You're bleeding! Oh God, where else are you bleeding?"

"Slow down, woman." He grunted, twin pains shooting down his neck and through the shoulder he landed on when he sat up.

"Wait, don't sit up! What if you're concussed? Or have internal bleeding? I didn't see what happened." She was becoming hysterical. "*Where are you hurt?*" she repeated on a shaky breath.

"Stop fussing." A shot cracked through the air, far too close for comfort, and sent enough adrenaline coursing through Joshua's veins to snap him out of the fog. Unfortunately, the adrenaline did very little for the throbbing pain in his jaw. Hopefully nothing was broken.

"Joshua!" Liv pulled one of his eyelids back to check his pupils.

"I'm fine!" Not entirely the truth but they needed to move. Being out in the open was a death sentence so long as there were still raiders with guns around. *Or Wheeler's men,* he thought with bitter rage.

"You're bleeding!"

"Where is Wheeler's man? And the other one?"

The question was answered for him before Liv could speak. Crumpled on the ground just beside him was the man who had been pummeling him moments earlier. A few feet away was a raider, his chest riddled with bullet holes. Was it wrong to be a little proud of the grouping? Joshua wasn't sure.

The only thing he was sure of was that Liv wouldn't be okay after this. Not for a while, anyway.

"I guess now we're even." Immediately Joshua regretted his words. Yes, she saved his life just as he had saved hers, but at what cost? She'd already seen so much, lived so much. He wanted to protect her from this, wanted to protect her from having to make that choice. For him, it was easy—probably too easy. For Liv, it would weigh on her for the rest of her life.

"They're dead. I shot them. I killed them." The trembling in her hands worsened. "I killed them," she repeated.

"Get my rifle and get up." He didn't have the luxury of comforting her now.

She obeyed, offering her free hand to help him off the ground. It didn't bode well that he needed to take it. She was right, he could be concussed. He was definitely bleeding and at least one of his ribs was cracked based on his painful inhales.

Joshua gritted his teeth and ignored the pain, focusing all his remaining strength on dragging Liv—she was struggling to stay upright worse than him—around the side of the nearest building and behind an old utility box. He winced when he crouched. His rib smarted again as he lowered Liv down beside him and took the rifle from her. She was in no shape to use it.

"Joshua?"

"Shhh. You did good, Squirrel." He repositioned himself so he could look at her. "And it was damn stupid. I'm pissed as hell at you right now, woman. How did you even get out here?"

"I climbed through the basement window." *Of course, she did.* The color returned to her cheeks, along with a deep scowl. "*You're* mad at *me*? I just saved your life!" A tiny hand came up to cover her mouth when she realized how loud she was speaking. "If either of us gets to be angry, it's me. You locked me in a room with a bunch of old people."

"To keep you safe!"

"If I'm going to risk my life, it's my choice. You do not get to make that decision for me." She stomped her foot.

"I'm always going to make that decision, even if you hate me for it."

"Why? What gives you the right?"

Joshua was trapped in her demanding gaze. There was a familiar fire in those eyes. She was furious. And scared. Even as she admonished him, there were tears gathering on her bottom lids.

He took a deep breath and answered more honestly than he thought himself capable, with words he never believed he would say to anyone.

"Why? Because I'm pretty damn sure I'm in love with you. Maybe that doesn't give me the right, but nothing is going to stop me. Do you understand? *I have to.* You're everything I've got, Liv, and I am not watching you die out here. I'm not worrying about the hundred horrible things those men could do to you. I couldn't live with myself if I let you put yourself in the middle of this and get hurt."

Liv leaned over and grabbed his hand with both of hers, pressing her thumbs in the center of his palm and rubbing gently. A soft, innocent smile played on her lips. "I shouldn't be smiling right now."

His own lips twitched. "You laughed when I told you that I'd killed men. I'm not sure which of us is more fucked up."

"I'm not fudged up," she said seriously.

Joshua had to suppress a chuckle, almost letting his twisted sense of humor get the better of him. Liv shot two men dead not twenty minutes earlier, yet she still refused to dirty her mouth. Such a strange, stubborn, perfect woman.

They quieted, noticing the surroundings had grown mostly still, the chaos coming to an abrupt halt. Even when it seemed the action was over, Joshua kept them hidden. There was no way to know which side, if any, had won and he couldn't take any chances. Not when neither of them was in a good state to defend themselves.

Fluffy flakes of snow had begun to fall sometime during the night. It was a little too warm for them to stick, which meant fat clumps were collecting on their clothes only to melt and slowly soak through. The sky was showing the faintest hint of grey, dawn finally making an appearance after a hellish night, but there was no sign of anyone in the street. Joshua wasn't keen on giving away their location, but he was acutely aware of Liv's increasingly forceful shivering.

"What do we do?" She leaned up to whisper in his ears. When her nose made contact with his neck it was so cold that he hissed.

"We wait."

"Do you think..." she swallowed and pulled her knees to her chest. "Do you think everyone is okay?"

It was the kind of question that reminded him just how innocent she could be. Liv wanted the world to be better than it was. She wanted to believe that nothing bad could happen to good people, even though she'd repeatedly seen contrary.

"No," his response was blunt. "I don't know if *anyone* is okay."

Liv cast her gaze to her shoes and sighed heavily. Joshua expected tears any moment, maybe a total breakdown, but it never came. She was always surprising him.

She tilted her head to rest it on his shoulder and said, "*you're* okay." When he didn't reply she nudged him and asked, "you are okay, right? Joshua? Tell me you're okay."

He answered by lifting her into his lap. The weight of her against his chest made his ribs ache but not nearly as much as the undiluted fear in her voice. It wasn't until she slipped her arms under his jacket, and he felt the heat of her breath on his neck that he realized how cold he'd gotten. Neither of them could stay out there much longer, not if they weren't moving.

On cue, a booming voice echoed through the center of town. Joshua carefully extricated Liv and leaned around the side of the building. The mayor was decked out in tactical gear that read "Sheriff's Department" across the back. He held a rifle and wore a handgun and a taser on his hip.

Beside him was a handful of militia men, some of them looking much worse for wear but none of them were bleeding too heavily. The mayor appeared to be doing roll call of his men.

Joshua let out a breath he'd been holding since yesterday afternoon and led Liv out from their hiding place. When he noticed Wheeler and two of his men joining the mayor, he made a point to stand tall, despite the stabbing pain he felt in his rib with every step. Not a single person made it through the night unscathed. There were bruises and bleeding wounds, some serious enough they could prove fatal if not attended to soon.

The sun crept along the horizon, unable to penetrate the thick cloud cover but offering enough light to reveal the carnage left by a night of battle. Bodies littered the road, blood quickly cooling and congealing in the frigid weather.

Joshua didn't know how many men had come to raid the town or how many militia there were to defend it but it looked like half a hundred people had died. It would take days to gather up the dead and they would have to work swiftly to beat the weather.

Fortunately, none of that was Joshua's problem. He only had one concern and she was huddled beside him.

"Don't look," he instructed when they stepped out into the open.

Liv shook her head and did exactly that. "I have to. It's our responsibility to bear witness, to remember them."

Her steps faltered as she gazed upon the gore. For a heartbeat there was a look in her eyes that he was sure matched the looks of soldiers returning from war, a look that no young woman should ever have, but it vanished almost as fast as it appeared. She closed her eyes and swallowed hard before reaching for his hand and squeezing it.

"You're okay," she whispered more to herself than to him.

"We both are."

"You sure you won't stay?" The mayor asked Joshua again as he carefully pulled his backpack over his shoulder.

The basement of the church and several outbuildings had been made into housing for people that chose to settle in town and those that were passing through. We'd both been awake for twenty four hours and though he was trying to hide it, it was clear that Joshua needed rest.

I understood why he didn't want to wait. There was a small risk of running into the few raiders that had escaped. To Joshua, that was nothing compared to the risk of not making it home. The snow had begun to fall quite steadily, and we would be lucky if we made it back to the farm without getting stuck or frozen.

By the way Joshua was eyeing Wheeler and the three armed men flanking him, I could see that there was more than one reason he didn't feel safe staying in town.

I was just as ready to be home as he was but that didn't stop me from worrying. He was favoring his left side and it was obvious that his pack was too heavy for his injuries. My pack was also full, far too full for me to offer to take any of his load.

"We're good," Joshua grunted.

"I can't thank you enough. If you hadn't come to warn us... We owe you a great deal, Joshua."

"Not my choice. It was all her." Joshua jerked his thumb in my direction, obviously uncomfortable with gratitude. God forbid they got the impression he might actually want to help anyone.

Mayor Flores turned his attention on me, his expression somber. "You saved a lot of lives."

"We have to take care of each other," I answered simply. "Otherwise, what's the point?"

Joshua tried to guide me to the gate, but I stopped him and shifted directions. He was confused and more than a little grumpy when I took his hand and dragged him back to the church.

"Liv, we're not staying." I could tell he was going for stern but there was a hint of doubt in his words. "Do you want to stay?"

"No." My response didn't seem to satisfy him, but he said nothing else.

It took me a minute to navigate through the church, but it wasn't long before I found my target. Asher was waiting with his sister and several other families. Tears were being shed, prayers quietly wept. I couldn't bear to look upon the faces of those who would be grieving for lost loved ones.

Without a word I waved Asher over and unzipped Joshua's backpack. Before Joshua could protest, I tugged the strap off his shoulder and lowered it to the ground. Both men voiced confusion—and a few curse words—when I started to stack wrapped packages of dried venison, small squashes, a cabbage, potatoes, apples, and several bags of nuts on a church pew. It was most of the contents of Joshua's backpack. Mine was still full, leaving us ample supplies if we got lost on the way and had to take shelter.

"Liv, we can't possibly take all of this," Asher balked.

Joshua began to speak but I interrupted him. "You can and you will. Share it with whoever needs it. Consider it a Christmas gift."

"Olivia." That was the sole protest Joshua offered, even though I was breaking one of his biggest rules. It spoke volumes about how exhausted and injured he really was. I was beginning to worry he couldn't make the trek home, even with an empty pack.

35
Promises

I had known many miseries since the blackout, but none of them rivaled walking miles through the snow in wet clothes after a sleepless night. My pack felt as if it weighed a hundred pounds, and my legs were so numb that each step was awkward and rigid. If we didn't make it home soon, we would both get hypothermia.

The temperatures dropped and the steady snow was now sticking, creating a carpet of resistance that hindered our progress. Joshua was right to worry that we would have been stuck in town, but I was beginning to question the wisdom of trying to make it home in our condition. He was flagging, more tired than I'd ever seen him.

Despite his weariness, Joshua still forged the trail, keeping me going with a muttered "almost there," and "not long now." If not for him, I never would have found my way. My compass and map still meant little to me, and I was so unfamiliar with the woods beyond the farm. It was his guidance and determination that had us standing in front of the gate by midday.

My gloves were drenched and my fingers too numb to untie my shoes and unzip my jacket. Joshua did it for me, his hands deft as ever. They must've been as cold as mine, but I couldn't tell. All I could feel was the faint pressure of his touch, every inch of my skin frozen.

"Strip," Joshua commanded as he did the same.

He was naked and halfway to the fireplace before I even unbuttoned my jeans. I stalled in my task, tears burning my eyes when I finally got a good look at him. The entire right side of his face was bruised, his ribs and sternum sporting matching purple marks.

So easy. It would've been so easy for him to die last night.

For the first time, I second-guessed my decision. Did we save lives? Or did I only put Joshua at risk? Maybe he wouldn't have sustained his injuries if he hadn't kept me from watching his back. Or maybe he would've been so distracted by my presence that we would both be dead. There were so many maybes, too many for my brain process without having a complete anxious breakdown.

I couldn't stop staring at his bruises, couldn't help but wonder if I'd made the wrong choice. My decision put Joshua in danger. I hadn't thought of that possibility, only of my own conscience. He seemed invincible to me.

"Why did you do it?" Why did he put himself at risk? Joshua was as risk averse as they come and, though it disappointed me, he cared little for anyone but himself. I was the exception, and I wasn't entirely sure why.

It wasn't because he was a terrible person, but because that was how he was made. For so long Joshua tried to tell me that was his nature, and I didn't understand it. Now I did and it left me more confused than ever.

He glanced over his shoulder as he crouched to start the fire and simply said, "for you."

"You saved people, Joshua. You did something good." I wanted to tell myself it was good. There was no choice but to fight fire with fire, taking a life to save one. That was how I was going to rationalize my own actions.

"For you." he repeated.

I was still standing in the doorway, stunned, too cold and tired to move when Joshua began carefully removed my wet clothes. He wrapped me in a blanket and sat me beside the fire. I watched him hang our clothes on the rack beside the hearth and rose to help. He needed rest much more urgently than I did.

"Sit."

"Joshua—"

"Sit down, Olivia."

"You're getting awfully liberal with this 'do as I say, Olivia' thing," I grumbled, but still obeyed.

"It works." His back was to me, but I heard the smile in his voice.

Joshua gingerly lowered himself to the rug beside me. I opened my blanket in invitation and he accepted, sliding closer to me, and breathing relief at the warmth of naked skin on naked skin. There was an unexpected peace humming between us, like all of the events of the last twenty four hours were completely imagined and we were still steeped in post lovemaking bliss.

Then my eyes glided over Joshua's quickly purpling jaw and reality opened a blackhole of anguish in my belly.

Fingers curled around my calves, I whispered, "Is it going to get better?"

Joshua studied me with hard, dark eyes. "Do you want my honest answer?"

I considered for two long breaths. "No."

"Everything gets better, eventually."

"You're just saying that to be nice." I tried for a teasing smile, but my face was too tired.

"I thought we went over this. I'm not nice."

"No, you're not." My lips finally found the energy to lift upwards. "But I like you anyway."

"Do you?" Rough knuckles followed the hill of my cheek. When he got to my nose, he straightened his finger and gently stroked from brow to tip. His affection was cautious and exploratory, nothing like I'd come to expect, yet there was a certain thrill to it. Every part of me, from scalp to sole, was new territory to be discovered.

"You should get some rest." My words contradicted my body, leaning to follow the warmth of his touch as it feathered down my throat to my nape.

"We both should," he agreed, though he too was in no rush to retreat from our nest in front of the fire.

I don't know if it was the adrenaline or the emotion that turned his touch incendiary. One moment his hand was on my neck, the next it was tugging my hips down to meet his. My fingertips dug into the muscles of his chest, provoking a wince that froze me.

"I'm so sorry, Joshua. We should—" I went to lift my weight from him, but he pulled me back, bringing my chest flush with his, lips inches from mine.

"No. I need this." He kissed me gingerly. "I need you."

Our eyes met, his colored with wariness and a vulnerability I'd only just learned to recognize. It wasn't something he wore easily, his body tense, once again looking like the stray cat that was halfway to fleeing. Joshua was expressing desire. He was asking for something for himself, something that *I* could give to him.

I needed it too, needed to feel the security of that closeness, needed the intimacy to banish the sick feeling that was quietly gnawing at my conscience.

Every inch of him was hard beneath me, taut with strength that was rooted much deeper than the muscles that built his big frame. The rise of his chest rocked me in gentle waves, his breath a warm breeze on my face. If I could go back and see him that first day we met, would I see all the ways I would come to find him beautiful?

Beauty probably wasn't a word a man like Joshua wanted to be associated with, but he had it. He was beautiful in the way that only someone you love can be.

And I did love him, so very, very much.

"Tell me again." I pressed my temple to his forehead, shifting my ear to brush his bottom lip.

"I love you, Olivia."

I sank down onto him with a shuddering breath, squeezing my lids together so he wouldn't see the tears trying to escape. They weren't tears of sorrow, but they weren't quite happy tears either. I couldn't explain to him why I was crying, couldn't find the words to describe the upwelling of relief.

Several heartbeats passed, another drawn out exhale, and I realized I hadn't moved. My face was still pressed to his, my thighs quaking with the exertion of my position. I wanted to burn this feeling into my memory forever, this connection that had become instinctual. When I'd had my fill of it, when I was filled with him, I pressed Joshua's back into the rug, and I rocked forward.

If I hadn't been watching his scowl untangle into a soft look of euphoria, I would have thought the gravelly sound that rasped from his throat was one of pain. He made another when I slowly slid back down until my hips met his. A very particular satisfaction warmed my lower belly as I watched his eyes roll closed. Those low, gratified noises persisted with every increased stroke of his body inside mine.

Gradually, his sounds became words, a murmur of my name, one of the harsh curses I'd come to find so endearing. His hands found purchase on my hips, cupping them with just enough pressure to make my desire burn hotter. What started as soft and comforting intimacy quickly became wild, bordering on desperation. Joshua tilted his back, rising to meet me every time I returned from my upward retreat.

I drove further, desperate for the release of that ever building pressure between my legs, but there was so much more I wanted from him, too. My hands feathered over his chest, fingers pressing into the firm muscles that encased his ribs. Lips met lips, cheeks, chins, the column of throats, and anywhere else they could reach. My want was not only for the primal pleasure from our frenzied movement. I wanted all of him.

The tension suddenly snapped, sending delicious vibrations up my spine and all the way down to my toes. Joshua stiffened beneath me, his tongue finding my name again, repeating it in chorus with each of my drawn out moans. It was different when he said it in a flare of passion, soft, almost a plea. His grip on my waist tightened, desperate for me to give him exactly what he'd given me.

"God, Liv."

I indulged him. I knew, probably long before now, that I would give him anything he asked for. I gave and I gave until he sat up, gasping. His arms came around me and he drew us together, our bodies so tightly wound that there was no beginning or end. My fingers buried into the muscles of his shoulders, holding on as if for dear life. In that moment, I felt that I would shatter into pieces if he let me go.

"I love you." It escaped my mouth before I could catch it.

Only after his thumb came to separate my tightly closed lips, tugging the bottom one and stroking the words off it like he could catch them in his palm and keep them, did I remember that I could say it.

"I love you," I repeated until I was breathless all over again, holding him as tightly against me as I dared.

"I know, I know." One big hand rubbed up my back, soothing away the pain he must have heard in my voice.

It was the good kind of pain, like the kind of tears that feel cathartic to cry. It was exhilarating, so thrilling that I almost cried out the way I had as we made love. The world was ending and nothing was okay but here, wrapped in wool and warm limbs, slick with sweat and completely sated, I didn't care.

I didn't care if everything outside that tiny cabin washed away. Let the snow keep falling until the earth was coated in it, until we were cocooned in silence and darkness, save for the crackle of the fire and Joshua's soft snores—he'd barely gone horizontal before he was out.

I leaned over him, watching his eyelashes dance while those dark chocolate eyes chased a dream. My lips settled on the pulse thrumming up his neck, shivering when the tight curls of his beard tickled my forehead.

I didn't move my mouth away from his skin when I whispered, "Joshua?"

"Mmm?" He shifted his head in my direction, but his eyes stayed firmly closed.

"You'll never have to be alone again."

A Note from the Author

Do you believe that dreams have meaning? One late autumn day I came home from a walk in the rain feeling feverish and tired. I fell asleep on the couch with a Dolly Parton song stuck in my head and dreamed of love in the face of tragedy. I dreamed of a young woman being brave in the face of her greatest fears, of a man with no heart finding it on the forest floor. I woke from that dream and immediately began typing away. Thus, Moonshine was born.

You haven't just finished reading a piece of my heart made tangible on paper (tangible-ish if you're reading the eBook). You're holding in your hands a dream that I've brought to life. I have words to describe many things—probably too many things—but none that can do justice to the way it feels when someone else enjoys my work.

As an author, it means the world to me when you reach out and let me know that my book kept you hooked. As an indie author, it means I can keep putting words on a page for your eyes to feast on when you let the world know that my book kept you hooked. If you have a moment, please consider reviewing Moonshine on Amazon or Goodreads. Reviews go a long way in making it possible for authors like me to support themselves.

Thank you for reading Moonshine and thank you for your support!

Until next time,

Kat Bostick

Acknowledgments

Writing a book is a journey and you meet so many amazing people along the way. I'm so grateful to everyone that gave their time and love to help me complete this project.

As always, I must thank my husband for putting up with the sound of the keyboard at three in the morning while I nursed our baby. I spent many of the precious few hours we got while our son was sleeping working tireless on this story and he never complained.

I'd like to thank my mom, my dad, my brother, and my sister for helping me as I waffled over cover designs. Your insights gave me so much clarity.

I have to thank the amazing Betsy Harloff for teaching me to use my baby carrier. It sounds like a small accomplishment, but it was the difference between me meeting my writing deadlines. Most of this book was written with a baby strapped to me!

Thanks to my ARC readers who jump at the chance to read my work. Your input and reviews fuel my craft.

A huge thank you to my amazing online author friends. Each and every one of you inspires me and keeps me going when I feel discouraged. What an incredible community of creative people.

And of course, I have to thank Dolly Parton for creating the music that filled my childhood with joy and inspired my latest creation.

About the Author

Kat has always believed in magic, if only the kind that flies from fingertip to keyboard and then onto paper, enchanting a reader and giving them a brief respite from the mundane world. She made her debut in 2019 with her first novel, Hunter's Moon. Like all of Kat's favorite stories, her books are packed with adventure, sprinkled with equal shares of humor and heartbreak, and finished with a healthy dose of romance.

When she's not writing Kat is a full-blown homesteading, crunchy-as-all-get-out granola mama, raising babies. She has a love for all things that grow in soil and spends many hours talking to the plants in her garden.

Find Kat on social @katbostickwrites